THE
PARTICULAR
CHARM

of Miss

Jane Austen

*We dedicate this book
to our friendship*

THE
PARTICULAR
CHARM
of Miss
Jane Austen

ADA BRIGHT
CASS GRAFTON

BROWN
DOG
BOOKS

FT
Pbk

Published under licence by Brown Dog Books and The Self-Publishing Partnership, 7 Green Park Station, Bath BA1 1JB

www.selfpublishingpartnership.co.uk

ISBN printed book: 978-1-78545-104-1
ISBN e-book: 978-1-78545-105-8

Cover design by Kevin Rylands
Internal design by Andrew Easton

Printed and bound by CPI Group (UK) Ltd, Croydon CR0 4YY

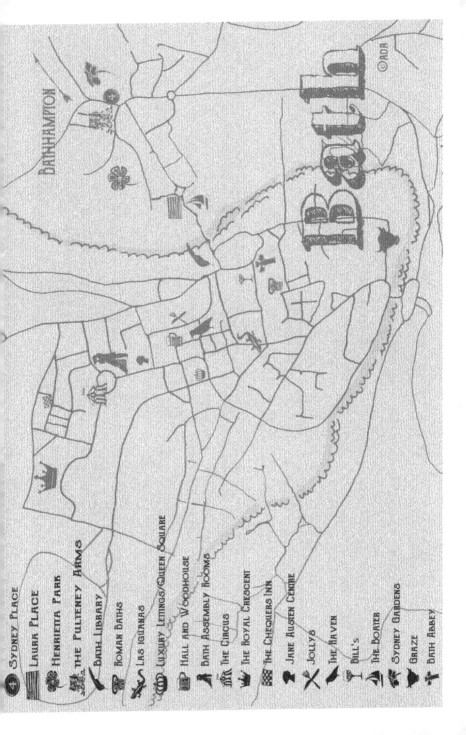

BATHAMPTON

Bath

©ADA

1 SYDNEY PLACE

LAURA PLACE

HENRIETTA PARK

THE PULTENEY ARMS

BATH LIBRARY

ROMAN BATHS

LAS IGUANAS

LUXURY LETTINGS/QUEEN SQUARE

HALL AND WOODHOUSE

BATH ASSEMBLY ROOMS

THE CIRCUS

THE ROYAL CRESCENT

THE CHEQUERS INN

JANE AUSTEN CENTRE

JOLLYS

THE RAVEN

BILL'S

THE BOATER

SYDNEY GARDENS

GRAZE

BATH ABBEY

CHAPTER ONE

September in Bath! Rosemary Wallace emerged at the top of the steps from her basement flat, delighting in the autumnal air and the dappled sunlight as it caressed the trees in Sydney Gardens, tinting their leaves with a hint of the gold and amber to come.

Turning her back on the temptation of the park, Rose set off determinedly, hurrying down Great Pulteney Street towards town but still finding time to admire the uniformity of the grand buildings, bathed in the sun's morning rays. How she loved Bath. It was her city, her home; always beautiful and sometimes a little crazy, the craziness having reached new heights this morning!

She ran through her 'to-do' list in her head. It was one of her busiest days of the year – definitely the worst day for oversleeping. It had been inevitable, though, with the smoke alarm in the flat above going off soon after she'd closed her eyes and then being too excited to fall back to sleep until just before dawn broke.

Walking briskly along, intent on making up lost time, Rose had almost passed by the man coming towards her until he stayed her with his hand.

'Hey, Rose! Hi!'

'Oh, Marcus. Hi – sorry!' She smiled widely. 'Late for work!'

Marcus glanced at his watch. 'I know you're dedicated, but it's only just gone eight.'

'Yes, exactly; I meant to be at my desk by now. I've barely slept, and what with the *Festival* kicking off tomorrow, we're manic with incoming guests *and* I've got a close friend arriving today for ten days...' She laughed. 'Not sure if it's the excitement or the madness, but it could be why I thought I saw the ghost of Jane Austen just disappear into thin air!'

Marcus laughed, too. 'You'll be fine once today is over. We're pretty booked up, too, so I'll be sharing your pain later. I'll let you get on, and perhaps–'

Rose's mobile interrupted them and with an apologetic smile, she pulled it out and glanced at the screen. It was her friend, Morgan.

'I'll catch you later.'

She exchanged a wave with Marcus as he walked on, then accepted the call and turned to continue her walk along Argyle Street.

'Morgan, hi! Have you landed?'

'Hi! Yes; I'm still on the tarmac. They don't seem to have a spot for us yet. I've tried telling them to just open up the emergency slide, and I'll make a run for it, but they don't think I'm funny.'

Rose grinned. 'How was your flight?'

'Great. So many accents. Everyone was too polite to tell me to shut up – it was glorious. So I'll get on the train and call you when I'm close.'

'Yes, perfect. I wish I could meet you at the station rather than your apartment, but it's a manic day of–'

'Don't even worry about me! I'll find my way. I don't want to cause you any stress. See you in a bit... Can you believe it?'

Rose couldn't. Her heart was more full than she could possibly express. A little breathless now, she sighed as she hurried across Pulteney Bridge. 'Why didn't we do this sooner?'

A rustling noise came down the phone – Morgan getting her things together. 'Because you had an idiot fiancé who didn't like me *or* want us to spend time together – or for you to spend time with anyone but him, come to that!' Rose's brows rose as Morgan paused. 'Did I say that out loud?'

Laughing, Rose waved at a friend having breakfast inside *Blue Quails Deli*. 'Yes; you did rather.'

'Sorry.' Morgan's voice softened. 'I'm just a little hyper – I didn't hurt your feelings, did I?'

Rose took a moment to reflect on the four-year relationship she'd ended in January. She could hardly muster up his face, much less any feeling of regret. 'Morgan, it's been eight months. I think any feelings associated with Jonathan are so far behind me, I can't even remember why I was with him in the first place.'

'Honestly, I think you thought you had a cranky Mr Darcy type on your hands that you could turn around when really you just had a normal jerk.' Rose laughed. 'Hey, they're making an announcement; I'd better pay attention. See you in a few!'

Rose tucked the phone back into her pocket before hurrying her steps again, smiling as she crossed the road and headed up Upper Borough Walls. If all went smoothly, Morgan's train was due into Bath around midday, and the sooner Rose got to the office, the faster the hour would come when the two friends would meet in person for the first time in their more than seven-year friendship.

A sense of anticipation, of excitement, urged Rose along, and before she knew it she was entering the building on Queen Square where she worked.

'Thank goodness you're here.'

'Yes, sorry; best-laid plans and all that.' Rose dropped her bag onto her chair and walked over to the large desk under the window. 'What's up?'

James Malcolm, owner of *Luxury Lettings of Bath* and Rose's boss, leaned back in his chair, stretching his long arms above his head for a moment – a familiar gesture to relieve tension – before sitting forward and waving a hand towards the two desks opposite him – both empty.

'Guess who can't come in today because of a bug?'

Rose blew out a breath. 'Bad timing.' She hurried into the kitchenette and set the kettle to boil. A strong coffee would sort James out.

'Let's have a drink, and then I'll round up some help.'

The morning whisked by in a whirlwind of phone calls, with Rose soon securing some backup help for checking in the many arrivals due that day and persuading the younger brother of a friend to run errands for her. Still, some part of her was keeping a close eye on the time, and when her mobile rang Rose snatched it up eagerly. 'Morgan? Are you here?'

'Um... no.'

Rose stood up, moving towards the door. 'What do you mean? Are you close? Was the train delayed?' She hurried down the stairs and out into the street to continue the call in more privacy.

'If I told you my train seems to be heading toward the wrong Spa, would you tell me that was a good thing or a bad thing?'

Rose paced on the pavement. 'Bad. Very bad. Where are you exactly – do you know?'

Morgan told her, including the spiralling story of exactly how she'd ended up on a train to Leamington Spa and when she'd first realised her error.

'Okay. Listen carefully. Get off at the next stop. Look for trains to Reading. You'll be able to pick up the one running between London and Bristol there, and Bath is a stop on that train. Just get on it and then call me.'

'Got it.'

'Okay.' Rose did some quick calculations in her head. 'Morgan?'

'Yeah.'

'Don't fall asleep on the train.'

'Not a problem. I'll find someone to talk to.'

Rose said a quick prayer for that poor, unsuspecting Brit and rang off, slowly rearranging her day in her mind as she went back up to the office.

With hindsight, it was lucky Morgan's arrival had been delayed. Neither she nor James had chance for a break at lunchtime, but as she fielded calls, organised the temps she had secured for the afternoon and liaised with various people to ensure everything went as smoothly as possible, Rose could feel an aura of contentment hovering. The annual *Jane Austen Festival* was always the highlight of her year – both at work and leisure – but with Morgan's imminent arrival, nothing could dent her mood.

As if on cue, her mobile pinged: a text from Morgan, proudly stating she'd managed to get on the train running between Bristol and London – only it was clear from what Morgan wrote she was going in the wrong direction.

Shaking her head in bemusement, Rose tapped in more instructions.

Get off at the next stop! Then, unable to stop herself, added: *Don't you have trains in America?*

Sure we do.

Have you ever used *them?*

Not really. I tried the subway in DC once. Eventually I just gave up and took a cab.

Why didn't you tell me you had trouble with directions?

Because I always get there eventually. Oo – I'm getting off the train again. Stay tuned. Okay, 8 minutes. I've got it now, I'm sure of it.

Text me as soon as you're sure.

You got it, boss.

'Everything okay?'

Rose looked over at James, who was eyeing her with concern. As she had been standing in the middle of the office furiously texting, she shouldn't have been surprised. 'Actually, no. One of our check-ins is delayed. Looks like she won't be here until about three.'

'This is the Laura Place check-in? Your friend?'

Trying to rework the schedule in her head, Rose nodded. Despite all her reorganisation, they now had two apartments due to receive guests at three, and all their extra help already committed.

Rose sighed. She would not let this stress ruin her day. 'Just when you think everything is going to go like clockwork.' She glanced at the sheet, noting the addresses and likewise the difficulty of checking Morgan in three hours later than planned near Pulteney Bridge and another booking due to check in on the other side of town, up near the Royal Crescent at exactly the same time.

'It can't be helped both Roger and Sarah have gone down with a bug; at least we didn't pick it up.'

James got to his feet. 'Yes, surprising, isn't it, how often they are knocked flat by the same malady, always on the same day?'

Rose frowned as he walked over to the small kitchenette and flicked the switch on the kettle; he was right, of course. Now she thought about it, both Roger and Sarah did spend an awful lot of time staring at each other, or talking in hushed voices. How could she have missed a budding romance her boss had noticed so easily? Not that she blamed him for his sourness towards love and relationships – after all, hadn't that shark of a woman put him through hell simply for caring about his own company, wanting to make a success of it?

Hearing the kettle switch off, she walked into the small kitchen, calling over her shoulder, 'More coffee?'

There was no reply. James stood at the window overlooking the square, clearly lost in thought. He was a striking figure, tall with broad shoulders and a head of slightly tousled hair – which Rose always called 'dirty blond' – that had a tendency to become more and more disarrayed as the day progressed, depending on his level of stress.

'James?'

He turned around. 'Sorry. Miles away. Tea, please, or I'll be bouncing off the walls.'

When Rose came back with the drinks, he had returned to his desk and was thumbing through a presentation, one with which she was very familiar. She had typed it up, made his many alterations and had then listened to him practise it over and over, honing it to fit into the precise 15-minute slot allocated by *Williams & Stock*. She knew how important it was to James to secure the tender for the newly renovated landmark building on the Paragon, a high-end range of apartments totally suited to their present portfolio and one that could lift his small company into something so much more substantial. The fact that the building had once been lived in by Jane Austen's aunt and uncle, and was somewhere she had often stayed, was what had drawn it to Rose's attention.

She had worked hard to develop a niche market for visitors to the city since she'd joined *Luxury Lettings*, and had always kept James informed of any apartments becoming available in buildings associated with Jane Austen, be it her visits on holiday, her residency or the two novels with key Bath associations, *Northanger Abbey* and *Persuasion*. She also worked hard on their marketing around key dates throughout the year which might attract fans of the famous author, such as the summer Regency costumed ball and the annual *Literary Festival*.

Placing the mug a safe distance from the precious presentation, she returned to her own desk, picking up the phone on its first ring. She put it down again five minutes later and sighed. More guests, ahead of time, now due to arrive at three instead of four. Thankfully, this booking was close to one of the others; she'd just have to sprint.

The ping of her mobile drew her attention: a new message from Morgan. It was a selfie with a fellow train passenger in which Morgan was proudly pointing to the digital readout above her head proclaiming 'Bath Spa'.

My friend says Bath is the next stop!

Rose checked her watch, assessing the difficulty of now being in three places at once and in two parts of town. She could only make it work if… Rose glanced over at James, who was mouthing words under his breath as he flicked through his presentation. She bit her lip. It was a long time since her boss had had to do a meet-and-greet, and he was hardly in the right frame of mind.

Well, there was nothing for it, and the worst of it all was it meant she would have to sacrifice checking her own friend in. The long-awaited face-to-face would have to be postponed, and she only hoped Morgan wouldn't be too disappointed. Glancing at the clock, she almost panicked. It was already approaching half past two. If she was going to make this work, she had to act quickly.

A little warily, Rose cleared her throat. No reaction. 'Er, James?'

No response. Getting to her feet, she walked over to stand in front of his desk and finally he looked up. She could tell from his face he was not best pleased.

'I am sorry, but there's a slight hiccup. Due to one earlier than planned arrival and one later, the only way we can meet our commitments to our guests is if you do one of these check-ins.' She waved the list, then held her breath.

He frowned. 'Are you joking? I have to be at *Williams & Stock's* by four.'

'Yes, yes, I know.' Rose rushed to placate him. 'It's just that I can't possibly do all three of these,' she waved the list again, 'and you have always said our customer service must be of the highest level at all times.'

'What about the temps we hired to help out? Can't one of them do some more?'

'Already out dealing with check-ins and fully scheduled for the rest of the day.'

James blew out a breath, then nodded. 'Go ahead, what do you want me to do?'

A wave of relief washed over Rose. 'It won't impact on your meeting at all. Here, look,' she turned to rummage through the papers on her desk, then walked over to place a booking form in front of him and he glanced at it.

'Morgan Taylor – your American?' He looked up with a frown. 'I thought it was a girl friend?'

'Yes. She is.' Rose resisted the urge to roll her eyes; she had stopped finding Morgan's given name strange years ago; Americans seemed to have a delight in odd monikers. 'My American, who is also a paying client, is now due to arrive at Laura Place around three. It's five minutes' walk from *Williams & Stock's* office, giving you all the time in the world to get there for four. She's five minutes away from the station, which means it should all come together perfectly.'

'Hmmm, okay. Well, you'd best call the other two arrivals and see if one of them is okay to wait half an hour. Aiden would be best, he's a regular.'

Rose paled; with the fracas over Morgan's arrival, she'd almost forgotten about who was arriving that afternoon. 'Can't *you* call him? He's a mate, isn't he?'

James looked at his watch. 'No time – if I'm doing this, I'd best get going.' He grabbed his presentation and placed it carefully into his briefcase, pocketed his mobile and took the booking form from her.

'Her mobile number's on there, though I'm sure you won't need it.' Rose hurried to the key cabinet and selected the right ones before opening the cupboard against the back wall and pulling out three sturdy carrier bags.

'Here.' She handed one to James, along with the keys. 'Remember you need to put these out in the kitchen before she arrives. Oh, and good luck with the presentation!'

He pocketed the keys, took the bag and with a reluctant smile turned for the door. 'Thank you; let's hope I don't need it.'

As he left the room, Rose dashed to the door and called down the stairs. 'James! Morgan is one of my best friends. Try and be nice!'

The only response was the sound of the door to the street as it closed behind him.

CHAPTER TWO

Conscious of the time, Rose hurried into the small cloakroom and stared at herself in the mirror as she washed her hands. Her tightly pulled back hair was fighting to be released from its restraint, but with no time, she quickly pinned back a couple of loose curls, applied a clear gloss to her lips and straightened her neat, formal jacket. It would have to do.

Grabbing the other two bags and the necessary keys from her desk, she slung her bag over her shoulder and flew down the stairs, trying to call Morgan, but the number just rang out and didn't even go to voicemail. Then with a yelp she saw the warning message now flashing on her screen: low battery. Frustrated with herself, Rose sighed. She was forever forgetting her charger; how could she not have thought about it this morning?

Walking out into the street, both carrier bags on one arm, she quickly selected Dr Trevellyan from her list of contacts, hoping her phone would hold out, then paused on the edge of the kerb, waiting for a break in the traffic and for the call to connect. She grabbed a moment to skip across the road as a car slowed to let her cross, raising a hand in thanks.

Hoping the call would go to voicemail, she hurried towards the steps at the far side of the square leading to a useful short cut to the area around the Royal Crescent. Her rapid breathing she put down to the pace she was making, but as she placed her foot on the bottom step, the tone ceased and a voice spoke, close in her ear: a deep, familiar masculine tone causing her throat to tighten.

'He-hello? Is that Dr Trevellyan?'

'Speaking.'

She could feel the old, familiar sensations returning as she climbed the steps, could picture his face, and she drew in a deep breath to steady her voice. 'Hi. It's Rose Wallace from *Luxury Lettings*. Dr Trevellyan, I'm so sorry; I'm running a little late. Do you still plan on arriving at three?' *Please remember me,* her heart pleaded.

'I'm here.' He always was a man of few words.

Rose's heart sank as she reached the top of the steps and set off along the walk at a rapid pace. 'At the property? I'm so sorry. I thought you were coming at three, not two-thirty.'

He muttered something unintelligible, then added, 'No, I meant in Bath.'

'Oh!' Feeling foolish, Rose could sense the telltale easy blush rising in her cheeks. 'Well, um, would it be okay if we met a little later at the flat; say, half-three?' There was silence. 'I – I really am incredibly sorry to inconvenience you…'

'No problem.' The line went dead before she could say anything further, and she tucked the phone back into her pocket before hurrying up the road towards Brock Street, anxious to reach the first apartment in time to check it over and lay out the welcome produce for the incoming guests.

Her anticipation of finally meeting with Morgan face-to-face after their many years of friendship had been at its height for days, but just for a moment, Rose's mind was full of nothing but Dr Trevellyan and wondering if he had changed at all since she had seen him in Bath last year.

By the time she'd settled the Hale family in on Brock Street, Rose was reminded, once again, why she loved her job. Mary and John Hale were visiting from the Lake District and keen to explore the local countryside.

Rose, however, had seen the elaborate bonnet they'd carried carefully in from the car and the telltale *Jane Austen Festival* programme sticking out of the lady's shoulder bag. Not for the first time, she wondered what the author herself would make of all of this pomp and circumstance so many years after her time on Earth. Then Rose pushed the thought aside to attend to the guests and, as she talked them through the local facilities, she made sure to mention a nearby restaurant, one Rose knew other festival-goers frequented.

Rose bade them a happy stay in Bath before making her way back out into the street. She walked briskly along and soon emerged onto the golden sweep of the Royal Crescent, pausing on the corner to drink in the view, one she never tired of. Had Morgan arrived in Bath at last? She hoped everything was going okay with James. Checking her phone quickly, she found no message or missed call, only the worrying reminder of the small sliver of red indicating what was left of her battery life.

Tucking the phone back into her pocket, Rose felt a momentary unease filter through her mind. Surely James wouldn't mention to Morgan precisely *who* Rose was checking in instead of her friend?

Morgan, of course, knew all about Dr Trevellyan and Rose's… *silliness* about him. Not that Rose had had any intention of letting anyone know about her crush, but Morgan had a way about her, a warmth and friendliness that encouraged people to admit to things they didn't intend to. Now, she just had to hope that if it did come up, Morgan would have the sense not to let any reaction slip in front of James. Even though they had never met in person, they had had sufficient interactions through social media and phone calls for Rose to understand Morgan was not known for subtlety.

This potential for embarrassment dampened her spirits a little but the distraction stood her in good stead, and it was only as she put the key in the lock to the outer door of the apartments that her imminent meeting with Dr Trevellyan resurfaced. Barely had she had time to recall it, however, when a male voice said behind her, 'Perfect timing.'

Rose blushed deeply. Plastering a smile on her face, she turned to face him, trying with all her might not to look as if she were about to swoon.

'Dr Trevellyan! I – er, I'm pleased you chose to stay with us again.' *Understatement of the year…* Rose bit her lip as he relieved her of the carrier bag and indicated she precede him into the building. Why was she always such a fool around him?

Conscious of the telltale colour in her cheeks once more and her heart pounding fit to burst, Rose hurried down the hallway to the door to the ground-floor flat. How could he be so… *gorgeous* and not be aware of it? Dark, intelligent eyes and brown, curling hair, only enhanced by the random strands of grey and oh, that deep voice… And he was so *cool*. A real grown-up – not like Jonathan, still as immature when they parted as he'd been when she'd first met him years ago. Rose smiled ruefully. Morgan had laughed when she'd called the doctor that, but she'd been just 24 the first time she'd seen him in person and the ten years between them had seemed a huge chasm. Her friend had brushed it aside; her father was more than twenty years her stepmom's senior; what was ten years between friends?

A voice cleared behind her, and Rose started and turned about.

Dr Trevellyan was juggling the carrier bag, his briefcase, a backpack and some folders with papers escaping in all directions. 'Any chance we could go inside before I have a mishap?'

'Oh, of course.' Feeling even more awkward, Rose clumsily opened the door to the flat and walked in, heading straight for the kitchen. There was no need for the usual introductory tour of the property; he had stayed in the same one for the past three years.

'Are the Janeites all in town?' He dropped the carrier onto the floor and placed his folders carefully on the kitchen table.

Rose attempted a nonchalant shrug. She had no desire for him to know how avid a fan she was herself. 'Yes, mostly; some tomorrow, too.' She tried not to stare at him as he shrugged out of his jacket and slung it on the back of a chair. 'Your – er – I believe your lecture is sold out again this year.'

He grunted, and Rose hurried to fill the gap in conversation. 'Is it to be a new topic?'

'Sadly not.' He stared at one of the folders on the table, then shrugged. 'Just the Steventon dig from a couple of years ago, with a few modifications.' He paused and glanced at Rose as if checking if he needed to clarify.

Rose nodded, unwilling to say anything. He had no need to know how much she knew about all Jane Austen's former residences. He certainly had no need to know she presently lived in the basement of the very home occupied by the Austen family from 1801 to 1804. Rose bit her lip; how she would love to let it all spill out, but she didn't dare. Dr Trevellyan rarely spoke beyond the common civilities, and she really wanted to keep him talking.

'Oh, I'm sure it will be welcomed. It sold out so quickly, and there were so many who couldn't get a seat.'

He pulled out a chair, swung it around and straddled it. Rose hoped intensely he couldn't read her mind.

'That's fortunate, then; otherwise, they'd be rather bored this year.'

Rose doubted anyone could be bored listening to his voice, but she kept the thought to herself, retrieved the carrier bag and walked over to the worktop with it. It would be easier to control her thoughts if she kept her back to him.

'You must know by now there's no minutiae too unimportant to fascinate Jane Austen's fans. You could veer off and ramble on whatever aspect you like, and they'll be interested.'

He grunted. 'If I give myself free rein, it will be about permits and flaky volunteers and the many, *many* frustrations of securing both. But you make a good point. I'll stick to the tried and tested.'

Rose glanced over her shoulder. He had opened his briefcase and pulled out a battered laptop and as he placed it on the table, he muttered, 'Familiarity breeds no contempt with me.'

'Is that why you always stay in the same apartment?' Rose hesitated; she wouldn't normally utter a word beyond the practicalities of the check-in. Perhaps if he didn't meet her eye, she might be able to hold it together quite competently. 'I know you said you appreciated the amount of natural light here.' She gestured towards the elegant drawing room across the hall with its full-height windows. 'I had the desk placed in its usual location, too. Oh, and I left you an extension cable.' Was she gabbling? Rose stopped abruptly as he looked up and met her gaze. 'Er – I'll just get these sorted, and then I'll leave you in peace.'

She turned away again and opened the bag, pulling out a huge bar of *Cadbury's* milk chocolate. Her heart sank as she peered back into the depths. There were *Oreos, Doritos* and, even worse, no sign of the locally made produce and the proverbial bottle of good wine always on offer to incoming guests.

'I prefer the fruit-and-nut variety.' Dr Trevellyan had come to stand beside her, and he retrieved the bag from her grip and peered inside. '*Love Hearts?*' He looked at Rose, a brow raised. 'A curious choice.'

Rose wished she could disappear through the smart Italian tiles under her feet. *Love Hearts* were one of Morgan's guilty pleasures, ever since Rose had included them in a birthday parcel some years earlier. 'Oh, Dr Trevellyan, this is the – I'm *so* sorry, I've mixed up the bags. We have a guest checking in today, from California. And – oh dear…'

He smiled slightly, a rare sight of no help whatsoever to Rose's flustered heart. 'Well, I can't fault her taste, but I'm not sure I can make it through all of these in just a few days.' He peered back into the bag and withdrew a bottle of water. 'No wine?'

'She doesn't like it; or tea–'

'Who doesn't?'

'My… this client. Look, I'll pop to the shop on Julian Road and get something. I'll be back really quickly.'

Rose held out the keys as she made for the door, but his hand closed over hers, forcing her to stop.

'Please don't bother. I can see there's tea bags in the caddy – that's all I need for now. I never eat the things you leave. In fact, I don't eat in at all when I'm here; the people-watching in restaurants is far too entertaining.'

He took the keys and let go of her hand, which felt warmer than possibly it ever had in her life, but Rose pursed her lips, not feeling any better about the mix-up. It was clear, however, he didn't want – or need – anything further from her, his attention already drawn back to emptying his briefcase. It was time to go.

'I will leave you to settle in.' She picked up the unwanted carrier and walked towards the door, and he waved a vague hand at her as he extracted a pair of wire-rimmed glasses from his jacket pocket and placed them on his nose.

Closing the door to the flat, Rose leaned back against it with a sigh. 'Welcome back to Bath,' she whispered under her breath. Then she hurried out into the street, relishing the cooling air as it brushed her still warm cheeks.

CHAPTER THREE

Rose had been back in the office for over an hour but still there was no sign of James. She walked to the window fronting onto Queen Square and scanned the street outside, then pressed her face to the glass to peer to the right, hoping to see him coming along Wood Street towards the office. Nothing.

She walked back to her desk and picked up her mobile. Damn. It was now completely dead. She couldn't try Morgan anymore, and she didn't know her number by heart, so she couldn't use the office phone. Thank goodness she did know which property she was in.

Glancing at the clock, Rose sighed as the phone rang again. She had been fielding calls ever since she returned from checking Dr Trevellyan into his flat, leaving her no time to reflect on how quickly she had succumbed to the charms he didn't seem to know he possessed, or whether Morgan was settling in okay to her flat. Rose knew to credit her friend with enough sense to cope, but it was her first time in the country and – despite being rather untravelled herself – she could imagine that the differences between one's homeland and another, even if they did claim to share a language, might be rather challenging on first encounter.

By the time she had dealt with the last of the calls, it was close to 6 o'clock and, impatient to find Morgan, she quickly shut down her computer and locked the office. The temps would go home after their last check-ins without returning, and seeing James's iPad on the desk, she knew he wouldn't go home without first coming back to work; he could set the alarm then.

Making her way through the streets, part of the endless flow of people heading home after a day's work, Rose dodged the tourists clogging the corner opposite Pulteney Bridge and hurried across it, jumping on and off the narrow pavement to avoid a passing bus and pedestrians alike. Despite her haste, however, she couldn't pass the florists on the bridge without browsing the array of gorgeous flowering plants and bouquets displayed outside.

Waving at the shop owner, who had spotted her through the window, Rose pointed to her watch with a smile and hurried on. She really didn't have a single space left in her tiny courtyard or on her steps for any more pots.

She fetched up outside Morgan's apartment in Laura Place out of breath but conscious of her excitement returning. This time of year – the run-up to and the 10 days of the *Jane Austen Festival* – always filled her with so much joy; she loved the atmosphere, the endless stream of Austen- and Regency-related events, the return of familiar faces and the fun of watching those who were new, but to have the added bonus of finally meeting Morgan was the icing on the cake. Perhaps not a fan to the depth Rose was, Morgan had sufficient interest in Jane Austen as an author to ensure they would both be able to get their equal share of fun from the upcoming week.

There was no response when she rang the bell. Rose frowned, glancing at her watch. The ground-floor windows were set a little too high, so there was no chance of peering into the flat to see if there was any movement. Could her friend have fallen victim to jetlag? From what Rose knew of Morgan's family it was very large, very loud, and very tied to North America, except for one black sheep of a brother who was travelling Europe at that very moment. It was possible Morgan had never experienced enough of a time zone shift to suffer from it.

Rose turned around and looked up and down the street. Could she have gone out? A middle-aged lady plodding past caught her eye, three overstuffed carrier bags straining in her hands, and the familiar logo put Rose's mind at rest. Of course! Morgan would have been given a bag full of things she could not – or would not – eat or drink due to the mix-up. The information folder in the flat would have indicated the nearest supermarket, which was no doubt where she had gone.

Feeling relieved and keen to get home and charge her phone so she could reassure herself Morgan was fine, Rose hurried down the steps and walked briskly along Great Pulteney Street, crossing over into Sydney Place and then pausing outside number 4 to extract her keys from her bag. She never failed to get a thrill whenever she stopped here, standing on the pavement where Jane Austen must have walked by so many times over two hundred years ago. Rose was about to flick the latch on the wrought-iron gate in the railings when a movement caught her eye and, glancing up, she saw a slender figure in one of the windows of the ground-floor flat above her own.

Whoever it was, they did not seem as though they wished to be seen; by the time Rose had opened the gate the figure had disappeared and for a fleeting moment she shuddered. Frowning, she hurried down the steps to the door to her flat. It wasn't the first time she'd noticed someone hovering in the shadows when she returned home in recent weeks, and she had meant to ask Marcus – who managed the boutique holiday apartments making up the remainder of 4 Sydney Place – who it might be. For a second, she recalled the figure in Regency costume she'd seen coming out into the rear garden that morning and then seeming to no longer be there. She felt goose bumps rise on her arms, then laughed at her own silliness as she put the key in the lock. There would be plenty of people in costume over the coming week and no doubt the visitor upstairs was just one of many of them.

Dropping her things onto the kitchen table, Rose spied her charger immediately and, grabbing her phone from her pocket, connected it before turning to put the kettle on. It would take a few minutes to come to life, so she hung up her coat and picked up the pile of papers on the table: all the tickets for the upcoming *Festival* events.

Again, a frisson of excitement ran through her, catching her almost by surprise in its intensity. Then she laughed. *Calm down, girl*, she cautioned herself. *It's just the combination of Morgan being here, the usual anticipation of the* Festival *and finally seeing the doctor again…*

Her insides made a strange lurch, and she dropped the tickets back on the table and turned her attention to the kettle. She needed to stop being such an idiot over him, and now would be a really good time to start.

Barely had Rose sat at the table with her mug of hot tea when the pinging sound of incoming messages alerted her to her phone now being live. Checking it quickly, she was unsurprised to see more than one missed call from James earlier but delighted to see a whole slew of messages from Morgan. At last! Quickly she scanned them, then laughed out loud.

There were several selfies again – including one with several very blond men captioned, '*I'm lost in Bath but with the nicest Germans – we're lost together and having a marvellous time!*' After that, there were a series of messages apparently detailing her path wandering the city.

It was no help whatsoever as to where Morgan might be now, but at least it confirmed she was in town and making friends already, though Rose did spare a thought for James. Did this mean Morgan had been late arriving at the holiday apartment?

Conscious her phone would not have much chance to charge before she needed to go out, Rose looked up Morgan's number in her contacts list – *just in case*, she muttered under her breath as she scribbled it in a small notepad.

She was about to grab her things and head back towards Laura Place when the phone bleeped again. It was a message from James.

Rose read it as she shrugged into her coat. *Result!* she whispered under her breath as she picked up her keys and headed once more for the street. She had no idea how her boss had come to have Morgan safely in hand in a bar just a few steps from the office, but she didn't care. Finally, they were going to meet in person.

Rose hadn't realised just how anxious she'd become about Morgan. Knowing she was fine meant she could really relax again, and she walked back down Great Pulteney Street with the lightest of steps as the mantle of worry slipped from her shoulders, taking the stresses of the day with it.

She ought to call James to say she was on her way, but with her battery so minimally charged, she didn't want to waste it. Soon she was crossing Laura Place, a wide smile on her face as she glanced over towards the flat where Morgan was staying. Ten whole days for them to hang out together. All these years of friendship, and finally they could be in the same place at the same time, with no one to answer to but themselves.

Morgan was quite a few years younger than Rose, who was 27, and only recently graduated from a small college in California, and she still couldn't understand how such a vibrant and outgoing person could find Rose interesting company. With Morgan being so full of the joy of life, she felt like a pale shadow by comparison. She'd spoken to her friend on video enough times to appreciate how genuinely lovely she was, with large, dark eyes, luminous skin and dark, shining hair. Rose had stared at her own reflection for some time after that first video-chat.

Her skin had the paleness – transparency, almost – of the traditional English rose complexion, but she couldn't ignore the smattering of freckles over her nose and dusting her cheeks. Her eyes were sufficiently lacking in blueness to seem grey in most lights and her tresses – long and curling beyond the control of any hair appliance – were ginger; soft auburn, her hairdresser always called it. It certainly sounded more elegant, but Rose was no fool; she knew ginger when she saw it.

Ultimately, it had taken Rose a while – a few years of deepening online friendship, in fact – to gather the courage to invite Morgan to visit, and as it was, she didn't have anything to worry about. Morgan was thrilled, excited and grateful for the offer, so much so that Rose had regretted the reticence preventing her from making it sooner.

The fact that Jonathan had so vocally discouraged Rose from taking the 'risk' had been one of the final straws in Rose's decision to end the relationship. All they'd waited for then was for Morgan to complete her degree and their plans were set.

Convincing Morgan's rather charmingly paranoid parents that Rose was a real, genuine person, their having met through an Internet forum, had been an experience. In the end, it was Morgan's father's company that had clinched the trip. Up until very recently, Dan Taylor's travel periodicals had focused purely on North America. Now Morgan had been offered a chance to spend a couple of months in the brand new London office, as the company had finally decided to expand into

Europe. After spending time in Bath with Rose, Morgan would be learning the ropes and reporting back to her father for a few weeks.

Rose found it touchingly sweet the family was so close, for her own was certainly lacking. Her friends had been the ones to caution her over meeting people online and being sure they were who they claimed to be; even James had had his say. She doubted very much her mother, whom she rarely saw, would care one way or the other.

Rose turned into John Street, avoided a group of young men standing outside the *Salamander*, and soon turned the far corner, taking the steps into *Hall & Woodhouse* two at a time.

The crowd instantly enveloped her, but she eased her way between the chattering couples and groups of friends, trying to catch a glimpse of James's tall figure, gripped by a sudden and totally irrational panic she might not recognise Morgan at all.

Two more 'excuse me's later and she had squeezed through the mass of people standing in the bar to emerge on the other side, close to where they tended to gather on the leather sofas, and there, exactly as Rose had hoped, was Morgan. To her surprise, she was curled up in a corner of one of the sofas chattering away to two young men, waving her arms around and making them both laugh; James, in the meantime, sat opposite, a faint look of surprise on his face.

Rose felt suddenly nervous, almost frozen in place, but just then Morgan glanced over her shoulder and their eyes met.

Normally shy in public situations, often quiet and introspective, Rose barely comprehended what was happening as Morgan leapt to her feet with a squeal and rushed over to throw her arms around her. Thankful for the melee and general noise around them, Rose realised she wouldn't have cared if they were in the middle of Milsom Street. Hugging her friend back, she felt a lump rise in her throat and, unable to stop them, tears spilled down her cheeks.

If this was making a scene, just for once, Rose didn't mind. They pulled apart and looked at each other, both crying and laughing at the same time.

Morgan looked just as Rose had expected… except that she was so much tinier! In all their communication – even over Skype – Morgan's personality shone through as just so big and to see her now, Rose wondered how so much life, so much energy and vibrancy could be contained within such a petite frame.

Morgan had fished a tissue from a pocket and was dabbing her cheeks. 'You're beautiful, Rose!'

'*Me?*' Rose shook her head in disbelief. Then she laughed. 'And I'm certain this wet-faced look makes things worse.' She wiped her face with her fingers, then smiled at her friend. 'But I knew you would be gorgeous. How are you? Are you okay? I'm *so* sorry I couldn't be there this afternoon.' She glanced over to where James was seated, certain he had just that moment turned his head away. 'Has James been taking good care of you?'

Morgan stepped aside and waved a hand towards the seating around the coffee table. 'Yes, James was my hero… a couple times already, and do you know these guys? We've been having a blast.'

Rose smiled faintly at the young men, then turned to James. 'I can't thank you enough. My phone died so I only just started to receive texts again.'

James shook his head. 'No problem. Do you want a drink?'

Rose nodded. 'Yes, please. Morgan? Can you last a bit longer or do you need to get some sleep? What about food? Have you eaten?'

'I feel wide awake now you're here.' Morgan beamed and gestured towards James. 'And I've been fed, too.' The young men seemed to realise they were surplus to requirements and excused themselves, and Rose and Morgan took their places on the sofa as James ordered the drinks.

Rose looked from one to the other. 'I have so many questions right now – for both of you – I don't know where to start.' She met James's eye. 'The meeting! Oh, how did it go?'

He looked slightly taken off guard, but said hesitantly, 'It went – I don't know. It was over very quickly. My first instinct is that I messed up – but Stock seemed to be trying to make me feel comfortable at the end – there were all sorts of undercurrents; I should've taken you along to translate.'

Morgan frowned. 'This is the meeting you were on your way to after opening up Laura's Place for me?'

'Yes, that would be after you locked yourself out – twice – but before you tried to burn the place down,' James said, obviously joking but clearly trying to steer the conversation elsewhere.

It worked; Rose gaped. 'You did *what?*'

Morgan rolled her eyes. 'You were able to let me back in, weren't you? And they were very small sparks and not even – I mean maybe just – a little poof of smoke.'

Rose's heart sank. What an awful welcome when her friend had travelled so far. 'Oh Morgan – where? How?'

Their drinks came, and James seemed content to distance himself, nursing his glass and letting the conversation flow between the two girls. After a full report on just how many wrong turns Morgan had made on her way from the station to Laura Place, Rose realised James was becoming increasingly uncomfortable. Yes, as suspected, Morgan had been late, and it seemed he didn't want it mentioned in front of her, which Rose found profoundly sweet of him, and yet she was genuinely worried it might have affected his bid.

Her chance to question him soon came, however, when Morgan took herself off to the bar to ask for more ice.

'I'm so sorry.' Rose felt incredibly guilty. 'You were late, weren't you?'

James glanced around as if to check Morgan was not within earshot and shrugged. 'A little. I think it ended up fine.'

'Really?' Rose persisted.

'Well, I think so. Let me take you through it.' He quickly recapped how the meeting had gone, and by the end Rose felt sure James had done admirably, with Morgan's lateness hopefully not hurting his chances – not by much, anyway.

'It does sound promising.' Rose wasn't sure who she wished to reassure most, herself or James, but his attention wasn't with her as he glanced around the room for the third time since they had started speaking.

'Look, do you think you ought to check on your friend? She's been gone a while, and she does seem susceptible to mishap.'

'Oh! Yes, it has been a while, hasn't it?' Rose frowned. 'How did you end up here with her?'

'Long story. She turned up at the office as I was about to lock up – had the folder with her as the office was the only address she had to hand, so I thought I'd best, well, you know. I didn't want you worried about her, and I didn't want her to get lost again either.'

'That's so kind of you.' Rose craned her head to see beyond the people surrounding them. 'It's just – she's always seemed so capable to me…'

A group of loud men – all very tall and very fair – were bearing down on their part of the room, obscuring her view of anyone else, but just as she was going to stand up to look for Morgan, Rose saw her friend dart out in front of the men and present them to her and James with her arms wide. 'It's my Germans!'

They gave a roar of approval, and Rose blinked. Morgan was so clearly proud, and the men so clearly pissed, that she struggled to keep from giggling as she turned to James for an explanation, but he just smiled tightly. 'She has Germans. It's another long story.'

The Germans brought a tray of shots with them, and insisted on them all sharing it. Rose wasn't keen, but one of the men – ash blond and charming, despite his inebriation – insisted. She spluttered and coughed, deciding enough was enough. This could get really messy.

James, who had disappeared temporarily, returned just as she was gathering her things to confirm he had paid the bill and, much to her relief, felt it was time to leave. 'Oh you didn't need to do that – but thank you.'

Morgan, who was now being taught a rather bawdy German drinking song, did she but know it, seemed to be leaning a little too heavily against one of her new friends, and, despite her game efforts to keep up with them, Rose could tell it was weariness and not flirtation.

'If you don't get her out of here now, someone's going to have to carry her.' James nodded at Morgan.

He held out Rose's coat for her, then walked over to retrieve Morgan from her new friends, handing over her bag and, after a momentary hesitation, helping her into the several jumpers she seemed to have with her.

The Germans expressed extreme, but fleeting disappointment. They were in full song by the time Rose, James and Morgan walked out into a now rapidly cooling evening, a blessing to Rose, and she drew in a deep breath, savouring the hint of autumn in the air.

Morgan, on the other hand, immediately started shivering. 'Someone's going to have to lead me. My best guess is that we're supposed to go... upwards?'

Rose laughed as Morgan threaded her arm through hers, cuddling up to her. 'Are you really that cold?'

'Fr-r-r-r-eezing.'

Rose's humour faded. 'Oh dear, do you want my coat?'

'No! No, the walk will w-w-warm me up. Where's James?' Morgan spun them both around until she could see him. 'Thank you so much for the rescue and the drink and the food – now I owe you three times.'

'Not at all, let's just get you–'

'Hey, James!'

CHAPTER FOUR

Rose tensed at the familiar, heart-melting voice, realising a man had come to stand before them. She swallowed quickly, grateful for the dusk, to hide not only her blushes, but also the traces of her earlier tears. She must look so unsightly.

James reached forward to shake the man's hand. 'Aiden! Good to see you back.'

'Good to be here.' His gaze swept over Rose and Morgan, who was still clinging to Rose's arm.

'This is a friend of Rose's from California, Morgan Taylor.' James indicated Morgan. 'Morgan, this is Doctor Aiden Trevellyan. He's an old mate.' The arm wrapped around her own tightened significantly, and Rose offered up the most heartfelt prayer that that was all her friend would do.

The doctor offered his hand. 'Please, the name's Aiden.'

Aiden? Morgan could call him Aiden within ten seconds of meeting him? She had known him three years, and he'd never once called her Rose or asked her to use his name! Before Rose could fully take this on-board, however, Morgan was speaking.

'Aiden. Yes, I know. I mean –' Morgan stopped and bit her lip, throwing Rose a lightning glance. 'Nice to meet you.' There was a pause, then, 'I'm from California.'

'So I heard. I believe I have you to thank for the *Cadbury's* and *Oreos.*'

Morgan looked at Rose in mock indignation. 'How could you?'

Rose couldn't help but laugh. 'It was an accident. You know I'd never knowingly give your goodies to anyone else.'

Thankfully everyone laughed, and James started to talk to his friend about the upcoming rugby game on Saturday, so Rose felt it was the perfect chance to escape, especially with Morgan pinching her arm and looking significantly between Rose and the doctor.

'Well, I'd best get Morgan to her bed; enjoy the rest of your evening.' Both men turned towards them. 'James, I'll see you in the morning.'

Rose turned away, steering Morgan along, whom she suspected wasn't far from falling asleep on her shoulder. They had gone but a few paces, however, when James fell into step beside her.

Rose frowned at him as they reached Quiet Street. 'You don't have to walk us back. It's the wrong end of town for you.'

James just shook his head and gave her a look telling her there would be no use arguing, but then she glanced over her shoulder. 'What happened to your friend?'

'Off to find somewhere to eat.'

Rose sighed under her breath as they walked on; how she would love to sit across the table from Dr Trevellyan and share a meal with him, listening to that lovely, deep voice and staring into those gorgeous eyes…

She shook her head. 'So – the Germans – what's the story?'

'*Oh*, weren't they the friendliest? When I was lost – the first time anyway – they were lost with me. We were lost twins. I wouldn't have gotten to Laura's Place without them.'

'Laura Place,' both Rose and James corrected in unison.

'Ooph!' Rose gripped Morgan's arm tightly as her friend accidentally tripped off the kerb, and she risked a glance at James.

His face was inscrutable, but his intention was apparent; he wouldn't leave them until they were safely home.

They maintained some desultory chatter as they walked, Morgan rambling on about all sorts of things, James making occasional observations about the parts of Bath they passed through, none of which her friend would recall in the morning. Rose merely listened and tried not to guess which restaurant had the pleasure of the doctor's company that evening.

Morgan's steps seemed to slow as they approached Pulteney Bridge, and Rose suspected her slight tipsiness had worn off with the walk and now plain old exhaustion was overtaking her, for her chatter had quietened down, and she kept apologising whenever she stumbled a little.

Finally, they came to Laura Place, and Rose took the key from Morgan's bag and opened the door, but before she could steer her friend over the threshold, Morgan turned around and gave James a hug and a whispered thankyou to him. He looked a little taken aback, and Rose tried not to smile as Morgan walked into the building, then waited, rubbing her hands together for warmth as Rose said goodnight to James.

'I really can't thank you enough.'

'You going to stay here tonight?'

Rose shook her head. 'I'll stay for a while, just to make sure she's settled. But I'm only up the road if she needs anything.'

'Right.' James's eye drifted to where Morgan stood. 'Make sure she writes your address down in case the office is shut next time she's lost.'

With a laugh, Rose nodded. 'I will.'

'Night, then. See you in the morning – heavy day. Let's hope the mysterious bug has passed, and we're back to full strength.'

Rose smiled at him. 'G'night.'

'Toodle-pip!' Morgan's voice called from inside the doorway; James looked at Rose in surprise, who laughed.

'It's a private joke – I'll tell you another time.'

She turned away and walked up the steps and into the building, taking Morgan by the arm and walking her along the hallway to her door, happiness welling up inside. Rose didn't know what to fully expect from the next ten days, but she was certain it would bring memories to cherish forever.

Something woke Rose long before her alarm the next morning, but the quality of light seeping through her curtains and the birds merrily beginning their dawn chorus quickly convinced her of the earliness of the hour. Stretching luxuriously, she rolled onto her side; no need to get up just yet.

She had been having a lovely dream, hadn't she? Closing her eyes, she tried to catch hold of the tendrils as they whispered through the far reaches of her mind, a sensation of warmth enveloping her body as faint remnants danced tantalisingly close. She'd been with Dr Trevellyan – were they dining together? Squeezing her eyes more tightly shut, Rose tried to remember the details… There had been the soft aroma of the food, the taste of the delicious wine, and the soft candlelight flickering on the doctor's bare chest…

Rose shot up in bed, eyes wide open now. *What?* Then she released a long breath and flopped back on her pillow with a small laugh. She knew perfectly well how *that* particular thought had seeped into her subconscious: Morgan! Barely had Rose crossed the threshold on the previous evening, when her friend had declared loudly he was '*adorable; the most gorgeous man alive!*'

No doubt it was Morgan, speculating shortly before they had said goodnight over how Aiden might look without a shirt on and then pondering how many children Rose and Aiden might have together, which had led to the dream...

Feeling her cheeks redden, Rose stirred uneasily in the bed. Had James been out of earshot before Morgan had said those words earlier? Trying to conceal the full extent of her obsession with all things Austen from her boss – her friend – was difficult enough, but revealing that would be preferable to him ever... *ever* finding out about her massive crush on one of his friends.

'Enough!' she cautioned herself. *'Think of something else, or you'll be even more gauche than usual next time you see the doctor.'*

Determinedly, the organised part of her mind began running through everything she needed to do at work later. So many people were checking in today, with every property they managed fully booked. She tried to think about what their contingency plan might be, should Roger and Sarah still be struck down by their mystery bug. Rose stifled a small yawn with the back of her hand. Seriously – how could she not have picked up on the subtleties of *that* little scenario playing out before her eyes, especially in such a small office?

A sudden loud thump from the flat above put paid to this line of thought, however, and throwing the ceiling a resigned look, she turned onto her side, her eyes falling on the half-eaten bar of chocolate by the bed.

Her friend had found her second wind once they were in the flat, so Rose had nipped down to the local shop and bought some replacement milk, *Oreos* and a range of thoroughly British confectionery before they had spent a couple of hours together. Morgan had finally unpacked her bags and, with Rose's willing assistance, had soon settled into her temporary home. Rose didn't think she had ever laughed so much in her life: at Morgan's ridiculousness about the doctor, as well as what her very Californian friend had packed for her trip.

Smiling widely, Rose felt fully awake now. Her excitement about the days ahead had lost none of its intensity; if anything, it was exaggerated, and despite the early hour, she flung the duvet aside and rolled out of bed, stuffing her feet into her slippers (prettily embroidered with a quote from *Northanger Abbey* – a gift from Morgan last Christmas) and grabbing her dressing gown from the floor.

Catching sight of her sleepy face as she passed the mirror, Rose paused and studied her reflection, then leaned over and flicked the switch on the light, throwing her features into stark and unkind relief.

'Ugh,' she muttered under her breath, before pulling a face at herself and flicking the light off. There were still traces of yesterday's mascara under her eyes, thanks to her tears and, no longer in the neat, formal style she used for work, her hair was as unruly a mass of curls as ever.

Rose was not envious by nature, but just for a second, she longed to wake up to such glossy, smooth hair as Morgan possessed, which in her mind's eye was no longer ginger at all, but a rich auburn – much more sophisticated, and surely more likely to catch the eye of Doctor Aiden Trevellyan…

'Stop it, Rose,' she admonished herself out loud as she crossed the hallway into the kitchen and put the kettle to boil. Catching sight of her mud-stained wellies in the boot box by the front door, she smiled.

Last night, she had been mystified as to why Morgan had thought she'd need *three* pairs of boots, including wellies – '*It always rains in England, right?*' – but had forgotten to bring a coat! September may have generally mild weather by British standards, but it was obvious Morgan wasn't going to be warm enough.

With a shrug, Rose picked up a mug, adding a tea bag from the caddy, just as another bump came from the flat above, and she glanced at the clock on the wall. It was barely six-thirty. Used to hearing a certain amount of movement from the flat above hers – people on holiday rarely thought about their neighbours; that was for everyday life at home – she rarely heard a thing in the early mornings. Tourists had no need to be up with the lark to get to work, after all, and this occupant – the one who seemed to have been in residence for some weeks – rarely made any sound, aside from the smoke alarm going off once or twice. In fact, had she not caught those occasional glimpses of the figure by the window, Rose would have assumed the flat was empty.

For a second, she recalled again the costumed figure drifting out into the garden above her yard as she'd popped out to put some rubbish in the bin, but she dismissed it lightly and grabbed the now boiling kettle and made that all-important first cup of tea of the day. She had just walked into her sitting room with her mug when a bleep from her phone (still plugged in for its overnight charge) distracted her.

A text from James: '*Call me soon as you're up. J*'

Rose selected his name from her contacts and set the call in motion as she settled on the squashy sofa, her mug in one hand, long legs tucked beneath her.

'You're up early!'

Rose laughed. 'Ditto! What's up?'

James grunted. 'I didn't want to text you last night, but I got a call from Ade when I got home. He's having problems with his laptop and needs some help fairly urgently.'

Feeling herself grow warm, sensing what might be coming, Rose slowly placed her mug on the coffee table and uncurled her legs. Why was the first thought in her normally sensible head whether the doctor's bare chest in real life was as good as she recalled from her dream?

'Rose? Are you there?'

'Er, yes; yes, I am. You want me to call on him later.'

'Don't hate me. I know you have tons to get through this morning, and I know how important it is for you to take your lunch break to see your friend.'

Rose blinked; how had he even remembered that when he was so busy himself? 'No, it's fine.'

'Well, you haven't heard it all yet. You have to go there now.'

'*Now?*' Rose felt panic grip her. 'But I *can't*. I only just got out of bed. I need to shower; wash my hair; get dressed and...'

'Calm down.' James was laughing. 'When I say 'now' I mean before you come into the office, first thing you do today. Even if you solve his problem with the laptop, he still needs some secretarial support, and I said we'd provide it. I've noticed our competitors offer it on one level or another, so I think we ought to as well.'

Rose fell back against the cushions, her mouth slightly agape but her heart racing fit to burst.

'Fine,' she said in a strangled voice. *And you chose today of all days to start offering?* 'But how can I fit that in with all we have to do? What if the others don't turn up for work again?' Her sense of duty, of professionalism, was warring with the desire to tell James to get off the damn phone and let her have as much time as possible to make herself presentable.

'I'll cross that bridge when I come to it. Damn, there's an incoming call waiting. You're a star, Rose. Call me when you're done with him.' The line went dead.

'Fine,' muttered Rose again, gulping down her tea as she headed for the bathroom. 'I'll call you when I'm done with him alright; in about twenty-five years' time, if not more!'

CHAPTER FIVE

With little financial support from her mother, Rose had spent the bulk of her holidays during her college years temping in a solicitors' office. Her main job had been to open daily packs of tax and other law updates, find the corresponding binder, put the old pages in the relevant archive, and insert the new ones. It was, by far, the most mind-numbing job she had ever had, but despite having spent the last few hours doing pretty much the same process for Dr Trevellyan, she was enjoying herself as she never had at *Wilkie, Logeroff & Frank*.

It wasn't just the subject matter – notes, photographs and slides about Steventon Rectory – interesting her much more than changes in law, it was handling Dr Trevellyan's notes and wallowing in (she couldn't describe it any other way) his adorable way of talking to himself as he organised his papers.

It hadn't taken Rose long to sort out the laptop, though she had been unable to retrieve the document the doctor had been working on. She longed to suggest he purchase a new one with more up-to-date software, but didn't have the courage. He'd been so intent on rewriting all his work from the previous day, including some new theories and additional finds from the dig, to ensure the latest version of his talk had some benefit to returning festival-goers, she hadn't wanted to disturb him.

Keen to catch up on himself, Dr Trevellyan had already been

scribbling away in longhand when Rose arrived, clearly oblivious to the thought she had put into what she was wearing – her smartest black suit and heels, her unruly hair completely tamed in a tight chignon – or the soft pink filling her cheeks the moment he opened the door.

After resuscitating the ailing laptop, Rose had begun typing from the notes he had quickly pieced together, and, watching him discreetly from under her lashes as she worked, she sighed softly. His hair was a tousled mess, but even with his wire-rimmed spectacles – very Harry Potter – perched on the end of his nose and the stubble on his chin and the red wine stain on his shirt, she found him completely adorable.

Finally, he was done, and he passed the additional slides to her before excusing himself to get showered. Rose, not wanting to think about what he was doing, hurriedly finished the notes and tried to focus on adding the slides into his presentation. She was just about to do a run-through of the slideshow when a muffled beeping sound penetrated her brain. Patting down the papers on the desk, she finally retrieved her mobile from beneath a copy of the doctor's own book, *Intrepid Archaeology*.

A text from Morgan: *Please tell me you've spilled coffee on his shirt and you mopped it up with yours and you two are locked in a passionate embrace right now.*

Rose almost squeaked aloud, dropping the phone as though it had burst into flames.

'Everything alright?'

Rose started, then glanced over her shoulder. The doctor stood in the doorway, and she swallowed hard. His hair was wet from the shower, the stubble had gone, and he was still buttoning a clean, white shirt. Hard on Morgan's text, Rose couldn't prevent the deepest blush from scalding her already warm cheeks.

'I – er, yes; I'm fine. Just a friend.' She quickly locked her phone to ensure the message was no longer visible on the screen and smacked it face-down onto the table. She turned back to the screen of the laptop, trying to pretend it wasn't just a blur of colour and letters and making absolutely no sense whatsoever. If she was not mistaken, he was looking at her in some concern.

Rose couldn't blame him; she had barely blushed all morning; now, she must look like her hand had been caught in the biscuit tin.

Dr Trevellyan said nothing, however, returning to his seat and soon lost again in his work. Rose gave herself a mental talking-to and forced her attention towards the slideshow. The morning had flown by, which was all well and good, but she really should check in at the office. Just then, her mobile rang and, half-expecting it to be James, Rose was surprised and a little anxious to see it was Morgan's number.

She glanced at the doctor; he seemed unaware of the interruption, but as she stood up and answered the call with a wary 'Hello,' she walked over to one of the windows on the far wall.

'How's Doctor Gorgeous?'

'Fine, fine.' Rose lowered her voice and hissed, 'Better than you will be when I get through with you.'

Morgan laughed. 'So he's still got his shirt on, then? Tragedy.'

Only just, thought Rose under her breath. 'Do you need me?' Rose was very conscious the doctor couldn't help but overhear her side of the conversation; she only hoped Morgan's voice wasn't audible, too. She wasn't exactly... quiet.

'Yes, I'm on my way to drag you off for some lunch because I'm starving. I've been to your office, and James directed me up here.'

'Oh! Yes, of course.' A momentary panic gripped Rose. 'But no need to come here – I'll meet you – where are you?'

'Just coming up to some huge, cream-coloured stone buildings.'

Rose furrowed her brow. 'Okay...'

'Oh – that doesn't help you? That's right, because *all* the buildings here are huge, cream-coloured stone.'

'Morgan–'

'I'm on the corner of Gay Street, according to the sign, so I guess I'm at the Circle place? What number are you on the Royal Crescent? I really need to see someone re-enact that annoying kiss from *Persuasion* so I can purge it from my mind. Do you think Aiden and you could oblige me?'

'Morgan!' Rose pursed her lips and tried again. 'Just turn around, go back down the hill and find number 40 – it's the *Jane Austen Centre*. I'll meet you outside.' Rose ended the conversation with a sigh of relief and went back to the computer, relieved to see the doctor still engrossed in his work, his glasses perched once more on the end of his nose as he made pencil notes in the margins of a document.

Quickly making sure all her own work was saved, Rose picked up her bag and then stood awkwardly for a moment before walking over to him. No reaction; then she cleared her throat.

The doctor looked up, then tossed his pencil onto the desk. 'Are you off?'

'Yes, all done. I left voice messages on the two calls as no one answered, and I've saved the presentation to a memory stick as well as on the laptop itself.' She held the stick out to him. 'Should I...' She glanced at the mayhem on his desk, then met his gaze. 'Do you want me to take it straight to the office and get it printed off?

'No, that's fine.' He took it from her and, to her relief, slipped it into his pocket just as the clock on the mantelpiece chimed the hour. 'I'll have a final read-through, see if I want to make any further changes first.'

Rose checked her watch. It was already two o'clock. 'Can I get you anything to eat? There's a nice deli just around the corner in St James's Square.'

'I know the one you mean – but no, thanks.' He leaned back in his chair and stretched. 'I think I'll take a walk around the local park, get some air, before I get back to this.' He waved a hand at the mess of papers on his desk as he got to his feet.

'And er – so there's nothing else you need assistance with?' Rose knew Morgan was waiting, and she'd also lost an entire morning on the busiest of days, but she simply didn't want to leave.

Dr Trevellyan shook his head as he shrugged into his jacket. 'No. Think I'm all sorted.'

Picking up her bag, Rose followed him out into the hallway, and he locked up before holding the street door aside for her. 'Hope it hasn't left you in too much of a mess in the office.'

Rose ducked her head as she passed him. 'I'm sure it's all fine.' She hovered a little uncomfortably on the step as he closed the door and then turned to stare out across the scene as he pocketed his keys. Having spent so much time with him, she felt completely at a loss as to how to end their meeting. Should she offer to shake his hand? No, surely that was too formal… *But at least you'd get the chance to touch him again.*

Feeling the moment stretch on, Rose cleared her throat. 'Well, goodbye, Doctor Trevellyan.' He gave a start, then turned to look at her, and she couldn't help but smile – he was always so easily lost in his thoughts.

'I filmed in Bath a few years ago – it was my first time on the TV, and my first set-up was down there.' He pointed to the field below the Royal

Crescent. 'Took me ten minutes to say my name like a rational person.'

How could Rose forget? The filming of an episode of *Time Travellers*, an archaeology show, haunted her. What an idiot she had been, applauding like some giddy schoolgirl when he held up his first find for the camera.

'I'm sure you aren't the only one who's been... irrational around a TV crew.' Was that her voice, squeaking?

He turned to look at her, and before she knew what was happening, he leaned forward and kissed her cheek. 'Goodbye – Rose.'

He turned then and walked off along the Royal Crescent towards the park as though he didn't have a care in the world, leaving a stunned Rose on the doorstep, her heart pounding as she raised a hand to where his touch had been.

CHAPTER SIX

The scene outside the *Jane Austen Centre* was much as Rose had anticipated. There was the usual melee of tourists, all lining up to have their picture taken, either with Martin, the costumed greeter – renowned for being the most photographed man in Bath – or the rather austere model of Jane Austen which had pride of place on the step in front of the building.

Today, however, there was the added confusion of a small group of people huddled around someone Rose couldn't see until she was almost upon them: Morgan! Surrounded by a host of new friends, she was chatting animatedly to them, all totally oblivious to their blocking the street. The moment she spotted Rose, however, Morgan excused herself charmingly, and they quickly fell into step together as they walked past *Hall & Woodhouse* and round the corner into John Street.

Morgan grinned at her friend. 'Well? How was your morning? Did you get him to pose for photos? Did he propose?'

Rose laughed as she shook her head. '*No!* Of course not.' She glanced at Morgan as they turned into Quiet Street. She'd had but ten minutes to compose herself since parting from the doctor, and she wasn't sure she could speak coherently. It was, after all, nothing. Yes, in terms of the three years she had known him, it was *huge*, but really, of no significance at all.

People kissed socially on the cheek all the time these days, didn't they? It had been a thankyou, that was all. She was only thankful he hadn't adopted the European influence presently infiltrating the normally restrained British culture of kissing on both cheeks. She had never managed to get it right, always going for the wrong side first. The chance of mishap and kissing someone – him – accidentally on the lips was way beyond any level of embarrassment Rose could imagine.

'You're blushing!' Morgan grabbed Rose by the arm and pulled her into a doorway between two shops. 'What happened? Was it the shirt? Did it come off at last?'

Rose stared at her friend as she recalled Dr Trevellyan standing in the doorway, fresh from his shower, buttoning up his new shirt with those long, slender fingers…

'Rose Wallace! You are becoming redder by the minute! You had better tell me everything, *now*.'

Glancing around, Rose shook her head. 'Come on,' she pulled Morgan along beside her. 'Let's go into *Jolly's* for a quick sandwich; it will be quieter in there at this time of day. I promise to tell you – and it's nothing, honestly; just… nothing at all.' She ignored Morgan's snort as they turned up Milsom Street.

Nothing else was said between them as they selected food and drinks and carried their trays to a secluded table in a corner, but Rose was conscious of Morgan's smug expression. She was worried she was going to disappoint her friend with how little had happened, and she sat down rather anxiously.

'So?' Morgan wasted no time. 'Tell me! Did he kiss you?'

Against her volition, warm colour flooded Rose's cheeks again.

Morgan's mouth dropped open, but she shut it with a snap. 'Wow; I was only joking!' She fixed her friend with a serious look. 'I knew it. How could he resist you? It's true love. It has to be.'

'Morgan! Shhh.' Rose glanced around the café, panicked in case anyone overheard them. 'It's not like that, not at all.'

With a sceptical look, Morgan applied herself to her food for a moment, then said, 'Perhaps you'd better tell me what it *is* like, then. Come on.' She took a swig of water from her bottle. 'Out with it; and don't leave out any detail.'

As succinctly as she could, Rose outlined her morning, including the doctor's wine-stained shirt – much to Morgan's amusement – and his parting gesture.

When she had finished, Morgan raised a knowing brow. 'Never uses your first name, you said. Probably hadn't even registered what it is, you said. Seems to me it's how he thinks of you, or he wouldn't have used it just now.'

Rose shook her head as she finished off her lunch. 'No – I think he's just absent-minded; he won't even be aware he used it, I am certain.'

'Whatever. I think we have lift-off.' Morgan piled the debris from their lunch onto their trays, and they carried them to the counter before heading back down the stairs and out into the street.

The afternoon was particularly fair for mid-September and the street full of people.

'Oh, look.' Morgan nodded across the street towards two people in full Regency dress. The costumes looked extremely well researched and made, even from this distance. A small group of tourists, cameras to the fore, were taking it in turn to have their photo taken besides the middle-aged couple, who seemed rather delighted with the burst of attention. Rose shuddered; she would have died of embarrassment.

'We'll see a lot of this now.' They turned down the hill. 'I'd best head back to the office. I've missed so much of the day, James will be going spare.'

They hurried down the street but then Morgan tugged on Rose's arm. 'Can we just go in here?' She waved a hand at a large bookshop. 'I really want to buy a few books about the city. It will give me something to read while you're working. Five minutes.'

They headed into *Waterstones*, where a helpful assistant soon directed Morgan to the section she required, leaving Rose to peruse the display of Austen-related books and materials on display. During the *Festival*, this was always expanded and more prominent, and she was unsurprised not to be the only person browsing through the books and goods on sale.

Once again, there were a few people already enjoying the opportunity to walk around in Regency dress, in particular three young women who were decidedly giggly and clearly a little self-conscious about what they were doing. Rose's attention, however, was soon drawn by a slender figure over near the permanent section of classic literature. Then she smiled; though dressed in normal clothes, albeit a little dated, the young woman clearly sported a close imitation of a Regency hairstyle. No doubt she had been practising, but had not felt brave enough to don the full costume yet.

Idly, Rose watched as the lady, who was staring fixedly at the top shelf where all of Jane Austen's published works resided, reached out and touched the spines, one by one, almost reverently. Definitely a true fan if ever she had seen one. Rose smiled; if she was not mistaken, the lady was softly saying the titles under her breath as her hand moved along the books…

'I'm done.' With a start, she turned around to find Morgan had returned, a small pile of books in her arms.

They walked over to the desk, but as Morgan chatted happily to the man taking her payment, Rose glanced back over to the lady, only to realise she had gone. With a shrug, she turned back and, with a little persuasion, finally managed to remove Morgan from the shop and leave the young man free to serve the next person in the queue.

CHAPTER SEVEN

'So – shall I call in on my way home later, or what?' Rose turned to her friend as they reached the steps up to No 13 Queen Square, ready to part company with her for the remainder of the working day.

'Nah.' Morgan shook her head, laughing, and lifted the carrier of books. 'I'll pop up with you and collect that folder from the flat – I left it here when I came looking for help yesterday and forgot to pick it up when your boss mentioned food.'

'Of course. Come on, then.' Rose led the way up the stairs to the office, but she was barely over the threshold when she picked up on the tense atmosphere. There was no sign of Roger – had he returned to work at all today? – and both James and Sarah were fielding telephone calls, the former with his usual, controlled professional manner, the latter looking bored rigid.

Meeting James's eyes as she crossed to her desk, he smiled briefly at her. 'The stopcock should be under the sink… no, not the blue wheel, the red? Yes, that's it. Okay, good. I'll get someone to you immediately.' He paused, his glance moving to Morgan who was hovering in the doorway. 'Not at all. No problem. Bye.'

Rose looked attentively to James for information as he replaced the receiver.

'There's been a small flood at Rivers Street.'

'In the kitchen?' Rose dropped her bag onto the floor by her desk as James rummaged through the papers on his own for his car keys.

'On the lower ground floor; sounds like a problem in the utility room. Thankfully, it's tiles, not carpet.' He glanced at his watch and gestured to Sarah to hurry up.

'Can you call *Overtons* and see if they can get there now? I'm afraid I've got to leave you with all the catch-up from this morning as well; I've a 3 o'clock appointment, and Sarah is due to go out on check-ins with the team.'

Rose waved him away. 'No worries. I'll look after things here. Morgan.' She looked over to her friend who remained by the door. 'Did you want to leave your shopping here and go and see some sights? There's plenty of them!'

'Absolutely not.' Morgan walked over and plucked a pencil from the collection on Rose's desk before tucking it behind her ear. 'I'll help you.'

Rose blinked, unsure whether Morgan was serious, but just then Sarah ended her call and, as James herded her ahead of him to the door, he glanced back at Rose.

'Let her help if she wants to – she was running the place while you were with Aiden this morning.'

Taken by surprise, Rose laughed, looking from one to the other. 'Really? How on earth did *that* happen?'

'Morgan can fill you in. I have to dash.' He looked over at Morgan. 'Feel free to use my desk.' He gestured towards it. 'If you can find it, that is.'

With that, he was gone, and before anything further could be said the phone rang. Morgan instantly snapped it up with a smile on her face and a cheery greeting for whoever was at the other end. Rose stared at her for a moment; it seemed her boss and her friend were developing a habit of running into each other. Rose put the thought aside, realising that, whatever the call entailed, Morgan was clearly adept at dealing with it, and she quickly logged into her computer and trawled through her contacts for their go-to plumbers. By the time she'd ended her call, satisfied they were on their way to Rivers Street, Morgan was on another one, busily scribbling notes onto a pad she had somehow retrieved from the mess on James's desk.

With a smile, Rose turned her attention to her inbox, which had filled up in her morning's absence. She resolutely closed her mind to her time spent with Dr Trevellyan; it had been wonderful but she would be a fool to hope it might be repeated, especially as she was on holiday the following week. By the time she returned, he would be gone again for another year.

This sobering thought was sufficient for Rose to relegate the memory to where it belonged, and instead she leapt back into being the coolly efficient manager she was known to be.

More than two hours later, having fetched a glass of water for Morgan and made herself a cup of much-needed tea, Rose sank into her chair slightly bemused by how the day had turned out. In some ways, she felt as if her whole world had been turned on its head since her friend's arrival and, what was more, that this was how it was supposed to be all along.

Like every Friday, she was helping mostly good-natured visitors to settle in, but this time not only were most of them Jane Austen fans like herself, but also Morgan was a few feet away at James's desk, helping to field incessant calls and talking animatedly to Rose whenever the phones fell silent. It was a huge improvement on exchanging instant messages across thousands of miles of cyberspace and several time zones.

When not chattering away to her friend, Morgan turned out to be excellent on the phone. She gathered information competently, got a quick answer from Rose if necessary, and responded with unquenchable friendliness.

More than once, Rose's mind turned to how very unhelpful Sarah and Roger were by comparison. Speak of the devil! She suppressed a sigh as Roger walked into the office, his mobile pressed to his ear as he loudly made plans for the evening ahead.

As soon as the call ended, Roger strolled over to his empty desk and threw himself into his chair with an all too familiar arrogance. His gaze had fixed on Morgan who was busily writing up a note about her latest phone call, and Rose couldn't help but think it a good thing Sarah was still out. The look he was giving her friend made it very clear he admired her.

Reluctantly, Rose waved a hand towards Morgan.

'Roger, this is a friend of mine who is over on holiday.' Morgan had looked up when Rose started to speak, a ready smile on her face, and she quickly got to her feet and offered a hand. 'Morgan, this is Roger.'

Roger was out of his seat in a shot and, in Rose's opinion, held onto Morgan's hand far longer than was necessary.

'Pleasure to meet you.' Only Rose saw the fleeting wink her friend sent across the room. Having retrieved her hand, Morgan sank back into the seat and picked up her pencil and notebook again, but Roger – tiresome man – didn't return to his. Instead, he perched himself on the edge of James's desk and started to ask Morgan about where she came from.

The sudden ringing of her mobile prevented Rose from hearing more than this and soon she was lost in the call, explaining the parking situation to a group in from Shrewsbury who were trying to discern whether they were indeed where they should be. Dimly she heard the office phone in the background, but to her annoyance when she finally ended her own call, Roger remained perched on the desk and Morgan was dealing with the caller.

'Roger,' he glanced in Rose's direction. 'Do you think you could find out from Sarah how the check-ins are going with the team?'

Expecting him to leap at the chance to speak to Sarah, he scowled. Rose stood her ground, however, handing him the check-in list, and with a loud 'tut' he snatched it from her, grabbed his mobile and walked into the kitchen.

Morgan, who had just ended her call, raised a brow at Rose, her gaze travelling to the doorway through which Roger had just passed. The message was as clear as it was silent between them: Roger was a waste of space. Turning to flick through her list of messages, keen to ensure she hadn't missed anything which needed sorting out before the weekend, Rose sighed. She would have to talk to James.

Thinking of him, Rose glanced at her mobile. There was a new text; he was on his way back to the office and expected Rose to pack up her desk and be ready to leave by the time he arrived. She smiled at the mild admonishment, knowing he was thinking of her. Their relationship was excellent and, though he was a hard taskmaster, working himself at least as hard as he expected his employees to do, he never failed to express his thanks or appreciation for a job well done. It was a shame neither Roger nor Sarah shared a desire to gain his approbation…

Voices filtered into Rose's consciousness, and she looked up. Roger had returned to the room and was now lounging on the edge of his own desk. Rose bit her lip. They seemed to have been talking about historical buildings – a safe enough topic in itself – but Morgan had assumed a blank, non-committal expression.

'It must be pretty hard to get your head around all the history in this country – or anywhere in Europe. Your lot think anything older than 50 years is antique.'

'What's the update from Sarah, Roger?' Rose glared at him, but he barely glanced at her, and before Rose could think of another way to shut him up, the door opened and James walked in, struggling with his briefcase, some loose files and a small bouquet of flowers. Rose looked at him in relief.

'Everything okay?' Rose took the files from him as he stopped by her desk. 'Do you want a cuppa?'

James didn't answer; he was staring over towards his own desk, a dark look on his face as his gaze roamed over Morgan and then to Roger, who had ignored the return of his boss and continued to utter inanities at her friend.

Had something gone wrong at James's meeting? He looked seriously displeased, and Rose got to her feet, unsure of her purpose but anxious Morgan might be about to get a double dose of bad English manners.

'And what is it, this messing around with vowels? The 's' and 'z' thing – fair enough, that's not too confusing, but really, I don't get how you lot chose to start dropping random letters from words.' Rose cringed with embarrassment; Roger had, it seemed, moved on from insulting American workmanship to picking on their language, and he was not finished. 'And why *do* you call aluminium *'aluminum'*? That's just plain stupid!'

James slammed his briefcase and the flowers down on Rose's desk and she winced as a few petals fell off. 'Perhaps it's because that's how it's spelt?'

Roger's head snapped around on hearing the tone of James's voice, and even he didn't have the gall to challenge his boss when he had that steely look in his eye.

With a sigh of relief, Rose watched Roger retreat behind his own desk to collect his things, and James walked over to speak to him in a low voice. Judging by the colour flooding into Roger's cheeks, he was not wishing him a pleasant weekend, and with a sour look in Rose's direction, Roger brushed past James and walked out, slamming the door behind him.

Rose and Morgan shared a quick glance as James turned around to face them. Then he smiled slightly, and both girls released a visible breath.

'Rose, anything new to – no, don't get up, Morgan.' He waved a hand at her friend as she made to stand. 'Anything need doing tonight?'

She shook her head, looking quickly through her notes. 'No – nothing that can't wait until Monday now. All the urgent things have been sorted.' She looked up. James had gone to stand beside her friend and was leaning over to log in to his computer. 'And Kathy is doing the two check-ins this weekend – she knows her stuff.'

'Excellent.' James straightened up. 'And next week? Anything I ought to be aware of?'

Rose shook her head. 'No, no. Everything's as done as it can be and, barring any maintenance issues arising, it should be a quiet week with all the expected guests already settled in.'

'Good – well, I'll just catch up on emails before I shut up shop.' He stood back as Morgan got to her feet. 'Thank you, Morgan. Your help is much appreciated – twice over.'

'I had fun.' Morgan smiled widely at him, all trace of her closed expression gone. 'Two favours repaid; one to go.'

Rose gathered her things, handed Morgan her bag of books, and they walked to the door as James sat at his desk, pulling his phone charger towards him. 'Have a fabulous weekend and enjoy your break. You will be missed.' James threw a knowing look in the direction of Roger and Sarah's desks, and Rose smiled sympathetically.

'Call me if you need anything or can't find anything, okay?'

James shook his head. 'I'm sure I'll cope.'

Both girls turned for the door, but then James called Rose back.

'Wait; I almost forgot.' He got up and picked up the bouquet from Rose's desk, still pretty and giving off a lovely scent, and handed it to her. 'You have been, as always, a star this last month, Rose. You never cease to amaze me. Thank you.'

Rose smiled widely, burying her nose in the flowers. 'They're lovely. Thank you, James. You didn't have to do that.' He did it far more often than he needed to, bless him.

He kissed her on the cheek. 'You're worth it; I'd be lost without you.'

To Rose's surprise, Morgan frowned, but before she could ponder on it, James turned to her friend.

'I'm sorry it's not as personal as flowers, Morgan, but thank you, too – here, it's the best I could do at short notice.' He handed her the information folder she'd left at the office on the previous day. 'I hope you enjoy it!'

Morgan looked taken aback for a moment, then she laughed. 'You're welcome! And thanks for this.' She waved the folder before shoving it into one of her carrier bags.

James opened the door for them both.

'Off you go and enjoy your evening. And Rose – forget about work for a week.'

CHAPTER EIGHT

Morgan seemed unusually quiet as they made their way down the stairs and into the street, and Rose cast her an anxious glance as they paused on the kerb, waiting for a chance to dash across the road.

'Is everything okay?' Rose touched her friend's sleeve to gain her attention.

Morgan looked surprised. 'Of course. Why wouldn't it be?'

'I wondered if – well,' Rose gestured helplessly with her hands. 'This wasn't exactly how we'd hoped to spend our first few days, was it?'

'Rose, you warned me it was a busy time – I'm not disappointed – I promise – kinda the opposite. I mean not that I wouldn't have been happy to have the time with just you.' She shrugged. 'But you are free now, aren't you? A whole week off work.'

Rose nodded, casting her friend another concerned glance. 'Yes – I am. But something isn't right. This may be our first meet-up in person, but I've known you long enough to know something's troubling you.'

'I love how British you are.' Morgan grinned. 'I suppose I am a little preoccupied – but I'm not *troubled*; not at all. I'm having a blast!'

'Is it Roger? He was so rude, I could've hit him.' Rose shook her head regretfully.

'Rose, Roger is not your fault. He's just –' Morgan rolled her eyes as she searched for the word she wanted to use. 'Clueless. He thought he was being funny. He *wasn't*. But, whatever. I think I'm made of stronger stock than to get upset by someone with those kinds of opinions.'

Rose shifted her bouquet of flowers from one arm to the other. 'Well, thank goodness James came back when he did. Roger was getting out of order.'

The thoughtful expression returned to Morgan's face. Damn Roger and his narrow-mindedness.

'Rose?'

'Hmm?'

'James… you've never thought–'

Rose frowned. Morgan couldn't possibly be upset by James, could she? 'Thought what?'

'He's a very attractive man… maybe not the romantic god that is Dr Aiden Trevellyan, but you and he seem… close? I mean, all that car boot stuff on weekends you once mentioned to me – the antiquing together...'

Rose's blush returned unbidden at the mention of the doctor. 'Oh no. That's something I've been doing forever – I just let him tag along when he was at a loose end over recent months. He's like… I don't know – a cousin to me? Maybe not as close as you are to your brother, but certainly – no, nothing like *that*.'

'Hmmm; seems to me like he's sweet on you.' Morgan nodded towards the bouquet, but Rose choked back a laugh.

'James? Good grief, no!'

'But he gave you flowers. *That* was sweet.'

'Yes, it was, but he does it quite often.'

'Really? And the kiss? I thought you Brits were into shaking hands.'

Rose rolled her eyes at Morgan.

'Seriously, we're good friends, that's all. And we work well together.' Rose glanced over her shoulder at the office. 'When I began working with him, he was already dating a woman called Mandy, and they seemed practically engaged. So honestly, I've simply never thought of him like that.'

'And – are they? Engaged, I mean.'

'Thankfully not.'

'But they're still together?'

'No, no. Thank God.'

'So – has it been long… since they split?'

'About six months?'

'Oh – right.'

Rose glanced over at her friend as the traffic slowed to a halt and they took their chance to hurry across the road. Morgan was displaying a marked curiosity about James. Was she… could she be *interested* in him? What would that mean?

'Where are we going?' Morgan gestured around at the milling crowds of people. 'Do we eat around here?'

'No; I booked us a table further up the town. Friday night is always so busy, but with the *Festival* people here and the home rugby game tomorrow, it's worse than ever. I wanted us to go somewhere we could hear ourselves think.'

'Good call!'

'Morgan.' Rose felt like she was missing something, but her friend's face was just as clear and open as ever. Rose shook her head. 'Never mind.'

They began to walk up the street, passing a gathering of people all dressed in Regency attire; for the most part, they were talking animatedly as they waited to enter one of the buildings on this side of the square, and Morgan caught Rose's eye and grinned.

'Looks like fun!'

'It's the pre-*Festival* get-together. They always hold one on the first Friday so people can reconnect with friends they've made here or new people can go along to meet others.'

'Did you ever go?'

Rose nodded. 'I did once. I had a few friends over attending, so I went along with them. It was fun, but I don't know that I'd have had the nerve on my own.'

They had almost reached the corner when Rose noticed the young woman she'd seen in *Waterstones* lingering by the railings. She was watching the commotion behind them, but this time she was dressed in full Regency costume herself, though Rose noted on passing it looked a little worn in places – perhaps second-hand or maybe she just attended lots of these events?

'Wait.' She tugged at Morgan's arm as they paused on the kerb again, waiting to cross, and Rose turned and walked back to the woman who took a startled step backwards when she joined her.

'Hi,' Rose said brightly, feeling far less confident than her tone implied. 'You should go in.' She pointed along the street to where the queue had diminished substantially now the door had been opened. 'I know it can be tough attending things on your own, but this is a great way to start making friends with everyone.'

She half-expected the young woman to bolt; there was something about her demeanour, her whole aura, which spoke of uneasiness. Perhaps it was the first time she had dressed up in public? To her surprise, however, she raised her head and stared at Rose with what could only be described as a curious look from surprisingly bright and intelligent hazel eyes.

She said nothing, however, merely inclined her head, and Rose gave a tentative smile, said goodbye, and turned to rejoin her friend. She had the horrible suspicion the young woman had been amused about something, and she had no idea what it might be.

As they crossed the road, Morgan threw her a curious glance. 'I thought it wasn't usual for Brits to make friendly overtures to total strangers?'

'It isn't, but somehow she didn't feel like one. I saw her earlier, when you were choosing your books. She's clearly an avid fan but, unlike most people here, she appears to be alone. I can still remember the first time I attended a costumed event. It's not easy on your own.'

Morgan frowned. 'It isn't?'

Rose resisted the urge to roll her eyes. 'Some of us don't find it comes naturally – it's not easy – to walk out in public dressed in a costume and especially to make small talk with strangers.'

'What, like Mr Darcy, you mean?' Morgan was grinning.

With a laugh, Rose nodded. 'Precisely. But not out of pride, I would add; from shyness or a lack of self-confidence. We can't all charm our way through life, Morgan.'

'What d'you mean?'

Rose gave her friend a resigned look. 'You've been in Bath for just over twenty-four hours, and I'm pretty sure you've made more new acquaintances than I did in primary school.'

Morgan laughed. 'Well, that's just cuz you're not trying. You could charm the pants off anyone – literally and figuratively – if you just gave it the old college try.'

Rose's mouth dropped open. 'The old *what*?'

Morgan laughed again. 'Oh Rose! Come on, I say the Doc is about two dinners away from being completely smitten by you. Can you really not see it?'

'You see love everywhere.' She dragged her friend around the corner and up Gay Street.

'I'm not the one who's been kissed today – twice!'

'On the cheek. Both times.' Rose shook her head as they headed up towards the Circus. 'My life was very normal and orderly before you dropped in.'

'I don't doubt that you *thought* it was. What I doubt is that you were paying the right sort of attention.'

The friendly debate continued as they walked, and before long, they had arrived at the *Chequers Inn,* a small but extremely popular pub, located slightly off the main tourist area in Rivers Street and therefore less likely to be found by the visiting Festival-goers. For just a few minutes, as much as she loved them all, Rose wanted a breather from the excitement and build up to have some quality time with Morgan and hopefully to hear what her plans were for her remaining time away from home.

Rose pulled open the door, standing aside for Morgan to enter. 'Here we are. Let's change the subject, shall we?'

'Sure, and while we're changing things,' Morgan swept past, deftly snatching Rose's clip out of her hair on the way.

'Hey, that hurt!' Rose ran a hand through her curls as they sprang back into life and rolled her eyes as she followed Morgan into the pub. It looked like there would be no let-up this evening.

The venue turned out a perfect choice. Tucked away in a corner so the comings and goings through the door didn't disturb them, the girls talked animatedly through their meal and before they knew it, it was time to order dessert.

'I'd like the Lemon Meringue, please. Morgan?' Rose turned to her friend, who had pounced on the menu with delight and still had her nose buried in it.

'Whose idea was it to forego an appetiser and have a dessert?'

'Yours!'

'Oh, yes, so it was!' Morgan peered at Rose over the top of the menu card. 'But it's so difficult. I mean, I'd like to try some of all of them, just to say I have. Except perhaps Eton Mess. I don't know what that is. Or should I play it safe with this Chocolate Delish thing?'

'We could make you a taster plate with a sample of 3 or 4 things if you like?' The waitress had been extremely helpful.

'Sounds like a plan.' Rose nodded encouragingly at Morgan who flashed her warm smile at the young girl by her side. 'It's a deal; bring it on!'

As soon as the waitress had disappeared with their order, Morgan fixed Rose with a compelling eye – one she was becoming familiar with.

'Now, where were we? Oh yes, your insistence that the lovely Aiden doesn't 'see' you.'

'As a woman, I said. I mean, I know he can see me, literally. He knows I'm there – sort of – like today when I was of use to him.'

'Really?' Morgan raised a brow.

'Morgan! Look at me.' Rose gestured to herself. 'I'm pale and uninteresting. What could someone… someone like him, find of interest?'

'Well, I dunno. You're striking, beautiful even,' Morgan persisted as Rose shook her head, feeling highly embarrassed by the praise. 'That jackass of a fiancé has scarred you! You're lovely, and more than that, you're friendly, kind – and funny.'

'*You* find me funny because I'm British.'

'Sure! But I've seen you make others laugh, too.'

Rose wished the subject could be dropped. Perhaps she should start talking about James, see if her suspicions were true? Before she could think of what to say, however, Morgan continued.

'Do you think the Doc ever figured out what you were doing taking all those pictures of him that first time you met?'

A wave of embarrassment swept through Rose – the force of which rendered all other embarrassments from the last twenty years of her life inconsequential. She instantly lowered her voice to a whisper. 'That could hardly be called meeting.' She sighed heavily. 'Though it was the first time I humiliated myself in front of him.' Then she smiled ruefully at Morgan. 'To be fair, I think the rapid photo bursts were nothing to the distraction of my applauding him like a frenetic seal later! And I told you, I never want to speak of it – ever.'

Morgan laughed. 'You do have it bad. We *have* to do something about this.'

Rose shook her head frantically, her insides lurching at the sheer thought of what Morgan might do. 'Can we please stop talking about him? Other than attending his lecture, I won't see him again until next year – and that's only if he decides to come back again. The last thing I want is to feel down about that on our first proper evening together.' With another sigh, she picked up her wine glass, unaware of just how melancholy her face looked. 'And the thought of not laying eyes on him *does* make me sad.'

Morgan snorted. 'Be prepared to be happy right now, then.'

Rose swallowed quickly on her mouthful of wine, then coughed. 'What? Why?'

'He's over there.' Morgan inclined her head towards the rear of the pub. 'At a corner table. Alone.'

It took all of Rose's willpower not to turn her head. 'We must leave,' she hissed at Morgan. '*Now.*' Her friend merely raised a comical brow at her. 'Did he just come in? Perhaps he hasn't seen me – us.'

'Why must we leave? Our dessert hasn't come yet! Besides, he's been there all along – oh, and yes, he *has* seen you – us.'

Rose blanched. 'How – how do you know?'

'Because...'

'Good evening.'

Heart leaping into her throat at the sound of his voice close behind her, Rose threw Morgan a frantic look and took another swig of her wine to try to ease the constriction.

'Hey, Aiden! How are you? Did you eat already?' Morgan was beaming her usual warm smile, and Rose drew in a quick breath. She felt incredibly flustered and could only put it down to the sudden recollection of their leave-taking and the way the conversation had just been turning. Had he overheard any of it?

'Just leaving. Thought I'd say hi and goodbye.'

'Won't you join us for a nightcap? Coffee or something?' Morgan indicated the spare chair at their table, presently playing host to Rose's pretty bouquet of flowers.

Aiden glanced at it, then looked from Morgan to Rose. 'No – thanks. I'll head off. Don't want to disturb.'

'Too late for that,' Morgan muttered under her breath at Rose, who went from white to red in an instant.

'Pardon?'

'Too bad. I just said it was too bad.' Morgan winked at Rose, who was trying very hard not to die of embarrassment.

He glanced at the flowers again. 'Nice bouquet. Someone have an admirer?' He was looking at Morgan, who smiled sweetly.

'Aren't they awesome? So pretty. James gave them to Rose; wasn't it sweet of him?'

'Very.'

'Are you sure you won't stay for a moment?' Morgan made as though to remove the bouquet, but the doctor shook his head.

'I shall leave to you it. Have a good evening.' He turned for the door, pausing on the threshold to raise a brief hand to them before disappearing out into the night.

CHAPTER NINE

Rose glanced at her watch: gone half-ten; time she went home. She waited for a pause in the conversation Morgan was having with her stepmother via Skype – it was quite a wait – then made her excuses.

'Bye, Mrs Taylor.' She waved at the lady sitting far away on the west coast of America, who beamed widely at her and waved back. 'Time I went home – lovely to see you again.'

'You, too, sweetie.' Mrs Taylor blew her a kiss. 'Look after our darling girl for us!'

'I will. Time's already going too fast – I intend to cherish every single moment.'

Rose was shrugging into her coat and bent down to pick up her bag.

'But wait. Didn't she–'

'I'll just see Rose out, Mom!' Morgan got quickly to her feet and followed Rose out into the hallway. 'This call could go on for hours. She wants to know every single detail of every single hour so far.'

With a laugh, Rose gave her a quick hug. 'I'll text you when I'm on my way down in the morning. Make sure you get some beauty sleep before the promenade.'

Five minutes later, Rose was back home and soon settled on the sofa with a small glass of wine and a book, and she sighed contentedly as she found her page and began to read. The peaceful moment was not to last, however, as the shrill bleeping of a smoke alarm emanated from the floor above.

Rolling her eyes at the ceiling, Rose sighed. The alarm had gone off twice during the evening in recent weeks. She would have to have a word with Marcus.

Discarding her book, Rose walked over to her iPod dock and pressed 'play', turning the volume up a little to hide the piercing beeping from above.

For a while, she lost herself in her book, but when she paused to reach for her glass, she frowned. The alarm normally stopped within a minute or so, but she had a feeling this time it hadn't.

She hurried over and turned off the music. Yes, definitely still going. Was there really a fire? Should she go up there? Visitors so often weren't sure how to operate things in holiday lets; how well she knew it.

Glancing at her book, Rose sighed and dropped it reluctantly onto the coffee table. It wasn't like she could get any sleep, so she may as well go and see what was up.

Relieved to see no sign of flames or smoke as she walked up to the door of No 4, Rose pressed the bell for the ground-floor flat. Looking upwards, the floor above was in darkness. The current holidaymakers were either out or very deep sleepers.

The door was opened cautiously, a pair of bright eyes peering round its edge.

'Hi! I live down there,' Rose gestured towards the basement flat. 'I can hear the smoke alarm. Is everything okay?'

Slowly, the door was pulled back to reveal the young woman Rose had spoken to earlier in Queen Square. She was still neatly attired in her costume, though her chestnut hair now hung around her shoulders.

'Oh! It's you.' Rose smiled and offered her hand. 'My name's Rose Wallace. It looks like we're temporary neighbours whilst you're in Bath.'

The lady smiled politely and took Rose's hand briefly. 'I am pleased to make your acquaintance. My name is Miss… Jenny; Jenny Ashton.'

There was a pause, with only the piercing bleep of the alarm to be heard.

'So…' Rose gestured towards the open door. 'Is there a problem? Smoke or something? We'd best call the fire brigade and quickly!'

'No, indeed.' Jenny shook her head, the shorter curls framing her face dancing around. 'Be not alarmed. There is no fire, merely a recalcitrant contrivance; it will not cease!' She glanced over her shoulder. 'I know not what I am to do.'

'Shall I take a look?'

With a relieved smile, the lady stood back and Rose walked into the hallway, then followed her along into the ground-floor flat, amused at the attempt to speak in Regency dialogue. Definitely the dedicated fan she had supposed.

There was no sign of smoke or flames inside the flat, but the beeping was incredibly loud and very persistent as they went into the bedroom. Rose stood beneath the alarm and chewed on her lip thoughtfully. Georgian buildings were all very elegant, but the high ceilings weren't as practical as modern ones.

'Are there any ladders here?'

Jenny shook her head. 'There is a spacious closet, but no ladder within.'

'How have you managed to stop it in the past?' Jenny raised a brow, and Rose added. 'I've heard it before.'

'Forgive me. It was not my intention to disturb.' She gestured towards the mantelpiece. It was covered in candles of all shapes and sizes, and though none were lit, Rose could tell from the smell in the room they had only recently been extinguished. Beside the bed there was an old-fashioned oil lamp, also not in use.

'I find the lighting pains my eyes. I am more accustomed to candlelight.' She waved a hand at the mantel. 'By dousing the flame, the noise would hastily cease. I find its continuance unfathomable.'

'Perhaps there's a fault.' Rose tried not to stare as she looked around the room for something to stand on and then peered into the adjacent sitting room, but it was impossible to miss the books piled high on every possible surface, including the floor. Jenny was clearly an avid reader!

'Might this suffice?'

Rose looked over her shoulder; Jenny was resting her hand on the back of a sturdy-looking chair at the desk by the fireplace.

'It might.'

Jenny stood aside, which Rose took as a hint she expected her caller to drag the cumbersome seat over to the opposite side of the room.

It was hard to miss the array of items stacked along the rear wall as she walked over to fetch it: neatly piled below the window and an old iron door set into the wall were small, wooden crates, the contents spilling out onto the floor – an array of antiques and collectibles. Perhaps she had some connection to the *Bartlett Street Antiques Centre* – a collector, or a trader or something...

Trying to curb her curiosity, Rose tried to pick up the chair. It was heavy, and it took all her effort to manoeuvre it into place below the still bleeping alarm.

Kicking off her slippers, Rose climbed onto it. She was tall enough, with the aid of the kitchen utensil quickly supplied by Jenny, to reach the cover of the smoke detector and managed to flip it open. The only answer for now would be to remove the battery, and with a little difficulty she finally managed to grasp it with the tweezers and it fell to the floor, narrowly missing Jenny who ceased her intent study of the quote on Rose's discarded slippers to jump out of its way.

Picking up the battery from the floor, she then studied it warily. 'Such loud disturbance from such small means.' Then she looked at Rose with a warm smile. 'I am indebted to you.'

'No problem!' Rose stuffed her feet back into her slippers and concealed a yawn behind her hand. 'I'll just put this back.'

Jenny stood aside again as Rose manhandled the heavy chair back into place by the desk. There was a writing slope on there – a lovely replica – a glass bottle of ink and what she supposed must be pens, though they bore little resemblance to the fancy quills with long feathers often depicted for the era! By contrast, there were also several bottles of eye drops next to them. Then Rose blinked. There was a piece of paper – rich textured – on the slope, and the writing on it was very familiar to her. Jenny was clearly trying to mimic Jane Austen's well-known hand.

Rose started at the sound of someone clearing their throat and spun around. Jenny was watching her from across the room, her expression keen, and, feeling as though she had stepped over a line, Rose blushed.

'Sorry! Too curious for my own good. You have some lovely things.' She gestured around at the silverware, old books and suchlike.

'One man's disorder is another man's treasure, do you not find?'

Rose eased past her and opened the door to the outer hallway. 'Er, yes, I suppose so. Make sure you let someone know you had a problem with the alarm as soon as you can, and I'm sure they'll get it fixed. 'Night.'

If Rose wasn't mistaken, she could have sworn Jenny almost curtseyed before deciding against it, merely inclining her head in almost regal fashion, and, keen to make her escape, she hurried to the front door.

'Do you think she's okay? Maybe she's just gone to the bathroom. I think…'

Rose looked up in surprise on hearing Morgan's voice as she closed the door to No 4 behind her, but the only person in the street appeared to be James. 'What on earth are you doing here?'

'He's with me,' called a voice from the steps down to Rose's flat.

'If only,' muttered James under his breath as Morgan hurried up to join them on the street wearing James's jacket. Rose, who had come to stand beside him, threw him an assessing look.

'What did you say?'

'I – I said, *phoning*. I tried to call you, but we could hear it ringing inside your flat and it just went to voicemail.'

Rose met his eye, then bit her lip. It wouldn't do to make fun of him, so she let it go. Besides, she was a bit preoccupied with everything she'd just seen.

'What were you doing in there?' Morgan pointed to the flat above Rose's, her hand barely visible in the overlong sleeve.

'Oh – just helping someone out. Smoke alarm going haywire.' She frowned and looked from her friend to her boss. 'More to the point, why are you both here at this time of night? And in your PJs, Morgan! Is something wrong?'

'It's me; I'm locked out again!' Morgan seemed decidedly proud of this fact, and James's lips twitched as he met Rose's gaze again.

Rose frowned. 'But you were safely inside when I left you. Come on; you'd best come in. Whoah!' She stopped suddenly as she made to pass her friend. 'What on earth is *that*?'

A movement had caught her eye as a tiny, furry head emerged from one of the jacket pockets and a pair of bright eyes peered out at her.

'Oh, it's so sweet,' whispered Rose, rubbing the kitten's head with her finger.

'I came out of *The Boater* just now and there she was out in the street, trying to rescue it.' James gestured towards the small creature. 'In her haste, she forgot to take her keys.'

'Can I camp out with you tonight, Rose? James doesn't have his work keys with him to let me back in.'

'Of course. Let's go in.' Rose led the way down the steps and into her flat. Her half-drunk glass of wine was still on the table, along with her discarded book and her mobile.

'Oh dear.' Rose bit her lip as Morgan tipped the kitten out of the pocket and it ran off into the kitchen to explore. 'I can't keep it here. Pets are strictly forbidden. And you can't keep it at Laura Place. No pets allowed there either.'

Morgan sighed. 'I guess not.' She looked rather crestfallen, however, but before Rose could come up with a solution, James shrugged.

'It's okay; I can take her... him... it.'

'You can?' Rose tried and failed to hide her grin, but James merely shook his head at her and went off in search of his new ward.

It was midnight before Morgan was curled up in a sleeping bag on the sofa, and she hid a yawn as Rose brought them yet another mug of hot chocolate.

'James really is my hero.'

Rose laughed softly. She wasn't a fool. She could tell her friend was very taken with her boss, and she couldn't really blame her. James was an intelligent, kind and hard-working man with strong loyalties. It wouldn't have passed by Morgan that he was also rather easy on the eye!

'Yes, very brave; rescuing a kitten.'

Morgan made a face, 'Well, *I* clapped for him anyway.'

Rose narrowed her eyes. 'Don't even bring that up!'

Morgan tried to look innocent. 'I don't think it was a big deal. No one ran screaming from you, did they?'

'It's all fine for you, you're American.'

'British people clap. I've seen it.'

'But only in very specific – ugh, I refuse to talk about this again.'

Morgan laughed. 'Fine, but James deserved the applause. He looked after me yesterday as well; and anyway, he *was* brave tonight. He scaled a locked gate in the railings to save the kitten, and now he's given it a home.'

There was a ping from Morgan's phone, one of several in the past hour, and Rose wasn't at all surprised when her friend chuckled before tapping a quick response.

'He's not too impressed with my choice of name.'

'And *he* would be James, by any chance?' Rose sipped her hot chocolate. 'Ha! You've gone pink!'

'It's the hot chocolate. It's making me warm.'

'The lady protesteth too much.' Rose smirked at her. 'So – what name did you give it?'

'Mr Darcy, of course!'

Rose laughed again. 'Seriously? It's going to sound a bit weird when he's at the door calling for it to come inside.'

Morgan spluttered into her cup, then drew in a deep breath. 'Haha! Especially from a man!' For a moment there was silence, then both girls dissolved into giggles.

There was another ping from Morgan's phone, and she snatched it up. 'Awwww! Mr Darcy is nibbling James's ear.' Then her eye met Rose's and they both started to giggle again.

CHAPTER TEN

'Wow! It's gorgeous; even more so than it looked in the photos you sent.' Rose held the dress Morgan had just removed from its wrapping up against her body and viewed herself in the full-length mirror. Then she laughed. 'It doesn't even reach my ankles! I think you're safe from me trying to steal it off you.'

Morgan grinned widely as she took the dress from Rose and tossed it onto her bed. 'Ditto. I don't think they make heels high enough for me to wear yours.' She lifted a fine silk shawl from tissue paper and something fell heavily to the floor. 'Oh! How could I have forgotten?'

Sweeping up the small package, Morgan turned towards Rose and grabbed her hand, pulling her to sit on the bed beside her.

'I got this for you.' She thrust the beribboned package into Rose's hands.

'Awww, you shouldn't have.' Rose didn't want to open it, it was so prettily wrapped, but Morgan urged her to hurry, and she quickly released the ribbon and tore open the paper to reveal a soft, suede pouch. Tipping its contents onto her palm, Rose gasped.

'Oh Morgan.' Her gaze flew to her friend's face, her eyes feeling suddenly wet and her throat tightening. 'It's… it's just *beautiful*.'

Resting on her hand was a stunning, hand-crafted yellow topaz cross on a fine gold chain – as close as it was possible to be to the one said to have belonged to Jane Austen herself.

'Wait! Look!' Morgan leaned over to the bedside table and opened the drawer. 'I have one, too, see?'

She held up another delicate cross and chain, a perfect copy of that believed to have belonged to Cassandra Austen. 'Now we can be 'sisters', too.'

Touched beyond words, Rose leaned over and hugged Morgan, sniffing back on her tears. 'It's the most beautiful gift ever. But how did you–'

'Remember when they started to make the replicas of the turquoise ring, and we searched everywhere online, asking every possible contact we had if they knew if replicas of the crosses had been made?'

Rose nodded, recalling her disappointment. 'We found those pretty ones sold in the shop at Winchester Cathedral, but they weren't quite the same.'

'Well, one of my college friends has a sister who is *big* into jewellery design – she makes bespoke pieces, so I commissioned her. Sent her photos of the crosses, and this is what she came up with. Aren't they awesome?'

'Beyond awesome! I *love* them.' Rose couldn't take her eyes off her gift, but Morgan nudged her and pointed to her watch.

'Hey, we'd better hurry up or we're going to be late meeting the others.'

Rose glanced at the time and let out a yelp.

A frantic 20 minutes later, she fastened the final button on the back of Morgan's dress and left her to put the finishing touches to her hair, which she had bundled up into a tousled bun through which she was now threading ribbons, repeating her regret she hadn't managed to buy a bonnet. Walking into the drawing room to admire her gift in the large, ornate mirror over the fireplace, Rose stared at her reflection. Her naturally curling hair for once was doing her a favour, with the soft tendrils she had left free from the pinned tresses at the back framing her face in a fair imitation of a period hairstyle.

Morgan soon joined her, and they admired the effect of the two necklaces for a moment, but then something caught Rose's eye, and she glanced out of the window. 'Hey, look. It's my nutty neighbour.'

They hurried over to the window, just in time to see the back of Jenny Ashton, impeccably dressed in Regency costume, as she disappeared into Argyle Street on her way into town.

Morgan grinned at Rose as they turned away. 'Off to the promenade, no doubt. So – how do you feel this morning about her? Do you still think she's forging letters to finance her candle fetish?'

Rose shrugged, feeling a little uncomfortable about their conjecturing during the previous evening. 'I'm not sure. I mean, she's a contradiction! Even you travel with books about Austen,' she nodded towards the books scattered over the coffee table, 'but I couldn't see a single one in the apartment. There were books everywhere, but they seemed to be more reference ones: history, science, medicine! A total contrast to writing letters starting '*My dear Cassandra*' in a fair imitation of Jane Austen's handwriting.'

Rose sighed as she picked up her reticule and shawl. 'There's something not right; she's beyond being an avid fan of the era. It's as if she's living the whole thing for real. D'you know what I mean? And the handwriting... well, it's just *too* accurate. How could anyone be that *good* at it?'

Morgan laughed and dragged Rose over to the open laptop on the coffee table. 'Look!' She quickly pulled up a familiar page. 'It's a font; we see it all the time on these blogs and things.'

'Yes, but–'

'No buts. Look, it's here.' Morgan grabbed the latest copy of *Jane*

Austen's Regency World Magazine from the side table. '*Her* name, written using *her* handwriting. Anyone could learn to copy it.'

'But not using a quill, surely? And proper ink, and paper that doesn't look like any paper *we've* ever seen.'

'So she's got a specialist supplier.' Morgan shrugged as they both picked up their accessories and headed for the door. 'Why does it bother you so much?'

'I don't know.' Rose shook her head. 'There's just something about her; I mean, yes, so she's a dedicated fan, but…'

'Yeah; she's obsessive. We already know that.'

Rose sighed. 'Yet there is still a huge great big 'but'.'

Morgan snorted, and Rose could not help but laugh. 'Not *that* sort of butt, you twit!'

'Come on, it's time we set off.' Morgan grabbed her keys. 'Let's not forget these today.'

Two minutes later and they were on their way.

'How long of a walk is it again?' Morgan had walked ahead of Rose as they crossed Pulteney Bridge, but now they were able to walk side by side and talk. Rose almost sighed with relief; she could almost pretend she wasn't walking through Bath city centre in full costume on a busy Saturday morning if she was chatting to her friend.

'It takes about an hour and a half from start to finish.'

'I hope these shoes last.' Morgan lifted her skirts and Rose eyed her very pretty, very impractical soft shoes warily.

'I told you not to try being too authentic, but you just had to listen to that Letitia woman.'

'She told me the least I could do if I was going to invade such a purely British event was get the Irene gal to do my costumes and supply the extras so I wouldn't embarrass the monarchy. She said –'

'Did she really tell you that?' Rose asked, distracted. Letitia and her friend, Irene, were avid Regency amateur historians, famous for being strictly accurate about *every* aspect of costume. Unfortunately, they were *so* strict that it tended to suck the joy out of anyone in their general vicinity who was simply trying to enjoy the *Festival* and, to be honest, didn't have limitless funds to spend on authentic Regency clothing and accessories.

'Well, not in so many words. It was the tone, though – believe me.'

'Oh I do.' Rose gestured to the right. 'Let's go this way – it's less congested.'

Morgan followed obediently, but Rose didn't miss her friend checking her mobile for about the tenth time in so many minutes.

'So – any word from James this morning?'

Morgan made an uncharacteristically nonchalant noise, as she stuffed her phone back into her reticule, but Rose stopped walking and pulled her friend into a shop doorway. 'Morgan, are you blushing?'

'I don't know what you're talking about.' Morgan winked but couldn't hold Rose's gaze.

A sense of joy bubbled up in Rose's heart as her suspicions were confirmed. 'I *knew* it. You like each other, don't you?'

'Well… I can't speak for him, but I'm pretty much a goner.' Morgan paused, then sighed. 'I'm sorry.'

'What? What on earth are you sorry for?'

'I swear I didn't come here to hit on your boss. I feel – well, I thought it was just – a flirtation – he's so nice, and he's tall and handsome and…' Morgan shook her head. 'Anyway, last night, when we found Mr Darcy, and we were walking to find you – I couldn't stop looking at his mouth when he spoke.'

'Oh dear, you are in deep, aren't you?' Rose grinned and set off again, Morgan in her wake.

'Oh yes, I'm glad you think it's funny – I'm lucky if he didn't notice since I got so distracted by the way his mouth moved that I stopped paying attention to what he was saying. I'll tone it down if we see him again, I promise, and obviously I will control myself if I end up...' A strange consciousness flooded Morgan's face as they reached the pedestrian crossing on George Street. 'Oh my God! I didn't tell you. I'm such a cow.'

Rose merely smiled at the friendly British insult they bandied around between them, but Morgan really did look quite concerned. 'What? Don't tell me he kissed you with his wonderful mouth and you've forgotten until now? Morgan – what? What is it?'

Morgan shook her head, but as the lights turned red and they began to cross the road, thankfully now seeing several other people in costume, Rose frowned. Swept along in the flow of people, however, there wasn't much chance to continue the conversation, until Morgan slowed to a halt at the bottom of Bartlett Street.

Realising she'd lost her friend, Rose turned around and hurried back to her. 'Are you okay?'

The steadying breath Morgan took only managed to scare Rose more as she turned to face her. 'These last few days have been great, haven't they? Barring, you know, me being a strumpet and the whole thing with your delusional neighbour trying to set the place on fire?'

Rose laughed. 'What makes you think you're a strumpet? Just because you like my boss who – so far as I can see – clearly likes you back? You're being very odd, Morgan; just spit it out!'

'Okay.' Morgan drew in a deep breath. 'How would you feel... if I told you my dad thinks a few weeks won't cut it. And that he's looking into getting me a visa-supported role – working for this new office he's just opened? You know what writing's like – you can do it anywhere.'

'So where – globally – are you talking about?'

'From – right here – England.' Morgan started to smile. 'Bath, if I want.'

Rose almost gasped. 'Honestly? Oh, Morgan! That would be… I just can't put into words how fantastic it would be! Is it – when will you know?'

Morgan shook her head. 'Not sure. He only mentioned it as I was packing to come here – which, obviously was ten minutes before I left for the airport. That's what my mom was all excited 'bout during our Skype chat – she seems to think it's a given.'

'You sound… you sound like you're not sure it's a good thing? Have we freaked you out, all us Brits?' Rose wasn't really serious, but she knew something was holding Morgan back.

Another cluster of costumed people walked past, and Morgan gestured up the hill. 'Should we keep going?'

'Yes, but only if you tell me what the problem is.' Rose fell into step beside her.

'It's not a problem – not a real one. I didn't want you to feel as if you should be responsible for me. But then, I've needed nothing but rescuing since I got here – 24/7 – which might be a lark for a little visit but now you're in danger of being stuck with me for a few years.'

'Don't be daft. I think it's brilliant. I can't believe you didn't tell me, but – now I almost wish I didn't know – I'll be on pins and needles until you know for definite!'

'Me, too. I know I had the cushion of the London office, but to be able to stay here for a while and be nearer you…'

Both girls exchanged tremulous smiles as they reached the top of the hill and joined the milling crowds around the Assembly Rooms;

it may have taken them years to finally meet in person, but neither of them was looking forward to saying goodbye, and this looked like a timely lifeline.

CHAPTER ELEVEN

Looking around, Rose drew in a long breath, unable to stop smiling. Ever since the *Jane Austen Festival's* inception, she had watched the opening event where hundreds of people would walk in full costume through the streets of the Georgian city, a fitting backdrop for such a picturesque and popular event. How she had envied their easy confidence in walking around in costume, surrounded by shoppers, day trippers, students and sports fans, all milling around the city as they always did on Saturdays.

But, even though it had taken Rose all these years to participate rather than simply watching from the sidelines, she had always been excited by it. This year, the walk with Morgan was something Rose was sure she would remember for the rest of her life.

Everyone was in such good spirits. The sky was cloudless and a light breeze lifted the curls around the ladies' faces and stirred their pretty shawls as they greeted friends, old and new, and prepared to set off. There were older couples, entire families, groups of young girls, friends of all ages and backgrounds all sharing this one common love – Jane Austen.

Cameras were pointed here, there and everywhere as locals, visitors, family and friends and even the local press all jostled to take photos of the beautifully attired gathering of festival-goers.

Gradually, all Rose and Morgan's friends who had travelled from various parts of the globe arrived, with hugs and introductions and lots of laughter surrounding them. Dresses and hairstyles were admired, but nothing caught the eye of their friends and total strangers alike more often than the crosses hanging around Rose and Morgan's necks. Before long, Morgan had run out of the cards she had stowed in her reticule giving the details of *Cascara's Custom Collections*, who no doubt was going to be very busy with repeat orders in the near future.

A group of very handsome Redcoats had gathered near the head of the slowly forming line, and they affably agreed to have their picture taken with Morgan and Rose and then, being American, Morgan asked for another in which they pretended to march her in custody.

Rose turned away smiling happily, only to meet the eye of Jenny who was standing apart from the general crowd. She waved at her, unsurprised when all she received in response was a quick inclination of her head, though she did at least give her a wide smile, too. Tempted to go and invite her to walk with them, something held Rose back.

She felt sad to see her always alone, but watching her now, it was clear she was perfectly happy, her bright gaze darting here and there, taking in the people, the costumes and every now and again, glancing at the festival programme and shaking her head in what appeared to be bemusement. Surely more a fan than a forger today, mused Rose, and she turned back to find Morgan being delivered back into the safe hands of her friends by the escorting militia.

Before she could point Jenny out to her, however, they were joined by a young man, stylishly attired in a smart uniform and performing a low bow over Rose's hand as he greeted them.

'Well met, ladies.' He turned to Morgan, and Rose bit her lip at Morgan's admiring expression.

'Morgan, this is Leo. Leo, this is Morgan, a friend of mine from the USA.'

Leo repeated his formal bow to Morgan, then offered them both an arm as the line of people began to move. Rose shook her head at the friends behind them, who were wolf-whistling and calling out to them, laughing at how quickly they had acquired a handsome male escort.

'This is great. Look at all these men with their wives on their arms. They don't look like they've been forced into it, either!' Morgan was looking this way and that as they walked. 'I hope they're getting *huge* bonus points.'

'I can't speak for all of them, but it's very possible they simply enjoy this as much as their partners.' Leo smiled at Morgan. 'There seem to be more men here every year.'

He was a very nice man, but Rose knew he was younger than her in more than years – very much a boy rather than a man – which didn't bother her particularly except she always felt on edge around him, as though any moment he would ask her out for a drink or a meal, and she'd have to reject him. With a sigh, Rose fixed a smile on her face and looked around, leaving Morgan to chat to Leo. She didn't miss Jonathan at all, but there were times when she missed the protection of being with someone, of having a ring on her finger as a barrier.

And Leo's not Doctor Aiden Trevellyan, is he? Rose looked quickly around. There was no denying she felt a little jittery whilst they remained at this end of the town. Thankfully, they weren't walking along the Royal Crescent this year – the thought of the doctor happening to look out of his window and see her traipsing past dressed like this made her skin go cold, despite the sunshine.

'Are you okay?' Morgan was peering round Leo at her. 'You look like you're going to throw up!'

'No – I'm fine.' Rose forced a smile as they left the Circus behind and walked along Brock Street, praying James wouldn't be out and about either. His flat was barely steps from the Royal Crescent.

'It's quite warm for September,' added Leo. 'It will be much more shady once we're on the Gravel Walk.'

'You're adorable, Leo. Are you single?'

'At the moment, yes.' He glanced quickly at Rose, who felt the easy blush steal into her cheeks and decided to become very interested in the people lining the route to watch the parade.

'Well, we're going to have to change that today.' Morgan patted Leo's arm. 'This is going to be highway robbery for you – you could sweep any girl here off their feet with your smart uniform and charming self.'

'Not sure it works on everyone...' Leo murmured, and Rose suppressed a sigh. He was a sweet boy, but just not right for her.

It was with relief that they crossed the road just before the Royal Crescent and headed back towards the town along the Gravel Walk, though the watching crowds hadn't lessened at all.

'This must be what it feels like to be famous,' called Chrystal, one of their friends in the cluster of people behind them. 'All these cameras going off on all sides!' She blew a kiss at some of the spectators. 'Y'all make me feel like a star!'

'You've *always* been a star,' laughed Sandy, who was walking by her side. 'It's just taken the British public till now to realise it.'

Swept along, surrounded by happy banter, smiling faces and her speculation over whether Morgan's dad would come through with the visa for his daughter, Rose sailed up Gay Street, back around the other side of the Circus and past the Assembly Rooms again, sparing no further thought for her potential embarrassment. She was enjoying the moment and simply didn't want it to end.

Before long, they had reached Milsom Street and were cutting a large swathe through the shoppers, again drawing lots of good-natured attention as the long line of promenaders made their way through the streets towards the lower part of the town. Even with Leo remaining steadfastly at their side, Rose couldn't fault a moment of this walk now she was into her stride. She'd stopped looking down, fearful of catching the eye of someone – anyone – who might make her feel a fool for dressing up like this. So infectious was the feeling of goodwill around them – even down to several rugby supporters, in town early for that day's game, giving them some gentle ribbing as they passed by – that she found herself able to relax and really enjoy the moment. She could hear Morgan's constant happy chatter as she regaled Leo with talk of her home and caught snatches of laughter and conversation from their other friends who followed in their wake. As far as Rose was concerned, she didn't want the walk to end.

It was as the procession slowed almost to a halt after passing the Abbey that something caught Rose's eye, and she glanced over towards *Cafe Retro*, growing so cold this time, she shivered, causing Leo to turn towards her in concern and pat her on the arm, giving her a reassuring smile.

James and the doctor were standing outside the coffee shop, cardboard cups in hand and deep in conversation with Marcus. James and Marcus, thankfully, had their backs to them, but the same couldn't be said for their companion.

Rose tried to shrink down a little in the hopes Tess, who stood directly in front of her, would conceal her with her bonnet. If only she wasn't so tall, or her hair such a recognisable colour.

Oh God… don't look over here, don't look over – no, no, no, no…

'Rose, what are you *doing*?' Morgan twisted around and stared at her, but to Rose's dismay, she then glanced up and said brightly, 'Oh look; it's James! And Aiden!'

Rose had seen Dr Trevellyan's indifferent gaze as his eyes roamed over the three of them, and there was nothing she could add to this other than a strangled. 'Yes, I know.'

Turning away, she tried to engage Leo in conversation, conscious she was babbling. She could only guess what her face portrayed – surely her crippling embarrassment had frozen her features?

'James is waving – at least, I think you could call it a wave.' Morgan waved energetically back, smiling widely. 'Though he looks a bit... surprised.'

Rose tried not hear, convinced her humiliation was complete, and thankfully the walkers began to move on again.

Morgan looked back, confused, pulling slightly on Leo's arm. 'Shouldn't we go back? Say hello?'

Rose pulled Leo's arm in the opposite direction. 'No, Morgan. No, we really shouldn't.'

Before long, they had reached the end of the promenade, and Leo reluctantly drifted away to join the battalion of soldiers whilst Morgan puzzled over the expression on James's face.

'He looked – well, you might have read it more accurately. You know him better.'

'What? Sorry.' Rose shook her head. 'James? I'm afraid I didn't see it. Was he – did he look... funny, then?'

'He just looked,' Morgan hesitated, then began to laugh. 'Like he couldn't quite believe his eyes. I take it you never told him we were doing this?'

Blowing out a breath, Rose shook her head again, then smiled reluctantly. 'No. I take it you didn't either?'

Morgan started to giggle. 'Seriously; his face was hilarious. Wish

I'd taken a picture!'

Thankful she *hadn't* got a photo of the doctor's blank expression, Rose turned with relief to talk to Marita who'd just come to admire the necklace. Dressing up in period costume might seem silly, and possibly a bit of an embarrassing thing to do with one's time, to some people, but a small part of her wished there had been something… some reaction, even if a negative one. She wasn't entirely sure he'd even *seen* her, or if he had, that he'd realised who she was, and that hurt.

Looking around at the happy, milling crowds in their wonderful costumes, Rose drew in a long, slow breath. There were musicians in the bandstand and impromptu dancing had begun. Friends were helping each other, adjusting bonnets or retying ribbons, and everywhere people posed for photographs, some with tourists who were delighted to find Bath overflowing with people in period dress, and Rose felt her spirits rise again.

This was what mattered; these lovely people, all her friends and most of all, Morgan – not a distant crush on someone who was never going to look at her and see the real Rose. It was enough of a reprimand to bring her to her senses.

'Morgan?' Turning back from taking photos, her friend smiled up at her. 'There's an open-air café over there; shall we go and find a nice cup of tea?'

CHAPTER TWELVE

'I can't believe we slept in so late.' It was almost one o'clock the next day, and Rose and Morgan were hurrying past the Parade Gardens but had to stop short when they came to the pedestrian crossing.

'I still feel drunk!'

Rose glanced fondly at Morgan as they waited for the lights to change to let them cross. 'You only had three drinks from when we met the girls for last night's dinner until we stumbled home in the early hours.'

'Ah, but I have a delicate constitution, don't ya know?' Morgan grinned as their chance came, and they hurried across the road and on past the back of Bath Abbey as it chimed the hour, heading for Cheap Street.

'Here it is.' Rose gestured across the street to *Bill's Restaurant*. 'I think you'll love it.'

'I love everything here. What's not to like?'

They hovered inside the doorway as the staff hurried to seat the people waiting in front, and Rose cast her eyes over the full tables. 'I hope someone thought to book a…'

'Hey! Over here!'

Rose grinned and waved at the people crammed round a table at the back of the restaurant, whispering to Morgan. 'We can't be as late as we thought! Marita isn't here yet.'

Morgan laughed as they followed a waitress to the booth. 'That's no consolation! Don't you remember her saying when she left last night that she was lunching with her family and would join us afterwards? Hey, Rose, look who's with them!'

Rose sighed as she caught sight of Leo's beaming smile. 'He seems to have taken to the girls.'

'Or to one in particular?'

Slapping Morgan's arm in playful reprimand, they greeted their friends and squeezed into the booth, Rose making sure to sit in the space next to Sandy and leaving Morgan to sit next to Leo.

'Hey, Rose, did you hear Winchester is closed?'

Rose blinked. 'What? The city?'

Sandy laughed. 'No. The cathedral!'

'Oh! I'm gutted.' Morgan looked it, too.

'How odd, especially during the *Festival*.' Rose frowned.

'Some sort of repair work. Think they'd have timed it better, wouldn't you?' Leo shrugged, but as the server arrived at that point for their order, they all hurriedly turned to the menus.

More than an hour later, having enjoyed a lengthy but hilarious brunch, Rose looked around, stirring her tea and conscious of a blissful contentment.

'Hey, look! It's her again,' Morgan whispered as Tess asked the waitress to bring more tea.

Rose followed Morgan's gaze. Sure enough, there was Jenny, alone as always, standing in the street outside the restaurant and studying something Rose suspected was a map. Turning back to face the booth, she sighed.

'It makes me sad.'

'What does?' Morgan pulled a face as she sipped the tea Chrystal had insisted she try, laying on a bet of five pounds as incentive.

'So many people around her, but she looks distanced from them. I have never seen her with anyone. She's always on her own.'

Dropping three lumps of sugar into her cup, Morgan laughed. 'Well, delusion thrives best in isolation, don't you think? Hey, have any of you met or spoken to that lady over there, the one outside? Don't all look at once! Jeez! Guys, real smooth.'

'Hey, there's Marita!'

Sure enough, out in the street their friend had stopped by Jenny and was pointing in the direction of the Guildhall, and as the lady set off along the street, Marita hurried into the restaurant and Rose scooted along the seat so she could squeeze in.

'What did our favourite fan want, Marita?' Morgan inclined her head towards the window. 'Was she in a chatty mood?'

Marita shrugged. 'Not really. She was looking for the market; said something about ribbons.'

Rose had become thoughtful as all the things about Jenny that puzzled her seemed to coalesce in her sleep-deprived mind.

'Something about her calls to me.'

'What d'you mean?' Tess waved the freshened teapot at Rose, who nodded and held out her empty cup.

'I think Rose just has a heart for the criminally insane.' Morgan grinned. 'For me, *I* think she's just...'

Anxious Morgan might find it amusing to share their ruminations over Jenny's purpose with the letter-writing, Rose spoke quickly. 'No – it's not just that.' She sighed; 'I think–' she lowered her voice and everyone leaned forward to listen. 'I don't think she's faking it – *any* of it. I think it's all completely real for her, as though she's living and breathing it.'

'Do you think she's escaped from somewhere – like an asylum?'

Rose shook her head. 'I wonder if – because she believes it, because she's obviously studied and read… I mean, she's even tried to get a look of Jane about her.' Rose hesitated. 'Okay, you're going to think I'm mad but, it's like she *is* Jane Austen. Or at least, the closest we could ever come to knowing the lady herself.'

Rose held her breath as a momentary silence descended. Such a wistful look echoed around the table amongst her friends, but it was enough for the absurdity of it all to fall into perspective, and Rose started to laugh, the others quickly following suit.

'Maybe we should just follow her around – get an autograph or two,' Morgan snorted.

As one, they all craned their necks to see if they could still see Jenny, but she had gone.

'I didn't really study her,' Marita said with a smirk, 'but she's looking pretty good for someone who's over 200 years old.'

'Yeah – shall we ask her what face cream she's using?'

'Or what vitamins she's on?'

They all laughed again, but Leo shrugged.

'Don't *all* you ladies think you're Jane Austen when dressed up?' He looked thoroughly unperturbed by their speculations.

'Oh no.' Chrystal shook her head. 'Some of us like to believe we're Elizabeth Bennet.'

Morgan nodded emphatically, and Tess laughed. 'She's right. Aside from the lucky ladies whose partners have come along with them, we can pretend we're searching for our own Mr Darcy.'

'Or Captain Wentworth?'

All eyes turned on Leo, and he raised a brow. 'What? He's definitely *my* favourite.'

Rose smiled as Morgan asked a passing waitress for the bill and, resolving to put her ridiculous suspicions where they belonged, she reached for her purse.

Five minutes later, they were all out on Cheap Street, but as they turned their steps towards the venue for the dance class Morgan nudged Rose's arm.

'Don't look now, but I think I spy the gorgeous Doc.'

Rose's insides did a somersault as she remembered his blank expression yesterday, and instinctively she stepped behind Marita and bent her knees, as though trying to hide.

'What are you doing?' Morgan was laughing. 'Don't worry, he's not coming this way.'

Rose straightened and looked over to where Morgan had gestured. Sure enough, there was Dr Trevellyan on the other side of the road, walking away from them. Rose sighed as she watched his broad-shouldered figure turn the corner and disappear from sight.

'Hey, come on, you two! We'll be late!'

'Coming!'

Thankful he hadn't seen her, though she couldn't account for why it mattered, Rose joined Morgan as they hurried to catch up with the others; it was time to relegate any thoughts of Dr Aiden Trevellyan to where they belonged.

It was possible every event at the *Festival* would become Rose's favourite – and the rest of the week still stretched before them!

Rose smiled happily as she moved elegantly – or so she hoped – along the line as they followed the instructions of the incredibly patient caller, a cheerful if emphatic lady called Diana. They had been at it for over an hour now, and Rose's cheeks ached with laughing, but, though it could hardly be said they were moving as one, they were definitely making progress.

Everyone was in good spirits, gamely stepping well out of their comfort zone, but Rose had been surprised to find Morgan hadn't mastered it in her usual quick way. Not that it dampened her friend's mood as she sailed off in the wrong direction once more. 'I think I got it that time. *No!*'

'Your *other* left!' Rose called over her shoulder as Morgan skipped straight into the next line over from them, laughing and apologising at the same time.

Rose was enjoying the swishing of her long skirt as it brushed against her ankles. Whilst there were a fair number of people in period dress, she had opted for a full-length but modern skirt and an Empire line top. Morgan had been instantly regretful for throwing on her jeans, and Rose and her friends had quite a job on their hands persuading her against grabbing one of the white cloths from the tables in the foyer to fashion a makeshift skirt of her own.

Stopping triumphantly on the final note of the music, Rose turned with everyone else to cheer their almost successful completion of a whole routine. Tess and Sandy, who were attending the advanced class later in the week, were watching from the sidelines and applauded enthusiastically. Morgan was high-fiving Marita, celebrating their survival of the set if not their dancing prowess, and Leo was bowing deeply to a blushing Chrystal. Turning back, Rose smiled – their second dance, if she was not mistaken.

It was exactly as she'd imagined it should be: laughter and music and friendship. She looked around at the happy faces and sighed blissfully. Just then, however, she spotted Jenny gliding towards the chairs lining the walls and taking a seat. Like Rose, she wasn't in costume today but wore a similar floor-length, full skirt, a neatly buttoned blouse and clutched a shawl in her lap. Making a sudden decision, and under the distraction of everyone grabbing cups of water – it was surprisingly warm work – Rose walked over to sit beside her.

'Are you going to join in? It's so much fun.' Rose gestured towards the milling dancers as they chatted and practised a few steps.

'Good afternoon.' Jenny looked briefly in Rose's direction, those bright eyes sparkling as always. 'It is not my purpose – no.'

'But it's a dance class.'

'A fine sport indeed.'

'So…' Rose turned in her seat to face Jenny, who glanced at her again but this time did not turn away, her eye caught by the necklace around Rose's neck. Then she raised her gaze to meet Rose's and smiled. There was something in her steadfast gaze…

'I'm curious; why did you come if you don't want to dance?'

Jenny glanced around the room. 'Is one obliged to participate? Did you never attend the theatre merely to enjoy the performance? Do those who follow the sporting endeavours of others join them on the field of play? There is ample amusement to be derived from observation and thus little need for the effort of partaking.'

It was the most Jenny had ever said to her, but Rose found herself wrapped in circles over what her actual meaning was. Perhaps she was best left to her own devices after all.

'Do not mistake me, Miss Wallace. I appreciate your interest, but please rest assured I am perfectly content.'

Realising the dancers were reassembling, ready for more mayhem, Rose stood up. 'Well then, I'll leave you in peace. See you later.'

'Had a nice chat?' Morgan grinned as Rose rejoined her.

'I asked if she planned to join in. But Morgan – I wonder…'

'Yes, you wonder a lot about her. Rose, let it go.' Morgan threw her a fond look.

'I'm trying but I just can't help but feel I'm missing something. And it's weird; when you talk to her, when she's got you fixed with her eye…'

'Her eye? Now you're making her sound spooky. She's just a mad crazy fan who learned how to write like a famous author – or… I dunno, maybe she's like an actress, playing a role. Hey, that's it!' Morgan laughed. 'She's one of those; you know, the ones who have to live the part they are about to play. What do they call it? Role immersion? No, wait – Method acting.'

Rose tried to apply it to everything she'd seen, to how she felt when in Jenny's company. 'I don't know. It's even more than that. It's not as if she's *trying* to live the life so much as – it *is* her life.'

'Well, that's the point of the Method, I think. It's that, or she's even more delusional than we first thought.' Morgan turned back to face the dance hall.

'But I don't want her to be delusional. I so want to believe in her.'

'What?' Morgan choked back another laugh. 'You want to believe she actually *is* Jane Austen? Rose –'

'No! Of course not. But I don't want her to be a criminal either.' She glanced over her shoulder, then back to Morgan. 'I feel some sort of – oh, I don't know… *connection* when I see her? Like she'd be fun to know?'

'Despite the possible forged letters you saw – and the candles and all the loot?'

'Maybe it's as we first thought and she's just something to do with antiques? She clearly loves the past and anything associated with it – and why not? Perhaps the letter-writing is something she enjoys, loves to indulge? What if she's pretending she lives in that era and because of her job, she's able to acquire the props to help her live the dream?' The more she spoke, the more sense it made to Rose.

Morgan eyed her sceptically, then grinned and waved a hand at the lines of dancers who were trying some new steps under Diana's careful guidance. 'You'd have thought she'd have leapt at a chance at this, then. Why don't we both go and see if we can persuade her? I still think her lack of interest does hint more at fraudster than obsessive fan, though.'

Rose looked around again, just as Jenny raised her head and they locked eyes. They stared at each other for a second before a flash of unease crossed the lady's face. 'Shit, she's seen us looking at her. I have to go and–'

Morgan grabbed Rose's arm. 'Where are you going? No! Are you kidding me? You can't just accuse her of being a fraud – or a loony!'

'I'm not going to,' Rose muttered. A whirlwind of images spun through her mind as she stared at Jenny: the inexplicable disappearance into thin air, the figure staring reverently at Jane Austen's books in *Waterstones*; her well-worn costumes and the curiously old-fashioned style she favoured at other times. Then there was the vast array of candles in the flat above hers, the boxes spilling their old yet suspiciously fresh contents over the floor, and the handwriting, using proper ink and a genuine pen of the era…

Trying to read the look on Jenny Ashton's face as she got slowly to her feet and picked up her shawl, Rose narrowed her gaze, her head swirling with all sorts of impossible thoughts. Then she murmured,

'*Jenny*. That was Mr Austen's pet name for his youngest daughter.'

Morgan rolled her eyes. 'Okay, look, just hold on. We don't want to scare her. Let's just–'

'She's going,' Rose said urgently as the lady turned to leave the room.

'Well, no surprises there. You've been staring at her! Enough to freak any normal person out, never mind Crazy Jenny!'

'I'm going after her.'

Morgan had to walk with a sort of trot to keep up as Rose strode out into the entrance hall and pulled open the door to the street. 'Rose, seriously.' And then, in a different tone, 'James!'

Rose stopped short in her run down the steps. Sure enough, walking past the sports centre was her boss, looking decidedly caught out. Distracted though she was, both by the culpable look on James's face and the glowing expression on Morgan's, Rose managed to catch a glimpse of Jenny's figure hurrying down the street towards Pulteney Road.

'I want to catch her before she disappears.' Turning back, she shook her head at James as he tried to waffle his way through how he happened to be there.

'So this is a – just a coincidence?' Morgan, for once in her life, sounded a little uncertain, and Rose looked from one to the other. If the colour flooding James's cheeks was any indication, coincidence had nothing to do with it.

Casting another glance down the road, just in time to see Jenny escape from view around the corner, Rose sighed. Interfering in her friends' personal lives went totally against the grain for her, but for a reason she couldn't quite explain, time seemed critical, as though she didn't have a moment to waste.

'Morgan – this is James. He's my boss and my friend; a lovely, genuine bloke, who wouldn't take anyone for a ride.'

'James – this is my very best friend, Morgan. She's great company, warm-hearted, adorable and would love to go for a drink with you.'

They both stared at her like a couple of deer in the headlights, and running out of patience, Rose rolled her eyes.

'Oh for goodness' sake; you have a *cat* together! Surely that's grounds for at least getting a drink?'

Morgan choked on a laugh; then she turned to James with a wide smile. 'Hey! Wanna help me find that big place with the huge stairs and all that glass? Wait, no. What about that other place – the one with–'

'How about we just… walk?' James gestured back towards town and Morgan nodded.

'I can still talk, right? While we walk?'

James smiled but said nothing, gallantly offering his arm to her, and Rose saw her opportunity.

'Off you both go then.'

Morgan narrowed her eyes at Rose. 'You're just trying to distract us so you can go off and play Nancy Drew.'

James frowned. 'What's going on?'

Morgan jogged his elbow. 'She thinks she's uncovered a counterfeit Jane Austen and wants to confront her. She's going to get herself shot!'

Despite her anxiety, Rose laughed. James, however, eyed Morgan seriously. 'This is Bath, Morgan.'

Morgan looked between them sceptically. 'I'm not in LA anymore, is that what you're saying, Toto?'

Rose held up both hands. 'I just want to ask her about some things. That's all.'

James shrugged. 'Fine. Then we'll all go.'

Rose turned away. 'No, James, don't be ridiculous. I'll be fine. This is my own… quest or… delusion or… *something*.' For a second, the image of Jenny's face from moments earlier appeared before her, and Rose gasped. 'And she *knows*.'

Morgan frowned. 'Knows what?'

'She knows that *I* suspect she's...' Rose stopped. What on earth *did* she suspect? 'Please bear with me! I have to find her, I have to talk to her.'

'Rose, she will think *you* are the mad one!'

'Then she and I will have to run mad together!' She attempted a reassuring smile at James and gave her friend a quick hug before turning and walking rapidly down the street in Jenny's wake.

Then she called over her shoulder as she broke into a run, 'But do not worry, we shall not faint!'

CHAPTER THIRTEEN

Jenny was quick on her feet, but Rose was catching her up. 'Jenny! *Wait!*' There was no response as the lady hurried across the road ahead and rounded the corner at the top of Great Pulteney Street. Putting on a spurt of speed, her long skirt clutched above her knees, Rose managed to be just a few paces away as her quarry took the step to number 4 Sydney Place.

Holding onto the railings bordering the steps to her own flat, Rose was out of breath, but she managed to summon enough to call, 'Jenny!' It was as though she was invisible and for a moment, Rose's resolve stumbled, but then she recalled the lady's formality. 'Miss Ashton? Please, could we speak?'

There was no response again as Jenny placed her key in the lock, and desperate now, Rose said firmly, 'Miss Austen.'

Sure enough, the lady froze. 'I would like to talk to you. Please?'

Rose held her breath, but slowly the lady removed the key and turned to look at her. 'I suspected as much – perchance it was inevitable. How may I assist you?'

Swallowing quickly, unsure whether she was relieved or not, Rose walked forward to meet her as she stepped back onto the pavement.

'There's something I have to know.' The absurdity of what she was doing struck Rose, but she pushed on. 'I hope you don't mind me asking. It's just – it's just I saw, you see.' She gestured towards the ground-floor flat. 'In the garden – and then, the other night; the letter on your desk, written in a fair imitation of Jane Austen's hand.'

The lady looked amused by this. 'It would be surprising were it not.' She studied Rose in what felt like an assessing manner. 'Yet these are mere observations; what is it you would wish to know?'

What *was* it she wanted to know? 'I – er – I just wanted to know that–' Rose grasped at straws. 'You – well, you have no plans to try and sell the letter.'

'I do not follow you. Why would I wish to dispose of a letter penned to my sister in such a manner?'

Rose blinked – *her* sister? Either this woman was as delusional as Morgan suggested, or she was so deep into living her upcoming role that she just refused to pull herself out of it. Nevertheless, Rose tried to plough on. 'I need to know you have no intention of pretending… to try and pass the writing off as…' She stopped. If this woman was *playing* at being Jane Austen, then she would consider her letters to be genuine, as far as it went.

'I cannot comprehend your meaning. There is nothing untoward in writing to my sister, in whom I have every faith, for she destroys each letter as soon as it is read. Is this your concern, that someone might discover what is afoot?'

Rose frowned. 'So you aren't writing them to sell them?'

'Most indubitably not. What a singular notion.'

'I'm so pleased.' Rose smiled in genuine relief, but it was fleeting. 'But wait! How did you plan to send it – to Cassandra, I mean? Is she also a – er –'

'You are acquainted with my sister? This is most singular.'

'No – of course not.'

'Yet you hesitate not to use her given name. Such informality is a little precipitous. 'Tis almost an impertinence.' Rose stared at her; then she narrowed her gaze. The lady was almost laughing at her. ''Tis but a tease, Miss Wallace. Forgive me.'

'Right. Okay.' Rose drew in a breath, trying to get back on track. 'So why do you write them, then?'

'To send intelligence of myself. Why else?' She peered at Rose. 'Does aught sicken you? Your faculties seem not wholly at your disposal.'

'Look, enough of this. I know what you are; who you are *pretending* to be.'

'Miss Jenny Ashton?'

'No – wait. Is that not your real name?'

The lady looked taken aback. 'You know it is not.'

'Yes, but then what...'

There was silence for a moment, a frown on the lady's brow. 'Is there a deficiency in your memory, Miss Wallace? Did you not acknowledge me not five minutes hence?' She gave a delicate shrug. 'So be it. 'Tis unfortunate, though long has Cass warned me of its inevitability and, to be sure, there is no little liberation in speaking of it at last.'

Rose stared at the lady before her. They were almost on a par for height and possibly age, yet there was a noticeable air of something *different* about her... A pair of intelligent, hazel eyes held Rose's steadily, and she was struck, now they stood in the natural light of day, by the hint of resemblance in her features to the descriptions and attempts at visual manifestations of Jane Austen. Yet it was as if none had been quite right. This was like the master bringing all those images into focus.

Feeling very glad James and Morgan had not come with her, Rose shook her head. Was she still slightly drunk? What was happening to her? Why did her skin tingle, right to the tips of her fingers?

Her voice came out in a whisper. 'I thought I saw you… disappear.'

The lady merely continued to hold Rose's gaze. 'And pray, when was this?'

'Thursday morning – early. You came out into the garden, and I was down in the courtyard. I convinced myself I must have blinked and you'd moved out of sight – the view is so restricted.'

'I see. I shall take more care in future. And this is common knowledge, hereabouts?'

'Not… exactly.' Rose wasn't sure if she was talking to a delusional woman or becoming one herself. This must be what being brainwashed was like. Was she saying she really *did* disappear the other morning?

Rose shook her head. 'It's not possible.'

The lady cautioned Rose with a finger to her lips. There was an elderly woman walking past with a small yapping dog on a lead, no doubt heading for Henrietta Park.

Once she had turned the corner into Sutton Street, Rose looked at her companion again. *This is not happening*, she chanted to herself.

'It is said all things are possible.' The lady reached into her pocket and withdrew a soft pouch. Then she smiled at Rose. 'How convenient are your pockets in comparison to ours. Oft one would be caught reaching for the recalcitrant thing in a manner most inelegant.' She tipped the contents of the pouch onto her palm and raised it for Rose to inspect. 'This is the means by which I come here.' It was a topaz cross and chain.

Rose caught her breath as she stared at it, mesmerised. 'It's very pretty.' Then she frowned, a hand raised to her own necklace. 'It's very similar to the ones belonging to Cassandra and Jane Austen. I've seen the real thing.'

The lady's shoulders rose and fell. 'As have I – and also the likenesses in books of the crosses they believe belonged to my sister and me, the ones they display, by all accounts, in a cottage in Hampshire where I go to live… or rather, once lived.'

'It's not true? They didn't belong to you – I mean, them?' Rose felt like a small part of her world was splintering.

'In part, but they numbered three. Why only two survive today, I know not. This,' she gestured towards the replica cross hanging around Rose's neck, 'is a copy of my mother's, not of mine.'

They both stared down at the cross, still resting in her palm, as Rose tried to grapple with all she was hearing. 'And this,' Rose pointed warily at it, 'this has been a – a way through time?' It sounded completely ludicrous when said out loud, but instead of looking at her as though she was stupid, the lady nodded.

'Indeed. I simply place it about my neck, and lo, I am either taken forward or back, dependent upon which way the cross faces. I only ever use it within the confines of the house and the walled garden.' She gestured towards 4 Sydney Place. 'For then, though it moves me from one time to another, the place remains constant.' Then she laughed. 'How well it would look, would it not, if I were to journey between time and arrive…'

A sudden burst of noise interrupted her, and they both turned quickly to see the small yapping dog, now free of its restraint, racing around the corner towards them, the elderly lady panting along behind and calling its name in a high-pitched squeal: 'Prancer! Prancer, you come here this minute!'

Prancer threw a disdainful look over his shoulder and kept running, unfortunately straight into the skirts of Rose's companion, who stumbled and, as she righted herself, the cross and chain fell from her hand.

Both she and Rose instinctively reached for it, but not soon enough. Snatching it as it fell, Prancer seized it in his teeth and with one quick swallow consumed it, disappearing immediately into thin air.

CHAPTER FOURTEEN

Rose's knees almost buckled under her for a second as an ice-cold sensation swept over her skin, and she grasped the security of the railings behind her. 'What – what just happened?'

The lady said nothing; her eyes were fixed on something over Rose's shoulder, and she spun around to see what it was. Something was different about the building, but she couldn't immediately detect what it was. Then, seeing Prancer's owner still calling for him as she walked up and down the street, the empty lead trailing behind her, Rose swung round.

'That dog just *disappeared* into thin air! Did you see it?'

'I did. And thus I must remain hereafter.' She met Rose's eye seriously. 'We were full aware of the hazardous nature of my undertaking.'

Rose was struck by both the calmness of the lady's demeanour and the finality of her tone.

'We? Who… no, wait! Why must you remain – stay, I mean?' Rose's skin was still tingling, and she put a hand to her head, then it dropped to her bare throat. 'My necklace! It's gone!'

'The power to come and go is beyond my reach, for my necklace is also lost to me, the portal forever sealed. I have no means of regaining my former life and must resign myself to my fate.' Rose didn't think she sounded particularly resigned at all. She seemed decidedly smug!

'But the dog! Can't it come back?' Rose's gaze followed Prancer's owner as she disappeared into Sydney Gardens, still calling shrilly for her pet.

'I suspect not. The charm passed from my hand to the hound, touched its throat; thus, it may have returned whence I came – to a street in this city more than 200 years ago.' She gestured around them.

'*May* have returned? I don't understand...'

'Perchance the hound travelled forward 200 years?' The young woman looked unconcerned. 'Whatever the outcome, the means to alert my sister is beyond me.'

'Your *sister*?' *Still*? This was ridiculous. Rose shook her head to clear it. 'I think I need a cup of tea and a sit-down. Would you like a cup of tea?' Her mind spinning, she turned towards the gate in the railings, trying to keep herself in check, but she was stalled by a hand on her arm.

'Do you not wish for me to tell you why and how?' The lady raised a brow. 'Did you not own to an excess of curiosity not a moment ago? Did you not make such haste to have this curiosity satisfied?'

Rose drew in a shallow breath. What she wished for was to say '*no, thank you, I think I've heard enough craziness for one day*'.

'No. I – er – I just thought a cup of tea might help. It's traditional, you know, in a crisis…'

She turned back to the gate and pushed; it didn't move. Rose glanced down, only to realise it was padlocked! She frowned, then as her gaze flew to the windows, she gasped. There was no sign of the pretty curtains she had hung so proudly in her kitchen the day she moved in, no photo frames on the sitting room window sill, and none of her carefully nurtured pots spilling their contents out over the steps.

'What the hell is going on? Is this some sort of joke?' Rose turned back, a sudden thought crossing her mind. 'Wait – is this one of those TV shows?' She looked up and down the street, then peered across at the foliage bordering the Holburne Museum. There were no visible cameras, but then, didn't they always conceal them?

''Tis neither quip nor jape, Miss Wallace.' Rose turned back to the lady as she spoke, her manner softer than before. '*This* is your home no longer.' She gestured towards the basement flat. 'You live elsewhere.'

Rose blinked. This could not be happening; it was some stupid dream. Had she fallen asleep at the dance class, bored with her want of a partner? She pinched herself hard on the forearm.

'Ouch!' No, definitely not asleep. She stared at the young woman in front of her, trying to take in what she was saying. 'But – but you can't be here. You can't be Jane Austen.' She bit her lip. It felt terribly insensitive to say it out loud, but she had to. 'She – you – died. 200 years ago. You were buried in Winchester Cathedral.'

'A building I much admire; yet it is a singular honour from which I take little enjoyment.' She sighed. 'Look.' She pointed at the front of the building, and Rose looked up. The plaque proclaiming Jane Austen's residence was gone, as were the smart box trees. Moreover, the ground floor was clearly an office, serviceable blinds covering the windows and the company name emblazoned on the glass.

'Much may be altered; you will see.'

Rose stared at her in disbelief. This was ridiculous; only moments ago, she'd thought there couldn't be anything more outlandish than her belief in this woman being Jane Austen. Now she was supposed to believe her whole life was entirely different, too.

Grabbing her bag, she opened it and rummaged around for the keys to her flat, pulling them out with a feeling of immense relief. It was quickly dashed. The keys were perhaps not that different, but the key chain held less than it should have and her usual mementoes were missing. In place of her pen and ink charm and Jane Austen silhouette was a small, stuffed owl sporting a Ravenclaw scarf.

Feeling almost sick with trepidation, she pulled her mobile from her pocket, staring in disbelief at the unfamiliar casing before quickly scanning her most recent calls. Where it should have shown Morgan – several times – James, her friends attending the *Festival* and even the doctor, the only names showing were her mother (who never called her), someone called Mary, and several from someone known as Lottie, both names she was unfamiliar with.

Rose closed her eyes. Her body felt weak and, used to being organised and in control of her life, she was at a loss as to what to do. She swayed on her feet and then felt an arm steadying her.

Her eyes flew open to meet those of the young woman, who smiled faintly. 'I regret I have no salts upon my person, or I would offer them.'

Shaking her head, Rose tried to summon a smile. 'I'm fine. It's just – unexpected.' She stuffed the mobile into her bag.

The lady nodded then looked around before turning to face Rose again. 'A dish of tea would be just the thing, but there are matters we must speak of. I do not think it would be wise to be overheard?'

'We could go into the gardens?' Rose gestured weakly across the road. She felt completely lost.

With a surprisingly firm grip, the lady took her arm. 'Come, then, let us make haste!' Leading a bemused Rose across the road, she steered her into the relative anonymity of Sydney Gardens and a wooden bench tucked away beside a tall hedge.

Rose stared at her hands in her lap. They appeared to be the same as always: pale skin, slender fingers with no adornment; neat, well-cared-for nails. She looked up. The sky was still there; blue with a smattering of clouds. The trees of Sydney Gardens continued to stand tall and proud, their leaves stirring in the gentle breeze and the faint rumble of traffic passing by on the Warminster Road could be heard in the distance.

It was all so familiar – yet so much had changed. She turned to look at the young woman at her side. She was also still there, her eyes free of guile or amusement, only an earnest plea in them for acceptance of all she had just told her.

'It is true, then. This is,' Rose swallowed quickly and waved a hand in the air. 'This is really happening. You *are* Jane Austen, and we *are* sitting on a bench in Sydney Gardens, calmly discussing how you managed to travel between living over 200 years ago and being here now.' She drew in a deep breath. 'And there is an iron safe built into the wall of your bedroom through which you and your sister exchange letters...'

Jane nodded. 'Indeed. I comprehend your confusion, Miss Wallace. It could be no more than mine when first I came here!'

'No, I'm sure!' Rose swallowed with difficulty. How was she to get her head around all this *absurdity*? 'And, er... how long has this–' A fleeting memory came of Marcus telling her about the new ground-floor visitor and how she was to stay for an indefinite period.

'I have been coming and going for some months now. Perchance I may not have tarried so long, had I not learned of the approaching *Festival* bearing my name. I will own to having been curious.'

Rose shook her head. 'It must have been the most bizarre time for you, but seeing all the people arriving lately, dressing up...' She looked at Jane again. 'I thought you were a dedicated fan!'

Jane's eyes twinkled as she smiled. 'I suspected as much.'

'And... and did you send your sister a copy of the programme through the safe for her amusement?'

She shook her head. ''Tis not possible. Objects may be brought forward from the past, but one cannot send back that which did not exist back then. Cass sends me ink and parchment so we may continue our habit of correspondence. Modern paper and ink will not pass through.'

'But virtually no letters survive from when you lived in Bath! It's always been said you and your sister were rarely parted during those years, or they were also amongst those Cassandra destroyed because…' Rose's voice tailed off as realisation struck. Jane merely raised a sardonic brow. 'And – and all those things in the apartment, in the boxes…'

'Are come from my sister; from our home: small pieces of silverware, even teaspoons, thimbles and suchlike, have acquired an astonishing worth, as do our books which are sought-after first editions here. I sell them at the antiques centre in Bartlett Street. It is how I fund my life.' She shrugged delicately. 'How else could I afford my expenses?'

'How else indeed,' Rose said weakly.

'But no longer. I am not sure what I shall do, but I must find a new home. All that remains are these,' Jane indicated the clothes she wore, 'and this.' She withdrew the leather pouch from her pocket. 'I knew the risk of becoming stranded; thus I kept this on my person – precious funds and a few other treasures. It seems they have remained.' She glanced around. 'I shall not be sorry to leave Bath, be it this century or the past.'

Rose felt suddenly cold and grabbed the arm of the young woman beside her, half-expecting her hand to go straight through it. 'Wait! Were you living in Bath then? What year was it… Oh no!' She started to shake her head as she released her grip. Jane seemed perfectly calm, as though it made little difference to her.

'You begin to comprehend whence I came.'

Rose stared at her, her head still moving from side to side in denial. 'It was in the year three. This very month.'

With a shudder, Rose closed her eyes. No! This could *not* be happening. She would open her eyes and she would be here alone. Jane Austen could not possibly travel through time to the future, and she would not be seated beside her on a bench in Sydney Gardens speaking words which were tearing Rose apart.

Cautiously she raised her lids. The dark-haired, hazel-eyed woman with an air of the past about her remained in her seat, her gaze steady.

Rose cleared her throat. 'You have disappeared in 1803 – eight years before your first novel was published. If there is no way back, then you were never published at all! The world has never heard of you, or *any* of your characters – this is a world without Mr Darcy?'

'Most indubitably.'

A silence fell as they stared at each other. Rose felt so agitated she half-expected to explode, but there was no sign of disquiet in Jane Austen's face.

Just then, the sound of music coming from Rose's bag made them both start, and she stared at it for a second, confused. She recognised the tune, but it took her a moment to realise it must be coming from her phone, and she snatched the bag up to find it.

It was her mother!

'He-hello?' she said cautiously.

'Where on earth are you? Your dinner has gone cold. I really don't know why I bother!' Before she could summon any response, her mother had hung up, and Rose lowered her hand, her eyes wide with surprise.

'I must still live at home!' She felt the colour drain from her skin, conscious of Jane's curious stare.

'Excellent.' Jane got to her feet gracefully. 'Here is where we part company, Miss Wallace. I wish you a good evening.' She made as if to curtsey again but stopped herself, which would have amused Rose greatly in other circumstances. As it was, she was gripped by a sense of panic.

'No – wait! You have to stay with me, at least for now.'

'And pray, to what end?'

'I don't know! But I need some time to think about all of this – the implications! I may have more questions. Besides, you have nowhere to go, do you?'

Jane met her frantic gaze with calmness. 'No. But I am resourceful, and I am in funds, which I have discovered eases many a path that might otherwise be obstructed. It serves just as well in this century as it did in the past.'

'No, no, no! You *must* stay with me – please! Come home with me.'

Rose got to her feet and looked around. They were still the only people in this part of the Gardens. She would fetch her car and… a cold sensation gripped her.

'Oh no!'

'What is it?'

'Where will my car be? It's normally in the garage in the mews I rent from Marcus, but if I don't live in my flat anymore…'

'You have your own conveyance?' Rose nodded, and Jane's eyes began to sparkle. 'I have longed for the chance to… Ah, I begin to comprehend your rather amusing air and countenance. You know not where it is.'

Rose simply stared at her. What else was there to say?

CHAPTER FIFTEEN

'Then we shall walk,' Jane smirked. 'For I am a great walker!'

'Yes, I know.' Rose would have normally taken the bus, but somehow boarding the No 4 to Bathampton with Jane Austen was just a step too far right now – not that it wouldn't have made the best ever selfie caption to post on Facebook! 'It's a couple of miles, though.'

Jane fell into step beside her as they headed for the top of the Gardens. 'I have walked all the way to Weston and back before now. It is one of the finer pleasures of Bath at this time of year, is it not, Miss Wallace? The country walks?'

How can she be talking about such mundane things as walking at a time like this?

'I can't believe I still live at home. This is a nightmare! And where do I work? How do I get to my job in the morning if I have no idea where I work?'

A sweeping sense of loss flowed through Rose, for her life, for James and her beloved job in the office in Queen Square... Even arrogant Roger seemed benign now...

'How is your place of employment so affected?'

'Because I only applied for *that* job because of where the office was located.'

'How very singular! Pray tell, what location had such a hold upon you?'

'Queen Square.' Rose sighed, and met Jane's amused eye. 'Number 13, to be precise.'

The lady brightened, 'How delightful! Oh, we passed the most pleasing stay there.'

'I know.'

'Of course you know. And there was a–'

'Black kitten playing on the stairs.'

To Rose's surprise, Jane tucked her arm in hers as they walked. 'I feel as though I have found a lost friend! This could be prodigiously entertaining, Miss Wallace! Your recollections are those of family or old acquaintances!'

Rose was feeling rather conspicuous walking along the Warminster Road with Jane holding her arm. Fortunately, there were few people about now, it being Sunday and early evening.

'Your mother will provide the necessary intelligence, will she not?'

'I can hardly walk into the house and ask her! She'll think I've gone mad – she may not be wrong!'

'This is not madness, my dear. This is just an altered reality.'

Rose had no response to this, and for a while they walked in silence until they paused to cross a road.

'It's not too far now,' Rose pointed ahead. 'The house is down in the village; we take the next turning.'

'What sort of person is she, your mother?'

Rose wracked her brains for something nice to say but came up blank. 'I get on her nerves. I used to think it was because I'm not like her, but in recent years I came to the conclusion I simply… irritate her. Nothing about me pleases her.'

'Then we have something in common.' Rose glanced at Jane as they turned into the street she had indicated. 'Oh, do not mistake me.

I love my mother, but she is not an easy person to please. She believes she gave up a great deal when she married my father, and though they seem content she does not conceal her belief in having given *all* the distinction to the union.'

As they neared the house, silence fell once more between them. Rose was being consumed by memories and the young woman walking by her side seemed to sense her disquiet, merely giving her arm a squeeze as they passed through the gate onto the sweep of gravel leading down to the house.

Staring at the pale stone façade of her home, Rose drew in a deep breath. She'd moved out over two years ago, something her mother had railed against, citing selfishness in her daughter. If Rose had thought her mother genuinely needed the generous rent she had been handing over for years, she would never have dreamed of leaving, but she didn't. Mrs Wallace had been well provided for by her husband, and though she worked part-time, it was purely for the social life, not because she needed the income.

Her mother had resented being left alone with a young child, and she had never hidden the fact she found Rose a burden – unwanted. Well, Rose didn't particularly want her as a mother, either, but right now, home was the only familiar thing left and it would have to suffice.

Resigned to her fate, Rose led Jane towards the house, noting her mother's flashy car parked in the open garage. There was no sign of her own car – where might it be? She had little time to contemplate this conundrum further, however, for they had reached the side door.

'Courage, Miss Wallace.' Rose turned and met Jane's eye once more, strangely reassured by her, and nodded before turning the handle and stepping into the kitchen.

'Rose Wallace! Look at the state of you! How will you ever find yourself a man if you persist in going out looking like that?!'

'Hi, Mum. This,' she turned to indicate Jane as she stepped into the kitchen to stand beside her. 'is Ja-Jenny. Jenny Ashton. She's... a friend of mine.'

'Charmed, I'm sure.' Mrs Wallace barely glanced at Jane. 'Your hair needs a good brush, Rose. Always so unruly.' She ran a hand over her shiny, blonde bob, then stopped to admire her bright nail varnish for a moment. 'I don't know why you won't take my advice and get it cut and dyed a better colour!' She walked over to the mirror on the far wall and applied some lipstick before turning to face the two silent young women. 'Now I am going out shortly. Your dinner was spoilt so I threw it out. You'll have to make do with what's left in the fridge.'

'Mum, Ja-Jenny needs somewhere to stay for a day or two. I said it would be okay to use one of the spare rooms?'

Mrs Wallace's gaze snapped back to Jane, and she eyed her up and down. 'Hmm, your friend needs a makeover as much as you do.' She frowned at Rose. 'I would have appreciated some notice, but – whatever you wish; you'll have to make the bed up and deal with your own meals. I've taken some time off work, and I'm off to stay with the Stewart-Lees from Tuesday.'

'That's nice.' Rose was torn between relief her mother was going to be away and pity for the Stewart-Lees, who were far too nice to have to put up with her mother. 'And – er – I'll be at work anyway, won't I?' She tried to ignore the roll of Jane's eyes at the faint question in her tone, but Mrs Wallace wasn't listening. She was checking the contents of her evening bag and singing under her breath.

Rose threw Jane a desperate look, but her new friend inclined her head towards the doorway opposite, saying quietly, 'Permit me to find the answer you seek.'

Hesitating on the threshold, Rose bit her lip, but Jane then said quite loudly, 'I will await your return. It is most kind of you to prepare a room for me, Miss Rose.'

Sensing herself dismissed, Rose started up the stairs, but stopped as she heard Jane address her mother.

'It must be pleasant to have an occupation, Mrs Wallace. Pray, what is your profession?'

A short laugh greeted this. 'Profession? I don't think I've ever heard it called that before! I work in a bar, love, in town. Great fun, keeps me young!' There was a slight pause before she added, 'You have a really odd way of saying things. Are you foreign?'

'This is a foreign land to me, most indubitably. And pray, what is your opinion of Rose's profession... at the – the–'

'At the library?' Mrs Wallace made a dissatisfied noise. 'My opinion is she's never going to catch a man's eye cataloguing mouldy old books in Bath Library; but she doesn't listen to me...' Mrs Wallace's voice tailed off, and Rose felt her throat tighten in anxiety. 'Why have you no bag with you? You aren't one of those hitch-hiker types, are you?' Rose could hear the frown in her mother's voice, could picture her expression.

'A 'hidge' 'hiker'? I am not familiar with this phrase?'

'Don't you have them where you come from? It's someone who begs lifts from people in cars, lorries; travel light and put their lives on the line to save a few pounds.'

Rose sank onto a stair, a hand to her throat. Was this really helping?

'Then no, I am no hidgehiker, though I will own to gaining enjoyment from travelling, and I find of late I have seized the opportunities as they present themselves. It is an adventure, do you not agree?'

Unsurprisingly, Mrs Wallace didn't seem to have a response to this. 'Where was it you said you were from, Jenny? I can't detect an accent, but—' The sound of a horn from the street outside interrupted her. 'Oh, that will be Giles. Right, I'm off.'

The side door banged as her mother left, and Rose got up and slowly walked back down into the kitchen to join Jane, who was eyeing the contents of the fridge with blatant disapproval.

'I comprehend your choice in making a home away from your mother. I find her manner most disagreeable, and her selection of victuals is most… singular.'

Rose sighed; but at least she now knew where she worked, and it was not in a profession completely foreign to her, such as working in the stock market or being – Heaven forbid – a doctor or hairstylist. At least she'd been spared from destroying someone's stock portfolio, causing medical complications or giving someone the worst bad hair day ever!

Agitated, she ran a hand through her unruly curls, then shook her head as Jane pulled a shallow bowl from the fridge and prodded the contents warily with one finger. *Was it too early for wine?*

A few hours later, Rose sat on the edge of her bed, still trying to come to terms with her new life. Somehow, she had managed to make them an edible dinner – at least, it must have been, for Jane had cleaned the plate put before her – before making up a bed for her guest in the room next to hers. It was the nicest guest room and, like Rose's, had its own bathroom, giving the lady the best possible privacy – something Rose suspected would be important to her.

A quick riffle through Rose's wardrobe and cupboards had produced some clothes for her unexpected guest – fortunately, they had a similar build and were not dissimilar in height – and Jane had then asked to be left alone for a while, something Rose was more than thankful for. She had gone downstairs only to wander around aimlessly, drifting from room to room, noting things that remained the same from when she left home and things that were different. Her mother clearly was not stinting on the redecorating and purchase of new furnishings.

It was only as she began to peruse the bookshelf – devoid of the usual set of Jane Austen's books which had long resided there – that she recalled her 'new' job, working in Bath Library. Walking out into the hall, Rose opened the wooden box on the wall where all the keys were usually found. The only identifiable car key was her mother's.

She pulled out her phone and quickly sent a text: *'Mum, where is my car key? Have you seen it?'*

Rose started to look around the room, lifting papers on the dresser and checking the fruit bowl – devoid of fruit, but piled with an assortment of bits and pieces – then grabbed her phone as it pinged: *'Don't be ridiculous!'*

'Why is it ridiculous?' Rose frowned as she tapped 'send', but five minutes later, she stood outside the guest room door knocking loudly.

'Come.'

'I not only don't have a car!' Rose muttered as she closed the door behind her with a decided snap. 'I don't know how to drive. Apparently, I've never learnt!'

'Oh dear.' Jane was standing by the window, still neatly dressed and failing to look remotely concerned. 'And this is a problem for you?'

'Yes! No – I don't know! I just don't understand how having *you* in my life has led to my no longer having a driving licence or a set of wheels!'

'Do you need to be conveyed to your employment?'

'Not if I work in Bath Library, no. But that's not the point!'

'I fail to see why it is *not* the 'point', as you call it.'

Rose dropped into a chair, her head in her hands. This was not happening to her. It was *not*! Then she slowly raised her head and met Jane's silent stare.

'I learnt to drive for James.'

'I have a brother called James.'

'Yes – I know.'

'But perchance you know not he is a crashing bore.' Rose let out a spluttered laugh. 'He is our mother's favourite, thus Cass says it is only fair he is not ours.'

Smiling properly for the first time in what felt like ages, Rose leaned her head back against the chair.

'Forgive my impertinence but, pray, who is *your* James?'

'Oh, he's not mine!' Rose shook her head and sat up straight again. 'He's my – he *was* my boss, before…' She waved a hand in the air, knowing full well it didn't begin to encompass everything that had happened in the last few hours. 'He offered me this job, one I wanted so badly, but on the condition I learnt to drive. You have to be mobile, you see, to be able to get around the outer-lying properties.'

'And must you leave directly when you awaken on the morrow – for the library? Shall I accompany you?'

'No, no, there's no need for that,' Rose said weakly, thinking of the difficulty of pretending she belonged somewhere with the added complication of Jane Austen wandering around.

'But I am fond of books, and have taken infinite pleasure from more than the content. The variety and richness of the scenes or characters portrayed on your book covers are sufficiently intriguing to occupy me!'

Rose shook her head. 'I am not due there tomorrow anyway. Mum just went into a rant about how could I possibly have forgotten I'd worked the Saturday shift, making Monday my day off this week, and she'd planned on my doing the washing and running several errands for her before she leaves for Gloucestershire, and how could I be so selfish as to choose work over helping her?'

'Is this not the 21st century? Do not permit your mother to rule you, Miss Wallace.'

'Rose. Please, call me Rose.'

'Forgive me; on occasion, I forget the swift succession to familiarity that is in the common way here.'

Rose smiled. 'Don't be too hard on yourself!'

Jane walked over to the mirror on the dresser and stared at her reflection for a moment. Then she met Rose's gaze in the glass. 'I am curious. Why did you introduce me as Miss Jenny Ashton?'

'I – errr…'

'You can use my real name, for it holds no familiarity in this world, and will draw attention from no quarter.'

The reminder of all she had lost swept through Rose as Jane turned to face her, but then she frowned. 'If nothing is left that relates to you – no books, no museum, no film or TV adaptations… *nothing* – then no one here in this… 'world' could possibly have heard of you.'

Getting quickly to her feet, Rose gestured with her hand between them. 'So why do *I* remember you – and all I *ever* knew about you and your life and works? How is it I know about Mr Darcy and his Elizabeth? About the trials of Elinor and Marianne? How can I have this knowledge if those things never reached the public – ever?' It was an appalling thought! 'And if this is the life I have lived instead,' Rose gestured wildly around. 'Why don't I know what that life is? If everyone else is just carrying on as normal…'

Jane said nothing for a moment; then she smiled. 'One cannot find all things fathomable, least of all when there is some form of enchantment afoot. How else might I be here? We should not let our astonishment overwhelm us, Miss Wallace, nor be surprised by the charm placed on the necklace extending its influence to anyone aware of its existence.'

'And this is why my memories remain? Including those of you – of who you are – of Jane Austen? Because I'm the only one who knows about the charm?'

'Is not all the evidence before you?'

As those words sank in, Rose could feel her world closing in upon her again. Only *she* knew what the world had lost?

'Excuse me.' She felt for the door handle behind her back. 'I – I need to just go and lie down.'

Chapter Sixteen

Glancing at her watch, Rose blinked owlishly, then covered her mouth as yet another yawn escaped.

Looking around the room, she grimaced. There were bright green Post-it notes everywhere, with scribbled details of anything she had been able to find online to help her find her feet in this strange new world – names, phone numbers, new passwords (she'd had to change every single one by choosing 'forgot password' time and again. Every one she used had a Jane Austen connection to it, so Heaven alone knew what she'd been using in this alternative life!). The realisation all her bank and credit cards would need new PINs for the same reason was just too daunting to think about right now.

Scanning her inbox for email pointers to what was happening in her life between her and her friends, Rose soon realised something else was missing: no emails from James. Her heart thumping wildly, she brought up the website, but her momentary relief at seeing the familiar lettering was short-lived. *Luxury Lettings* was still based in Queen Square, of course, but the website itself was… *basic*! It seemed to be a much smaller company, with much the same property portfolio as when she'd joined years ago. On the plus side, it was still James's company. How well did they know each other in this life? He'd been a very casual acquaintance back then, before she joined the firm…

Rose got to her feet and stretched before walking over to the window to draw the curtains. A perfunctory examination of her wardrobe revealed a serious lack of her usual work clothes: the smart suits, dresses and heels. With a sigh, she closed the door on the sight of some familiar and many not so familiar outfits. It looked like the dress code at the library was a little more informal than she was used to.

Then she turned to the shelves and studied again the books spilling onto the desk below. The shock on entering her room had been profound; it had been like entering a slightly warped time capsule. So much was as it had been when she was in her late-teens and early twenties and studying at school and college, with a proliferation of fantasy titles littered around the room, quotes from books by Tolkien, Rowling, Pullman and Lewis – classics new and old – on her mouse mat, her slippers, her walls, the mug on the bedside table...

But all her books by or about Jane Austen and her life were gone. All those joyful hours of reading and rereading, wiped from the face of the earth. Hours and hours of browsing at book fairs and along the dusty shelves in second-hand shops, building up a collection of as many different versions of Jane's books as she could – just a memory. Trying to keep a hold on her emotions, Rose turned slowly on her heel, surveying the room.

The DVD collection stacked by her television was no consolation. Gone were the many adaptations of Jane's books, both the period and the fun, modern ones: *Bridget Jones's Diary*, *Bride & Prejudice*, *Clueless*... Her heart heavy in her chest, Rose turned away.

Everything spoke of Rose living a fairly reclusive, introverted and quiet life where she lost herself in the worlds of her other beloved books. *And a lonely life*, whispered a voice in her head, and she welcomed it like an old friend.

It was true. How could she have known what a love of Jane Austen's writing had brought her: the friends, the life choices which had led to a job she loved, a slow but steadily growing confidence in herself as someone of value?

She felt like someone had died, the sense of loss was so severe. Time and again she had turned to Google and searched: Jane Austen, the names of her oh-so-famous novels, Chawton House, the museum in what was her last home, the Jane Austen Society – nothing. It was all gone.

So had the many forums and blogs she had religiously visited and followed, where she had met people – made friends – who could talk as endlessly as she about all things Jane Austen. This is where she and Morgan had built on their early acquaintance and become the very best of friends, soul sisters for each other, because for all her extended, multicultural family, Morgan had confessed years ago to Rose about how adrift she felt, even amidst the loving family around her.

Morgan! Turning quickly back to the computer, Rose tapped the space bar, pretending not to notice the tail of Harry Potter's broomstick as the screensaver sailed out of sight. She scanned the recent history of the pages she had visited, trying not to see the link to the New Zealand Embassy in London. Was she in such a bad place in her life that she was really thinking of emigrating to the land of elves, wizards and hobbits?

The last Harry Potter book had been out for several years, as had the last film; surely she didn't still frequent any of those forums? But if she did…

There was nothing in her recent history, but she had never forgotten the web address of the site where she'd first met Morgan and she quickly entered it and brought up the *Hidden Tower*. The announcement (in all caps) that J.K. Rowling's *Fantastic Beasts &*

Where to Find Them would be turned into a trilogy was the top thread. But there was nothing in the conversational thread from Morgan, so she clicked on the Member List and selected her screen name: CAgirl. Her last post had been several years ago.

All this time? She had spent so many years in this life without Morgan around to talk to, any time of day or night? It was too much to take in, and either through exhaustion or shock, Rose was unable to stop the tears as they began to flow steadily down her cheeks.

Just as dawn was breaking, Rose had fallen into a deep sleep. Feeling quite spent from her burst of tears, she had lain back on her bed, her mind reeling with all she had learned, and tiredness had suddenly swept through her as she had fallen into oblivion.

When she finally awoke, just for a fleeting second, Rose thought she had had the strangest of dreams. She lay still, her lids closed, barely daring to breathe; then a hard rap on the door and her mother's voice thrust her back into reality. It wasn't a dream; none of it was.

Opening a reluctant eye, she glanced at her bedside clock; it was almost midday. Drowsily, her head emitting a dull ache, she crawled off the bed and wondered out onto the landing, her eye immediately drawn to the door of Jane's bedroom. The house was incredibly quiet. Was she in her room or downstairs?

Rose hurried back into her own room and showered before pulling on some clothes automatically and pausing outside Jane's room again as she passed, wondering whether to knock or not. She felt weary and decidedly unrefreshed, despite having slept so long.

Her mind was full of all the things she'd spent years wishing she could ask her favourite author, but half of them hadn't even happened to Jane yet – not back in 1803.

Why didn't she publish *Persuasion*? What made her put it aside after completion and start a new work in *Sanditon*? Did she really intend it to be called *The Elliots*? It was widely said that her brother, Henry, had named both that and *Northanger Abbey* (had she intended, after changing the heroine's name to Catherine, to call it that instead?) And what of the world-famous silhouette, said to be Jane Austen but not 100% proved? It was drawn around 1815, found pasted into a copy of *Mansfield Park* – another book she had yet to write. There was no point in asking her if it really was Jane, or who had produced it and labelled it '*L'aimable Jane*'.

No answers, just so many questions. Rose drew in a shallow breath and tapped lightly on the door – no response. A firmer knock went unanswered, so Rose poked her head around the door to find the room empty. Downstairs, she found every room in a similar condition. The only note was from her mother, saying she had gone to the beauty salon and telling her to empty the dishwasher and move a load of washing into the tumble dryer as soon as the cycle ended.

A momentary panic gripped her, and she was suddenly wide awake. Grabbing her bag, she looked around wildly for her car key, then remembrance struck her and with a muttered curse under her breath, she rushed out of the house. Where might Jane have gone? How on earth would she find her? What if she didn't *intend* to be found?

'*No!*' Rose admonished herself as she hurried up the road towards the nearest bus stop. '*I am the only person who remembers Jane Austen's novels, her wonderful stories, her well-loved characters... I will not lose her as well.*'

But where to begin searching? As the bus rumbled along the road towards the city, Rose ruminated on where Jane might have gone. Perhaps she was at the antiques centre? Did she have more valuables from the past tucked into that leather pouch?

The bus pulled to a halt at the next stop and, realising where they were, Rose hurriedly picked up her bag and dismounted. She would cut through Sydney Gardens. Surely there was a chance Jane had merely come out for a walk? If she had come into town on foot, she would have passed by here and its familiarity may well have drawn her in.

After 20 minutes of walking up and down every path, however, Rose realised the futility of her search. There was no sign of Jane anywhere, though sadly there were posters of a missing dog fastened to a lamp-post as she resignedly left the Gardens behind. She crossed the road but had gone barely a few paces along Sydney Place when she realised there was someone on the step outside No 4, about to press the bell, and her heart leapt. It wasn't Jane Austen, but there was something familiar nonetheless about the petite figure.

'Morgan!'

The woman's raised hand fell to her side and she spun around. Yes, it was definitely her, despite the neatly fastened hair and trendy glasses.

The shock of recognition was clearly one-sided, however, as she studied Rose cautiously and without any familiarity.

'It's me, Rose!' She hurried along the pavement to join her friend on the step to 4 Sydney Place, refusing to look at the empty space where the plaque once rested.

'I'm sorry,' Morgan was shaking her head. 'Rose who?' She eyed Rose carefully. 'How did you know my–'

It was galling to be treated like a stranger by her best friend. Then, saying a silent prayer for the Internet history links she'd browsed on the previous night, Rose summoned a smile. 'I'm Ginger Weasley.

From the Harry Potter forum?'

Morgan's brow furrowed for a second, then her gaze shot to Rose's face and she laughed. 'Oh – my – God! It *is* you.'

She dropped her overlarge shoulder bag onto the ground and wrapped her arms around Rose in a hug before letting her go, and Rose felt a prickling behind her eyes. So soon after her first meeting with Morgan in reality – and that heartfelt hug in *Hall & Woodhouse* only days ago – the enormity of what she had lost was hitting home.

'Wow!' Morgan was shaking her head again. 'That was a few years ago. I don't think I ever went back to the forum after the last book came out.'

Rose, who knew they'd moved on from chatting on a Harry Potter forum two years earlier than that – exactly when they'd discovered they had a mutual love and admiration for Jane Austen's works – merely nodded. What could she possibly say?

'Wait a minute,' Morgan eyed her warily. 'How did you... you recognise me? My profile pic then – well, I was a teenager.'

'Yes, and I said you looked about 10.'

Morgan laughed. 'I remember! I tried to be offended, but you weren't the only one to say it.'

Rose's mind was in overdrive. What should she do? She couldn't tell Morgan everything that had just happened. She would think she was mad and would give her a wide berth. She needed to build on this small reintroduction, keep Morgan part of her life whilst she tried to work out what could be salvaged from how things used to be.

'So, umm,' Rose gestured towards the door of number 4. 'Did I interrupt you? Sorry.'

'Oh – no.' Morgan threw a cursory glance over her shoulder at the building. 'I can come back. I'm not expected, it's just one of the stops on my trail.'

'You've just arrived in Bath?'

'Yes, this morning. I've been in London for a few days, but that was vacation. Now I have to start work.' She glanced at her watch. 'Hey, do you fancy grabbing some lunch? I'm feeling kind of ...well... foreign surrounded by all these British accents. After all the Harry Potter and Doctor Who immersion, I honestly thought I'd fit in a bit more than I do.'

Rose nodded quickly, grateful for the natural reprieve. 'Of course. Let's go round the corner, there's a really nice café where we can catch up and eat at the same time.'

CHAPTER SEVENTEEN

They fell into step along Sydney Place, and Rose threw Morgan a curious glance. 'I didn't realise you wore glasses.'

'I don't.' Morgan winked at her as they reached the corner of the street. 'It's clear glass. I bought them for the job, thinking I'd look a bit more serious… studious, you know? It's just that it's hard enough to get respect as the boss's daughter – I thought – what do you think? Too hipster?'

Despite the strangeness of everything, Rose could not help but laugh. Whatever else had changed, this was still the Morgan she knew and loved. She only hoped her friend would come to cherish their friendship in this new life as much as she had in the previous one.

She led her around the corner to a small café on Bathwick Street, and they were soon settled with cold drinks and awaiting their sandwiches. Morgan, however, was giving Rose that wary look again and she braced herself for whatever might be coming.

'I still can't believe you recognised me earlier. It's amazing, Ginger. Just like a movie…' Morgan blinked and her mouth dropped open slightly. 'Wait! Did we know real names on the forum? I don't recall your…'

'Oh, I'm sure some of us did,' Rose said hastily. 'I mean, I can't remember really, but we must have, mustn't we? What sort of job are you here about? Are you working for your father, then?'

Morgan nodded slowly, then she smiled. 'I must try to remember to call you Rose. Yes… you know – I can really see it's you now.'

'Hmm, the hair?'

'No – no, it's something else. I feel I know *us*, if you know what I mean.'

Rose knew precisely what she meant, but thankfully their order arrived just then and the moment passed as it was laid out before them.

'Anyway, yes – I'm working for my father. Well – it's more like he throws me at unsuspecting people who need a bit of help. Like someone sends him a proposal for a story – but they don't have the time to do the research nitty-gritty – Dad sends me in.'

'You must learn the most interesting things. Have you travelled all over, then?' Rose paused and frowned. 'Is there something wrong with your sandwich?'

Morgan had moved around the bread on her plate as if wondering what was underneath it, but she shook her head. 'It's fine – is this bacon?'

Rose couldn't help but laugh at Morgan's expression. 'You should've said you wanted it burnt to a crisp.' Then she stopped. Would Morgan wonder how she knew that was how she liked her bacon? She bit her lip, but thankfully, Morgan was more intent on removing the thick slice of bacon from her BLT sandwich and laying it aside, wiping her fingers on her napkin.

'So right, what was I saying? I've learned some interesting things – but most of the research I'm asked to do is stuff that can be confirmed with a well-timed phone call. People submitting to the science magazines generally have all the research assistants they need – so I get stuck dealing with the travel writers who can't read their notes so I need to spellcheck names and such. But this story I'm working on here: this is another kettle of fish entirely.'

Rose was intrigued, despite the awkwardness she was feeling. 'And it's brought you here to Bath?'

'Oh right, you asked if I have travelled. The answer is: yes; but only all over the US. But this is the first time I've been scheduled outside the States.' Morgan took a sip of her drink. 'So, yes. A real mystery set right here in Bath. Wait! Do I remember correctly? Weren't you born and bred here?' Rose nodded. 'Awesome! I'd love to talk to you about it – you might even be able to help. Can I record you?'

Rose had difficulty not choking on her sandwich, but managed to nod again as she watched Morgan choose an app on her phone and prop it up between them.

She put her hands under her chin in what Rose suspected was one she used with people she didn't know but whom she wanted to put at ease and also get information out of. It didn't put Rose at ease in the least. 'Have you ever heard of the Lost Lady of the Gardens?'

'Er – no, not that I can recall.'

Morgan laughed. 'I'm not surprised. I'm starting to feel like she's about as easy to find as Waldo.' At Rose's face, Morgan chewed on her lip. 'The *Where's Waldo?* books? Do you have them here? Never mind. Anyway, I've done the obvious background research, of course, family records, that kind of thing, but there is very little to go on.' She shrugged and smiled her warm smile at Rose. 'That's when the guy I'm working for…' Morgan paused and pulled a face. 'He's not easy; too intelligent for his own good. Anyway, he suggested I come here. This is where the story begins and ends.' Morgan clapped her hands lightly. 'Daddy agreed, after some serious begging, and here I am.'

She started to question Rose about the history of Bath, something she was more than willing to discuss, but it was only as the conversation turned towards the Regency era, which naturally led her mind back to Jane Austen, that Rose faltered, unsure of herself, her sense of bewilderment returning with a vengeance.

There was a strange sort of unreality about Morgan being here, yet their friendship no longer had the history she knew and loved. A pang of homesickness struck her; where was James? She had known him a little, of course, outside of the work connection. And what of Dr Trevellyan? He would still have been on that infamous dig in town, but she wouldn't have seen him, wouldn't have embarrassed herself. Well, at least she'd discovered something positive about her new circumstances.

The sing-song ringtone of Morgan's phone caused her to start, and her friend grinned at her as she answered it.

'Excuse me,' Rose gestured towards the WC sign. 'Won't be a sec.'

Morgan waved at her, turning her attention to the caller.

Leaning back against the wall in the corridor, Rose's mind was in turmoil again, the sense of loss all-pervading. So many important things in her life – people – just... *gone* from it, beyond her reach. She was still grappling with it all: Jane Austen was here in the 21st century, and currently staying, for Heaven's sake, in the spare room in Rose's mum's house. And no one – not *one* person other than Rose herself – seemed to recall there ever being such a person in the world.

Her cosy home was hers no more, her beloved job was in someone else's hands, many of the friends she had made all over the world through a shared love of the author were lost to her – except for Morgan. Dear, wonderful Morgan... Despite the situation, the inexplicable circumstances, this one fact grounded her, brought her back to herself, and she drew in a steadying breath.

Come on, Rose. Get a grip. You have to make sure you don't lose sight of Morgan – find out where she is staying.

Back at their table, Morgan was still on her mobile.

'That's awesome!' She winked at Rose as she flopped back into her seat. 'Yes – I'd love to. Hold on,' she put the phone down to rummage in her bag, pulling out a leather-bound notebook. 'Yes... yes, I've got that.' She scribbled in the book for a moment, then glanced at her watch. 'Yes, of course. I'll come now. And thanks!'

She dropped the phone back into her bag before draining her glass. 'Sorry. I have to get to this meeting for two o'clock. I've been waiting on the call all morning.' She laughed. 'He sounded cute.'

'No problem. It's been... it's been great to see you – again.' Rose signalled for the bill. 'Are you staying locally?'

'I'm at that big Crescent place?'

Rose's heart leapt, thinking of the apartment she had checked Dr Trevellyan into. 'In an apartment?'

'No, it's a hotel. Here,' she pulled a card from her pocket. 'I took a stack of these in case I can't find my way back and need to grab a cab ride.'

Rose went to take the *Royal Crescent Hotel* card, but Morgan held onto it. 'Hold on.' She scribbled on the card before handing it over. 'My mobile. Call me. It would be fun to have dinner or something.'

The waitress dropped the bill on the table, and they both fished in their purses for money, then got to their feet.

'Hey, can you point me in the direction of...' Morgan squinted at the words scrawled across her notepad. 'Manvers Street?'

'Yes, of course – it's about ten minutes away. I'll walk with you there, if that's okay?'

Morgan gave her a curious look as she shrugged into her jacket and picked up her bag. 'You bet! You're the only person I know in Bath.'

Not for long, mused Rose under her breath as she counted out some change for a tip and turned to follow Morgan into the street. *Based on recent experience, I'd say she'll know at least a dozen people by nightfall.*

Leaving Morgan at the police station for her meeting, Rose wandered somewhat aimlessly along Manvers Street. On the corner, she looked back, but Morgan had disappeared inside the building and a fleeting dread filled her. What if they didn't meet up again? What if Morgan had somehow written her number down wrong, or Rose couldn't decipher the writing?

Then she took herself to task. There was no need to panic. Bath was a small place; she would not lose Morgan. It was just too perfect that she was here in the first place – fate obviously didn't intend for this friendship to be lost forever. Rose put her fears out of her mind and focused on the problem at hand: finding Jane Austen.

With a renewed sense of purpose, she scanned the people milling around on the corner of North Parade. Perhaps the sensible place to start, with Sydney Place and Gardens drawing a blank, would be the parts of Bath she knew Jane was familiar with. After all, had she not used them liberally in *Northanger Abbey* – or *Susan*, as Jane currently thought of it?

She set off along York Street, but as she passed the *Tourist Information Centre* by the abbey, she found herself drawn into the busy interior, brimming as always with tourists looking for advice, tickets or souvenirs. Her suspicions were quickly confirmed: there were no longer any Austen-related items on sale, nor any of the many books about her which normally jostled for pride of place on the shelves with other books about the city.

Hurrying back into the street, Rose refused to glance at the window. It had recently been filled with *Festival* paraphernalia – programmes, mugs, accessories and the like – and she had no desire to see what had taken its place.

Rose walked and walked, passing more signs of Jane's absence from the world – number 40 Gay Street housed a legal practice, not the popular *Jane Austen Centre* – there were no people hanging around outside the building, waiting to have their photo taken with Martin, the Greeter, or the model of Jane herself.

Turning away, she dodged between the traffic and walked along the northern side of Queen Square. She could not bear to look down towards No 13. *Luxury Lettings* was no longer part of her life.

But the past was not easy to shed, and characters from Jane Austen's two novels set extensively in Bath haunted her as she walked. How bittersweet it was to be accompanied along the Gravel Walk by Captain Wentworth and Anne Elliot, knowing the precious words of his letter were gone from the world forever? How sad was it to think of Jane Austen never creating those characters or those words?

A sense of desperation swirled through her, and Rose hurried her pace to emerge onto the Royal Crescent. It looked much as it always did, and she walked quickly from one end to the other, but there was no sign of Jane. She paused only as she came to No 14. Standing by the railing, she looked at the windows of the ground-floor flat. There was no sign of life. Did the doctor ever come to Bath or would he have no need if he was no longer on a dig or coming to speak at the *Festival?*

Rose sighed, and moved away. Perhaps she would never see him again. That thought brought little comfort, and she walked more slowly along Brock Street, full of a sense of foreboding and casting a regretful look at the door where she had left the Hales only days ago, happily settling into their flat.

Round the Circus and down to George Street traipsed Rose, her eyes scanning every passing face for the features she sought. Pausing at the top of Milsom Street, her eye was drawn to the wooded outcrop known as Beechen Cliff. Would Catherine Morland never walk there now? Feeling sick to the heart, the ever-present sense of loss taking an even firmer grip on her heart, she hurried down the hill.

It was as she passed *Waterstones* and recalled her first sighting of Jane – was it only four days ago? It seemed like she had lived a lifetime since then – that she considered it worth entering a shop. Jane was fond of reading, wasn't she, and had already mentioned discovering *Toppings* and *Mr B's*. Perhaps she should check on all the bookstores methodically.

A quick tour of the ground floor showed no sign of the missing author, and Rose negated the basement, knowing it housed travel books, maps and the like and was probably the least likely to hold Jane's attention.

Climbing the stairs, her nose was assailed by the rich smell of freshly roasted coffee, and she inhaled deeply as she quickly checked the first floor. Many of the books here might have caught Jane's interest, but there was no sign of her perusing the shelves, and Rose turned around and walked back towards the stairs.

Mr B's Emporium was just around the corner; she'd try there next, and then… Rose fetched up short as she reached the stairs. Seated on a large sofa adjacent to the café area was Jane, her nose tucked into a book which she was reading closely.

CHAPTER EIGHTEEN

The rush of relief was almost overwhelming, and she hurried over. Jane did not seem to detect her presence, and with a half-smile, Rose took in the half-empty cup of tea on the nearby table along with several books. As she suspected, they covered a wide range of topics, from crafts and needlework to weightier subjects like history and science. All, however, had one thing in common: they had been discarded in favour of the novel she now held.

'Miss Austen – Jane.'

The lady started and looked up, then smiled, lowering the book into her lap. 'Good afternoon, Miss – Rose.'

Rose had caught a glimpse of the cover of the book, and her heart leapt into her throat. 'What are you doing?' she croaked.

'Partaking of some tea. The taste is most particular, but I find I am becoming accustomed to it.'

Rose shook her head. 'No – I meant, what on earth are you reading?'

Jane turned her book to show the cover to Rose, who paled further and grabbed it from her.

'This is not polite behaviour, Miss Wallace – Rose.'

'I'm sorry. Really, I am, but I just don't think you're ready for this one yet!'

She dropped the copy of *Fifty Shades of Grey* onto the table.

'But I have barely begun. I enquired of an assistant for something popular with young women. She explained 'Grey' was one of the people in the book, so I anticipate an interesting study of character.'

'Yes, well – maybe... when you're – I mean... just trust me. Look, are you finished with your tea? Would you mind walking back home with me?'

Jane got up to leave with her easily enough, then turned back and picked up a small card from next to her teacup.

'A kind lady in there gave me this.' She waved a small card with *Waterstones* emblazoned across it and two small ink stamps on it. 'When I have had ten cups of tea, I am allowed one for no charge. At first, I thought I must consume all ten in one sitting, but she assured me it is not so.'

'Very exciting,' Rose agreed and led the way out into the street and fresh air. Unfortunately it did nothing to clear her mind. Now that she had Jane firmly in tow, the fears that had been going around and around in her mind burst out with a frustrated, 'Could you not have left a note?'

Jane shrugged her shoulders lightly. 'My pen and ink are both lost now.'

'We have pens in the house.' Rose huffed. 'I was worried; I had no idea where you were.'

'Does it signify? I cannot remain at your mother's house indefinitely. I must find my own situation.'

'But – you can't just stay here!'

'In Bath? No, nor do I wish it. I aspire to a small house in the country.'

'No – I mean *here*. This century.'

'My dear girl, as I have explained, I have no choice.'

Aghast, Rose stared at Jane as they paused on the kerb to let some traffic pass.

'But there must be a way – we *have* to find a way…'

'Why is it so important to you?'

'Your books! Your beautiful words, your characters – I cannot bear the thought of all the people who must now live without them. And what about other writers who came after you, who were inspired to write *because* of your stories, whose writing was influenced by yours?'

'But they have no comprehension a loss has befallen them. As for myself, I have yet to create the stories or the characters.' Jane set off across the road, and Rose hurried after her.

'Not all of them. You've already done a first draft of *Pride and…* I mean, *First Impressions* – and of *Elinor and Marianne*.' She felt bereft, as though feeling her way in the dark. 'And *Northanger Abbey* – *Susan*. You revised it *here* – in Bath – and sold it to a publisher. I've read about it, and–'

Jane stopped on the corner of New Bond Street and turned to look at her. 'And I am sure you comprehend it all. The book was not destined for publication before I… during my lifetime.' She seemed quite unperturbed, but Rose could feel herself sinking and put a hand to her head.

'But what of Anne Elliot? And Captain Wentworth and *that* letter?'

'What letter?'

'From *Persuasion*. Quite possibly the most romantic letter *ever* written.'

Jane eyed her sympathetically for a second as they both fell into step again. 'But I have yet to compose it. I could not even bring myself to read the novel. Oh, I did make a beginning.' She turned away as they walked across Pulteney Bridge.

Rose could not imagine what it must have been like, to peruse words written long ago by one's own hand but not recognise them. Then Jane turned back. Her eyes were wide, and Rose suspected she was experiencing some emotion and trying to keep it in check.

Swallowing visibly, Jane raised a hand to her throat. 'I – I could not read beyond Anne's reaction to having to leave her home: Somersetshire and Kellynch, so dear to her heart, her childhood home.'

'It resonates with your own memories of leaving Steventon.'

Jane nodded. 'It is but a story to others: the history of my life. And yet Papa retired barely 18 months ago, and one cannot recover in haste from such a wrench. One does not.'

Feeling terrible for reminding Jane of something clearly still painful to her, Rose sought desperately for something to say, but she was continuing.

'But I am not formed for ill humour.' Jane waved a hand at the buildings around them as they continued along Great Pulteney Street. 'And Bath has – had – its compensations.'

Rose tried to curb her curiosity, but failed. 'It's been said, and often written, that you didn't like Bath. Some people have even said you hated it?' She held her breath. Bath was her home, and she loved it with all her heart.

Jane laughed. 'How quick come the reasons for approving or disproving what we like.' Then she glanced at Rose, who was relieved to see all sign of sadness gone. 'I liked Bath well enough as a visitor – who could not? To be a resident brings all manner of alteration.' Jane paused as they reached Sydney Place and looked over towards the Gardens. 'Yet, it had its rewards, and I found pleasure in many things.'

'Walking, for one.'

'Indeed. And being so well situated, I was able to take full advantage of the country hereabouts. There was ample amusement to be had from our proximity to the Gardens.' She waved a hand at the trees across the road. 'Though they were more to my liking then than now.'

They turned to continue, and Rose felt she could understand. Although still a peaceful enough haven for present-day visitors and residents alike, with trains thundering through every so often and many of the features from its original layout long gone, the Gardens must seem very different to someone who knew them 200 years earlier.

Still, she was happy to have asked the question, and they continued their walk back to Bathampton in good spirits, as Jane happily talked about her time in Bath, in both the past and the present.

This had to cap every other moment in her life for nerves, thought Rose as she slowly mounted the stairs to the main entrance of *Bath Central Library*. Forget first days at school, the occasional first date, interviews and even the first day in her job at *Luxury Lettings*. At least then she had known what she had applied for, had at least an inkling of what to do, what the offices looked like, the name of her boss.

She hovered on the landing. The library had yet to open its main doors. Glancing at her watch, she realised it was only a quarter past nine. But shouldn't she, as a member of staff, be able to get in before the general public? She studied the screens in front of her. The main floor of the library was visible beyond and people could clearly be seen moving about.

Rose frowned, looking even harder for some sign of entry for staff but there was nothing. She had no choice; she would have to wait for the doors to open for business and perhaps pretend she'd missed her bus?

Two hours later, Rose really was wishing she'd missed the bus. Her morning had taken on nightmare proportions ever since she'd walked in and been frowned at for not using the usual entrance – she'd have to watch carefully at lunchtime and follow someone to find out where it was.

Barbara, apparently her direct supervisor, was off that day, which at first had seemed a relief until she realised it meant everyone pretty much left her to her own devices, assuming she knew what she had to do.

Having spent the first half-hour walking around in a daze – at least as a library user she was familiar with the general layout available to the public – she had been taken aside by a young woman whom she had heard being called 'Mary'. That at least accounted for one person on her missed calls list.

'Are you okay, Rose?' She had looked most concerned. 'You are so pale, and… well, sort of jumpy.'

Rose glanced around, certain that the two members of staff on the main enquiry desk had suddenly looked away and pretended to be busy.

'I – er – yes. Sorry. Bad night. Feeling a bit… distracted.' She tried to summon a normal smile but was pretty certain all she managed to do was bare her teeth in a frozen sort of grin.

Mary looked unconvinced, but she patted her kindly on the arm. 'Why don't you pop upstairs and put the kettle on? The first tea break will be coming up soon. I know we usually make our own, but take a few minutes to do something routine and see how you feel afterwards. If you're no better by lunchtime perhaps you should go home.'

Right then, Rose could think of nothing better than being sent home, but knowing it wouldn't solve anything, she thanked Mary and watched her walk away. Her new dilemma was which door to go through to get to the staffroom; plus all the doors had key codes…

'Er – excuse me?' A member of staff who had been tidying away books in the *Children's Area* was walking past.

She smiled at Rose. 'Hi, Rose; how were your days off?'

'Oh. Quite… unusual. Lots going on.' There was a pause, as if she was waiting for Rose to say something. 'And – er – and you? Did you have a great weekend?'

The smile disappeared. 'I thought I told you on Saturday. We had to bury our beloved cat. It was terrible.'

She stalked off, leaving Rose feeling dreadful, but she looked up to meet Mary's eye across the room who mimed pouring a kettle into a mug and pointed towards the door to her right. She would have to pretend she'd had a mental blank over the code and ask for it, but she knew which door to go through at least.

CHAPTER NINETEEN

Rose had never been so thankful to see five o'clock finally come round as her shift ended. Trying to ignore the concerned look on Mary's face as she muttered a quiet goodnight and hurried towards the main entrance, Rose quickly descended the stairs and emerged into the fresh air.

Northgate Street was as busy as ever, bustling with traffic and shoppers jostling with workers going home for the day. Automatically, she turned left, thinking of the sanctuary of her flat in Sydney Place, only to stop immediately. It was no longer her home; she had no choice but to go back to her mother's house in Bathampton. The thought of walking past her old flat brought a lump to her throat; perhaps she should take a bus this time?

'May I walk with you?'

Turning around, Rose was unsurprised to see Jane. After all, had she not just spent several hours in the library herself? Then she sighed. What did it matter? Nothing mattered anymore.

'Yes, of course.' Rose blew out a frustrated breath as they began to walk. 'Well, *that* was a day from hell.'

'And pray, why is that?'

'Why?' Rose glanced at Jane. 'Where do I begin? There are codes on all the doors to access the offices, staffroom and so on.' She grunted. 'I've had to ask what they are; everyone thinks I'm mad. I've been there three years, but couldn't understand how to use or find anything. I got locked out of the computer because I had too many guesses at what the password might be so I spent the morning demoted to shelving books and making tea for everyone during their allotted breaks until IT got it sorted.'

'A challenge indeed.' Jane's dry tone did little to help soothe Rose's frayed nerves.

'And I gave everyone the wrong mugs. Then…' Rose sighed. 'Just when people had stopped asking me if I'm okay or sickening for something and giving me either sympathetic or wary looks, *you* turn up. I am stuck in a surreal library which holds no reference at all to Jane Austen or her works but in which she herself is walking around perusing the shelves and muttering about finding a book which is obviously long out of print and occasionally making derogatory remarks about the other people.'

'Forgive me for supposing one might find a particular book in the library. Do you suggest I frequent the park on the morrow in the hope it may deliver?'

Rose threw her a look. 'My whole world has turned upside-down. I've no idea who I'm friends with and who I'm not.' She tugged her mobile from her pocket and waved it at Jane as they began to cross Pulteney Bridge. 'Other than my mother, my most recent calls are from a Mary, who I now know is a colleague, and several missed ones from a girl called Lottie. I don't know anyone by these names!' Rose stopped as they reached Laura Place, and Jane did, too. Then she raised a hand to her head. 'Could it be… I wonder if it's one of my best mates from college; it could be Liz.' Rose bit her lip. Though flooded with hope, she shied away from making a call to someone who might not turn out to be who she thought. The strain of the pretence of the day was enough; she wasn't in any mood to pretend she knew someone else she didn't.

Jane frowned. 'I fail to see a connection.'

Rose started to walk again, refusing to glance in the direction of the flat Morgan had so recently inhabited, and Jane fell into step beside her.

'Liz – Elizabeth; we met in school. Her mother was a great reader.' She glanced at Jane. 'You were her favourite author, and she named her daughter after Elizabeth Bennet. Now I have no idea what her first name might be.'

'And why do you think it might be this… Lottie?'

'Because her mother's second-favourite author was Charlotte Brontë.'

Jane looked blank but then why wouldn't she? The now famous author of *Jane Eyre* was only one year old when Jane Austen died.

They continued in silence for some distance, though both of them cast a meaningful stare at No 4 Sydney Place as they passed, but as they reached the Beckford Road and began the ascent, Rose turned to Jane again.

'Does the noise bother you? The road? This is a main route to Warminster and beyond and has such heavy traffic.'

Jane smiled. 'Much is altered.' She looked around and gestured with her arm. 'Naught but open fields bordered the Gardens.' Her expression sobered. 'My disinclination for our removal to Bath was much compensated for by our pleasing situation in Sydney Place. One does not – did not – feel so confined by the city on its outer edges.'

'Then shall we walk along the canal?' Rose pointed to the gap through which the towpath could be seen, winding its way towards Bathampton. It was a route she had often trod in the summer months when still living at home.

'As you wish.'

They fell into step again, continuing to walk side by side at first for the width of the path permitted it.

'I did not answer your question.' Jane glanced at her, and Rose frowned. 'Noise emanating from these modern conveyances does not trouble me, for it is merely different. The constant rumble of wheels over cobbles, the clatter of hooves is not so much lower in volume than your modern conveyances. 'Tis why I prefer the country; the disturbance of silence has a more natural source: birdsong, flowing water over stones, the bray of a lamb… these things I miss more than any other.'

Rose glanced around. It was peaceful by modern-day standards on the towpath, with a few ducks swimming in the canal and very few people about, but just then a light aircraft came overhead, it's engine chugging away, and she glanced at Jane as they walked.

'And what do you make of our 'modern conveyances'? You must have seen the trains passing through Sydney Gardens, too, if you've been here a while, and noticed the planes flying overhead?'

Jane looked up as the small plane sailed out of view. 'If I may fly through time, why should man not have discovered how to fly through air?'

Why not indeed, mused Rose. She could only hope she would apply such matter-of-fact logic to things if she ever found herself in a situation like Jane's. The reminder of their circumstances was unsettling, however, and she decided to change the subject.

'Why are you so keen to find the book you were looking for? There's so much reading material in the library…'

Jane glanced at Rose as they walked side by side. 'I am an avid reader, as you may recall.'

Rose laughed. 'Yes – I don't think I'll ever forget the sight of all those books piled high in your flat.'

'So much to learn. Two hundred years of words, of knowledge, to consume. There is so much to absorb, to think of, to feel.'

'So why do you want this old book, then?'

Jane smiled ruefully. 'It is whimsy, perchance. There are moments when I am quite overwhelmed – what is history to you, is for me intelligence of vast import; the relentless succession of discoveries in science and medicine; wars won and lost, monarchs come and gone… and novels. So many stories, and so many ladies writing openly, without restriction. There is much to absorb, and my mind feels at war with itself. Barely do I sleep at night, my imagination too full for repose.' She paused as they stood aside for a cyclist to pass before continuing side by side. 'I wish for something familiar.'

'What were you reading when you – well, when you last travelled here?'

Jane glanced at Rose. 'A guilty indulgence, I fear: a gothic romance Cass acquired for me from *Marshall's*–'

'*Marshall's*?'

'One of the circulating libraries on Milsom Street? I had but one volume to read, and a notion for finishing it, hence my desire to locate a copy.'

'Would this be an Ann Radcliffe novel?'

Jane smiled widely. 'Well done, Miss – Rose. Indeed it was.' She sighed. 'But it was not to be. I could find naught of Miss Radcliffe, despite hours of searching.'

'I may be able to help you.'

'Truly?'

Rose nodded. 'Here, we need to go down these steps.' She indicated the stone steps leading down to the road by the *George Inn*. 'We just have to cross over the bridge, and we're nearly there.'

They made their way into Bathampton before Rose continued. 'There must be some store of older books in the library. Today, I didn't have a chance to really find my way around much, but I did pick this up.' She pulled a piece of paper from her bag. 'It's a plan of the library I came across which indicates what each room holds – there are several, you see, beyond what is on the main floor. I am sure I may be able to find something of interest to you.'

Jane expressed her appreciation emphatically, and Rose realised she'd been fairly dismissive of how the lady might be feeling – she seemed so capable, so calm and collected on the surface, and so accepting she had no choice but to stay. It made her determined to do what she could to help her. If only Rose could become as adjusted to her fate so easily.

As soon as they were home, and conscious of Jane's desire to find a lighter book to capture her attention, Rose took her into her room. She studied the shelves of books for a moment, but sensing Jane's attention was elsewhere, she turned around.

'Pray, what is this?' Jane gestured to the many Post-it notes still liberally scattered over Rose's desk from her attempt at research the other night.

'They're little notelets – sticky, see?' She tore a fresh one off the pad and handed it to Jane who touched it warily. 'You write on them, things you don't want to forget or things you want to tell someone – and then stick them somewhere... useful, to remind you.' Rose looked at the pile of notes on her desk, all stuck on top of each other. Yes; very useful.

'Should I have a notion – a character, perchance – I make a notation?'

Rose nodded. 'Here.' She picked up a fresh pad from her shelf and handed it to Jane. 'They may come in handy. Now, let's find you something diverting to read.' She studied her shelves thoughtfully, then pulled an old favourite from the bottom shelf. 'There you go.'

Jane took the book cautiously. 'Is this not a child's text?'

Rose glanced affectionately at her well-thumbed copy of *Harry Potter and the Philosopher's Stone*. 'Yeah, we all made that mistake. Try it. It's as much about fantasy and magic as our present situation, so I reckon you'll enjoy it.'

With renewed interest, Jane examined the cover. 'How diverting. I took much enjoyment from discovering the world created by Mr Tolkien when first I came here.' She glanced around the room, clearly noting Rose's interest in the story as well before meeting her gaze. 'I thank you kindly for the recommendation of Mr Rowling's storytelling also.'

'Ms Rowling,' Rose corrected automatically, then smiled slightly at Jane's raised brow.

Once Jane had gone back to her room, Rose slumped onto the bed. She longed for the comfort of losing herself in a favourite book, but all this did was reinforce the unhappy situation: her favourite book of all time no longer existed.

'I am half agony, half hope'. Were such precious words gone forever? Would it be up to Rose to make sure Jane rewrote her stories in exactly the same way as she once had so they could be restored to the world?

Sitting up quickly, Rose pushed her hair back over her shoulder. How much could she remember? What if Jane's experiences had changed: how she would write the books? She might not want to write exactly how she had in the past. What if she... tried to modernise everything?

Rose's heart sank as she got slowly to her feet, the weight of Jane's lost legacy threatening to crush her. She was going to get a migraine if she didn't do something to take her mind off things.

She grabbed her bag and left the room. She needed time to think

– or rather – not think about the impossibility of her situation. Rose fished around in her bag as she hurried along the landing, retrieving the card Morgan had given her and pulling out her mobile. If her friend was free for dinner, it would be the perfect distraction from her present worries.

CHAPTER TWENTY

Having made a quick meal for Jane and left her fully engrossed in her book in the conservatory, Rose caught the next bus into town. The day was improving as it passed into evening. Not only had she come home to find her mother had already left for her week away, but Morgan had sounded pleased to hear from her.

Soon, she was walking up the steps into *Hall & Woodhouse*, but couldn't help wishing wistfully for it to be last Thursday. Thursday; a day when she had been so happy, a combination of excitement and nervousness swirling around inside her over the imminent meet up with Morgan. Rose straightened her shoulders, pushing open the door and stepping inside, feeling the twin tugs of fate and déjà vu. She was here to meet Morgan again, wasn't she? This was no time for regret over what had been.

Thankfully, it wasn't as crowded as last week, and Rose had barely taken a few steps across the room before she spotted her friend. She was on the same sofa as when Rose had first seen her, talking to whoever was next to her. Of course she was talking to someone. Rose shook her head; Morgan was *always* talking to someone.

Then, with a lurch of her heart, Rose stopped in her tracks – déjà vu indeed. Morgan was talking to *James*! Goose bumps prickled Rose's arms as she took in the scene, then, drawing in a steadying breath, she walked slowly towards them. Morgan was talking animatedly, her arms waving around as she recounted some tale or other to the man at her side. As Rose drew near, however, he looked up and smiled in surprise.

'Hi, Rose! Haven't seen you around in ages. How's things?' Not her old life then. The small sliver of hope filtering through her faded away.

'Oh – you know.' Rose shrugged. *Or at least, you might have some idea if a dog hadn't swallowed a necklace two days ago.* She resisted the urge to sigh. 'Much the same as always.'

Morgan had turned around with a wide smile. 'Ginger! You found me.' She gestured towards James. 'I was lost – couldn't find this place at all, and I accosted these lovely people as they were passing and they took pity on me and brought me here.'

People? Rose's gaze flew back to where James was seated only this time she saw who sat on the other side of him: *Mandy*! Nooo. He was still trapped in his toxic relationship?

'Mandy, you remember Rose Wallace?' James got to his feet, the easier to talk to everyone.

Mandy's frosty expression didn't melt at all as she looked Rose up and down. 'How could anyone forget that hair?' She all but shuddered, and Rose almost laughed. Some things certainly hadn't changed.

'It's awesome, isn't it? She'd be on the cover of one of my dad's magazine's if he ever saw her,' Morgan said, winking at Rose, and James smiled fleetingly at her, a gesture Morgan returned. 'Crazy, isn't it? I had no idea we'd have friends in common.'

'Friends? I think passing ships would be more accurate.' Mandy sipped at her drink. Rose hoped she would choke on it.

'Rose was at school with Jo,' James told Morgan. 'My sister. They're still mates now.'

We are? thought Rose. *We never saw each other much in my other life!*

'How's the library?' James grinned and turned to Morgan. 'Jo always said Rose would need a job where she could be surrounded by her precious books.'

Rose didn't want to think about her current job; the loss of her place at *Luxury Lettings* caused a physical pain in her breast, and she felt an irrational swoop of envy for whoever had been given the job instead of her.

'Well, shall we head up, Morgan?' It was unsettling and almost distressing being in their company like this, and Rose felt the need to escape. 'We have a table booked for dinner,' she added to James.

Goodbyes were quickly said, with Morgan repeating her thanks again for their help.

'Do you have a thing for him – that James?' Morgan asked, looking back over her shoulder as they climbed the spacious, curved staircase.

'No. Why?' Rose followed her look; if she was not mistaken, James had just then averted his eyes from them. It made her heart sink even lower.

'You seemed all flustered around him,' Morgan said, looking all around as they went up the impressive staircase as though she was visiting the palace of Versailles. 'Wow, look at all this glass!'

'More likely it was Mandy. She's poisonous, and he's a nice man – *really* nice. He deserves better.' *Someone like you, Morgan*, her mind whispered.

'But she clearly doesn't like *you*. Does she think you're competition?'

Rose almost tripped on the top stair. 'Hardly! Mandy never liked anyone. I'm not even sure she liked James.'

'Liked?'

'Likes. I meant likes.'

They were quickly seated, the conversation falling naturally between them, due to Morgan's inherent friendliness, and Rose was thankful she could almost be herself. In fact, just for a moment, everything felt normal, and she smiled as she watched Morgan questioning their waitress, who seemed unable to resist her friend's warm and open manner. Currently, they were discussing the young girl's nephew and what he liked to receive for his birthday.

'Oh, that's so cute. I have four nieces myself – and only one nephew – but they all love Bob Shea's books – do you want me to write down his name for you? He has this book called *Big Plans* that's my favourite. Every time I read it I walk around announcing that I've big plans. 'Big plans,' I say! Like the character in the book. I can't help myself.'

'Shea, I'll remember. But – were you wanting anything besides your water?'

Morgan scrunched up her nose in thought. 'No, thanks – Ginger?'

Rose shook her head. 'I've already ordered.'

'Oh yes – of course! Well–' She had clearly thought of another question but the waitress had this time smartly made her escape, and Morgan took a drink from her glass before turning to Rose. 'So – what do you do for a living? I feel like – if I remember – the last I knew you were in school – is that right?'

Rose sighed inwardly; no it was not right at all, but it would have to do.

'Yes, at college, I think. I work at the library here in town.'

Morgan's eyes lit up. 'Oooo, the library? That's on my list. Would you mind – could I come visit you?'

Rose thought again about the learning curve she was having, trying to act naturally in a job she was supposed to already know.

'Yes, of course. Drop by anytime.' After all, it would be good to see a familiar face!

Morgan beamed at her. 'Perfect, absolutely perfect. Would you have old newspaper clippings and such?'

Your guess is as good as mine, thought Rose. 'Yes. We definitely do.'

'I watched that show – I know you had it here first, but I watched the American version anyway – *Who Do You Think You Are?* – have you seen it?'

Rose pursed her lips. 'Well – I watched the episode with J.K. Rowling and the –' Rose stopped – there had been one with Julia Sawalha, the actress who played Lydia Bennet in the much-loved 1995 television version of *Pride & Prejudice*, but would she be as well known in this... life? Rose blinked as she suddenly thought of Colin Firth, pretty much *the* Mr Darcy of most fans' dreams. He'd already been in several British films when he got the role, but had his international film career blossomed quite so much without his much-loved portrayal and that famous wet shirt scene or – 'I think – has Colin Firth done an episode?'

Morgan frowned. 'Colin Firth? Who's he? Oh, is he that older guy in all the serious stuff? I don't think so. I'm not sure he's that well known in the US.'

Rose spared a moment of silence for the hundreds and thousands of women across the world who had no idea their favourite leading man and his iconic role were history. Well, perhaps a good amount of them had found him in whatever roles Morgan meant – at least his acting career had been successful – just different.

Then she shook her head. 'Oh, well – you were saying?'

'Yes – well, the best part of that show for me is when they find these sensational stories about their ancestors in the local papers. It's crazy what they used to print; I mean it basically amounted to full-on gossipmongering. Which is perfect for this project on the lost lady. I'm looking to find out what the town thought happened to her. Rumours perhaps too unsubstantiated or ridiculous to have been mentioned in the police report.'

Rose waited, but when Morgan seemed to think she'd made herself clear she had to ask, 'But won't that just perpetuate the falsehoods?'

'You sound just like my current boss. No! They add a piece of flair before I crushingly debunk them. If I can. I struck out online finding anything about my lady in the papers, but I did find something interesting.' Morgan fiddled with her phone for a second and turned it around to show Rose a picture of an old newspaper headline proclaiming *The Mysterious Disappearance of Owen Parfitt*. 'This happened not far from Bath in 1765! Just imagine – he disappeared into thin air and was never seen again, alive or dead. Remind you of any lost garden ladies?'

For the first time since the world had changed, Rose found herself truly distracted. 'That's – really interesting.' Rose was about to say how proud she was of her, but felt that might be a little too intimate for now, and before she could continue, a woman stopped as she passed by their table.

'Ah, hello, Rose.'

Rose didn't recognise her. *Here we go*, she muttered under her breath.

'Er, hi!'

'Thanks for covering last Saturday; you won't mind doing the next one as well, will you? We're so short-staffed.'

The woman nodded briskly at them both and whisked away, and Rose met Morgan's amused glance.

'Colleague of yours?'

Rose simply nodded. What was there to say? She didn't know the woman from Adam, and she certainly hadn't been at the library during her first day! Quite possibly, she was the elusive Barbara!

'I can't tell you how lucky I feel that I ran into you.' Morgan beamed at Rose, but before she could question her further, their waitress arrived, looking very much as though she hoped to deposit their order without being noticed.

No such luck. Morgan turned and greeted her like an old friend. 'So, Emily, how long have you lived in Bath?'

Morgan had somehow persuaded Rose into taking her on a tour of some of the more unique pubs, but Rose had only agreed on condition she go home first to charge her mobile and change. Rose's motivation was twofold – aside from what she told Morgan, she really wanted to make sure Jane hadn't decided to move on in her absence.

Making a beeline for the mobile charger plugged in near the kettle, Rose tried not to make it too obvious she was looking around for a displaced 19th-century author.

'I'll just go up and change – did you want anything to drink?'

'No thanks; mind if I snoop around your bookcase?'

'Not at all. Here,' Rose led Morgan into the drawing room. 'Make yourself at home.'

'Hey, look! You have *Spooks!* I have it, too, but obviously it's called *MI5*.'

'Sorry?' Distracted, Rose whipped a Post-it off the TV screen ('*Vast box with infinite variety of speaking images; inconceivable*') and turned to see what Morgan held. 'Oh, yes.'

Morgan had picked up a DVD from a nearby shelf and was brandishing a copy of an early series of the show with Matthew Macfadyen on the cover.

'You all have excellent taste in leading men. I loved this first guy, but I liked the blond who came next, too, and I'm not usually cool with big changes like that.'

Rose suppressed a sigh as her friend innocently hit another sore spot. Losing Jane's books had been a body blow; no longer being able to watch the adaptations couldn't compare, but it was still galling to think of the loss of yet another beloved Mr Darcy and a Captain Wentworth, too. Not wanting to dwell on it, Rose turned around just as Jane emerged from the conservatory. 'Oh, thank God!'

Jane stopped dead. 'I beg your pardon?' She looked over her shoulder. 'Is aught amiss?'

'Nothing.' Rose remembered her other guest and looked between Jane and Morgan, who had taken up her 'pleased to meet you' expression. 'Just glad you're... here. Ja-Jenny–'

Jane walked over to join them. 'My staying is quite tolerably fixed.' She eyed the DVD in Morgan's hand with a curious gaze.

'He is well-looking, is he not?' She pointed to Matthew Macfadyen, then looked up at Rose with a small smile before turning to stare at Morgan.

'Are we acquainted?'

Rose shook her head quickly. 'No, no. This is Morgan Taylor, a friend from America.'

'A revolutionary!' Jane's tone was somewhere between excited and astounded, and Rose hesitated; she hadn't thought of the added cultural complications. She looked back at Morgan's openly friendly face and tried to be optimistic. After all, who could not like Morgan?

'California to be exact. We're a breed of our own.'

Jane's eyes widened, her expression almost as eager as Morgan's. 'I am not familiar with this place; what is your lineage?'

'My – oh, well, it's complicated. My mom was German, and

my dad is Italian. But Mom died, and Dad remarried a wonderful Mexican lady with two daughters, and then my dad and she had a little boy together.'

'I am all... astonishment!'

Rose broke in. 'Morgan's a researcher for a magazine, Jenny.'

'Indeed?'

'Yes; she's investigating some old mysteries from the West Country, including one set in Bath many years ago. I'm sure it would interest you.'

Jane met Rose's look in silence, and Morgan took the bait. 'Oh, are you a fan of history? How long have you lived in Bath?'

'There is no easy answer to this question.' Then Jane shrugged lightly. 'Sufficient time to own to some familiarity.'

Morgan smiled widely. 'I hope you don't mind my saying, but you have an unusual way of expressing yourself.'

'In this I am not alone.'

Rose choked back a laugh, relieved to see Morgan's smile widening. 'Yeah, I'm discovering lots of differences in our so-called common language.'

'Yes. So... Morgan has travelled all this way in order to get more information for her story.'

Jane was staring at Morgan with avid curiosity. 'Why does she still have her coat on?'

Rose bit her lip. 'It's very warm in California – she's feeling the cold.' Jane looked as though she might have something to say to this, so Rose turned quickly to Morgan. 'I don't think you ever told me the rest of the story you were working on – you said it was a missing person case?'

Morgan looked between them again, but said, 'Yes. Well – there was this woman; she disappeared into thin air. No trace of her was ever found! Her family is pretty well respected, right, but no one knows a lot about them. They keep themselves to themselves. So – picture it – it's the beginning of the 19th century. There isn't a lot a respectable woman in England – or well, anywhere, really – could do without a companion back in 1803, but she must have gone somewhere–'

Rose blinked, gripped by a strange sensation. It was as if her insides were turning to ice. Jane had paled, her lips slightly parted. It couldn't be – but there were a lot of things recently that Rose had thought impossible that had proved more than.

'Did you say 1803?'

'*Yes!*' Morgan took her hands out of her pockets. 'So here's the deal – the family – this woman lived with her parents and older sister – are, like, all worried and report her as missing. Then they back off, refuse to make any further comment. Granted, the law enforcers of the time weren't the most popular people, but the whole thing strikes them as so weird they actually wrote a report on their conversation with the family. And it still exists, though it's in very poor condition. Someone did track it down for me, but I had to go into the station to get a look at it; couldn't touch it or anything.' Morgan grinned at Rose and then Jane. 'Isn't it fascinating? They suspected the family knew exactly what did happen, but for whatever reason, they're just not saying. No body was ever discovered, so there is no proof of foul play, and the family – again – seems pretty well above reproach, so the most logical assumption is that this woman simply ran off, most likely with a lover...'

A small squeak escaped from Jane at this point, and Morgan nodded excitedly. 'Yes! I know! Scandalous for the time. I can just imagine it, though – can't you? It's no wonder the family kept quiet. It would have ruined the other daughter by association. Maybe he was someone far above her class, and his family didn't approve and so under the cover of night –'

'How… alarming! Such wild speculation!' Jane had gone even paler, and Rose glanced at Morgan who seemed unfazed.

'Well, yes – maybe it makes a better story if *she* is the higher class and runs off with the butler.'

Jane put a hand to her head and sagged against the worktop. 'It is to be hoped your investigations do not end in disappointment, but I fear they may.'

Morgan shrugged. 'Well… anyway – I'm looking forward to trying to figure it out.'

Rose decided it was time to make a move.

'Right, come on, Morgan. Let's go. We can catch the next bus and it will drop us by the abbey which is as good a place to start as any.'

'But what about Jen?' Morgan smiled at Jane. 'You want to come with us? We're going pub hopping!'

'A pleasure all the more enhanced for not having any notion of what you speak,' Jane began, but catching Rose's urgent eye, she paused. 'But I must forego your generous offer and resume my reading. It is most gripping. Mr Potter is in danger of discovery by the surly custodian's feline despite his concealment by a cloak of invisibility.'

'Mrs Norris,' Rose supplied, fondly remembering the moment Jane described.

'Mrs Norris? You're out of practice, Ginger. Filch's cat's is Mrs Marmaduke, remember?' Morgan admonished, and Rose's gaze flew to her friend in surprise as she turned to Jane eagerly. 'You're reading *Harry Potter*! Is it your first time?'

'Indeed.'

'I wish I could read it all for the first time. Well, in order at any rate. I read book 3 first, you see.'

'No – I do not.' Jane smiled gently, softening the words. 'Good evening, ladies.'

'See ya! Okay, Rose, let's go!'

Rose was still staring at Morgan in confusion. Then realisation struck. If there was no longer a novel called *Mansfield Park*, then there was no longer a character called Mrs Norris for J.K. Rowling to choose as the name for the busybody cat in her Harry Potter series.

Morgan stayed Rose with a hand as she turned blindly for the door. 'Wait, weren't you going to change?'

'I decided against it.' Rose waved a hand at Jane who turned to leave the room and, if she was not mistaken, had winked at her! Rolling her eyes, she followed Morgan out into the cool evening air. Jane Austen was turning out to be more than a handful.

CHAPTER TWENTY-ONE

Rose hurried from her room the next morning and down the stairs, already running late, only to fetch up short as she saw a Post-it note stuck to the telephone in the hall.

'*Why such predilection for placing people in boxes?*' Seeing the familiar hand of Jane Austen in such a way was just too bizarre to take in so early in the day, and Rose walked through the kitchen, grabbed her house key and let herself out. There were two more Post-its: one on the fridge, saying '*Ice house (life of provisions extended; oft to no advantage)*' and one on the electric kettle saying '*Do not place on stove; mayhem may ensue*'.

Having watched carefully the previous day, Rose managed to not only find the staff entrance at the rear of the building but also, on the third attempt, to get in without assistance. It felt like she had scaled Everest, and she entered the staffroom with a smile on her face.

'Hey, you look much better.'

Mary was making herself a drink by the sink and Rose dropped her bag onto a nearby chair and walked over to join her.

'I feel better, to be honest.' She reached for a mug from the rack on the wall, then stopped, remembering everyone had their own. Thankfully, Mary was busy putting her tea bag in the bin, and Rose quickly opened the cupboard under the sink to find a spare mug.

'Aren't you putting your bag in your locker?' Mary frowned as she met Rose's gaze.

'Er – yes! Of course. I'll do it on my way down.'

Five minutes later, she opened the door to the locker room with caution. Did everyone have their own lockers? Some of them were closed, some had keys sticking out of them – a distinctive, thin key. Rummaging in her bag, Rose unearthed her keyring and found one that matched the same style and after three attempts found the matching locker.

A further five minutes, and she was down on the main library floor, trying to look busy with a shelving trolley. At least that was one thing she'd had ample experience with on the previous day.

'Rose! Barbara is asking for you.' Mary sailed past, her arms laden with books, and looking over towards the main desk, Rose saw the woman who had spoken to her the previous night in *Hall & Woodhouse*.

Here we go, she muttered under her breath.

By mid-morning, Rose's head was reeling again. Barbara – whose patience had run thin after the umpteenth time Rose asked for help with the in-house cataloguing system – had told her to leave it and oversee the public computers and deal with any printing from the main desk and also to assist any customers with the copiers. She had also advised her to see a doctor.

The desire to grab her things and leave after tea break was strong, and only the inducement of Morgan coming along to do some research gave Rose the courage to return to the main library floor. Before any sign of her friend came, however, her attention was caught by a familiar voice, and she walked slowly towards the area she'd been overseeing earlier which housed the computers for public use.

There, talking far more loudly than permitted, sat Roger, her colleague at *Luxury Lettings*. He was clearly doing something on one of the computers but also holding court with the poor people either side of him. Edging a little closer, Rose busied herself tidying up some abandoned printing which had been left on a nearby table.

'Thought I'd move on. When you're good at what you do, you can walk into a job pretty much anywhere.' He turned back to the screen and tapped a few keys.

No one appeared to be paying him much attention, but Barbara must have heard voices for she came around the corner and glared at Roger's back. Then, seeing Rose, she gestured at her to speak to him and walked off.

As Roger didn't know her outside of her job, Rose felt confident enough to go over and request he speak a little more quietly so as not to disturb other library users.

'Who are you but some public service minion? You can't tell me what to do.' Pretty much the same Roger, then. 'I've just sent a document to the printer. Get it for me, will you?'

'I'm afraid you'll have to come to the desk for it. We charge per sheet of paper and once you've paid, you can have your copies.' Rose walked away before she said something she might regret.

Taking Roger's pages off the printer, she could see it was his CV. Had James been driven to fire him at last?

'That's private!' Roger snapped at her as she met him at the counter. He handed over the necessary money, and Rose refrained from pointing out that if he wanted privacy, he shouldn't come in to use the public computers. *He* may be looking for a new job, but she preferred to cling to this one for now.

One of the men who'd been sitting at an adjacent computer joined him at the counter then, just to let Rose know he'd sent something to the printer, and Roger put the CVs into a folder and turned to address him.

'Mark my words: that James Malcolm is a loser. Fancy giving up your business just because your girlfriend wants you to move to London! I'd never do that for a woman!'

And with this parting shot, he walked out of the library with his usual arrogant strut.

In a daze, Rose dealt with the man's request. *James was leaving Bath?* But he loved it here. It meant as much to him as it did to her. And his business – he was giving it all up?

This is Mandy's doing, Rose muttered under her breath. *I can't believe it; it's so sad!*

And what about James and Morgan? Rose walked slowly out from behind the main desk. There hadn't seemed much likelihood for their initial mutual attraction to be rekindled in this strange new world, not with Mandy still around, but somehow Rose had not given up hope of romance somehow finding a way. But not now…

'Hey!' Morgan came breezing into the library and waved as soon as she saw her, a wide smile on her face.

'I was expecting a really old building – you know, dusty shelves, ancient tomes.'

Pushing aside her regrets, Rose laughed. 'You were expecting Hogwarts' library, then?'

'I suppose I was.' Morgan looked a little disappointed as she glanced around, but Rose steered her over to a vacant table on the far side of the library and sat her down.

'So, where *do* you need to start?'

Morgan rummaged in her cavernous bag and drew out some sheets of paper.

'There's very little available; seems the constables of the day had more pressing matters of crime than a missing eloping woman. I have a few details from my kind police contact. I scribbled some notes on the family interview because I couldn't have a copy. Everything was in a very poor condition.' She laughed and wrinkled her nose. 'Smelt bad, too. Don't think anyone had opened that particular archive in hundreds of years.'

'Do you still want to see old newspapers?'

'Yes! When I phoned here, they said I'd have to come in person to see ones from the year I was interested in. They have copies on microfilm, too. I'm seeing my guy in charge at one for a catch-up lunch, so it would be great to have some new stuff to show him.'

'I've an idea where the microfilm is stored, and I'm sure we can work out how to use the reader. Can you let me know what it is you're looking for exactly?'

'I think the best place to start is with the local paper – the *Chronicle*, I think it's called? Just whatever there is for around September 1803?'

'Okay. Bear with me.' Crossing her fingers behind her back, Rose walked off to the section where she'd seen the digital microfilm readers, hoping the cataloguing system wouldn't be too difficult to master.

With help from Mary yet again, Rose had finally found the right microfilm and then worked out how to feed it into the reader before leaving Morgan to her research. She didn't see much of her, as she was stationed at the computer area on the opposite side of the library. But as one o'clock neared she walked back over only to find Morgan still engrossed in her work.

'Hey, aren't you meeting the man in charge?'

'Yikes! I didn't realise the time!' Morgan began stuffing papers into her folder and shoving pens and notebook into her bag. 'I'll be late, and he'll be cranky about it.'

Rose felt a pang of regret; every time Morgan left her, she felt bereft, desperate to hold onto the only tangible thing connecting her real life with this strange alternative one – other than Jane, of course, but that was an avenue she didn't want to think about.

There had been no sign of Jane in the library this morning, much to her surprise, and she was torn between the relief of not having to keep an eye on her as well as continue her pretence of a job and wondering where she might be. She wasn't overly confident Jane wouldn't just take it into her head to move on and, even though she had no idea how they were going to find a way for her to return to the past, she knew if she lost her, it would be the end of *all* hope – she'd be stuck in this world forever; *this* would become her life.

'Hey.' Morgan stood up and swung her bag over her shoulder. 'Come with me?' She swept her hair up into a neat, practised bun and fastened it quickly, then fished in her pocket for the fake glasses. 'He can be so... I dunno... intimidating?'

Rose laughed, quietly delighted Morgan wanted her company. 'I can't imagine anyone intimidating *you*.'

Morgan grinned. 'Okay, perhaps not intimidating. I just find it hard to be myself around him; he's so – serious. And quiet. Doesn't seem to want to chat unless it's work-related.'

'Well, I'm sure you make up for that.'

Giving Rose a gentle thump on her arm in reprimand, Morgan fixed her with a serious eye. 'I mean it; please, Ginger? For old times' sake? Come with me and it will help the meeting pass so much more quickly.'

Rose walked towards the doors with Morgan. 'I thought you were lunching with him, not having a meeting?'

With a shrug, Morgan smiled ruefully. 'I am – but the food is secondary to whatever it is he will want me to do next. I don't feel like I've made that much progress, so I'm hoping he isn't too grumpy about it.'

'Okay. I'll come. Where are you going to be? I need to just go upstairs and grab my things and if he's a stickler for timekeeping, you'd best not hang around!'

With another worried glance at her watch, Morgan nodded. 'He said to come to the *Roman Baths Kitchen*. Is it far?'

'Just turn left out into the street and head for the abbey. It's right there, in front of the abbey and Pump Room – you know where those are?'

Morgan was at the top of the stairs. 'I'll ask someone! See you in a minute.' And then she was gone.

Rose arrived at the *Roman Baths Kitchen* barely five minutes after Morgan and soon spotted her at a corner table. She was alone and waved eagerly when she saw Rose, beckoning her over.

'He's just popped outside to take a private call he's been waiting for. Probably the most words he's ever spoken to me outside of work stuff.' Morgan winked. Despite her earlier words, she didn't seem too cowed.

As there was a set of keys and a battered leather notepad at the place to her left, Rose took the seat opposite and picked up the menu to see what was on offer. Moments like this were so precious now, she wanted to savour every one.

Barely had she given the menu a cursory glance, however, when Morgan kicked her under the table. 'He's back,' she hissed, straightening the glasses on her nose and giving Rose a wink.

Rose bit her lip to hide her smile and got to her feet.

'My apologies,' said a familiar deep voice as a figure came to stand beside her. 'You must be Rose.'

CHAPTER TWENTY-TWO

Every nerve tingling, Rose turned slowly around.

'This is Dr Aiden Trevellyan.' Morgan had also stood up.

'Yes – I know. I mean, hi! Pleased to meet you… Dr Trevellyan.' Tentatively, Rose held out her hand, only for it to be grasped in his and given a firm shake.

'Aiden. Please, call me Aiden.' He smiled as they took their seats.

Feeling the easy blush stealing into her cheeks, Rose sat down quickly, only to notice the frown on Morgan's brow. When Rose sent her a questioning look, however, she shook her head and mouthed, 'later'.

The waitress appeared then and took their order, and Rose strove to rein in her mind, which was careening out of control in a mist of hows, whys, whats, none of which she was able to voice. She took a deep draught of her water. The doctor had ordered a bottle of wine to accompany their lunch, and she would probably need the Dutch courage to get her through. Glancing at him, Rose swallowed quickly. How she had longed to join him for a meal, but perhaps not quite like this.

Flicking through his notebook, the man at her side then turned to Morgan, but he paused and glanced back at Rose. 'I'm sorry – we've some things to discuss. Will you excuse us?'

'Yes, of course.' Rose welcomed the respite. It meant she could continue to sip her water and study him discreetly – finally something good about *this* life, she wasn't just someone who checked the doctor into an apartment once a year; in *this* life, she was on an equal footing, able to call him by his first name.

Did he look any different? Not really; but then, why would he? How welcome was the sound of his voice as he ran through Morgan's progress with her. Being familiar already with his brevity and his intense concentration over his work, she could understand why to Morgan it made him seem unapproachable. She was so used to being able to work her magic on anyone; her friendliness and warm smile never failed to bring people out, and she no doubt found Aiden's reticence alien to her.

Rose listened to them whilst pretending not to. They were discussing Morgan's findings at the police station as she showed him her notes on the family interview. Rose carefully moved her knife and fork a few millimetres along the table, then refolded her napkin, pretending she was otherwise occupied, but in reality taking in every word, unable to stop glancing at the man at her side, or study his hands as he flipped through Morgan's papers.

Then she frowned. Why would he be interested in a long-forgotten missing person case? Wasn't he an eminent archaeologist? His interest in Jane Austen related merely to the Steventon dig of a few years ago, just one of many in his career so far, so it was unlikely his working life had changed in any particular way in this world.

Just then, their order arrived, and Morgan broke off in mid-sentence. Rose had been right – it didn't matter that he did little beyond place probing questions and study Morgan's notes. There were no periods of silence, for her friend had something to say about everything.

The doctor poured them each a glass of wine, and Morgan took a cautious sip. 'Okay. And what did you find out at Sydney Place?'

Rose met her friend's frantic look, realising she had never returned there after the other morning.

'Oh! Not much…'

Aiden frowned as he picked up his knife and fork. 'Did you speak to each tenant, as we agreed?'

'I'm afraid I put paid to that, Dr Trevellyan.'

Rose sent him an apologetic look, but his only response was, 'Aiden.'

Grabbing her glass, Rose took a hasty slug of her wine. 'Yes, of course. Sorry.'

'And?'

Morgan was mouthing '*I told you so*' at her across the table; thankfully, Aiden's attention seemed to be firmly with her, so Rose drew in a quick breath and nodded.

'Yes – you see, we've not been in contact in such a long time, and Morgan was just about to pay the first call when we bumped into each other. There, I mean; at number four.'

'I will get on it this afternoon.' Morgan smiled widely at Aiden, but he merely grunted.

'If none of them has any information on the family – and that's highly likely if they're all tenants – try to find out who the owner of the building is.'

'Yes, sir!'

Aiden stared at Morgan as if he wasn't quite sure how to take her, and Rose cleared her throat.

'So – Dr Tre- Aiden. I was really interested in the dig you led in Somerset a couple of years ago. Are there any plans to revisit the site? I remember reading an article on it, and I'm sure you said there was so much yet to uncover there.'

To her surprise, Aiden entered willingly into a discussion on the project. His enthusiasm for his subject was infectious, and even Morgan seemed to warm to him a little as he recounted some anecdotes from the dig. Having heard him talk at the *Festival* in previous years, Rose knew already how different this side of him could be from his usual manner. It was as though he came alive when talking of his work.

Feeling her confidence grow, Rose began to relax as they finished their meals and ordered cups of tea and a dessert for Morgan. After all, as far as Aiden Trevellyan was concerned, he and Rose didn't know each other at all. She wasn't sure if it was the wine with lunch or just some devil-may-care attitude that seemed to be rising within her, but she felt her self-confidence rising.

'May I ask, then, how or why you became involved in the job investigating this disappearing woman? It doesn't seem to be of archaeological interest from what Morgan has told me so far?'

A shadow crossed Aiden's face so swiftly, Rose wasn't sure if she'd imagined it. 'Not on its own, it's not.'

There was a small interruption as Morgan's dessert and the tea arrived, along with a slight delay as Morgan chatted happily to their server.

Rose wouldn't normally have had the courage to press someone for answers, but her curiosity over why and how Aiden might be looking into Jane's disappearance was at its height. 'So – this disappearance – why does it interest you?'

'I suppose you could call me a closet detective.' He grinned suddenly; it made him look years younger, and Rose nearly dropped her teaspoon. 'I'm fascinated by unsolved mysteries – especially those unearthed during a job. Something came up on the recent project that led me here to Bath, and I couldn't resist it. That's it in a nutshell.'

'I love it! And there are so many more mysteries I could help you find.' Morgan had let the young man return to his work now, and looked hopefully at Aiden, and for the first time, he smiled in her direction.

'A tempting offer, though as an archaeologist I shouldn't admit to such flights of unscientific curiosity.' He grimaced and lifted his empty glass. 'Must be the wine and the company.'

The girls laughed, and the conversation turned to more general things as they finished their tea, after which Aiden, who insisted on paying, walked over to settle up. Rose couldn't help but look over her shoulder to watch him, then turned back quickly, colour flooding her cheeks. He was leaning against the bar and staring straight at her!

Morgan fixed Rose with a semi-serious eye. '*Well?*'

Rose blinked. 'Well, what?'

'He just totally checked you out!'

'He did not!'

'Rose Wallace! Don't you act the innocent with me. *And* I heard you say '*I know*'. How do you know him if he doesn't know you?'

'I've heard of him. Read a lot about his projects before now.'

'Really? That's it? Yet the minute you laid eyes on him, you knew it was *him*?'

'Well, I've seen photos, and he was the guest archaeologist on an episode of *Time Travellers* – it's all about historic excavations and so on.'

'And recorded him, too, I bet. Did you keep watching him on rewind – you know, do the slow motion thing?' Morgan waggled her brows and laughed, and Rose shhhhed her as the doctor returned to the table.

'I must get back to the library.' Rose got to her feet, feeling flustered and strangely happy at the same time.

'And I must, too.' Morgan slung her bag over her shoulder.

'Don't forget your glasses.' Aiden indicated the abandoned spectacles. Morgan had taken them off to read a piece of her handwriting to the doctor when he couldn't decipher it and forgotten to place them back on her nose.

She snatched them up and replaced them. 'Thanks! Always doing that. Well, we must be going.' She grabbed Rose's arm and all but dragged her across the room towards the staircase. 'Thanks for lunch, Dr... Aiden.'

Unable to help herself, Rose glanced over her shoulder again as they left the room. Aiden was still standing by the table, watching them, and he raised a hand before turning back to gather his things.

Sailing down the staircase, Rose followed Morgan out into the street with only one ear on her friend's muttering about the amount of research Aiden had given her to do. The day was definitely feeling a little brighter than it had an hour ago.

'Hey, look; isn't that your friend, Jen?'

Rose raised her gaze to follow Morgan's hand as they rounded the corner by the abbey and paused on the end of Cheap Street to let a car go by.

An open-top tour bus was sailing past, and sure enough, on the top deck was Jane. She looked extremely happy, and when she saw them she gave a small wave.

Rose's hand dropped to her side as she and Morgan continued their walk, a frown on her brow. Unless she was much mistaken, Jackie Herring – the Director of the *Jane Austen Festival* in her other life – stood at the front of the upper level of the bus, talking into a microphone!

As soon as they returned to the library, Morgan settled herself back in front of the digital reader, and Rose – allocated the job of tidying the fiction shelves by Barbara, who was still eyeing her with caution – welcomed the chance to dwell on lunch whilst still appearing to work.

Until, that is, about an hour later, when a familiar face appeared by her side: Jane Austen.

'So how was the guided bus tour?' Rose smiled in response to Jane's animated face.

'I am all eager delight; a most informative lady was our genial hostess.'

'I'm sure she was; her knowledge of Bath is extensive.' *You have no idea*, Rose muttered under her breath. Then she realised Jane was holding a small piece of paper out to her.

'I was advised by a lady.' She waved a hand in the direction of the main enquiry desk. 'I must complete this if I seek a rare title?'

Rose took the *Request Slip* from Jane. There was something quite surreal about seeing the familiar handwriting there in front of her.

'Your pens do not please me.' Jane held up a biro then studied her fingers. 'To be certain, one's skin does not stain, yet I feel oppressed by the continuous flow of ink.'

Rose almost laughed. 'You are intimidated by this?' She pointed at the cheap pen.

'There is no opportunity for pause, no moment of reflection, whilst refreshing one's pen. I like it not.'

Rose shook her head and studied the form. 'Okay. Let me go and ask someone how I do this. Why don't you go and find a seat somewhere?'

Jane looked around the room, her mood visibly sobering. 'It is not a pleasing place. I do not find it conducive to reading. The light is too strong, too bright, and pains my eyes.'

'How about over there?' Rose pointed to a corner reading nook. 'There are windows so the light will feel more natural? I'll find out what I can. I don't know how long I'll be.'

'As you wish.' Jane walked over to the other side of the room, studying the shelves as she went, and Rose hurried over to where Mary was. 'Please can you help me? A lady has just asked if we have a copy of this.' She passed the slip to her; Mary was turning out to be a good source of information without questioning too much why Rose's knowledge was so vague.

Mary frowned. 'Ann Radcliffe? If we do have a copy, it will be in the Local Store.' She glanced around. 'You'll need to speak to Anne.'

'Er – Anne?'

Shaking her head, Mary took Rose by the arm and turned her around. 'There.' She pointed over to the shelves housing local history books. 'Anne – the *Local Studies Librarian*, remember?'

'Oh, of course. Sorry!' Rose smiled as genuinely as possible, silently begging Mary to forgive her, and she grabbed the slip and walked quickly over to the *Local Studies Area*.

'Hi – er, Anne? I was wondering if you might help me find a book for... a customer.'

Anne took the slip from Rose and studied it thoughtfully. 'We do have it, but I'm not sure it's available for public use. Is the customer waiting?'

'Yes, she is.'

'Then I'll go and look now.'

Rose hovered near the door through which Anne had gone – not far from where Morgan was still peering intently at her screen – and within five minutes Anne returned, handing over two aged volumes.

'This is all I can let you have of Radcliffe's story right now. There's another volume to this one, but it's unfit for production.'

Rose took the two books carefully. 'I can't thank you enough.'

'Not a problem,' Anne waved away her thanks with smile and a reminder to ensure the customer handled them with care and returned them so they could be put back in the store.

Rose found Jane in a corner seat, a small pile of books on the table beside her and one in her hand which she held towards the light coming in through the window as she read.

Looking up as Rose took the seat opposite, Jane smiled. 'Do you have pleasing news?'

'Sort of. What are you reading now?'

Jane raised the book and showed the cover to Rose: *Maritime History of the World.* 'I find it most engrossing.'

'Are you happy enough continuing then? I have this for you.' She waved the old books and Jane's eyes shone as she put her existing book back on the table and reached for those held by Rose.

She studied the spines, then opened the front of one of them. '*The Romance of the Forest.*'

'Is it another gothic romance?'

Jane looked up from studying the two volumes. 'Indeed.' She frowned. 'Do you not have the third volume?'

Rose shook her head. 'I'm afraid it was in too poor a condition. I'm so sorry – it was the third you were reading, wasn't it?'

'It is of little consequence. I shall begin over.' She gave a small smile, stroking the hard and well-worn cover almost reverently.

'I can't check them out, Jane, because they're not lending stock and can only be looked at here in the library, so you'll need to leave them with a member of staff – or me – when you leave, okay?'

Whether she was heard or not, Rose wasn't sure, for Jane had already opened the first volume.

The rest of the afternoon passed in a whirl as Rose continued to try to learn as much as she could. Morgan, having spent too long staring at the digital reader, decided she needed a break and left to make appointments to visit the various occupants of Sydney Place. Other than trying to keep an eye on Jane in her corner by the window, her nose glued to her book, Rose found herself at liberty to relive her conversation with Aiden over lunch as many times as she wished, and in fact, was so enjoying doing just that as she shelved some books in the fiction section that she only realised it was time to leave when one of her colleagues bade her goodbye and left for the day.

'Rose!'

She looked over as Barbara called to her from the main enquiry desk. 'There's a call for you?' She waved the phone, and Rose frowned as she placed the remaining books back on the shelving trolley and hurried over. Her mobile was in her pocket, so surely anyone who knew her would use that?

'Hello?' She spoke hesitantly, conscious of Barbara nearby as she tidied things away prior to the evening shift.

CHAPTER TWENTY-THREE

'It's Aiden Trevellyan.'

Rose's eyes widened, colour flooding into her cheeks, and she turned her back on her colleague. 'Oh! Hi. Did you want Morgan? She left about ten minutes ago, and–'

'I – er – no. I have her mobile.'

Of course he does, you idiot. Rose bit her lip; *play it cool, stop acting like a schoolgirl with a crush.*

'I just wondered – well, you seemed quite interested in the Lopen dig. I have some great photos on my laptop; if you wanted to – well, I mean – I don't expect you're free, but–'

'I'm free. When? I mean, did you mean today?' *Yes. Very cool. How old are you?*

'Yes. I have some time to kill before my train; I wondered if you fancied meeting after work?'

Rose sighed; no chance to go home and get into something sophisticated and try to improve her unruly hair, then. She shrugged; sophisticated wasn't a word she could apply to the wardrobe she had inspected the other day. 'No. I mean yes, of course. I leave at five – now, in fact.'

'Good. Excellent.' He cleared his throat. 'I – well, I'll be waiting outside.'

~o0o~

Because Aiden had a train to catch, Rose had suggested they walk down to *Graze* which was adjacent to the station, and as it was a fine evening, she walked out onto the terrace at the back to find a table whilst Aiden went to the bar.

Despite the initial frisson of excitement at being asked to meet him, even if only to talk about his work, her confidence had wavered a little during their walk. Conversation had been a little awkward and sporadic, partly due to having to cross so many roads during rush hour and partly due to her realising that without Morgan's comforting presence it was not quite so easy to be relaxed in Aiden's company.

She was still struggling to adjust to the new balance in her acquaintance with the doctor. Having adored him from afar for so many years, she was finding it difficult to be herself.

Just then, he came through the door onto the terrace, a glass in each hand, his gaze skimming over the tables. Rose waved a hand, and he saw her and smiled, and her heart dropped several inches and then leapt back into place. Swallowing quickly, Rose glanced down. Good grief, he'd better not do *that* too many times.

He deposited the glasses on the table before swinging his bag off his shoulder and dropping it into the chair beside Rose.

'Great spot.' He looked around appreciatively as he sat down. The terrace overlooked the platforms, so all the comings and goings of the station – trains and commuters alike – were there for their entertainment. 'I love people-watching.'

I know, her heart whispered. She reached for her drink. 'Thanks for this. Yes, me, too; I like to come here for a cup of tea sometimes and just watch the goings-on.'

He raised his glass to her, saying, 'Cheers,' and she did likewise.

There was silence for a moment as they both looked at each other, then, typically, they both spoke at once.

'Did you want–'

'What is the–'

'No – please, Rose; go ahead.'

Still savouring him saying her name, it was Rose's turn to smile. 'I was just wondering what the current project you're working on is?'

Aiden leaned back in his seat and stretched, then sat forward. 'It's a fairly routine dig: a small Hampshire church burnt down in the mid-1800s and rebuilt. They want to identify the footprint of the original church, so I'm overseeing the small team doing the excavations to see what can be found.'

Rose's skin tingled. 'And… and where is this church?'

'A small village south of Basingstoke. Chawton? Charming place, bit off the beaten track since they built the A30 bypass.' He didn't seem to notice the paleness of Rose's skin as she took a sip from her wine glass.

'Oh, er yes, I know it, actually… Chawton.' Rose stuttered, 'I didn't realise it was connected to your being here in Bath.'

Aiden shook his head. 'Well there is an off-chance it isn't. But I'm certainly curious.'

'The story you are working on with Morgan?'

He hesitated, then took a drink of his beer. 'Yes.' Then he smiled at her again and Rose was incredibly thankful she was sitting down. At close proximity it was even more overwhelming. *Get a grip*, she admonished herself. *You're supposed to be cool, calm and collected, remember?*

'And – er – what was it you were going to say?'

'I wondered if you wanted to see the photos I mentioned?'

'Of course! But,' Rose glanced at her watch. 'When is your train?'

'Not for an hour.'

He pulled his battered laptop from his bag and as he fired it up, Rose felt a pang for her old life. How she had loved that morning working for him, doing what she could to restore his computer, watching him discreetly as he focused on the work he loved so much. It hadn't mattered that he didn't even '*see*' her; she had just felt so thrilled to be in his company.

'Right.' He fished his glasses out of his jacket pocket. 'Here, let me come to you so I can show you.' Before she could realise what he was doing, he'd stood up and moved his chair round next to her, sat down and pulled the laptop across the table to face them both.

Rose could feel the telltale colour rising, and took a hasty swig from her glass of wine, letting the cool liquid slide down her throat to ease a sudden tightness.

Half an hour later, she was so fully engrossed in listening to Aiden talk through the articles and photographs with her, along with the relating of some amusing anecdotes from the dig, she'd become more accustomed to his closeness and had actually stopped staring in fascination at his long, slender fingers as they pointed out various things of interest on the screen.

'Thank you so much! That was incredibly interesting.'

Aiden sat back in his chair and eyed her with a curious look. 'Really?'

She nodded quickly.

'It's not that I doubt you; I just don't often come across anyone who's genuinely intrigued. There's a surface interest, of course, but not for further knowledge, more explanation. It's… refreshing.'

Rose had edged her chair back a little, too, the better to be able to see him now they were side by side. His words emboldened her, and she gestured towards the now closed laptop.

'What drew you in? Why archaeology?'

Aiden smiled again, a genuine wide smile that lit up his dark eyes, and Rose grabbed her glass again only to find it empty.

'Here, let's have another whilst I bore you to death with the history of my life.'

There was nothing Rose wanted more, but with the constant arrival and departure of trains to their right there was no way of forgetting he had to leave, and soon.

'What about your train?'

He shrugged. 'There'll be another.'

Another half-hour later, Rose was stunned at how much she was enjoying herself and how relaxed she was beginning to feel. Aiden had talked about being born in Cornwall, a county steeped in myth and legend, and how that led to a love of the supernatural and fantasy stories as he grew up. It had appealed to him even more than history, which had led him to study English literature long before his thoughts turned to history itself, and ultimately archaeology, for his Master's.

He had, in an endearingly self-conscious way, admitted to having been a massive *Lord of the Rings* fan in his late-teens and early twenties – a geek, as he put it – though he said he'd drawn the line at dressing up and attending conventions.

Rose had been unable to avoid blushing at this, though thankfully he didn't seem to notice. Her embarrassment of being seen by Aiden during the promenade on Saturday still lingered.

In her turn, Rose had admitted to an equal interest in JRR Tolkien's world amongst others, and he had turned to her enthusiastically, caught up in his story, his face animated in a way she'd only ever seen when he was delivering his talks at the *Festival*.

'I honestly believe it changed my life, changed *me*.' He smiled self-deprecatingly. 'Some people think you're mad when you say an author's words have done that, but it's true. I think I will always be that same geek who was entranced with Middle-earth. It's what drew me to archaeology in the end. I was mystified by the past, fascinated by Tolkien's mythology and the world he created; I wanted to explore ancient culture, ways of life…' He paused, then shrugged. 'I'm going on too much. But you can see how it led to where I am today.'

Rose smiled, her heart swelling with something she couldn't quite define. Perhaps it was admiration for his passion for his subject?

'I think I begin to see why an old myth about a woman disappearing into thin air might intrigue you.'

'One of the first things we do on a job like this is a geophys analysis.' Rose nodded as he explained the purpose of it, not wanting to reveal she already knew from her avid following of *Time Travellers*. 'You can imagine, with it being hallowed ground, we wanted to be very respectful and careful in our investigations.' Rose merely nodded again, unwilling to interrupt him. 'Well, the findings were disappointingly inconclusive from the project's point of view, *but* something else was thrown up, and no one else seemed remotely intrigued… but it really spoke to me, do you know what I mean?' He looked expectantly at Rose.

'Yes. I'm sure I do.'

'At the back of the churchyard, next to the church, were these three graves. Two of them had fairly traditional headstones and were linked to each other – members of the same family. A bit of local research revealed it was a Hampshire family whose youngest daughter had gone missing – completely disappeared without any further trace – when they had been living in Bath for a few years.'

'Cassandra and Mrs Austen.' The words came out before Rose could stop them. Damn the wine!

Aiden stared at her. 'How on earth do you know those names;

where those people were laid to rest?'

Rose bit her lip. 'Oh! I must have seen them in Morgan's notes; at least, I think I did?'

He studied her for a moment and, sensing her courage would fade if she didn't press on, said, 'You were going to tell me what you found?'

'Yes; yes, I was. Well, it was blatantly obvious from the geophys results the third stone wasn't marking a grave. It was made to look like it was, that there was a third member of the family there, but there was something about the stone – it was much smaller and entirely different to the ones behind it – and its wording was... well, it was a bit weird to be honest.'

Rose's curiosity was at its height. What, in this strange world, had been put on a headstone in Chawton churchyard?

'I've dealt with Dan Taylor at *Taylor Transmedia* before when I've worked in America, and I knew he'd just opened up an office in London. So I got in touch – told him I'd like to research a grave that wasn't a grave and a disappearing act from 200 years ago. I thought it was a long shot, to be honest, but he went for it in a big way. Apparently, in addition to the new global emphasis, he's been trying to get his daughter more involved in the company, and he thought it was a good project for her so here I am...'

'Trying to find out what happened to the missing daughter – to Jane Austen.'

'Yes. And...' He stopped. 'Look; tell me what you think of this. It seems to have gone straight over everyone else's head, but not yours, I think.'

Rose bit her lip as Aiden opened the laptop again and coaxed it into life. Her anxiety over what he might be about to show her was warring with her sheer delight at how relaxed he seemed around her;

how at ease *she* felt.

'Here.' He had opened up another photo and Rose edged her chair a little closer to look at it. It was clear that the patch of open grass in front of the graves of Cassandra and Mrs Austen – ones she had visited many a time – now held a smaller, arched stone. It looked at least as old as the others. The photo was replaced by another, a close-up of the wording.

'I can't make it out.'

'No, it's not easy – and therefore easily overlooked. This...' he pointed to the upper words, 'says '*Jane Austen*', and below it is '*Loving and Much Loved Daughter and Sister*'. Nothing odd about that, though there are no dates. This, however,' he lowered his finger down to the base of the stone, 'was what caught my attention and set me off on this trail in the first place. Can you read it?'

Rose peered closely at the screen, slowly mouthing the words at the bottom of the memorial stone. Being nearer the ground and less exposed to the elements, they were just about decipherable. Then she gasped and sat back. 'Oh my!'

'Oh my, indeed.' Aiden closed the laptop and turned to face her.

Rose's voice was a whisper. '*Lost?*. I don't understand – why... how...'

'How did a line from a well-known Tolkien poem end up on a headstone which is over a hundred years older than when the author published *The Lord of the Rings*? Why is it there?' Aiden shrugged. 'Told you I love a good mystery.'

'It must have been put there to commemorate Jane, even though she'd... disappeared. I can't imagine how the family coped. How sad.'

Aiden frowned. 'You're very well-versed in Morgan's research. You must be helping her a great deal.'

Still reeling over the implications of the wording on the stone,

Rose blinked. She hoped her unexplained knowledge wasn't reflecting poorly on her friend. 'Not at all! Morgan's doing all the hard work, but she likes to talk.'

'Doesn't she just.' He grimaced. 'She's a little… unusual.'

'You shouldn't be too harsh on her. She has this wonderful warmth and friendliness, this amazing ability to bring people out, to have them tell her things they never intended.'

Aiden studied her thoughtfully for a moment. Then he smiled briefly. 'You're quite right, and I'm wrong to say otherwise. It's just a little… difficult? Awkward? You know, having the boss's daughter handed to you as your assistant?' Then he shrugged. 'I'm already relying on her to find out as much as she can about the silent family. After all, they're all we have. It's not like we can talk to the missing woman.'

Jane! Rose's hand shot to her throat, and she glanced at her watch: almost eight o'clock. How could she have forgotten about her for so long?

'I – er – do you fancy getting some food?' Aiden waved a hand at the falling dusk. 'It's getting late.'

'Oh, I couldn't. You must get back, it will be so late and your friends will be concerned.' Just like I'm concerned about my… *friend.*

Aiden met her worried gaze steadily. 'I'll text them.'

CHAPTER TWENTY-FOUR

Rose stared at him, mesmerised, desperately wanting to stay, but the moment was broken as her phone began to ring. Sending Aiden an apologetic smile, she glanced at the screen.

'It's Morgan. Shall I...?'

Aiden nodded and got to his feet. 'Go ahead; I'll nab a couple of menus.'

'Hi, Morgan. Are you okay?' She watched the doctor talking to a waiter through the glass windows.

'Sure! Hey, random; I just saw your friend – you know, the slightly odd one, who's staying with you – Jen, is it?'

Rose's skin went cold. 'Oh no! Where was she? Is she okay?'

'She looked great! She was sitting outside *The Pulteney Arms* with a couple other people. Seemed to be enjoying herself!'

A small sound escaped Rose, but Morgan was continuing. 'I've been round the corner at Sydney Place; got loads of photos, so that's cool!'

'This late?' Rose frowned at her watch.

'Apart from the offices on the ground floor, they're all residential – some students as well. No one was home until evening. I'm just going to call Dr T and let him know. Should stop him implying I'm not doing what I should be.'

'Oh, right.' Rose's eyes slid unconsciously towards Aiden who had just retaken his seat.

'What? You sound weird.'

'Sorry, it's just – er – I can hand him the phone if... that would be easier?' Rose met Aiden's questioning eye with a slightly anxious smile.

'You're with Dr T? As in *now*?'

'Hm-mm.' Please don't let her say anything too –

'Oh my! Did he ask you on a *date*? Am I interrupting – did he try to kiss you yet?'

Pink in the face, Rose couldn't look at the doctor. 'Morgan! I'm passing you over now.'

Aiden's conversation with Morgan was brief, but long enough for Rose to start panicking. What was Jane doing outside a pub, albeit a friendly, neighbourhood one? How could she have forgotten her – totally? And what of the valuable volumes she had handed to her? Did she leave them in the library, as she'd asked her to? What if they were just sitting out on a table and not returned to the store and Anne saw them before she could do anything about it...?

'Here.' Aiden handed back her phone, and she tried hard not to notice his fingers brushing hers as he did so. He didn't seem to notice, turning to study the menu card, but Rose was getting to her feet.

Aiden looked up, and she turned to grab her jacket from the chair back, unable to meet his eye.

'I'm so sorry, Dr... Aiden. There's something... just come up. I have to go.'

For the briefest moment, he looked completely taken aback; then he assumed a blank expression reminiscent of when he'd seemed to stare right through her at the costumed promenade, and regret flooded through her.

'That's fine.' He shrugged and drained his glass before getting to his feet.

Was it possible he was disappointed? Outlandish though the idea was to Rose, she couldn't leave without making sure he knew she didn't want to go, but no words came. Before she could think about it, Rose took a step forward and quickly kissed him on the cheek. His gaze flew to hers as she stepped back, and she smiled tentatively.

'I'm really sorry.' She turned away but he stayed her with his hand.

'Tell me it's not me, and I'll catch my train hungry but content.'

Rose drew in a shallow breath, then shook her head. 'No, it's not you. I've had... it's been... brilliant. It's just a – problem I need to sort.' With that, she left; if he'd tried to persuade her to stay, she might just have thrown caution to the wind and left Jane to fend for herself a little longer.

The weather had turned when Rose got up the next day, all hint of the late summer sunshine washed away by a steady downpour, but she couldn't bring herself to care very much. The pleasure of her evening with Aiden was still filling her up. She was certain her pulse hadn't yet calmed down – not simply because of how wonderful it had been to spend time with him, but because of all they'd spoken about.

One side of her relished every moment of the evening: their conversation, his opening up about his interests, the clear indication he was disappointed she had to leave, but the other was in turmoil, tormented by what Aiden had said about the grave that wasn't a grave in Chawton. If there was truly nothing there, merely a headstone of remembrance, it meant Jane had never been able to return. Her works *were* lost to the world. Now it was evident why only two of the three crosses remained; Jane's was clearly never seen again.

As she had lain awake during the early hours dwelling on both the precious moments and the horrid finality of the situation, she had been gripped by a sudden urge to talk to Aiden, to tell him about Jane, about life as it had been, about… *everything*. She'd always known him to have an intelligent mind, but now she understood his mind was open to all sorts of things, including a long-held love of fantasy and of the inexplicable. But Rose shied away from the thought. Much as she wished it, she didn't know him well enough to take such a risk; sadly, it was a risk she didn't dare take with Morgan either.

The recollection of how precarious her reacquaintance with Morgan was sobered Rose somewhat as she got ready for yet another day at the library, and with a sigh she threw her reflection one last glance, grabbed her bag and walked out onto the landing, only to come face-to-face with Jane, who had likewise just emerged from her room.

'Good morning.' Jane inclined her head gracefully, and Rose smiled at her. At least she had managed to curb her instinctive urge to curtsey.

'Morning. Did you sleep okay?' Jane had been full of tales when Rose finally got home and found her in the conservatory reading by candlelight. She had clearly enjoyed her evening meeting people outside *The Pulteney Arms* after being deserted at the library. This remembrance, however, was sufficient to trouble Rose. 'Do you have the books with you? I really need to try and replace them before it's noticed they are missing.'

Jane raised her hand, in which she was clutching the first two volumes of *The Romance of the Forest*. 'Forgive me for taking them; I would not wish to bring trouble upon you, but I longed for the simplicity of words with which I am more familiar.'

They turned to make their way downstairs, and Rose was reminded of the unusual wording in the photo Aiden had shown her. She mulled it over as she quickly made some toast for them both, but Jane looked miles away as she munched, and uncertain whether or not it was wise, Rose decided to share with her what Aiden had shown her.

There was silence for a moment, then Jane sighed. 'Then 'tis final, is it not? I will own to some regret. 'Twas all a vast adventure; yet I find I begin to miss my daily correspondence with Cass. How little we value the minutiae of life until we have it no longer.'

'I'm so sorry, Jane.' Rose felt helpless to know what else to say. They were both trapped, and she just couldn't see how they would ever be able to overcome it. 'So – you did write to your sister about Tolkien's works? I know you said you couldn't send any books back to her that were more recent than 1803.'

'I did. My sister is fond of poetry, and I often sent her extracts of poems I enjoyed.'

Wishing she could tell Aiden, so he could fit another piece into his mystery puzzle, Rose glanced at the clock. It was time to go to work.

'Here, let me put the books in my bag so the rain doesn't damage them.'

Jane handed them over willingly. 'I have no further use for them; I finished the second volume again in my bed last night.' Then she sighed. 'It is most vexing the third volume is not available.'

'If you come into the library later, I may be able to find out if we have a copy in one of our other libraries. My colleague said the actual volume was not fit for production – that means we can't let it be handled.' Rose frowned, thinking of the rows and rows of drawers housing microfilm. 'I wonder if it's on some other media…' Then she smiled at Jane. 'But if not, we'll just have to order a modern reprint, though that will take a day or so to come, so there'll be a wait.'

Jane smiled in return. 'One does not truly *wait* for aught in this life, least not as one does in the other.' She looked happily out of the kitchen window. 'The rain is a pleasant change, is it not? I shall walk into town with you.'

Rose laughed as she put their plates in the dishwasher and reached for her coat. 'I think you'd find very few people who'd agree with you on that.'

They walked out under a large umbrella to the bus stop, but Jane kept putting her arm out so that the rain splattered her bare fingers.

''Tis most invigorating! It is so… fresh.' She glanced at Rose and smiled. 'Whence I came, rain draws vapour from the city rooftops, mingling with smoke from the numerous chimneys.' She looked up at the rooftops now, glistening with shiny wetness. 'No. I like this rain very well; and…' She inspected her fingers, glistening with raindrops. 'I am become accustomed to forgoing my gloves.'

Rose sighed as they reached the bus stop as words from *Persuasion* drifted through her mind, words that were lost now, of arriving in Bath in the rain: *'the first dim view of the extensive buildings, smoking in rain'*, and Lady Russell's reflection on the ceaseless clink of pattens – though, to be fair, she had found this a pleasure rather than a pain.

CHAPTER TWENTY-FIVE

Once they arrived at the library, Jane insisted Rose keep the umbrella and wandered off along Green Street, and Rose turned and headed for the back of the building and the staff entrance, appreciating the reprieve from having Jane there at the start of her day. Things may have become a little easier as the week progressed, but she was still far from firing on all cylinders, and Barbara wasn't the only member of staff still keeping a cautious eye on her.

This 'surveillance' did make it difficult to do anything out of the ordinary and, knowing she needed someone – and most likely Anne's – help to replace the books and find out if the rest of the story existed in some form or other, Rose decided being as close to truthful as possible was the best policy.

Anne had been displeased, obviously, when Rose admitted she had 'forgotten' to ensure the valuable old volumes were returned to the store the previous evening, but because they were both clearly safe and in the same condition as when they had been retrieved, she took them from Rose and let it go with a reminder to be a little more careful in future.

'I know you said the final volume of the story was very fragile? The customer who wanted to read it is really disappointed not to be able to finish it. Are there any other ways of finding a copy? Like those early copies of the Bath Directory? Or can a copy be ordered from another branch or could I order one online?'

Glancing at her watch, Anne nodded. 'All possibilities. I can have a look through the card catalogue, but it will have to be later. I have a local journalist coming in at ten to do some research and that will probably take me a few hours.' Then she pointed over to the *Study Area* at the back of the library. 'In the meantime, you could try the microfilm archive.'

'Okay, thanks.' Rose's spirits lifted; keeping Jane; amused meant one less thing to worry about at the moment. Finding an elusive volume of a more than 200-year-old book might be a bit like looking for a needle in a haystack, but at least she could give it a go.

About an hour later, Jane finally appeared in the library.

'Do you not admire my new shawl?'

'Did you need one?'

'Not at all; and indeed, I cannot take credit for finding it. The rains became heavier, and I took shelter in the nearest establishment and lo, there it found *me*.'

'Well, it must be our lucky day for finding things.'

Jane smiled, her eyes sparkling, as she took off her – or rather, one of Rose's – wet coat. 'You have a copy for me.'

'In a manner of speaking, yes.' Rose steered Jane over to the *Study Area* and sat her down at one of the microfilm readers. For a moment, Jane stared at the contraption in front of her, and Rose couldn't really blame her. Despite the digital screens, they were rather cumbersome in appearance and had various dials and knobs.

Although fairly straightforward to operate – the film was fed into the reader pretty much the same as old cine film would be into a projector – even that technology was beyond Jane's experience, so it was a while later before Rose was able to leave her to settle down to read the opening chapter of the longed-for third volume.

She had barely turned away, however, when Morgan appeared.

'Isn't the weather great?' Morgan beamed at Rose and then at Jane who had swivelled in her seat to look at her.

'Then we share a common trait, Miss Taylor.'

Morgan's smile widened. 'Call me Morgan. I just love the rain here.'

'Is it polluted whence you came also?'

Rose and Morgan exchanged a quick glance, and the latter laughed. 'I suppose it is, but I don't care. We rarely get rain; I love the smell of it.'

Jane smirked at Rose before turning back to the screen. 'Something in common indeed!'

Dropping her bag on the floor, Morgan sat down at the machine next to Jane's.

'Well, just one more thing to check and I think I'm nearly ready to do a draft of the article to put before Dr Grumpy!' Rose walked round to the other side of Morgan and took a seat. 'I spoke to him this morning.' She frowned. 'I'm having trouble persuading the Doc we have all the data there is and that this is as far as the story goes.'

Recalling Aiden's deep interest in his findings in Hampshire, Rose doubted he felt quite so ready to prepare his paper yet, but as Morgan switched on the machine next to Jane's and opened her notebook, she knew there wasn't anything she could say about that.

Part of her felt the only thing keeping her sane was still having Morgan to hold onto, and Rose still clung to her past reality as the *real* one, despite everything pointing to it being permanently out of reach.

'What? Why are you staring at me? Do I have something on my face?' Morgan looked over from the screen she was now squinting at.

Rose shook her head, dispelling her gloomy thoughts. 'You know, I think you might actually need glasses.'

'This is a vile thing to do to the written word.' They both looked over at Jane who was also squinting closely at her screen.

Morgan raised her brows and leaned over, and Jane muttered, 'I believe there is a creature in this machine, one that bites me if I apply even the slightest more pressure on this knob than it thinks I should.'

Reaching for the controls on Jane's machine, Morgan smiled. 'Has it got away from you? It's so easy to do; I used to do it all the time. Here, do you remember what page you were on?'

'I have barely begun; I am just on the opening chapter.' Jane looked over her head at Rose. 'Is there no alternative than using this unforgiving contraption?'

Rose shook her head apologetically. 'I'm sorry, I'm told the volume is simply too fragile. I know it's frustrating but, other than waiting for an online copy to be delivered –'

'Is this it?' Morgan pointed at the screen, and Jane turned to peer intently at it.

'I thank you; it is.' Jane gave her usual gracious inclination of her head.

A silence then settled over them for a while, with occasional mutterings from Jane, the scrawling of Morgan's pen as she took more notes from the screen in front of her and the quiet sorting of books by Rose, who had brought one of the shelving trolleys over so that she could be on hand whilst still being seen to be doing some work.

'So... Ginger?' Rose glanced up; Morgan had spoken quietly and was still staring at the wide rectangular screen. 'How long was your date with Dr T last night?'

Rose's lips twitched. 'Not very long, and it wasn't a date!'

'Did he ask you to take a look at his bone collection?' Morgan's lips curved up in a wicked smile. 'Or maybe offer to take you on a walk in a nice, dark graveyard? You could have a dainty faint and be in his arms in no time.'

'You're being ridiculous.' Rose shook her head, but Morgan had hit close to home with the remark about the graveyard. Glancing at Jane, she bit her lip – she had seemed so alive, so... resolved to her situation and, in fact, almost relishing it at first. Had she done the wrong thing in telling Jane about the memorial stone in Chawton? Was she dwelling on how long Cassandra lived without her? How long her beloved sister suffered?

A sudden bleep caused Rose to start, and she dropped the book she was holding. Morgan fished out her mobile and then looked questioningly at Rose as she picked the book up from the floor. 'Hey – if I were trying to get to Italy, which airport would I be best to fly out of?'

Rose felt her stomach sink. 'Heathrow, most likely. Are you – are you going to Italy, then?'

Morgan was busy texting on her phone, but she nodded. 'Yeah, just as soon as Dr Grumpy is done with my services. I'm joining my brother in Rome. He was wandering Europe for the summer and has deigned to meet up with his big sis.'

'That's... exciting.' Rose tried to smile, but disappointment was rising within her. *What did you expect? She is here for a specific reason so why would she hang around? She's not here to see you, to have a holiday or any of the things that brought her here in the old world.*

'It's *not* the old world, it's the real one.'

Both Jane and Morgan turned to look at Rose. Had she said it out loud?

'Sorry.' She waved a book and hastily stacked it on the trolley. 'Just a quote from a book.' She could feel colour invading her cheeks at Jane's knowing look.

Morgan sent another text before putting her phone away and

turning back to her screen, and Jane did the same, only to exclaim seconds later. 'This infernal machine has returned me to the beginning yet again.'

'Do you want me to find your place?' Morgan looked up from her notebook, but Jane waved her away.

'Please do not trouble yourself; I am in no humour for this box and *it*,' she jabbed a finger at the screen, which, being a touch screen, immediately zoomed in on the page before her. 'Is clearly in no humour for *me*.'

Morgan grinned up at Rose before extracting a pencil from behind her ear and scribbling some words into her book.

'Soooo.' Rose tried to sound as casual as possible. 'How long do you think that might be – until you leave for Rome?'

Morgan looked up again. 'Oh, I think I have a couple days yet.' She gave Rose a knowing look. 'Plenty of time for another dinner – unless you're planning on cosying up in a nice crypt with the Doc anytime soon.'

Rose tried to laugh, but panic gripped her throat, and it came out rather strangled. Thankfully, Morgan didn't seem to notice.

The hint at seeing Aiden again was alluring, but Rose wasn't blind to it all being a pipe dream. She hadn't forgotten how invisible she actually was to him in the real world, but the thought of Morgan leaving Bath tore her apart. She and Jane were the only things she had left to hold onto, the only things in this strange life which resonated, meant something to her, right now. She swallowed hard and blinked away the sensation of tears rising.

She was about to give herself a stern talking-to when she happened to notice Jane's face. 'Jenny? Are you okay?'

Jane was staring fixedly at the screen before her, unblinking, a hand to her throat, and, concerned, Rose walked round to her side and crouched down.

'What is it? Are you feeling ill?' *Please don't be ill*, her heart begged. *I can't cope with the responsibility of an ailing Jane Austen on my hands just now.*

Shaking her head, Jane pointed towards the screen, and Rose turned to look at it. The machine had skipped back to an image of the frontispiece of the book, which bore little more than the title and the note of it being a work of three volumes, this being the third. She frowned, and glanced back at Jane, who whispered, 'Take heed... below the title.'

Rose leaned closer; the text itself was faded, but in its enlarged form, there seemed to be some words pencilled below it.

'What is it? What does it say?'

Jane shook her head. 'I cannot decipher sufficient of the lettering to be certain, other than of one thing. My sister wrote this; whatever these words are, they came from her.'

CHAPTER TWENTY-SIX

Rose spared a glance at Morgan who could surely hear them. 'What do you mean?' she whispered.

Touching the screen warily this time, Jane stared at it as the page magnified again, then turned to Rose. 'This is Cass's hand; I would know it anywhere.'

Rose blinked and stared at the words. Very little survived of Cassandra Austen's letters, so the writing style meant nothing to her and the words were almost illegible, the ink so faded and the transition to microfilm not helping either. 'Does that say something about 'the end'?' She frowned – so it was the final volume; of course it was, and even if Jane was right – and she wasn't entirely certain Cassandra Austen was prone to defacing library books – what difference did it make?

Jane shook her head. ''Tis not certain.' She was peering very closely at the screen now and probably in serious danger of damaging those fine hazel eyes if she wasn't careful.

'You guys okay?' Morgan spoke quietly on the other side of Jane.

Rose nodded, wanting to discourage Morgan from asking any more questions just now. 'Yes, fine. Just looks like someone has scribbled in the front of the book, nothing more.'

'Nice to know graffiti was all the rage even then.' Morgan laughed and started to straighten her papers.

Slowly, Jane sat back in her seat and drew in a shaky breath. 'I – I told you, did I not, this was the book I was reading the last time I left. I collected it from the circulating library earlier that day; Cassandra must have hoped I would seek it out.'

'You think this–' Rose waved a hand at the screen, 'is the actual copy? That it's a *message* from her?' She could sense Morgan's interest was with them, even though she appeared to be engrossed in packing up her bag, and lowered her voice even further. 'Can you read any of it?'

Jane shook her head. 'I shall endeavour to make it out; I make no guarantees.'

Morgan stirred, and Rose glanced at her as she got to her feet and swung her bag over her shoulder. 'Well, I think I'd better get going. Rose – call if you want to meet later.'

'Wait, I'll walk with you.' Rose glanced back at Jane as they walked towards the library entrance, but she was still peering intently at the screen in front of her.

'Is everything okay?' Morgan stopped as they reached the doorway and inclined her head back towards the *Study Area*. 'Your funny friend – she seems a little wound-up today.'

'She's fine – I think.' Rose shrugged. 'Look, is there any chance you are free tonight? If you're leaving Bath so soon, I don't know when I'll see you again.' It was an effort not to sound too needy, but Morgan didn't seem to notice.

'Sure! I'm just off to take a few more photos at number 4 – indoors, thankfully – but I'm free tonight. Should we do dinner again? Last time was fun!'

Feeling she'd been granted a reprieve, Rose nodded quickly. 'Perfect. How about–'

'Rose Wallace! There you are!'

A dark-haired young woman came hurrying into the library to join them, a wide smile on her face. It was Liz – or was it Lottie? Thankfully, she at least looked exactly as she normally did, and Rose smiled at her, but in response she got a finger wagged in her face.

'What's going on with you? I must've tried calling you a *dozen* times this week and it just keeps going to voicemail.' She turned to Morgan and smiled. 'Rose is useless, always letting her phone battery die.'

'I'm sorry,' Rose was so grateful for the sight of another familiar face, but despite that she felt on very uneven ground. 'This is my friend, Morgan, from the US.' *Please, please, please introduce yourself so I don't have to get Liz's name wrong.*

Liz held out her hand and Morgan shook it. 'Lovely to meet you. I'm Lottie.' She grinned at Rose. 'We went to college together a few years ago and then kept going with some evening classes.' She laughed. 'Some were not quite as successful as others.'

'Awesome! What did you study?' Morgan was immediately interested in this new acquaintance, but Rose was already wondering what might be coming. The only class they'd started together was an English Literature one, at Rose's persuasion, and Liz had left within weeks, trying her hand at a language course before giving up on it, saying it wasn't the same without Rose there.

'Oh all sorts. Rose here was a dab hand at most things, but I just can't apply myself.' This was sufficient encouragement for Morgan, however, who soon had engaged Liz in conversation, with Rose trying hard to keep up and see what else may have changed other than her friend's name.

'Forgive my intrusion.'

Rose turned around to find Jane at her side. Her colour had returned to normal, but her expression remained serious. 'May we speak?'

Concerned, Rose glanced at Morgan and Liz who were chatting away happily. 'Yes – of course. What is it?'

'It is imperative I see the book in its original form. Cass's words were meant for me, I am certain.'

'But it's just a line. What can one line tell you?'

'I know not; yet I have a longing to see my sister's hand. Pray, indulge me in this, Rose?'

Jane looked as serious as Rose had ever seen her and, although she had no idea what it would achieve, she nodded. 'Okay; let me just say goodbye.'

Interrupting Morgan in full flow wasn't easy, but once her friend had noticed Jane, she saved Rose the trouble of introducing her as well by doing it herself, before starting to question Liz further about her job as a junior solicitor.

Liz, however, was as adept at extricating herself from situations as Morgan was at gaining information from people, and she smiled apologetically at Morgan. 'You'll have to excuse me; I only popped in to check with Rose that everything's all okay for Sunday. It is, isn't it, Rose?'

Rose blinked. What was happening on Sunday, for Heaven's sake? Liz was looking at her expectantly, however, and she suddenly recalled the engagement party invitation sitting on her mantelpiece in her flat. Heaven alone knew what she'd done with it at her mother's house. 'Of course.'

'We're so looking forward to seeing the cake.'

Rose's relief wavered as Jane said, 'Pray, what cake might this be?'

'It's for our engagement.' Liz waved a hand bearing a sparkling ring in front of them. 'Rose makes the most amazing cakes. Really beautiful, and I told Tina we had to have one for our party.'

If Rose's mind hadn't gone into overdrive at the idea of making a cake when she couldn't bake, she might have been amused by the look on

Jane's face. She summoned a smile, however, as Liz turned to walk away.

'See you Sunday, Rose. Oh, and don't forget the wording we agreed!' With a wave of her hand, Liz was gone, and Rose put a hand to her head. Could things really get any more complicated?

*

CHAPTER TWENTY-SEVEN

There was a constant bustle of people in the library after lunch, with a children's reading hour, a well-attended local history display in the exhibition room and a student group working on their coursework. As soon as a suitable moment arose, Rose and Jane slipped through the door leading to the lower floor unnoticed by any of the other staff.

Her legs feeling weak, partly through anxiety over taking someone into a domain she probably shouldn't have access to, but also over Jane's potential disappointment, Rose quickly ushered her down to the lower hallway and then stared at the row of doors. The book hadn't been on the electronic system, and Mary had had to show Rose how to use the card catalogue to identify its specific location, but which door led to it?

Jane was looking up and down the windowless corridor, her face alive with interest. 'It would be preferable to work down here, would it not? I find the light more to my liking.'

Rose blinked. How could Jane be so easily distracted from their purpose?

The sound of a door slamming somewhere out of sight made them both start, however, and Rose grasped the first door handle, whispering over her shoulder, 'It should be – just in here I think.'

The room was a stationery cupboard, and they both backed out quickly.

'Okay, perhaps not.' Rose turned around, trying to remember the day she'd come down with the plan to try and familiarise herself with things. 'Here, let's try this one.'

With relief, the second door – labelled unhelpfully *'Bookstack 2'* – led into the local store and, using the identification markers on the floor-to-ceiling shelves, Rose quickly located Bay 11.

'It should be in here.' She grasped the lever and turned it several times so the shelving unit parted, closing the first row in the process as the shelves of books by local authors slowly revealed themselves.

Stepping forward, Rose glanced at the reference number she had written on the back of her hand, but before she could move further, a hand gripped her arm. 'Good heavens!' Jane was staring wide-eyed at the vast metal shelving unit. 'Is it safe? Is one not at risk of crushing?'

Rose shrugged. 'Hopefully not. It's a manually operated rolling system, see?' She pointed to the lever. 'And we are the only ones down here. Besides, what else are we to do?'

Jane released her arm, but followed her along the row rather warily, constantly looking back towards the room beyond their confined space.

'Okay, it should be here somewhere.' Rose scanned the shelves. The books were of all shapes, sizes and styles, and many were of much more recent publication than the volume they sought. She crouched down and scanned the lower shelves to no avail, but as she straightened, she caught sight of something of interest. 'Here! These are really old. Look.'

Rose pointed to the name written on the shelf, above which were several very old-looking spines. *'Radcliffe, Ann.* Now, which is the right one?' She ran a finger along and soon found the volumes of *The Romance of the Forest* she had returned to Anne earlier. Next to it, and noticeably in a far more delicate condition, was the final volume, and Rose eased it carefully from the shelf and opened it, her insides swirling with guilt.

Jane peered over her shoulder. 'Look, see?' Pointing to the red mark in the top corner of the front cover, Jane nodded. 'This is, to be certain, a lending copy. That is the shelf mark.'

The book was in very poor condition, unlike the other volumes, and had an even more musty smell. The pages looked very tattered and browned, and Rose turned to look at Jane who stepped beside her and nodded.

Reverently, she turned the first page and there, in a neat and precise hand, were the words they had seen on the microfilm, only this time, though badly faded, they could just about be made out.

Oft, the end befits the beginning. CEA

Rose looked at Jane. 'What does that mean?'

Jane said nothing as she reached out and traced the faded words, her finger lingering over the final letters. 'Cass would oft read the conclusion of a book 'ere she began. Did I not tell you? 'Twas a most singular habit, and we fought most amicably about it.'

'Okay, but why would she write these words *here*?'

'Before all was altered, she may have desired to send it to me? It is in her nature to remind me of our quarrels.' Jane held out her hand for the book, and Rose closed it and passed it to her.

Jane stared at it for a moment, stroking the battered cover. Then she opened it up, and read the words again, before flicking through the pages to the back of the book, where she studied the closing lines of the story. 'I felt obliged to read the end, in case there was aught here for me. How Cass would have laughed at such an outcome.'

Rose frowned. A line from Cassandra Austen sent in teasing to her sister hardly helped them. 'What do you mean, aught – what did you expect?'

Jane shook her head. 'I know not; perchance more of her hand, but to what purpose? Those words were likely penned before the moment the portal closed.' Then she smiled ruefully at Rose. 'I know not for what I hoped.'

'But surely Cass... I mean, your sister, could hardly write much in a library book and expect it to go unnoticed for two centuries!'

With a delicate shrug of her shoulders, Jane closed the book. 'Lending copies were oft liberally covered with annotations, even illustrations by some industrious hand.'

Taking the book from Jane, Rose opened it carefully again, reading the faint lines under the title and then easing open the backboard, which clung tentatively to the spine. Then she frowned.

'Why is there a bookplate in a library book? It doesn't make any sense.'

'If in all of this you seek sense, Rose, I fear you are destined for disappointment.'

'Okay, but why is it on the back cover? Weren't they usually stuck inside the front?' Rose angled the book to catch the best of the light, which was limited inside the shelving unit. 'There are some letters on it, too. There.' She pointed to the faint markings.

'Plates profess ownership – one owns the front and back as much as one owns the pages within.' Jane took the book from Rose and glanced at the worn bookplate, which was coming loose on one side. 'Though 'tis rare in a lending copy.' She went to close it, but then gave a small gasp.

'This lettering you mention... it is Cassandra's mark; of that I am certain, though 'tis sadly distorted. Look.' Jane pointed to the faded letters. 'These are her initials.' She flicked to the front of the book where '*CEA*' followed the wording, and then to the back cover, and Rose stared at it. Was it wishful thinking that the lettering she thought she'd seen were those actual letters?

Jane, in the meantime, was running a hand over the book, examining the spine and then returning to the back where she touched the frayed edge where the bookplate had been attached.

'There is something concealed beneath.'

A shiver passed through Rose as some of Jane's palpable excitement reached her. Could she be right, or was she just indulging in a ridiculous hope? 'What – I mean, how can – how can it?'

'Do not undervalue my sister, Rose. Cass is… *was* a resourceful and able woman.'

Jane returned her attention to the back of the book. In its damaged state, the edge of the bookplate was already worn thin in places, and Rose held her breath as Jane pulled at it, expecting an alarm – moral if not actual – to go off at any moment at such sacrilege, but nothing happened.

With the paper so frail, it did not take long for Jane to peel back enough of it to reveal a small piece of folded parchment, pressed entirely flat by two hundred years of constraint. Rose swallowed hard and whispered, 'Take it, Jane. It must be for you.'

'Long had I foregone all hopes of a letter from my sister; perchance there is some intelligence of home.' Jane, her hands clearly trembling, carefully extracted the paper just as the door to the archive room opened.

Rose quickly closed the book and tucked it back onto the shelf before hurrying to the end of the row to peer out and see who was there.

'Rose!'

'Barbara!' Rose's voice came out as a squeak as she grasped for words – any words that might help. 'You gave me a start!'

'What are you doing down here?' Barbara frowned as Jane emerged from the shelving row to stand beside her, one hand tucked into her pocket. 'And who is this? Rose, you know we do not allow the public down here.'

'Er… yes, I was just remembering that and saying to… to this customer.' She gestured towards Jane. 'We'd better get back up to the main floor and talk to you first.'

'Yes, well – good.' Barbara smiled kindly at them both, waiting for something, and Rose raised a brow in question.

'What was it that you needed that required permission to come down here with this lady?'

'Oh!' Rose forced a laugh. 'Yes; sorry. Well, Miss Ashton here, she specialises in antiques, so she's interested in the restoration of old books.'

Barbara frowned. 'Well, our priority of course is preservation, but with the right grants and resources that's certainly a possibility. In fact, it's a passion of mine. Is it something you're also interested in, Rose?'

Rose's guilt over their recent abuse of a valuable book came out as a very convincing, 'Yes, very much! Especially works from the early 19th century.'

Barbara's smile widened. 'That's nice to know. But next time, you really must get permission to access anything in this area, Rose.'

'Absolutely.'

They all three stood around nodding at each other for a moment, until Jane nudged Rose in the back with her elbow. 'Forgive me for taking up so much of your time, Rose. Shall we remove to the upper floor?'

'Yes, of course!' Rose turned to Barbara. 'Thank you so much for understanding. It won't happen again.'

Rose and Jane edged their way past Barbara and out into the corridor, closing the door behind them and then, in silent agreement, walking rapidly back to the stairs and the anonymity of the busy main library floor.

CHAPTER TWENTY-EIGHT

Looking no less guilty as they emerged into the room than they had earlier on leaving it, Rose led Jane to a nearby table, then turned on her heel only to be stopped by Jane's hand on her arm.

'Where are you going?' she hissed. 'You cannot leave me – not now.'

Rose shook her head. 'I'm not; I'm just going to the cookery section. You forget I have a gourmet cake to bake by Sunday!'

Jane glanced around. There was no one near them, and she patted her pocket. 'Are you not intrigued? Do you not wish to comprehend what we have found and whether it is indeed from Cass?'

Rose tried to push away the memory of first reading *Northanger Abbey* and Catherine Morland's late-night find of crumpled parchment in a hidden drawer in the imposing chest in her chamber.

'More than anything, but we look suspicious enough as it is. I'm going to pretend I'm actually doing my job for a few minutes and let you read it. Then,' Rose drew in a shallow breath, trying to keep her hopes in perspective. 'I'm going to come back and see what it is we've found. I only hope it isn't just an old laundry list!'

Jane blinked, then smiled widely. 'Your recollection is admirable.'

Rose's intended ten minutes of activity in full view of other members of staff had stretched to twenty by the time she returned to Jane, due to having to find a specific book for a customer. Though the break may have done enough for her reputation in the library, however, it had done little to calm her nervous anticipation. What had they found? Was it of any value, a letter deliberately left by Cassandra for Jane, in the hope it would reach her across time, or was it merely a scrap of paper with no connection to the Austen family?

With some trepidation, Rose rounded the corner of the cabinets screening Jane from view, only to find her staring into the distance, looking pale but clearly suppressing some emotion, the yellowed piece of folded paper on the table in front of her. As she took the chair opposite, however, Jane turned to look at her and, understanding Rose's silent request for permission, slid the paper across the table to her.

Unfolding it carefully, it was clear it wasn't a letter, but a poem, and she glanced quickly up at Jane who merely nodded encouragingly. Rose's lips moved as she slowly mouthed the words to herself – words that, though faded, were still perfectly decipherable, despite the old-fashioned lettering.

> In hopes of you, ere long I tarried;
> Instead there came a hound.
> But then I saw that which it carried;
> The charm, it has been found.

~ ~ ~

> Without it, you are lost to me;
> A way back here you lack.
> I laid it in its usual place;
> Behind the door so black.

~ ~ ~

To keep it safe, one must conceal;
Thus only you can it reveal.
And so, I leave, for you to find;
This rhyme our lives to re-entwine.

Rose had never been any good at working out puzzles and conundrums, but something about it excited her, and she passed it back to Jane. Some more colour had returned to her cheeks, and she was leaning earnestly across the table, her bright eyes fixed on Rose.

'Can you not see?' She pointed at the opening lines. 'Prancer! How it could be, I know not; yet Cass *must* have seen him appear in the street, for how else might she comprehend?'

Rose spared a momentary thought for the elderly lady who had lost her pet. She wasn't sure if Jane's theory was sound or not, but it was no time to debate the finer detail. Something was stirring in her insides, and it felt very much like hope.

'So why hasn't your sister come here, brought it back to you?'

'My brother claimed it would only perform its magic for me – or when passing from my hand to another.'

'So she laid it in its 'usual place' – the safe?'

'It draws the most perfect sense, does it not, for her to return it to the portal through which we exchanged all things?'

'Perfect sense indeed,' whispered Rose faintly, wondering if she could somehow repress the hope suddenly rising in her heart as her pulse began to race. 'It's what we've been hoping for – it's the impossible made possible!' Rose stared blankly at the letter. 'But what do we do now? How can we get the necklace back?'

Jane looked wistful for a moment. 'You cannot be of the illusion

— surely, you cannot believe it remains these many years on? The world… the landscape… all is vastly altered; progress is all-consuming and stone neighbourhoods have issued forth from the meadows I once walked. Naught of the past remains truly as it was.'

'I know it won't be that straightforward. Before being a holiday apartment, the ground floor of 4 Sydney Place was – *is* – an office. We can hardly just walk in off the street and demand they open the safe for us, but–'

'We must endeavour to be content, Rose.' Jane placed a gentle hand on Cassandra's poem. 'Through Cass's efforts, we are able to comprehend much we were left to speculate upon. With this we must be satisfied.' She picked the piece of aged parchment up and folded it reverently.

Rose sighed, her tentative hopes all but faded. 'But that doesn't mean we can't try, does it?' She chewed her lip; Jane was eyeing her warily. Then her eyes lit up. 'Morgan!'

'Your American.'

'Yes! She'll have made best friends with everyone there when she visited. Perhaps she could check for us? But I don't see how that solves things; I mean.' Rose ran a distracted hand through her hair. 'Supposing by some miracle the necklace is there? How can she justify taking it?'

Jane raised a brow. 'If the necklace remains where it was first concealed, then the door will not have yielded.'

'What do you mean?'

'Part of the charm's protection; in the future, only my hand may access the safe, should the contents sealed within be destined for me.'

'Sooo – if we can just, somehow, get you in there with her, to open it? She can convince them we're part of a club – *The American*

Fascination with Old English Iron Ware club?' It all sounded totally ludicrous, but if anyone could pull it off, it was Morgan.

Jane eyed Rose thoughtfully for a moment. 'I am not well acquainted with... Morgan, as well you know.'

'No – of course.' Rose nodded, understanding. 'This is something I have to sort out.' Then she brightened. 'Well, we are having dinner tonight, so I'll try and find a way of saying... something.'

CHAPTER TWENTY-NINE

They were quickly seated in *Las Iguanas*, Morgan's choice of restaurant as she was missing Mexican food, but although Rose held the menu card in front of her, she saw none of the words. Her intention of somehow convincing Morgan to approach an almost stranger and basically ask if a friend of a friend could look inside his safe fell at every attempt to put it into words. How could she ask such a thing without any explanation at all? She sighed softly as her normally sensible self fought with the familiar voice in her head, urging her this time to take a leap of faith in her friend.

But I don't know how to begin, she whispered under her breath.

'Sorry?' Morgan's bright smile appeared over the top of her menu card. 'Did you say something?'

'No – sorry, no. Just reading out loud.'

By the time Rose was halfway through her starter, however, she realised she didn't have the energy to pretend to have an appetite anymore. Morgan had made a valiant effort to keep their conversation up despite Rose's quietness, but even she had now fallen silent. Then, before she could stop herself, Rose put her fork down and blurted out, 'Can I tell you something?'

Morgan raised her brows. 'Of course.'

'It's going to sound ridiculous.'

'No – I'm sure–'

'It's going to sound ridiculous because... it *is*. Completely ludicrous.'

Morgan's lips twitched. 'Try me; I'm from California, remember?'

Rose dropped her napkin in her lap and shifted so she sat straighter in her chair. 'This woman you're investigating?'

'Yes...'

'I know her.'

'Wow, really?' Morgan leaned forward eagerly. 'Did you hear about the legend in school, then?'

'Yes – I mean, no.' Rose huffed, annoyed with herself. 'I mean I *know* her.' She took a sip from her wine glass, trying not to see the frown forming on Morgan's brow.

'Is this one of those moments when I don't understand you because you're British?'

Rose laughed shortly. 'If only.' Then she sighed; in for a penny, in for a pound. 'Okay. This woman whose disappearance you're researching was a brilliant writer. She wrote six books, all of which are world-famous and one is often voted the nation's favourite novel of all time. It's called *Pride & Prejudice*.'

'Well, Jeez, this is going to be really embarrassing to admit, then – I've never heard of it.'

'That's because she disappeared before she could write them.'

'I'm confused.'

Rose sighed. 'I told you; it's ridiculous.'

Morgan blinked her large eyes and put her hands in her lap. 'Well. It *is* certainly feeling a little crazy. How do you – I mean, okay, yeah that's the question I'll start with – how do you know about the books if they've never been written?'

'It's all to do with Jenny.'

'Well, she's definitely a bit odd, so I can see she might fit into something you think is ridiculous, but never mind her for now – can we go back to the lost lady? You said–'

'She isn't Jenny Ashton. Her name is Jane Austen.'

'But that's the name of the missing woman!' Morgan looked excited. 'Why didn't you tell me?' Then she frowned. 'Hey, did the Doc put you on to this? Is he not happy with my work and now he wants you and – whatever her name is – to get involved?

'No! Not at all.' Rose shook her head. 'I'm just telling you her real name: Jane Austen.'

Morgan looked a little sceptical and leaned back in her seat. 'Is she a relative of the family? Does she know things about it? Wow!' Leaning forward again, Morgan grinned. 'Hey, this could make the article even better.'

Rose nodded. 'Yes, she knows all about it. You see, Morgan, she *is* the lady who vanished into thin air over 200 years ago. She was in possession of a necklace that allowed her to travel back and forth in time and –'

With a laugh, Morgan took a sip of her drink. 'Okay – a necklace? So no TARDIS, then? How does she fit inside?'

'Yes – just a necklace. But – you see, everything's changed because she lost that necklace four days ago. Now she can't get back to 1803, but as her first novel wasn't released until 1811, none of her books were ever published – do you see?' Rose looked anxiously over at Morgan, but when her friend didn't respond, she continued quickly. 'And my world has completely changed, because I was one of her avid fans – both she and her writing have been a big influence in my life. *Huge.* You loved her, too, and… I know how bizarre this sounds, but I'm so… *upset.* I want my life back. I want *us,*' she gestured between them, 'back to where we were.'

Morgan's mouth was slightly parted. 'Um – Rose... I don't – I mean – that's very flattering but–'

'I'm not in love with you!' Rose tried to laugh, but this was all too important. She swallowed hard, trying to ignore the unexpected tears rising. 'Morgan – in the normal world – where your lost lady wrote the books I loved, you and I were *best* friends. We did meet on the Harry Potter forum, but sometime later – a few years ago – we both discovered a mutual love of *Pride & Prejudice* and moved over to a community of Jane Austen fans and – we've become the closest of friends. If you want me to be honest, you were the best friend I've ever had. And – I thought maybe fate or God was giving me this wonderful gift by having you be here in Bath and that maybe I could recover your friendship in this world or time or... I don't know what to call it. This hasn't ever happened to me before as you can imagine.'

'We've got that in common,' Morgan said dryly.

Rose drew in another breath. 'Look, I wouldn't have told you – I would've just – I don't know, pretended I didn't have your email and asked for it, pretended the whole friendship was just starting over with you, but something has happened today; something potentially significant, and it's given me hope. And – I just realised, now, struggling to make small talk about such inconsequential things right now, that I had to include you in...' Rose waved a hand in the air. 'All this! I *need* to include you, even if you think I'm crazy. So–'

Morgan said nothing, just stared at her with her big, brown eyes.

'Listen, did you ever watch the film '*Big*' with Tom Hanks? Of course you did. Everyone did. Well, do you remember him trying to convince his best mate that he was still just 12-year-old Josh in the body of a 30-year-old man?' A slow nod was the only response to this. '*That* is what this is!'

'You're a 30-year-old *man?*' Morgan pushed back in her seat, looking wary.

Rose couldn't help but laugh, but quickly sobered. 'No! That's not what I meant! I mean *this*.' She waved a hand between the two of them this time. 'Is one friend trying to get her best friend to believe in her, to accept what she's saying, even though it's *un*believable, incredible, beyond rational acceptance?'

Half-expecting Morgan to make her excuses and disappear into the night, Rose sent up a silent thankyou for her friend's pioneering spirit as she reached over the table to squeeze Rose's arm. 'Now, now… you're just a little tired. Why don't we skip dinner and get you home to your mom?'

Rose shook her head. 'Oh no, she's one of the worst parts of this. My family isn't close like yours, Morgan. I know your stepmum stepped in when your mum passed away, but my own mum never stepped up to begin with.' Rose started to smooth the tablecloth nervously. 'Somehow, having the writings of Jane Austen in my life enhanced it, had a profound effect on it and, more importantly, it was because of her you and I bonded and became such good friends. You've been a huge influence in my life since we met online; I've learned to be more confident, to stand up for myself, to strike out on my own. And I've used my knowledge of her life and her works to develop a role I love very much – working for James.' Rose paused. 'You met James – he helped direct you to –'

'I remember.'

'Good – then you know –'

'Wait! Hold on, hold on, hold on. How do you know about my family?'

Rose inhaled quickly. 'Because I told you, *this*…' She gestured all around them. 'This isn't the way things normally are. I've Skyped with your parents. Your brother, Calvin, is a real flirt and always promises to take me dancing in Paris. He loves to travel, unlike your stepsisters who are both married and–'

Morgan had gone very pale and put out a hand. 'Stop.'

Rose did. Then she swallowed hard on a rising restriction in her throat. 'I know this has come out all wrong. I meant to be more patient, had almost begun to resolve myself to the way things had changed.' For a fleeting moment, Aiden's face was before her, and she faltered. 'But that's not who I want to be. I want to go back to being *me*, back to the life I had.'

There was no answer to this, but she could sense Morgan detaching herself, easing back in her seat, and Rose was gripped with a sense of panic.

'Please, just listen; there's more. You see, Jane and I found something today that might just change things. For the first time in days I have hope I haven't lost everything I once had or – hoped I might have.' Once again, Aiden's image appeared in her mind but this time it gave her strength – she didn't want to have to choose between him and her old life. Wasn't there a chance here she might just be able to have everything? She looked straight into Morgan's worried eyes. 'Look, you don't have to believe me, but I *know* you. You might be a brilliant researcher in this reality, but well – you're a great writer in mine. The journalist in you must have some curiosity. If you would just… not leave.'

Morgan opened her mouth to reply when the waiter deposited her dinner plate in front of her, removed Rose's starter and asked them if they would like anything else. Rose said no and Morgan very uncharacteristically just shook her head. There was silence between them and finally Morgan looked at her. 'We never did share our names on the Harry Potter forum, did we?'

'No.'

Morgan shook her head. 'Are you some sort of hacker, then, or…?'

Rose laughed, despite the tension at the table. 'No! God, no.'

Morgan tapped a finger on the table. 'You've only told me things any good data miner could find. Tell me something that couldn't be found, something not public knowledge.'

Trying not to hope too hard or too fast, Rose nodded. 'Yes. Okay – but –' She blinked as she wracked her memory for everything she knew about Morgan, seeking something only a friend would know, something likely only ever said between them. 'I don't know how much your life has changed because of Jane's disappearance, but–'

'Let's park the disappearing woman for now, and her life. I want to understand how you know about me – about *my* life.'

The fear of rejection gripped Rose's throat. Her heart was pounding in her chest, but she knew from the determined look on Morgan's face that she was giving her one chance to prove it.

'Okay, okay… I know you always struggled more at school than the rest of your family and your dad always thought it was because you were too busy socialising but actually you're dyslexic. He – they, your family, all felt terrible once you were properly diagnosed, and so as not to hurt them more, you pretend that time in your life didn't upset you, but it really did.' Morgan was staring at Rose, unblinking, and she hurried on. 'I know you hated your brother's last girlfriend; you had a fight with her out on the patio of some restaurant in – I don't know, some surfer restaurant where they let you drop peanut shells right on the ground.'

'*Long Boards.*' Morgan had as gone as white as her linen napkin, now discarded by her plate.

'Yes!' Rose nodded. 'And… you have a lot of first dates, but no one has ever compared to how you feel about the relationship in *The X-Files*, so you never go on second dates.'

Morgan's eyes grew impossibly wide. 'I don't think I ever… connected… that…'

'No, because you never realised it until *we* were talking about it after your first date with Eric the pizza guy.' Rose leaned forward, her courage rising. 'Morgan, I'm not crazy. I just have to try and put things back to how they were… and it would be really incredible if you'd help me.'

Morgan's hands stilled on the table. 'Rose…look…this is all a bit–' She stopped and reached for her bag. 'I'm just going to the bathroom. I just need… a minute.'

Rose almost begged her not to, but quickly reined herself in. 'Yes, of course. Take all the time you need.'

The time ticked away, and Rose stared miserably at the salad in front of her. She hated salad, but at least she could hardly complain her food was going cold. She glanced over her shoulder: no sign of Morgan. Then she sighed. Why on *earth* couldn't she have just asked for Morgan's help getting into 4 Sydney Place? What had come over her to spill it all here… now… like *that*?

Rose looked around the room at the other people enjoying varying degrees of pleasant dinner conversation and wondering if Morgan was already halfway to the Royal Crescent… or… worse – the police station. It was as though someone had dropped ice cubes down her back. How could she possibly explain to the rest of the people in this mixed-up world what she'd just blurted out to her friend? It had been meant only for Morgan's ears… for the friend Rose still believed Morgan could be.

Rose looked at her watch again and, with a heavy heart, she pushed back from the table. There was little point sitting here waiting for someone who wasn't going to return...

CHAPTER THIRTY

'Sorry – there was a line.'

Relief rushed through Rose so fiercely as Morgan dropped her bag on the floor and resumed her seat she almost wept. Instead, she took a slug of her wine and waited.

'I'm not saying I believe you,' Morgan said slowly, and Rose felt a flutter of hope. Surely there was a 'but' coming? 'But you've definitely got my interest.'

'Thank you for not leaving.' Rose's throat was tight with relief.

The corner of Morgan's lip rose. 'Do you know, I've never told anyone about what happened with Nicole. But *she* may have – so I can't just take your word; do you understand?'

Rose nodded again, and cleared her throat. 'If you spoke to Jane...'

'Just... – one crazy lady at a time.' Morgan smiled, taking the sting out of her words and then stared at her cold plate of enchiladas. 'Okay, you might not believe me – or maybe you will after what you just told me – but I'm hungry. Let's order something fresh and while it's cooking, you can tell me about us and how we got from Harry Potter to....' She waved a hand towards the window. 'Bath.'

Two hours later, Rose was finally beginning to believe the next words she said would no longer be the trigger to finally send Morgan running for the door. They were currently trying to work out what, if anything much beyond her friendships with those in the Austen community, Rose included, had changed in Morgan's life. But so far, almost everything else seemed the same other than her specific job description within her father's magazine.

All this gave plenty of weight to Rose's story, because she knew so very much about Morgan's life – but it was also making Rose feel a little melancholy: wasn't this simply more evidence, stronger confirmation she really was the only one left who remembered the joy and influence Jane Austen's writing had brought to the world? It was simply unbearable.

Morgan considered Rose from over the chocolate fudge cake they were sharing. 'It seems to me that you're my Jane Austen.'

Rose quickly swallowed the fudgy spoonful in her mouth. 'I'm sorry?'

'Well, your version of me seems pretty happy.'

'You seem happy here – now, as well.'

'I'm not; not really. Believe it or not, grumpy Dr T is one of the nicest writers I've worked with so far. I'm just fact checking for other people's work. I'm not even sure I know what I would write if I had the opportunity; which I won't, because my dad doesn't want it to look like nepotism.' Morgan stopped, then shook her head. 'Honestly, I'm feeling a little hopeless here.'

There was no missing the catch in Morgan's voice, and Rose hated that she couldn't go and hug her as she would have done before now. Then she frowned. 'But you're an amazing writer! As soon as anyone reads your first article they'll know nepotism had nothing to do with it.'

Morgan smiled briefly. 'I take it this vote of confidence comes from remembering my attempts at fan fiction?' She let out a breath. 'That was all about practising, to be honest, at first, I can't say I ever wrote anything beyond a few long posts extolling the virtues of Sirius Black and how J.K. Rowling would never kill him off.' Morgan winked. 'And we all know how well that worked out.'

'*That's* what's different then.' Rose bit her lip, a pang of regret sweeping through her for the lost years of friendship. 'We wrote loads for the online Austen community. You were such a fan of Jane and Bingley.' The pang deepened at Morgan's blank look. 'Never mind; trust me, you loved them, and you wrote beautiful stories about them. We even had our own archive where we shared our stories with people who became real friends of ours.'

Morgan stared at her in disbelief. 'We did? How on earth did that ever start?'

'We were online one night – at least, it was the early hours for me – and I was having a rotten time with my mum, yet again, but it had made me really low, and you wrote me a silly and hilarious story about Anne de… another character in one of Jane's books to cheer me up. From there – you just never stopped. I – if I think back, it was probably while you were still at university. Maybe it influenced your direction; all I do know is that your confidence in your writing grew and grew, even though you never did get to grips with spelling.' Rose paused, then smiled ruefully. 'That's something you have in common with Jane Austen.'

'Crazy lady?' Morgan laughed. 'Who'd have thought it.' She met Rose's anxious gaze, and then shrugged. 'Okay, what's this big discovery you made with your 19th-century buddy?' She held up a hand when Rose grinned. 'I'm still not saying I believe you about her. But… let's pretend I'm starting to. Catch me up.'

Rose reined in her rising hopes and nodded resolutely. 'Yes! Well, you're never going to believe this, but Jane's sister–'

'Cassandra Austen.'

'*Yes!*' Rose leaned forward. 'Cassandra found the necklace – and that in itself is a long story which – yes, I will tell you in a second

– no, wait – I've started at the wrong end. We found a note to Jane from Cassandra in an old book in the library. It's a poem, and we think, I mean, we're pretty certain it's a message telling Jane she put the necklace back in the safe at the house where they lived at the time.'

'At 4 Sydney Place?'

'Yes!' Rose said triumphantly.

'There's a safe at 4 Sydney Place? Where?'

'It's black cast iron, and it's built into the wall in the bedroom… I mean, the back room. It's probably just another office right now.'

'Yes – it is.'

'Well, that's where it is; right there in the back wall. And this is where I – we – need your help, why you need to be included in this. You've met the people in that office, so we thought perhaps you could give me an introduction, I don't know, something, some way in for us so that Jane can try to open the safe and check if by some miracle the necklace has survived all these years right where it was–'

Morgan's face had taken a dramatic turn, and Rose felt her stomach drop.

'What? I swear we wouldn't take anything else from the safe or take advantage of your friendship in any other way but –'

'No, it's not that. Rose, I'm happy to help you get in there, but –' She smiled sympathetically. 'I'm sure there's no safe.'

Rose shook her head slightly. 'Yes – there is – I've seen it myself – Jane used it to correspond with Cassandra – they would send letters and supplies and –'

'But I was there for two hours and took at least four hundred images – all of which I've already sorted and edited to show the Doc. There's no safe in that room, or anywhere else in the building that I can recall.'

Swallowing quickly, Rose grasped at the remnants of her hopes as they drifted away from her. 'There must be–'

'I'm so sorry, sweetie.'

Unable to bear the disappointment having seemed so close to a resolution, Rose blinked back a sudden rush of emotion. It really did seem like they'd come to the end of their leads, the end of any hope – however flimsy – that there was a solution to be found.

There seemed very little more to be said on the subject, and with the hour now so late, the girls agreed it was time to go. Morgan had said she might pass by the library on the following day to put the finishing touches to her research presentation, but Rose had remembered her rota and said she would be at home instead. Despite the hug Morgan gave her as they parted on the corner of Queen Square, Rose watched her friend walk away with a heavy heart.

Now she had poured all that out to Morgan, who was about to leave Bath anyway for Italy, what chance had she for restoring their past friendship? Time had run out on her, and so, finally had hope.

CHAPTER THIRTY-ONE

After a long and restless night, Rose woke unrefreshed but thankful she didn't have to face yet another day in the library. Helpful as everyone had been to her, despite what must have been seen as odd behaviour, the strain of appearing to be comfortable in an unfamiliar environment was beginning to take its toll.

For a moment, she lay still, her eyes closed as everything that had happened the previous day circled around in her brain. But as much as she wanted to reclaim the hope inspired by Cassandra's poem, she kept coming back to Morgan's assertion she had seen no sign of a wall safe during her visit to Sydney Place. 'I don't want to think about it,' Rose whispered. 'I don't want to give up.' Morgan had taken hundreds of photos, hadn't she, over the four accessible floors of the building? Surely she couldn't remember in detail every one?

She opened her eyes, blinking at the light filtering through the curtains. Though it had had its fraught moments, she had some comfort to draw from the evening. Her friend's open-mindedness had surprised her at first, even though she knew it shouldn't, but somehow, because their friendship wasn't quite so solid in this world, she'd experienced some doubts as to whether everything else about Morgan would be the same. She'd forgotten her passion for tales of time travel and, whilst her friend was intelligent enough to know that these were just stories, she'd seemed at last to believe that whatever

Rose was telling her, she wasn't mad.

Morgan's main disappointment was it probably wasn't something she could include in her story – for who on earth would believe her? Rose had reflected likewise it wasn't something she could speak of to any other living soul.

What about the Doc? Didn't you feel that connection with him the other night? No; she could never tell him. That was a foolish girl's dream, but as thoughts of Aiden swept through her, Rose's insides did a loop and she rolled over and hugged her pillow.

Crushing on him, a distant unattainable figure, for three years had been a source of painful pleasure, exciting when he came to Bath – an unreachable fantasy but one she'd held onto. Now, something had changed.

Had he felt it, too, that strong connection as they'd talked almost without pause the other evening? Or was she deluding herself? What would he see in quiet, unworldly Rose?

With a sigh, she rolled onto her back and stared at the ceiling, still covered in the fluorescent stars she'd put up when she was 14. What did any of it matter? Aiden would take Morgan's research and write a completely fascinating but false article on his findings, and she would possibly never see him again – and as for Morgan? How long would she be in Europe? Had she done enough to make her want to stay in touch online when she left?

A tentative knocking came at the door, clearly not her mother's sharp rap – thankfully, Mrs Wallace was still away visiting her friends – and Rose leapt from the bed to open the door.

'Good morning.' Jane was already dressed and held Cassandra's note in her hand. Rose wondered whether perhaps she'd held it all night long, so attached did she seem to it.

'I know you think it's pointless, but did you have any bright ideas – you know, how we're going to get into Sydney Place?' By the time Rose had returned home the previous evening, Jane had gone to bed; she didn't have the heart to tell her Morgan's belief of there being no safe.

Jane shook her head. 'I have taken part in some home theatricals but am no actress – as you have seen.'

'You do really well. I am not sure I'd be able to pass myself off credibly if I suddenly found myself in the early 19th century.'

'Oh things were so much simpler – just different.' She glanced around the room, her gaze landing on Rose's computer. 'Much is altered here, but I find human nature remains the same.' She smiled at Rose then. 'It amuses me greatly.'

'I'm sure it does.' Rose gestured at her nightdress. 'I'll get ready and join you downstairs, shall I? We can talk over breakfast about what we're going to do next.'

'As you wish.' Jane turned away, but then she looked back over her shoulder. 'Do not forget you are a master confectioner.'

Rose paled as she closed her bedroom door and turned around to lean against it. The cake for Liz and Tina! Everything that had happened lately had swept it from her mind.

Half an hour later, after a quick breakfast, Rose made a thorough inspection of her mother's pantry which revealed a surprising array of baking things, not only a wide range of flavourings and decorative items, but also piping bags and nozzles, cookie cutters in various shapes and sizes and a stack of shiny baking tins and trays. Clearly, in this life Rose took her baking seriously.

Despite this, the one recipe she had copied at the library the previous day required a couple of missing ingredients and soon they were walking to the local shop.

Jane had been silent as they walked; since the discovery of Cassandra's note, she had withdrawn into herself a little and it was only as they were making their way around the narrow aisles in the shops as Rose looked for vanilla essence and a box of eggs that she roused herself to take any interest in her surroundings.

'I am not familiar with this type of purveyor; has he no specialism? I am used to a baker's, a confectioner's, a milliner's or a haberdashery, not a shop with a small selection of all these things and more. What can its purpose be?'

Rose spied the vanilla essence and tossed it into her basket. 'These local shops try to stock a little of everything so that if you've forgotten something in town you don't have to go all the way back to get it. You can find almost anything in them, they're amazing.' Seeing a stand holding various items of stationery, Rose added a couple of packs of Post-it notes to her basket. 'They tend to be known as 'convenience' stores.'

Jane poked a finger at a roll of plastic bin bags, then eyed up some cards of assorted buttons next to colourful rolls of cotton. Beyond that was a large display with sunglasses, sunhats and sun lotion – all on sale, due to the time of year – and then a small fridge stocked with fresh meat, cold cuts, cheeses and beyond it a shelf filled with balls of string, boxes of nails and tubes of glue.

'Pray, how is this a convenience store? One can barely turn about, 'tis so narrow, and there is no logic to the produce on display. I find naught of convenience about it.'

Rose shrugged; it was an argument she couldn't win, and she picked up a box of eggs and headed for the till, trying not to laugh as Jane continued to stare around at the variety of items filling every shelf.

As they walked back to the house, however, Rose began to feel anxious. Perhaps it was because she was now wide awake and in Jane's company again, once more facing the uncertainty of each day, but she was being visited by doubts over the wisdom of her confession to Morgan.

What had she done? If there was no safe in Sydney Place, then this really was the life Rose was going to have to live. And she'd just admitted to the one person she had hoped to reclaim as a close friend that not only did she believe in time travel but that she presently had a time-travelling woman living with her – not only a once-famous woman, but the very person Morgan had come to Bath to research. How would Morgan feel in the cold light of day? Would she avoid her like the plague; and even if she didn't, would her manner towards Rose have changed? How could it not? After all, what would Rose's reaction have been had the circumstances been reversed...?

CHAPTER THIRTY-TWO

With her eyes fixed on the ground and a silent Jane at her side, Rose sighed. Well, the first thing she was going to do, if she was stuck here, was move out of her mum's house. She had no idea what working at the library paid her – she hadn't even checked her bank accounts to see if she was solvent, let alone that she still had savings – but somehow, even if she ended up in a garret, she was leaving as soon as…

'I stopped by and when you weren't home, I figured I'd wait for you. I hope you don't mind.'

Rose looked up to see Morgan leaning against the gatepost outside the house, her coat and bags on the ground by her feet. Her relief jostling with uncertainty, Rose gave her an uncertain smile. *Please don't let her have come to say goodbye!*

'Ah, the Revolutionary.' Jane inclined her head towards Morgan in her typical fashion, but instead of her usual eye-roll or smirk in Rose's direction, Morgan simply stared at Jane and said nothing.

Rose gathered her courage, waiting with bated breath as Morgan gathered her things from the floor. 'Of course I don't mind. I'm … glad to see you. I was worried that maybe, in the light of day, you might…' Rose raised both hands in a helpless gesture.

'That I'd run away with my hands over my ears?'

'Something like that.'

'Well, I nearly did – but hey, I like you.' Morgan winked; her smile was genuine, not forced at all. 'And you don't seem like a crazy person – well, aside from everything you said – so I thought, why not stick with the curiosity and see where we get to.'

'I appreciate it. Morgan, you have no idea how much I do.'

Morgan met her eye seriously this time. 'You're wrong; I think I do have an idea how much, and that's why I'm here.'

Rose swallowed hard on a sudden rush of emotion, then drew in a deep breath.

'Excellent! So, let's go in, shall we?'

Rose gestured to Jane to walk ahead down the gravel drive to the house, and Morgan fell into step beside her.

'So you're –?'

'Do you suffer memory loss, young woman? We have been acquainted some days now.'

Bringing up the rear, Rose sighed. 'Jane, I've told Morgan who you are. Who you *really* are.'

They had reached the side door now, and stopped as Rose fished out her key.

Jane eyed Morgan with a raised brow. 'How this affects you, I know not. For myself, whom I was is who I am, thus I suffer little inconsequence.'

She stepped into the house as the door swung open and Rose turned to Morgan.

'Please, come in – won't you?'

'Sure.' Morgan's lips twitched, 'You know the British have a reputation in my country for being a tad curt. I think now, you've all mellowed considerably in the last two hundred years.'

Rose sighed, shaking her head as she followed Morgan into the house. 'She's really a romantic at heart – honestly. She's just a bit stressed today.'

'I'll give you the benefit of the doubt.' Morgan patted the bag slung over her shoulder. 'I brought my laptop so you can see the pictures I took. Who knows, maybe it will give you some insight into what to do next.'

'Perfect! Thanks so much – though, in all honesty, I have no idea what can be done if the safe has been removed. We will never be able to trace it and even if we could, there is no way it would still have anything in it.'

Rose steered Morgan into the dining room so she could unpack her laptop onto the table. It was as they passed back through the hall to the kitchen that she spotted and quickly snatched up yet another Post-it note stuck to the cover of a *Grantchester* DVD left on a nearby chair: '*His air and countenance please me; a suitable likeness of Mr Charles Bingley?*'

Rose smiled to herself. Who would have thought the appeal of James Norton would transcend the centuries?

Jane had disappeared up the stairs, and Rose pulled the vanilla essence and eggs from the carrier bag and placed them by the cake recipe as Morgan came to lean against the worktop.

'Apparently, in this reality I bake things – not professionally, for friends and so on, but it seems I've got quite a good reputation.' She opened the pantry door and took out the flour, sugar and cocoa powder. 'Rather inconveniently, I've also apparently promised a cake for my friend's engagement party on Sunday, which is a bit of a problem to say the least, when my baking experience begins and ends with the making of some teeth-defying scones at school and a bad experience once with some pre-made frozen pastry.'

Morgan grinned at her as Rose deposited her finds next to the eggs.

'Oh dear. Well – be thankful you aren't married with kids in this world – what would you have done?'

Rose stopped in the process of pulling an electronic mixer from a cupboard, her lips parted in surprise. 'I don't even want to think about it. Oh no! What on earth would I have done? How could I …'

Morgan reached forward and nudged her in the arm. 'Sorry – don't freak out – it didn't happen – that's a good thing.'

Rose nodded, but the thought of all the possible complications – and embarrassments – was almost horrifying. Perhaps this life as it stood wasn't so bad after all!

Just then, Jane came back into the room and Morgan smiled brightly at her.

'So – Jane? May I call you Jane?'

Jane walked over to the recipe and picked it up, then turned to face Morgan. 'You may; it is my given name. I found no use for the alias to begin with, though it had familiarity in its favour – my father often calls me Jenny.' She glanced over at Rose with a small smile. 'I counselled Rose there was no need, as she alone had awareness of my name in this world.'

Morgan held up a hand cautiously. 'Well – I had, too. I was researching your disappearance and would definitely have found it more than a little odd to have run into a woman with the same name by coincidence.'

'Perhaps. Yet of what consequence might it have been? What might you have supposed, pray?'

Morgan raised her brows then turned to Rose. 'She has a point.'

Rose put her hands on her hips. 'Well, what would *you* have done? To me, Jane Austen was the absolute most familiar name to me, and to many of the people around the world. It was instinct to try and come up with a different name, one can hardly prepare for it. At no point in my lifetime have I been dreaming up strategies for if I find myself in an alternate reality.'

'And everyone in America thinks the school system is so superior here.' Jane frowned, but Rose knew Morgan was joking and grinned. The teasing was a good sign. 'But,' Morgan continued, 'I would certainly have taken you for a relative and asked you *way* too many questions.'

'Do you have butter, Rose?' Jane held out her hand and Rose passed it over. 'Forgive me the impertinence, but if I have sufficient comprehension of your character, I fully anticipate the same henceforth.'

Morgan grinned. 'Are you giving me free rein?'

'A satisfied curiosity will oft lead to calmer nerves.' Jane eyed the modern set of scales warily as she dropped a chunk of butter onto them, and Morgan and Rose exchanged an amused look. Morgan rested her elbows on the worktop dividing the kitchen from the breakfast area.

'So... Rose has told me there were three necklaces given to you, your mother and your sister by your brother?' At Jane's nod, Morgan added, 'And where did the necklaces come from exactly?'

Rose ushered Jane round to sit on a stool at the worktop and took the bag of sugar from her.

'To be certain, I cannot say *exactly*.' She paused, then smiled at her interrogator. 'My brother, Charles, bought them whilst in Gibraltar on his return from a tour of duty in the Indies. He wrote to us of them, but said little beyond the stones being topaz and the chains of gold. We scolded him, of course, for spending his winnings on the females of his family. He has a family of his own to support, you see.'

Morgan frowned. 'Well – did your brother warn you when he gave them to you, they might have – oh I don't know – magical properties?'

'Not at first; he wrote of the purchase, but he only sent two of the three – my mother's and Cassandra's – preferring to bring mine in person next time he was in England.' Jane seemed lost in a memory, staring into nothing, but her eyes sparkled with a return of their usual vivacity and a faint smile touched her lips. 'He spoke privately to me, told me he knew full well my frustrations, my desire for something more than living quietly at home, mending and sewing, managing the household accounts and waiting... waiting for something – *life* – to happen rather than being able to seek it out.'

'And then what?' Rose was captivated; Jane had never spoken of this to her, and she laid aside her spatula. The cake could wait!

'He told me my gift alone held certain qualities – magical properties, as Morgan calls them. He had met by reputation a woman believed to have certain powers, and she had bestowed some upon the cross and chain but it was essential it passed from his hand to mine and no other.'

Morgan's eyes were wide. 'And this spell or whatever it was... it transported you through time?'

'Your powers of deduction are astonishing.'

'Jane!' The warning note in Rose's voice did not go unnoticed, and Jane gave a rueful smile.

'Forgive me; you have an unfathomable tendency to state that which is obvious.'

With a shrug, Morgan grinned. 'What's evident to one person is often unthinkable to another.'

'Touché!' Jane laughed. 'You are a formidable adversary.'

Morgan's smile widened. 'So – did the other two necklaces do anything – have similar abilities?'

Jane shook her head. 'They displayed nothing beyond the traditional accomplishment of jewellery; inanimate but quite pretty nonetheless.' She threw a mischievous look at Rose and then Morgan. 'Though how Cass and I wished they did! Imagine our disappointment when first Mama placed her chain about her neck and failed to disappear.'

Laughing with the others, Rose broke a couple of eggs into a bowl and started to whisk them around with a fork.

'Of course, I have never been able to wear my own cross and chain merely for pleasure.'

Rose's eyes widened. 'Gosh! I'd never thought of that. How sad – you should have a replica made.'

Jane smiled, shaking her head. 'It is of little import. Mama did not consider the semi-precious stone to be good enough for someone who had connections to the Leighs of Stoneleigh Abbey, however, tenuous, and bestowed hers upon me. 'Tis perchance the reason it is oft mistaken for my own.'

She and Rose exchanged a quick glance, and Morgan frowned, but before she could say anything, Jane turned to her instead and fixed her with a compelling eye. 'May I now be given the liberty of addressing *you* with a question?'

With her usual warm smile, Morgan nodded, and Rose picked up the flour again and began to pour it into the mixer, forgetting that measuring it out might be a sensible first step.

'Did no one consider commencing one's nation with the wanton waste of one's own supplies might not be a fortuitous beginning?'

Morgan looked blankly at Rose who shrugged. 'I think she means the Boston Tea Party.'

'Oh, that. Well,' Morgan pursed her lips together, clearly trying not to laugh. 'We're still known to be a little rebellious and it has definitely been a double-edged sword. Um, were you particularly against American independence?'

Jane shook her head. 'Not at all. But tea is secured under lock and key. I shall never forgive the shocking wastefulness of dispatching such a valuable commodity into the sea.'

'Well, that answers that.' Morgan grinned at Rose as she walked out to her laptop. Then she called back, 'The pictures are up, if you'd like to see them.'

Wiping her hands on a tea towel, Rose hurried across to the dining room, Jane in her wake. 'Not particularly – if they are going to confirm what you have already told me.'

'What has she told you?' Jane looked from Rose to Morgan and back, but it was the latter who answered.

'I didn't see a safe in any wall when I visited, but I took loads of photos. You can see for yourselves.'

'Perhaps you just didn't register it, you know?' Rose refused to give up hope, even though she knew deep down it was futile.

Morgan ushered her into a chair and with her friend's encouragement Rose started to scroll through the photos.

'Do not be despondent, Rose.' Jane patted her reassuringly on the shoulder. 'Three of the stories you know so well remain firmly in my head, and I am just as capable of writing in this century as I was in the past – perchance even more so with such modern conveniences.' Jane frowned. 'Or perhaps not, for here, young women are obliged to complete all manner of chores in addition to their profession. Household duties I am somewhat familiar with, but I do not care for these convenience stores.' Jane's voice perked up. 'How much pecuniary recompense must I command in order to pay someone to procure my provisions?'

Rose rubbed her hand across her forehead. 'Er, we'd have to look it up. Gosh, Morgan, you *did* take a lot of photos. How long were you there?'

Morgan laughed. 'Hours, I think. I was busy chatting, too, you know.'

Yes, Rose did know, but just now she was caught up in the flickering images as she swept each one across the page.

'Oh, you even went down to the basement! This is where I live – lived. I had these adorable curtains – I made them myself... they really...' Rose stopped as her throat tightened, and she quickly scrolled through until she got to the ground-floor office. There it was, the flat in which Jane had been staying, alien with its office supplies everywhere and yet familiar in layout. As the photos of the back room – Jane's bedroom – came onto the screen, Rose could sense Jane peering over her shoulder. There was the rear wall with the window out onto the garden, and just as Morgan had said, there was nothing but a wall: smooth and unobstructed.

CHAPTER THIRTY-THREE

Disappointment rolled through Rose in waves. 'I'd been holding out hope there was some picture covering it – or filing cabinets – to explain why you hadn't seen it.'

Morgan put a comforting hand on Rose's shoulder. 'I'm so sorry.'

With a shrug, Rose got to her feet. She didn't want to stare at that blank wall any longer. 'It was a long shot. The family left the house in 1804 and who knows how many residents came and went before the safe was pulled out?'

'Or the necklace could have been moved by the family or, if they left it – taken by any number of people.'

Rose shook her head. 'Jane says that's not possible.'

'I know your crime rate is low here, but if I buy a house and there is a pretty necklace left there, I'm only going to go through so much trouble to return it to its rightful–'

'No, it's not that. The safe is protected, enchanted in some way – only Jane can open it if the necklace is inside.'

'No way!'

Rose was too disheartened to share in Morgan's awe of this new evidence of magic. 'When we found Cassandra's message I just – it seemed like it was all working out – like a story… it can't end like this.'

Morgan squeezed her arm as she walked back to the kitchen. 'Hey – nothing is ending. You heard Jane – she's going to write her books again here in the 21st century. And maybe now she won't die so young so – maybe this isn't far from the fairy tale you were hoping for. This way – she might actually write more. Maybe she'll find the love of her life here and live happily ever after.'

Jane, who had followed them into the kitchen, looked at Morgan. 'I am warming to you on continued acquaintance, though one and forty is not considered a young age to leave this earth; least, not in early 19th-century England.' She then turned to Rose with a small smile. 'Perchance you recall the speculation over my death – was it one of numerous possible diseases or was it accidental poisoning? I do not fear death, but nor am I predisposed towards it. Whatever the cause, all the suppositions are incurable in my time. I am confident your doctors might aid me better.'

Morgan nodded encouragingly. 'See? Jane wants to stay. What do you like best about–'

'Living in a world brimming with advances in medicine, science, technology?' Jane looked around the room, a small smile on her lips. 'Things of infinite variety.' She grabbed a stack of Post-it notes from the fruit bowl, but this time she didn't write anything on them. 'This.' She tore one off and stuck it to the hot water tap, then another and stuck it on a roll of aluminium foil before a mischievous look crossed her face, and she walked over and stuck another on Morgan's jeans.

'Some advances are more personal; how is one to find aught amiss in a world permitting women of all ages the wearing of trousers.'

Morgan laughed, but Rose sighed. She understood; truly, she did, but she missed Jane's writing so much, missed everything it had given her.

'Enamoured though I am of many things, I will own to a dislike of your inclination for placing people in boxes.' She waved a hand at the mobile phone on the nearby worktop. 'One should only be placed in a box when one has paid the debt of nature.'

This time, Rose rolled her eyes. She knew, despite her words, Jane had found her first adventures with a television screen and a phone fascinating, if beyond her initial understanding.

'Can I see the note you found?'

Rose glanced at Jane, who nodded and took it from her pocket. She offered it to Morgan, who studied it curiously, then looked up, first to Jane, then to Rose, who tried to summon a smile.

'You said last night you needed my help. Well, I don't know how I can help with all we've found out so far, but let's talk it all through together while we get this cake in the oven.'

'Oh, can you bake? You could be a life-saver.'

Morgan laughed. 'Definitely not! I've never tried. But we have three heads on it, and it can't be *that* difficult, can it?'

Rose peered into the mixing bowl and bit her lip. Those could well be famous last words.

Rose closed the oven door on their third attempt at making a chocolate sponge cake and turned around to survey the mess. There were ingredients spilling out of packets and mixing bowls, spatulas and measuring spoons scattered across every work surface. It was a good thing her mother was still away.

'The consistency is much improved, is it not?' Jane indicated the oven. 'It bodes well, I believe.'

With a sigh, Rose nodded and then grabbed her phone as it pinged. 'Oh thank goodness!'

'Your friend – she has the intelligence you seek?'

'Yes! She thinks I need help for my poor memory, but at least we have the wording.' Rose turned the screen to show Jane who peered at it for a moment, then reached for a notepad and pen which hung on a hook by the phone on the wall.

In her neat and curling hand, she wrote the words, '*Reader, I married her. A quiet wedding we had*', muttering under her breath about the plastic pen she held.

'How singular!'

'It's almost a famous quote – from *Jane Eyre*. Liz-Lottie will have chosen it as a nod to her mum.' Jane eyed Rose warily. 'Don't worry about it; probably in the other world, it's a quote from one of your books instead!' Rose glanced over at the oven. Was the cake they had made big enough for such a quote? 'Ah well, let's hope this one works! I expect it needs to cool a great deal before we attempt to ice it.' Rose threw a troubled glance over the mess on the worktops. 'I'd better start clearing some space.'

'I do not see the need for such haste. To be certain, resting the cake overnight would be preferable, would it not?'

'I have absolutely no idea.' Rose laughed, though she wasn't particularly amused at her present situation. 'Besides, I have to work all day tomorrow; I daren't leave it until the evening in case we have to start all over again.'

'We can figure it out for you.' Morgan's voice came from the other room where she was busy editing her article on the laptop.

Rose glanced at Jane who waved the notepad. 'We have the wording – we shall be industrious in the kitchen whilst you toil at your occupation, and by the time we meet again, all will be answered.'

'Are you sure?' Rose wasn't too convinced an early 19th-century author and a 21st-century Californian's ideas of how to decorate a cake would coincide, but then at least she wouldn't be around to observe the fallout.

'We'll be fine,' Morgan called from the other room, and Rose walked across the hall to stand in the doorway just as the clock on the wall chimed six o'clock. The day had flown by, what with their repeated efforts to produce a cake that didn't fall apart as soon as they tried to take it from the tin and, during cooking times, their ceaseless speculation about where the safe might be now, if it hadn't been sent for scrap.

After a moment, Morgan looked up. 'Come and have a look at this.' She pointed to her screen and Rose, expecting to read the finished article, took a seat next to Morgan on the sofa. 'I did a list of previous owners and the like for the house in Sydney Place for Dr T, going right back to the Austens' day. See?'

Rose studied the document Morgan had opened. 'Maybe if we work through and track down these people or their descendants, someone has kept the safe as some sort of display piece.'

'Yes, and maybe like the locket in *Half-Blood Prince* it will just happen to be with someone we know.' Despite her despondency over Cassandra's note being yet another dead end, Rose could not help but laugh. 'You're such an optimist, Morgan!'

Morgan grinned at her. 'Well – we all knew it was Regulus the moment we read his initials so *yes*, of course I am. I'll rub off on you eventually.'

Rose turned to look back at the screen. 'You already did; years ago. It's just that I'm struggling to maintain it at the moment.'

'I'm not sure if it's freaky or nice that you remember more about me than I do.' Morgan gave her a fond look. 'Right then, we need to give you something to do. Why don't you start with the Austens' letting agents, this *Messrs Watson & Foreman* at Cornwall Buildings? I bet you can find something tomorrow in the library archives about them, trace the landlord and his family forward.'

Feeling a frisson of interest, Rose stared at the names, then raised her eyes to Jane who had come into the room.

'Their office is… *was* in Walcot. I recall it quite distinctly, though I did not of course venture inside when Papa called upon them.'

'Yes – I know Cornwall Buildings. Jane, what is the name of your landlord in Bath?'

'It is – was – a Mr Pinker. He was most obliging when we took the property, for he was bound to paint the two first floors and an agreement was reached which satisfied all parties.' Jane smiled, a distant look in her eyes. 'We travelled to the West Country and passed a most enjoyable summer on the Dorset and Devon coastlines whilst the house was duly prepared.'

Morgan laughed. 'Isn't it fascinating how some practices are no different today than they were then? It's standard where I come from for rentals to have some work done before the new tenants move in! The last apartment I had at college was completely renovated, and–'

Rose leapt to her feet. '*Renovations!*

CHAPTER THIRTY-FOUR

Morgan stared up at her. 'Er – it wasn't *that* exciting. Just a new–'

Trying to think clearly as memories flooded in, Rose shook her head. 'No, I mean I remember, when I moved into my flat… Marcus told me–'

'Who's Marcus?'

Jane walked over to join Rose. 'My present landlord? He is a most respectable gentleman with pleasing manners.'

Rose nodded quickly and looked down at Morgan, who was gazing from her to Jane in confusion.

'Morgan, in the old time – the *real* time – I mean in *my* real time, all the floors above basement level of the house in Sydney Place are holiday apartments. Marcus's company manages the property, and when he learned about my interest in Jane Austen – which is why I even applied to rent the basement flat in the first place – we talked in detail about the building and about some of the discoveries they made during the renovations. Before, it had been a combination of offices and student lets, you see – much as it is now – and needed a thorough upgrading.'

'I'm still not getting where you're going with this.' Morgan got to her feet, too, and placed the laptop on a nearby table, but excitement was rising in Rose and she put a hand to head.

'I can't believe I never thought about it… Anyway, he told me that when they brought an architect in to design the holiday apartments, he worked out that one of the walls in the ground-floor offices had been built in front of the original.'

'A false wall? Now we really are getting into gothic material.' Morgan looked a little sceptical. 'I still don't see how that helps us track down the missing safe.'

'Don't you see?' Rose looked eagerly from Morgan to Jane and back again. 'Marcus said that when this wall was removed, they discovered something behind it – built into the original wall!'

Jane's eyes widened. 'The safe.'

Morgan studied Rose thoughtfully. 'So… you think there's a chance the safe might still be there – just hidden? That the wall – the false one – is still in place today?'

Rose nodded, trying to rein in her rising excitement. Her hopes had been dashed once too often in recent days, and she wasn't sure how many more falls she could take. 'Marcus said there was every indication the additional wall was put up when the building was fairly new. It was pretty substantial and took some removing. And the cornicing and skirting matched the rest of the room; there was no indication at all it was a secondary wall. What if–' Rose turned to look at Jane. 'What if your family *hid* the safe – knowing Cassandra had placed the necklace in there to find – by building a false wall?'

Jane blinked. 'The building is – was – but a few years old; a match of the materials is entirely feasible.' She nodded slowly. 'Most indubitably the best way to preserve the necklace in its hiding place.'

'That's what it means – the end of the riddle she left you!' Rose watched as Jane pulled the old piece of parchment from her pocket again.

'*To keep it safe, one must conceal; thus only you can it reveal.*' Jane looked up.

'We thought it meant it was concealed *in* the safe; what if it means the *safe* was concealed as well?' Rose's skin prickled and she rubbed at the goose bumps rising along with her anticipation. 'We've got to check if that back wall is the original, as we had assumed from the photos, or if the secondary wall is still in place.'

'Yes!' Morgan nodded and turned to shove her laptop into her bag.

'But how? We can't go now.' Rose glanced at the clock. 'They'll be closed; we'll have to wait for Monday.' The thought of having to pass the weekend not knowing if they were onto something at last was disappointing to say the least, but as her enthusiasm waned, another thought struck Rose, and she turned to Jane. She was white as a sheet.

'Come on!' Morgan was heading for the door. 'What are you waiting for? This is no time to nap on the job.'

Rose took a breath and said carefully, 'Jane.'

'Rose.'

Morgan looked between them, confused for a moment before raising her brows and saying, simply, 'Oh.'

'Jane, I understand your reasons for being content here. You know I have selfish reasons for wanting to return to the reality I know. And I don't want to trivialise this decision for you, but... if we can make this work... your sister. You were all she had.'

Rose held her breath as the silence stretched between the three of them, the poignancy of the moment almost overwhelming. Finally Jane nodded.

'Do not despair, Rose. I have not forgotten my family, though perhaps it seemed I had, nor am I immune to what you have lost. I miss my sister beyond words. Though often separated, we wrote to each other every day when apart, and,' Jane drew a shaky breath, 'I would have that back above all things.'

Rose couldn't even be embarrassed by the wetness in her eyes. She smiled tremulously at Jane, mouthing, 'Thank you.'

'So, if we're going to do this–' Meeting Morgan's cautiously enthusiastic gaze, Rose reluctantly shook her head. 'It's no good. It's a listed building – like almost all the ones in Bath. Even internal alterations need formal permissions or permits, and that can take weeks, months even. We could be waiting six months or more to have the wall removed and that's without any guarantee the safe was left in place or that there is anything still in it if it was.'

'Then there is no point in waiting for Monday, is there?'

'No.' Rose felt suddenly despondent again. 'Besides, what right have we to request the wall be removed? We aren't the owner or the tenant.'

'Exactly; but then, in the real world, *your* real world, none of this is relevant, is it?'

'What do you mean?'

'If the false wall is still there, and if the safe is there, too, *and* if the necklace is still in it, then as soon as the door is opened to reveal it, this... this time travel portal is reinstated!'

Rose stared at Morgan. 'That's a heck of a lot of 'ifs'.'

'Sure is! But *if* so, the world you talk about will reform instantly, the offices will disappear, along with any damage we've done, and it will be Jane's apartment again.'

Jane nodded. 'We know my sister placed the charm in the safe; if the safe has not been removed in the intervening years, it will remain inside.'

'This is too incredible. We *have* to find out if it's there.' Morgan picked up her laptop bag and slung it over her shoulder.

Rose was wavering. It all sounded so improbable; there was so much that could go wrong. 'But the only way of finding out if it's there is... well, we'd have to knock a hole in the wall.'

'Where is your sense of adventure, Ginger? Harry was doing this all the time – breaking the rules to set the world to rights.'

'Yes, but *he* had an invisibility cloak. That would be really helpful right now!'

'More importantly than that: he had loyal friends who helped him no end. So did Frodo – he'd never have coped without Sam.'

For a moment, Rose stared at Morgan, but there was no denying her words rang true, and she met her challenging gaze full on. 'You're right – except of course, we don't have magic to assist us, of our own or our friends.'

'No, but we do have something none of them had – cellphones.' Morgan fished hers from her pocket and waved it in the air. 'This is *our* secret weapon! I've got Adam's number – he's one of the guys working from that office – I'll text him and say I think I left a lens cap over there the other day and can I just come by to grab it?'

'You don't think someone will notice when we start hammering at the plaster?'

Morgan had already started texting. 'I'm sure he won't be there – he told me he usually shuts up shop at 5 and the cleaners are there by 6 – they do the offices and the communal areas on all floors. I met them when I was there late the other day. They're real friendly.'

Still having serious misgivings, Rose started when her own phone began to ring, and she quickly fished it out of her bag. It was an unknown number, but some instinct prompted her to connect the call.

'Hello?'

'Er – hi. Rose? It's Aiden… Trevellyan.'

'Oh! Hi!' The easy colour flooded Rose's cheeks and Morgan smirked at her as she put her phone back in her pocket.

'I was just wondering if you were busy all weekend.'

Feeling two pairs of eyes on her, Rose edged her way out of the room and into the kitchen where the fallout from their day of baking still remained. 'A bit.' Where had her ability to form words gone?

There was a pause, and Rose wracked her brains for something witty or clever to say. 'I may be tied up with some of my friends.' *Nice. Very clever.*

'Oh, I see.'

'Rose!' Turning around, she saw Morgan and Jane in the doorway. Morgan was pointing at her own phone and giving a 'thumbs-up' before gesturing to her to wind up the call. Rose looked at Jane. She was saying nothing, but there was a message in her eyes. She knew it was time.

I want both worlds, Rose thought in a sudden panic. *If I can just get him to tell me what it is about me now that has stopped me being so invisible to him…*

She drew a breath for courage and turned her back on the others. 'Aiden, I'm not imagining it, am I? You do…' She swallowed hard. 'You do quite like me?'

He cleared his throat, and she held her breath. 'Quite – a lot.'

She tried, but even behind the obscurity of a phone call rather than facing him, she couldn't bring herself to ask the questions raging through her mind: *what do you see in me in this world that you don't in the other? Why do you want to spend time with me?* If she only knew the answers, perhaps she'd know how to change things in the other life… if she ever got it back.

'What I mean is,' he was continuing, albeit with some hesitation in his voice. 'You are – you listen, you ask intelligent questions. I don't know, you seem genuinely interested in me – I mean, in my *work*!'

A slow smile formed on Rose's lips. 'I *am*; genuinely interested, I mean. And I will see you… soon. I'm so sorry, I wish I could explain, but for now I have to go.'

'Er – okay. Bye.'

'Bye.'

Rose frowned at the screen as she turned back to Morgan and Jane. 'How on earth did he get my number?'

'He asked for it! I didn't think you'd object, somehow!' Morgan winked at her. 'Also asked whether you had a 'significant other', to quote him.'

There had to be hope for them, didn't there? If they really did manage to restore life to how it was? Fired up by the conversation with Aiden, Rose drew in a deep breath. It was definitely time.

CHAPTER THIRTY-FIVE

She turned to Jane. 'Are you okay? You've turned awfully pale.'

Jane nodded. 'I am perfectly resolved, though I find this plan fraught with danger. I come from a world where one can be deported for stealing little more than an apple.' She gave Rose a rueful smile. 'I too wish to regain my former life, but there is part of me who would remain. I am uncertain of my true destiny. Is it the life I once had, or is *this* where I am meant to be?'

Rose shook her head. 'I wish I knew. There are so many things here in this century that makes life... easier, cleaner, *safer* for you.' Then she smiled. 'But I know how much you love your family, and if we can restore things to how they were, surely you can continue to enjoy both? And Cassandra must miss you terribly.'

'I fully comprehend; it is a sound wish, a hope we both share.' Jane followed Morgan out into the hallway, then turned back. 'But if the constables arrive, and we are despatched forthwith to the magistrate, I shall declare you both kidnapped me.'

Rose waved her hand. 'Morgan can handle the police.'

Morgan looked surprised as they lined up by the front door. 'I can?'

Rose smiled at her. 'With one hand tied behind your back. You talk yourself out of speeding tickets all the time.'

'How do you... Oh, right. Well, that's just a mix of respect and apology...'

Rose grabbed her bag from the table. 'Anyway – it won't matter. If the safe is there and the necklace is inside, the world should revert to its normal form.'

'And we will be back in a Sydney Place we are familiar with, Rose.'

'Not me.' Morgan's face had become very uncharacteristically serious, but Rose smiled at her as they walked out into the driveway.

'No – but trust me, you will be having a great time.'

'What do you know?'

Rose laughed; she could barely keep herself from bouncing on the balls of her feet. 'It's a long story – but trust me, Morgan; you're having a lovely time in the real world. Now come on, are you two with me or not? We've got to get there before the cleaners leave!' And Rose set off at a steady pace down the drive. Little did she know it, but Jane Austen was about to take her first ride on a bus!

Rose's bravado lasted all through the bus ride into Bath, and continued even when they realised they had nothing with them suitable for knocking holes in walls.

With a shrug, Rose had told Morgan and Jane they wouldn't have found anything at her home either (her mother always paid someone to do any maintenance to her house), and they'd made a quick detour into Bathwick Street once off the bus to another local shop where they managed to buy a small mallet. To both Rose and Morgan's amusement, Jane had seemed very impressed with this, remarking as they walked back out into the street that the 'convenient' store had, for once, lived up to its name.

Once outside 4 Sydney Place, however, her confidence waned

somewhat, and she was thankful Morgan was taking the lead, showing the cleaner who came to the door the text from Adam giving her permission to go into the building and, in fact, greeting her like an old friend.

With a quick grin over her shoulder, Morgan gestured for them to follow her inside. 'Claire has been cleaning here for nearly ten years. Oh, and that's Bonnie!' Morgan waved cheerily at a young girl presently lugging a vacuum cleaner up the first flight of stairs. 'She only joined Claire a couple months ago.'

'Well, we'd best get on, dearie.' Claire nodded to Rose and Jane and turned to face Morgan. 'Where d'you think you left this cap thingy, then?'

'Can we go up to the top landing? It was the last place I took photos, so I'm sure it must be up there.'

Waiting until they had disappeared round the corner on the stairs, Rose and Jane could still hear Morgan chattering away loudly.

'Oh of course, feel free to keep up with your cleaning. I'll just let myself out.'

'Come on! We don't have long.' Rose pointed at the door to the ground-floor offices. It was ajar and lights were shining from inside. They hurried through the front room and then through the door into the back office where they both stared at the plain, featureless expanse of the back wall; then, after exchanging a glance, they moved forward in unison.

Rose put her hands on the plaster. 'Here, do you think?'

Jane stared at the window to the right of where Rose stood, then walked over and put her own hands just to the side of Rose's. 'Here. I would know it with my eyes closed.'

Pulling the mallet from her bag, Rose drew in a deep breath, then let it out in a rush as they heard a vacuum start up on the floor above.

It was now or never. She tapped the mallet against the wall, making a very small dent in the plaster.

Jane rolled her eyes. 'Unfathomable! We are seeking a safe, are we not, not a sixpence?' She took the mallet from Rose and swung it in earnest at the wall, and a large chunk of plaster fell away, but all it exposed was a matted mass of wattle and daub. Jane whacked it hard with the mallet, but it barely moved, taunting them with its solidity.

Handing the mallet back to Rose, Jane smirked. 'I believe it is now your turn.'

'But we'll never break through this! No wonder it's lasted centuries. And we only have as long as Morgan can distract the cleaners upstairs.'

Jane glanced at the ceiling where the sound of a vacuum cleaner could still be heard. 'Then make haste, else our mission fails us.'

Attacking the wall with every ounce of strength she could muster, Rose finally managed to make a breach in the old wall and using the handle of the mallet, finally broke right through just as the noise from upstairs ceased; without the sound of the vacuum to cover for them, who knew how long they'd got.

'I've never done anything like this in my life!' Rose whispered.

'Nor I. It is most invigorating, is it not?'

Invigorating? Rose looked down at her dust-covered clothes and her dirty nails. Perhaps the meaning had changed over the centuries.

They both began pulling shreds of plaster and debris from around the opening, conscious of the noise they were making but powerless to stop now. The dust was excessive and they were both spluttering and coughing but neither of them gave up until finally they had made a gap large enough to see through.

The safe was there, albeit likewise covered in dust, but that was the first hurdle scaled. But there was no time to celebrate. Grabbing the mallet from the floor, Rose attacked the wall again with increased energy, but a sudden clattering on the stairs and a voice shouting alerted them to someone's approach and they stared at each other in horror, both frozen to the spot.

'I think they're onto us,' Morgan was breathless as she charged into the room. 'Fortunately, I'm a bit quicker on my feet than Claire, and Bonnie – actually, I don't think Bonnie has noticed!'

'Is there a lock on the door?'

Morgan slammed it shut, forced a bolt across, then turned slowly back to stare at them both. Her face had gone uncharacteristically pale, and she looked quickly to Rose, then over at the wall behind her where the black face of the safe could be now be seen.

'It's all true. What you said.' Her voice was faint, and Rose turned around quickly to see what she was looking at. 'I mean, I *wanted* to believe you; I convinced myself I *did* believe you, but now I really, *really* do!'

'Indeed. The safe remains intact. All we must do is open it, and if the necklace rests inside…' Jane gestured around the room. 'All will be well.'

Aware time was running out, Rose looked over at Morgan, who still looked stunned. Claire appeared to be hammering on the door, and then was heard yelling at Bonnie to phone the police.

'You're going, aren't you?' Morgan's voice was tremulous, and Rose walked over and hugged her, trying to ignore the sting of tears rising as she was hugged fiercely in return. This was ridiculous. If it worked, she would see Morgan again very soon. And if it didn't, they'd be sharing the same cell in Bath police station for the night.

'If the safe still holds the necklace, then yes, I think so.' Giving Morgan one last hug, she swallowed hard on the sudden restriction in her throat, and walked back over to Jane, who stood near the newly revealed safe, before turning once more to meet Morgan's wide brown eyes.

'I'll see you,' Rose mouthed to her, and Morgan gave her a little wave just as a siren was heard in the street outside, followed quickly by the heavy pounding of feet in the room beyond the door.

Rose turned to Jane. 'It's time.'

Jane nodded solemnly. 'You will not be sorry to leave this life behind.'

For a moment, Rose remembered Aiden, the sound of his voice on the phone earlier, and she smiled faintly. 'No – but it had its compensations.'

'Open up! Open up in there. This is the police!'

With one last look across the room at Morgan, Rose nodded at Jane, who reached into the hole for the brass handle and tugged at the door to the safe.

CHAPTER THIRTY-SIX

Rose gave an involuntary shudder as once again the ice-cold feeling swept over her skin, but this time she welcomed it as the room around them seemed to dissolve and reform.

For a moment, she and Jane stared at each other; it had gone incredibly quiet, the cacophony of sound silenced in one all-important second.

Cautiously, Rose looked around the room; a room she was entirely familiar with as Jane's bedroom, with boxes full of silverware and rolls of parchment spilling out onto the floor and oil lamps and candleholders on every surface. Of Morgan, the police or the cleaning ladies there was no sign.

With a gasp, Rose raised a hand to her neck: her replica cross was back! She spun back around to face Jane, a wide smile spreading across her face.

'We did it!'

Jane had extracted a small leather pouch from the safe and was peering inside. 'Indeed.' She wrinkled her nose. 'It is to be hoped Cass did the necessary upon its retrieval!'

Rose's smile widened. 'Just hold onto it – firmly!'

Jane slipped the pouch into the larger one she kept on her person, then looked down at her dust-free skirt. 'I do not think I have had so much fun since Cass and I sewed up the sleeve lining in my sister-in-law's pelisse. It seems we are returned to our former selves.'

Rose looked down at her now debris-free fingers. 'I know... at least... hold on; I just need to check something.' Hurrying out into the hallway, she tugged open the street door, before releasing a pent-up breath. There was the brass plaque announcing the building as Jane Austen's former home, and *there*, she noted with increasing delight, were all her plant pots, their contents cascading down the steps to Rose's own front door!

She glanced at her watch, then frowned. It was showing a time more than an hour earlier than when they had made their raid on the office, and Rose slowly walked back into the building and closed the door.

If it wasn't the same time, was it the same day? She tugged her mobile from her pocket; the leather case with the elvish markings had gone and in its place was the familiar peacock cover. Rose pressed a kiss on it, then flipped the cover open and stared at the screen: Sunday 13 September!

'Jane!' Awash with relief, Rose hurried back into the apartment. 'Jane, we didn't just do it! We did it *all!*'

'Of course we did.' Jane was over by her desk, and Rose joined her. 'Why would it only work in part?'

'I don't know. I suppose I thought time would have moved on during our absence.'

Jane was sifting through the papers spread across the desk, and Rose tried to calm rising agitation. She didn't know what she was feeling: happiness, excitement, bewilderment all jostled for her attention.

'I need to go home,' she whispered, suddenly overwhelmed by a rush of relief, of gratitude, for *this* life. 'Downstairs, I mean. I just need to...'

Jane looked up, then smiled, her warm, hazel eyes sparkling again. 'You wish to be assured of many things, and there is much to ponder;

it was an adventure beyond all others, was it not?'

'Yes!' A whirlwind of images from their time in the other reality swept through Rose's mind, and she shuddered. 'Though I'm not sure I'd want to repeat it anytime soon.'

'Nor I.' Reaching down, Jane extracted a plain piece of paper from the roll at her feet. 'Besides, I am long overdue in writing to Cass, and thus I shall wish you a good evening.'

Rose made to turn away. 'Goodnight, Jane.' Then she hesitated before turning back. Her throat felt strangely tight. 'I can't think of anyone else I'd rather have been on an adventure with than you and Morgan. Your sister is so lucky to have you.'

She gave Jane a tremulous smile and quickly made her way out into the street again, where she stepped down onto the pavement and then stopped, drawing in a deep breath of the cool evening air. *Calm down*, she admonished herself. *It's all going to be okay now.*

Slowly, Rose turned around in a circle, soaking in the sights and sounds of *her* part of Bath: the grand, terraced houses of Great Pulteney Street, the Holburne Museum nestled in Sydney Gardens, and then Sydney Place itself, her gaze falling once more on the plaque beside the door of number 4.

It was barely six o'clock, and the sound of laughter and voices caught her attention. Looking back across the street, she saw a group of women of varying ages walking up the gravel path to the museum, mostly dressed in full Regency costume. Of course! The *Festival* was still in full flow, and tonight was the night of '*An Evening with Mr Wickham!*' Never in her life had Rose expected to be relieved that *that* man existed.

'Wait, wait!' one of them girls shouted, waving her phone. 'Group selfie before we go in!'

The laughter intensified as they all jostled to fit into the photo.

'Sylvie's bonnet is blocking my face!'

'Clarice, move your fan! I can't see!'

'Come on, we'll be late; Helen – hurry up!'

Shoving the phone back into her reticule – a common, if rather bizarre, sight at the *Jane Austen Festival* – the young woman hurried after the others as they poured into the museum and out of sight. Struck with a sudden thought, Rose tugged her own phone out of her pocket again and flicked it open.

There were the photos she had been taking at the *Festival* before things had changed, and... she tapped again... *there* were her contacts, her latest call list, all looking exactly as it should!

There were a few missed calls, too, mainly from Morgan and one from James. Rose turned and walked to the gate in the railings. Despite appearances – not just the pots but also the familiar curtains – she wasn't totally convinced her home had returned until the gate swung open freely, and she sighed with relief as she hurried down the steps to her front door. She didn't quite trust herself to call Morgan just yet; tugging her keyring from her bag, she opened the door and stepped inside.

First... before anything else... she had the overwhelming urge to check one more small detail.

Ten minutes later, curled up on the sofa with her copy of *Persuasion*, Rose finished rereading Captain Wentworth's letter, releasing a soft sigh as she came to the end of it.

She placed the book reverently on the side table and picked up her mug of tea and looked around the room in contentment. Letting herself back into her own flat had filled Rose with so much joy, she had almost wept. There were all the familiar things: her comfy sofa, the furnishings she had so carefully chosen, her shelves and shelves of books, crammed with titles from all stages of her life – her old friends – and on the wall, an elegantly framed quote, a gift from Morgan.

'You pierce my soul. I am half agony, half hope.'

Her friend! It was still Sunday evening, and she'd not long since left Morgan and James outside the dance class! Rose chewed her lip. Could she talk to Morgan without sounding like a complete lunatic? Laughing at the insanity of it all, she picked up her phone and flicked it open, but as she went to connect the call, she remembered exactly *how* she had left her friends – and her parting words of advice to them both. Getting to her feet, Rose paced slowly to and fro as she tapped in a text, not wanting to intrude in case… well, just in *case* she was intruding!

Then she curled back up in her seat and picked up her book again, quickly becoming lost in the familiar words and language. The sudden ping from her phone caused her to start, but she snatched it up eagerly.

'The next time you go chasing a delusional criminal please try to update me a bit quicker!'

Rose winced as she read Morgan's text. She had almost forgotten their speculation over Jane and their suspicions about her. With hindsight, it felt the height of absurdity and also a bit of an affront to her favourite author! Then she shrugged; there was no way she could tell Morgan exactly what the truth was.

'*So sorry,*' she typed in quickly. '*Luckily it was all a misunderstanding. I hope we'll laugh about in twenty years' time. You okay? You're not lost?*'

The response came back immediately: '*What?! A misunderstanding? How?*'

Rose swore under her breath; then, relieved Morgan couldn't see her reddening face, tapped in: '*She's not doing anything illegal – just likes to practise the hand, likes trying to use authentic things like the pens of the day and so on. Please, can we literally never speak of it again?*'

Morgan was clearly typing a response, so Rose pre-emptively keyed in quickly: '*So? Did James gather the courage to hold your hand?*'

There was a pause, then: '*A lady never tells.*'

Rose's mouth curved into a smile. '*Oh?*' she texted back, then crossed her fingers, hoping the previous topic was well and truly behind them.

'*James brought me safely home.*' Rose's smile widened, and she silently cheered.

'*Did he now? How kind of him! And is he still looking after you?*' She held her breath, waiting; then the phone pinged again.

There was no message, just an emoticon of two small faces *kissing*!

'I *knew* it!' Rose laughed and put the phone aside. Time to leave them in peace. *Time* – she had all the time in the world now, and she'd catch up properly with Morgan in the morning.

When Rose had finally fallen into her bed, she sank into its warm, comforting familiarity with a sigh of pleasure. She tried to start reading *Pride & Prejudice* again, but her lids soon grew so heavy she was asleep before she could even close the pages.

The ping of her phone brought her awake with a start the next morning, and for a moment she was completely disorientated, convinced she was still at her mother's house and facing a long Saturday at work in the library. Then, as she sat up and peered sleepily around the room, she remembered. They had done it! Against all the odds, they had managed to put things right!

Sinking back against the pillows, she realised she was lying on something hard and extracted her phone. There was a new text from Morgan: *'Call me when you wake up!!!'* followed by a string of hilarious emoticons indicating she was in a sunny frame of mind!

Smiling to herself, Rose closed her eyes and thought back over the previous day spent with her friend and Jane, culminating in their raid on 4 Sydney Place and the breaching of the false wall. *Aiden!* Rose's eyes flew open as she remembered his call, and her heart began pounding in her ears. He had called her, had wanted to see her again! Feeling heat stealing into her cheeks, Rose threw back the covers.

That hadn't been happening in this life, had it? Not yet... She had to find a way, find the courage to make a beginning. Who knew what might come of it?

She glanced over at her alarm clock and wished she had thought to set it: it was already 11am! Restless now, and desperate to reconnect with Morgan and Jane and, dare she even think it, attend Aiden's talk later, Rose swung her legs out of bed and headed for the bathroom. Was it possible to merge the two versions of her life into one happy whole?

Half an hour later, she walked through the ever-open door to 4 Sydney Place, eager to see how Jane was and hopefully have her curiosity satisfied over Cassandra's actions. She smiled as she reached the bottom of the stairs; how different did it feel to the previous evening, when they were facing uncertainty over the success or otherwise of their mission? After all, they could have been waking up this morning locked up in a cell at Bath police station! *That* would have been something for Jane to write about!

Rose whispered a heartfelt '*Thank you, Cassandra*' under her breath, then noticed the door to the ground-floor apartment was ajar, and she pushed it aside. 'Jane? It's me, Rose!'

There was no answer; she walked down to the kitchen, but it was empty, so she walked back to the closed bedroom door. Tentatively, Rose knocked. There was a shuffling sound and then it was swung open by a woman dressed in an overall.

'Oh, hello, love. Did you want someone?'

'Er, no. I mean, yes. The lady who is staying here?' Rose peered over the woman's head.

The cleaner pulled the door wide open, a duster and can of polish in her hand. The bed was stripped and there were no boxes on the floor, nor any lamps or candles in sight. Rose's heart lurched. Had Jane gone so soon?

Feeling almost dazed, Rose walked up to the safe in the wall and placed her hand on it. It felt real and solid, and reaching out, she grasped the brass handle, much as Jane had on the previous evening, and tugged. The door swung open easily but there was nothing inside.

'Good morning, Rose.'

Relieved, Rose turned on her heel. 'There you are!'

Jane stood in the open doorway to the drawing room, and she beckoned Rose to join her before closing the door firmly. It was only as they settled on the sofa she realised Jane was dressed in one of her Regency outfits, her hair appropriately styled. Slowly Rose looked around the room. It wasn't empty like the bedroom, but all the piles of new books had been stacked neatly against the wall and next to them were two rather battered-looking old suitcases.

'I trust you found naught of distress on your return home?'

Rose's gaze snapped back to Jane. 'Not at all! Everything was exactly as it should be!' Then she frowned; Jane looked pale and tired. 'Are you – is everything okay?'

'Not entirely. For myself, I will own to gaining little sleep. Barely – or so it seemed – had I closed the door upon my letter to my sister, when there was a response, and thereafter followed many an exchange, both lengthy and not conducive to a sound night's rest.' She smiled ruefully. 'I long to reassure her – in person, not merely by my own hand – of the success of her endeavours and of my own well-being.'

'You – you're leaving? Going back? I mean, I know that you *do* at some point because everything is back how it was. What I meant was, you're going right now?'

CHAPTER THIRTY-SEVEN

Rose gestured towards the cases and books, knew her voice sounded wistful.

Jane smiled kindly at her and took Rose's hand. ''Tis not only for Cass I must return. As we suspected, my family has become well-versed in all my... dealings. My desire to journey here cannot be tolerated or enjoyed without their forgiveness for my former secrecy and their blessing for its possible continuance.'

'And she – your sister – did she fill in the gaps? I mean, how she even knew about Prancer, worked it all out?'

'Indeed.' Jane gestured to a small pile of letters on the table, but Rose's eyes were caught by what lay beside them: the cross and chain, resting on top of the soft leather pouch. 'Cass was drawn to the window by the sound of an animal in distress. The cross had become lodged in Prancer's throat – he could not extricate himself without her aid.'

Drawing her gaze back to Jane's, Rose nodded. 'And now?'

'He remains with Cass.' Jane smiled. 'My sister has long wished for a pup, though she may regret taking him into her care. It seems Prancer has a propensity for stealing stockings!'

'But what about your family – your mum and dad? How did they find out you simply hadn't gone missing?'

With a sigh, Jane's smile faded. 'Cass's sorrow went unremarked at first by the family who understood her to be grieving for her missing sister, but our parents' decision to involve the local magistrate forced her into confessing the whole to them.'

'Followed by the family's backtracking.'

Jane nodded. 'Further, Cass knew that if the necklace was placed within the safe, I could open it in the future. Being at least half as sensible as I ever give her credit for, she comprehended aught must prevent me from doing so, or I had assumed the charm lost without trace and thus ceased to try. With little to guide her, she felt her only way was to leave a message in the hope it would find me.'

Slowly exhaling, Rose nodded. 'Or you would find it yourself!'

'My father was persuaded of the need to conceal the safe, for Cass was full aware how many years it must keep its secret – and thus the wall was built. Beyond this, all she could do was hope and pray we would find our way back to each other.' Jane paused, then took Rose's hand. 'Thanks to you, Rose, we did. Without your persuasion, your persistence, I would not have found a way home. My sister – my whole family – is in your debt.'

'Yes, but,' Rose swallowed on the rising lump in her throat. 'You're going back to an untimely death, when you could still live a long and fruitful life here.'

'My life will be fruitful, will it not? My literary aspirations will be realised, and I am most fortunate: an unpublished author, yet I comprehend the outcome before I have begun!' Jane paused, then laughed. 'Perchance I am become more like my sister!' Then she patted Rose on the arm. 'Be free of your agitation. What was done was done for the best. Now – I am in need of an emissary. During the night, I have been able to convey to Cass those possessions which came through the usual means.' She nodded towards the door into the room with the safe. 'But for aught acquired here, I must leave instruction on its disposal. Would you pass this to my landlord?'

Feeling her heart dip, Rose took the letter from Jane. 'Disposal? You are – I thought… I thought perhaps you'd come back. You know, once you'd sorted things out with your parents.'

Jane smiled faintly. 'I have learnt sufficient in this time to comprehend my family will need me in the coming years, and thus I must remain with them for the foreseeable future. Perchance once we are happily situated in Hampshire, I will take out the necklace once more.' She got to her feet, then held out her hand. 'To be certain, if I choose to do so, I shall seek you out. You have been a good friend to me, Rose.'

A tightness gripping her throat, Rose stood and took Jane's hand. 'I can't even send you back with those drops to help your eyes.' Then she gasped, recalling the poisoning theory on Jane's death. 'Wait! You don't use arsenic at all, do you?'

'Only on those I find disagreeable.'

'Jane,' Rose pleaded. 'Be serious!'

Jane drew in a short breath. 'I will own to our having Fowler's Solution at home. It is recommended for rheumatic pain. But…' She met Rose's anxious gaze and squeezed her hand gently. 'I promise to take care.'

'I wish I could do – could've done – more.' Rose sniffed.

Jane's eyes softened. 'It is impossible to do justice to the hospitality and care of attention you have shown me. You did more than any other could.'

There was nothing more to say, so she responded firmly to Jane's shake of her hand, knowing she would expect nothing less, and sniffed away the threat of tears.

'I wish you every happiness; I only wish I could've sent you back with something to help you when you become ill.'

'Do not concern yourself over me. I have much to accomplish in the coming years, and who is to say what may or may not occur in our lives in the interim?'

Rose nodded, her eyes wide. 'Goodbye, Jane.'

'Goodbye, Rose; my gratitude is beyond words, but I will carry you here.' She touched her heart. 'Always.'

Unable to respond as the lump in her throat threatened to choke her, Rose nodded again, then she hurried from the room. Glancing back as she closed the door, she saw Jane had turned to stare out of the window. Rose, unable to stop a tear sliding down her cheek, walked out into the hallway and pulled open the heavy front door, wiping her sleeve across her eyes and blinking as she stepped out into the sunlight.

Then, drawing in a shaky breath, she straightened her shoulders and stepped down into the street. The large windows of the drawing room in the ground-floor apartment gave a full view of the interior as she passed – it was already empty; Jane had gone.

With a sigh, Rose turned away, but before she could push open the gate to her own flat, a sudden breeze lifted the curls on her shoulders as a voice whispered behind her, '*Be not melancholy*'. Spinning around, Rose knew there would be no one there but she felt strangely comforted, and she hurried down the steps to her flat, intent on calling Morgan – *her* Morgan. It was time she picked up the threads of her life – this life she had missed so much!

Barely had Rose ended her quick call to her friend when her own phone began to ring.

'Hey, Liz! Hi!'

'Rose! I was hoping to catch you! I know you're tied up at the Festival all week, but can I ask a favour about the cake for next weekend?'

Rose's eyes widened. *Are you kidding me?!* squeaked a small voice in her head.

'Er – yes? Go ahead!'

'I called the people making it at the weekend because I hadn't heard from them, and guess what? They've messed up! Taken on too many bookings and now they won't be able to do it!'

'Oh! That's a shame. Er – you do remember I can't bake, don't you, Liz?' Rose held her breath.

Thankfully, Liz laughed heartily. 'Do I ever! Anyway, I wanted to ask if you could let me have the details on whoever made that gorgeous cake you organised for your company's fifth anniversary? You posted a photo on *Instagram* at the time, but now I can't find it.'

'It was *Tara's Tarts & Teacakes*; she's usually pretty good at fitting in last-minute orders. Hold on, let me check my contacts for her number.' Almost giddy with relief, Rose quickly relayed the details to her friend. 'So, how are the plans for the party coming along? The invitation was beautiful!' Rose's gaze drifted over to the mantelpiece, and she saw the card exactly where she'd left it, tucked behind the clock.

'Ugh! Stressfully!' Liz laughed again, and Rose grinned, she had missed hearing it so much! 'Tina wants to be involved, but every time I give her something to do, she either forgets or does it wrong!'

'Best not let her get involved in the wedding planning, then!'

Just then, Rose remembered her friend's change of name in the other reality. 'Hey, Liz – have you ever wondered what your parents might have called you if your mum hadn't loved *Pride & Prejudice* so much?'

'What? Is this one of those *Facebook* quizzes?'

'No!' Rose laughed but her skin tingled in anticipation. 'It's just… I recently was in a situation where I was trying to understand the legacy of Jane Austen's writing on the world… and then I realised your name might be – *have* been – different, if Elizabeth Bennet hadn't been created!'

Liz chuckled. 'I dunno!' She paused. 'Oh dear! Think of the possibilities! Something from *Jane Eyre*, perhaps. Jane would've been okay; Bertha?' She went off into peals of laughter. 'That would have made me Bertha Bottomley!'

Rose laughed, too.

'Thank God for *Pride & Prejudice*, right, Rose?'

'You have *no* idea how much I agree with you!'

'Alright, mate; let me go call this lady and see if she can help me out. Probably won't see you before Sunday, what with the Festival and your friend over. Hey, feel free to bring a guest if you like! Bye!'

Rose's immediate thought was not of Morgan, and she put the phone down hastily, relieved Liz couldn't see the deep blush filling her cheeks.

Barely five minutes later, Rose walked quickly down to Laura Place to meet Morgan, trying hard to keep a control on her sheer joy at the world being back to normal; if her friend thought anything unusual about the ferocity of Rose's hug when they met, she didn't comment on it.

They had walked into town to enjoy a leisurely lunch with Morgan filling Rose in on her evening with James. He had invited her out to dinner, and then they'd had a nightcap back at her flat, and it was agreed, from whichever cultural angle you looked at it, this constituted a proper date!

It was a lovely September afternoon, and Rose had persuaded Morgan to take a stroll around the streets of Bath to enjoy the weather, finding it hard to suppress her delight on discovering the

Jane Austen Centre returned to its usual place and the window of the *Tourist Information Centre* once again displaying its Austen-related merchandise.

Bumping into some of their friends, two of whom were beautifully dressed in full costume again, they agreed to take afternoon tea in the Pump Room. They weren't the only table of festival-goers in the elegant building, and there was plenty of banter being thrown about the room as the musicians played a suitable musical accompaniment, and Rose had looked around contentedly.

Morgan's holiday still stretched before them; a Morgan who couldn't stop talking about and exchanging texts with James; a James who clearly wasn't feeling his usual workaholic self! On top of all that, this evening was Aiden's talk. She would be seeing him, albeit at a distance, for the first time since things had returned to normal!

Before that, however, there was a talk on *Regency Social Etiquette* to attend where, typically, Morgan ended up at the front as soon as a volunteer was asked for, and threw herself into the role of a Regency lady giving the 'cut direct' to the other volunteer, much to the audience's amusement.

After that, they'd met up with Sandy and Tess for dinner, before splitting up, their friends to go to a musical recital at the Holburne Museum, and Rose and Morgan heading for the venue where Aiden would be doing his presentation.

A little of the euphoria which had carried Rose through the past 24 hours had faded by the time they arrived outside the Theatre Royal. She'd been living in a blissful haze, so wrapped up in the delight of being back where she belonged, and with all things Jane Austen back in their rightful place, too, that she hadn't thought too much beyond it.

Now, standing in a long queue, virtually all-female, waiting to be let into the theatre, she was filled with misgivings at the thought of seeing Aiden.

'Wow! This must be a sell-out!' Morgan winked at Rose.

The woman in front turned and grinned at them. 'It usually is. Last year, there were people sitting on the floor because they'd run out of chairs!' She gave a pronounced wink. 'That's the draw of the gorgeous Doc for you!'

'He used to talk at the Mission,' added her friend, nodding her head down the road. 'But he's too popular, so they've put him here this year.'

None of this was news to Rose, but it was sufficient encouragement for Morgan to begin chatting in earnest with their new friends. Rose was silent, her anticipation jostling with her trepidation and turning her insides into a tight knot.

The last time she'd talked to Aiden, he'd been asking her on a date – sort of. Did that Aiden exist anymore? *Of course he does – he is exactly the same person. Not taking part in a dig in Steventon or doing talks about it occasionally doesn't change him as a man! It's only the manner of your acquaintance that is different.*

Easy for you to say, thought Rose sourly. Here she was, about to come face-to-face with him again and this couldn't be further from a date! No, she was merely one of the crowd today… Rose turned to look around at the swelling sea of women of all ages waiting in excitement for his lecture. Did any of them care at all about what he was saying, or were they only there to stare? What were the odds now she could still have both of her worlds?

'Hey, Rose, come on!' Rose started as Morgan began to move forward. 'The doors are open!'

There were no allocated seats, so there was a mad rush as people tried to get the best ones, pouring in all directions down to the stalls. Rose had planned to sit in the back row so she could enjoy watching the presentation without being noticed. As Aiden had never so much as shown a flicker of recognition when she'd attended his talks in the past few years, she had no reason to expect today to be any different, but after her recent experiences with him, that was going to hurt.

'Nope! No hiding for you.' Morgan grabbed her arm as Rose made to step along the back row. She went up on her tiptoes as she tried to scan the stalls, thwarted by a melee of hurrying bonnets and fans, then waved. 'Damn, they can't see us!'

Putting her fingers to her lips, Morgan let out a loud whistle, then waved again.

'We've saved you seats,' called Marita. 'Over here!' She pointed to her right, where Rose could see Marita and Chrystal, and she bit her lip. They were in the front row!

Her protests to Morgan went unheard, and she was dragged to the front – though thankfully at one end and not the centre of the row – and found herself sitting almost at eye level with the stage, which was equipped with nothing but a large, portable screen and a small table bearing the doctor's familiar and battered laptop.

Remembering her morning working with him, helping restore his files and then his going for his shower just as Morgan called, the telltale colour stole into Rose's cheeks and she sighed softly.

Morgan was turned around in her seat chattering to the women behind when her friend's mobile lit up. Rose almost rolled her eyes; she could make out James's name, and she gave Morgan a nudge and nodded at it.

To her surprise, however, Morgan ignored her phone and turned to face Rose; then she leaned conspiratorially closer to her. 'You know

I love you, right?'

Giving a small, rueful smile, Rose nodded. 'Yes.'

'Did you also know you've been a little weird today?'

After everything that had happened, or nearly happened, Rose could hardly say she felt surprised at the observation. 'I know; sorry.'

Morgan was peering closely at her. 'Are you getting all overexcited about seeing…?' She inclined her head toward the stage. 'You Know Who? And no, I don't mean *Voldemort*.'

Swallowing quickly, Rose shook her head. 'No, I think I'm a little tired.'

'Earlier, it was like you were on some kind of high – like, *unnaturally* high, like you'd had one too many sodas. But now, you're… well, I can't put my finger on it – are you anxious? Are you nervous?! Is it about me? Have I said something or – No? Phew. Okay, so if not me then did your mom call or something?'

'Don't you think you'd better stop wasting time nagging me and answer lover boy's text instead?' Rose grinned and nudged Morgan affectionately. 'If you don't respond within seconds, he'll think you're lost or in danger or something and come tearing down here to rescue you!'

'I don't know what you're talking about!' With a grin, Morgan turned her attention to the incoming text, responded quickly and then switched off the phone, tucking it into her pocket as the lights on the stage went up.

Then she leaned towards Rose and whispered. 'Rose Wallace, something has gotten into you!'

'I have no idea what you mean.' Rose whispered, her gaze locked on the stage now. Rose loved Morgan, too, but she wasn't about to try and explain how she'd spent several days in the company of Jane Austen herself, a slightly different Morgan and an attentive doctor! Nor could she tell her she was now living those same days again – this time emotionally exhausted but overjoyed because she had helped to save novel writing and romantic literature from a dire fate and her own normal life to boot. There were some explanations best not put into words.

Just then, there was a crackle as the loudspeakers came to life, and a disembodied voice made a brief announcement about fire exits, switching off mobiles and a request not to take photographs, particularly of the presenter. This was greeted by a loud groan from one section of the stalls, followed by much laughter from everyone else, but then there was a lull as all eyes turned to the stage and Aiden walked on.

There he was; in the flesh. He looked exactly as always, and Rose smiled faintly at the collective sigh from around her as he shrugged out of his jacket and tossed it on the chair before pulling his wire-rimmed glasses from his shirt pocket and putting them on.

The disappointment she'd known would come as his eyes scanned the audience briefly, passing over her and Morgan without a hint of recognition, hit much harder than she'd expected, and her hand flew to her throat as it tightened threateningly.

Morgan leaned in again, no doubt to tease her, but then she stopped and patted Rose's hand awkwardly. 'Hey, are you okay?'

Rose nodded but didn't look at Morgan in case she spotted the hint of tears in her eyes. 'Yes, of course.'

With another reassuring pat on her hand, Morgan sat back in her seat again, and Rose swallowed hard, her gaze fixed on the white, portable screen, unable to look over to where Aiden was sorting through his slides – slides *she* had been working on only days ago…

CHAPTER THIRTY-EIGHT

'I'm sorry to keep you waiting.' As his familiar voice rang out, Rose chanced a quick glance in his direction. He had perched himself on the edge of the small table, placing his slides and even the laptop in peril. 'I had a slight mishap on the way in.' He reached down and waved the broken strap of his bag. 'It left things slightly out of order on the pavement.'

A general murmur of reassurance spread through the room, with someone calling out, 'You're always worth the wait, Doc!' followed by a ripple of laughter.

Aiden smiled self-consciously and ran a hand through his already tousled hair. 'Ah… right.' He got to his feet and walked round to his laptop, hitting a key and picking up the remote and pointing it at his screen. An image appeared on the large screen on the stage, a familiar drawing to Rose, of Steventon Rectory when Jane used to live there.

'Sooo.' Aiden stared at the image for a second, then turned to face them. 'Let's talk Steventon, shall we?'

'We can talk *anything* you like, Doc!' A few people laughed again, but most were watching him expectantly.

'Okay; so, I think I recognise some of you from previous years.' Aiden scanned the faces turned up to him, then smiled faintly. 'You'll be pleased to know, therefore, that this year, I'm sharing some new facts with you, along with images of formerly unseen artefacts, a couple of which we can accurately date to the period the Austen family lived in Steventon.'

There was a frisson of excitement at this as, once again, Aiden's gaze roamed over the crowd, and Rose watched him, unaware she was holding her breath. 'If you're a well-behaved audience…' He paused deliberately, 'I might even let you in on a few of my secret discoveries!'

As people smiled and a few cheered, he suddenly turned his head towards the area where Rose and Morgan sat and for a fleeting second – so fast she wasn't quite sure it had actually happened – their eyes met. She swallowed quickly, but he was already launching into his presentation, the first slide flashing onto the screen. If it hadn't been for Morgan singing '*he's so into you*' under her breath, she would have been convinced she had imagined it.

Rose didn't hear a word after that – not that it mattered. As she had typed up his notes and re-created half of the slides, she knew the talk by heart, even if it was mainly new to the rest of the people there.

As always, when Aiden was talking about history, about his work in particular, he was a heady mixture of animated intelligence and intensity. Glancing quickly to her left, she could see the rapt faces, all silent now, drinking in his every word – though whether it was because of the content or simply because he had such a lovely voice, she couldn't tell. She didn't dare glance in Morgan's direction, and just hoped her own face was arranged in some semblance of polite interest, because her heart was doing flip-flops in her chest. She had never met anyone who had this effect on her.

Rose felt unsettled; she didn't like being part of this sea of devotees – she wanted to be special. But honestly, more than anything, she wanted to have the chance to be near to him, to talk to him and spend time in his company again. With a sigh, she tried not to watch him, staring fixedly at the slides as they flipped onto the screen. Her eyes, however, seemed to have a will of their own and returned time and again to where he stood, reeling off the prepared words of his talk, or rambling off at a tangent as something would strike him, his hands moving expressively as he expounded on one theory or another. *He had such lovely hands*, mused Rose, watching keenly as he gripped the edge of the table for a moment to reach for a map to show them.

Lovely hands. Rose sighed, then flinched as Aiden stopped suddenly, the unfurled map hanging loose for a moment. Morgan made an involuntarily sound and then coughed to try to cover it, and Chrystal threw her a startled look before smiling at her. *Oh. My. God. Did I say that out loud?!*

Rose's skin went cold, then really warm. Morgan had her hand over her mouth trying not to laugh.

Meanwhile, Aiden had barely missed a beat and was holding up the map to the audience now as he wound up his talk – was he done already? More to the point, was there a chance, the slightest, teeniest chance, he hadn't heard her? Had she spent the last hour simply staring at the man? So much for scorning those who came to stare rather than listen!

'Now, before I open up the floor for questions, is anyone taking the tour to Hampshire in the morning?'

Rose glanced around; there was a fair show of hands. The escorted trips to Jane Austen country had become so popular over the years, they now did two, and sometimes three, during the *Festival* to accommodate the demand.

'Good; good.' Aiden stared into the distance for a moment as a hush settled on the audience. Then he seemed to recall where he was, and blinked. 'Right. Well, if you're on that trip, I've got a team on a dig in Chawton I need to check in with; probably find me by the church, as we're working on a project there. Feel free to come and say hello.'

A buzz of noise followed this, and Rose frowned. That wasn't on the official programme! She turned to Morgan, who grinned at her.

'Good job we chose to go on Tuesday's tour, huh, and not Monday's!' Then she laughed, keeping her voice to a whisper. 'He might regret inviting people to say hi, though! Doubt he'll get a chance to do much work once the bus arrives!'

'Right – any questions?' The doctor had perched his glasses on his head, clearly pleased by the number of hands shooting into the air. 'Yes – the lady there,' he pointed into the audience. 'In the… er… blue bonnet – yes, the one with feathers rather than fruit!'

There was a murmur of laughter.

'Are there any seats left on the coach tour?' The laughter increased, and Aiden smiled, causing Rose's heart to flutter alarmingly again.

'I believe it's already sold out.' Most of the hands were reluctantly withdrawn as a collective 'Awwww' could be heard.

'Er – anyone else? Any*thing* else?'

He fielded a few questions about the dig, but most of them were about him: what had drawn him into archaeology? What find had given him the most pleasure? Where was he going next?

'This is more like a chat show than a Q&A!' Morgan hissed in Rose's ear. 'Ask him one of your intelligent questions; go on.' She nudged Rose hard in the ribs.

Shaking her head fiercely, Rose glared at Morgan, who simply smirked back at her before returning her gaze to the stage.

Sinking back in her seat as the questions continued to come, Rose sighed. The lecture was as good as over; with Aiden heading off to Chawton tomorrow on what was clearly his current project, the likelihood of him returning was slim. Was this how it would end, like any other year?

'Right. If that's all the questions, I'll say thank you and—' Aiden's voice broke into her thoughts, and Rose looked over to where he stood on the edge of the stage. 'Yes? The lady at the back – you had another question?'

'Yes, I wondered if you had any photos of the metal comb you mentioned finding? I'd love to see it.'

There was a general murmur of approval to this, but Aiden frowned. 'I do, but I'm not sure if I brought them…' And he turned and looked straight at Rose. 'Do you remember seeing them when you were sorting through things?'

The surprise left Rose speechless for a moment, but her heart began to race under his stare, and she could feel warmth filling her cheeks as so many eyes turned in her direction. Morgan nudged her foot and Rose sat up a little in her seat and cleared her throat. 'Yes – yes, I do.'

There was an expectant pause, and then a smile almost touched his lips; it was all she could do not to sigh out loud again.

'And, er – can you, by any chance, remember where this was?' There was some gentle laughter at this.

'Sorry. Yes, of course. At the back of the blue folder,' Rose pointed over to the small table. 'I think it was the section labelled, *Day 3 Finds*; I put them in order according to their catalogue number.'

Aiden turned to flick through the folder for a moment, and Rose sank lower into her seat, trying to breathe slowly, evenly. *That did not happen; it didn't.*

Morgan was grinning at her. 'You said, '*I do*' to the Doc!' she whispered. ''Fraid that's it – you're man and wife now, in front of all these witnesses!'

'You're incorrigible!' Rose muttered, her heart slowly resuming its normal pace.

'Here we are!' Aiden turned back to face the room, waving some photographs in the direction of the lady who had asked the question. 'I've got something I need to be doing this evening, but I'm happy to stay until…' He glanced at his watch. 'Say, 8.30? So if anyone has anything else they'd like to have a look at, please come up to the front. Thank you, everyone.'

There was a loud round of applause and a few more whistles from around the theatre, and people began to get up and gather their belongings.

'Doctor Trevellyan! Aiden, excuse me!' Rose's skin went cold. 'What you are *doing*?' she hissed at Morgan, who was waving at Aiden and beckoning him over.

'Let's not waste the opportunity!' Morgan winked at her as Aiden came to stand in front of them at the edge of the stage.

'Oh, hi!' He smiled at Morgan. 'Did you have a question for me?'

'Yes, but not about archaeology!' Morgan's smile widened as she quickly moved her leg, Rose's kick misfiring as her foot connected with the front of the stage instead.

No one else seemed to notice the thud, though Rose would swear Aiden's eyes had flickered and… was he *smirking*, or had she imagined the edges of his mouth curving upwards slightly?

'Great lecture! Good to see you again. Wanted to let you know – Rose, James and I are all heading over to *The Raven* now. You're welcome to join us if you're up for it.'

He didn't answer straight away, and Rose, who had been staring anywhere but at Aiden, slowly looked up. He wasn't smiling, but he was watching her, and for some reason, it gave her a little courage.

Swallowing her trepidation, she said as cheerfully as she could muster, 'We'd love to see you there.'

Aiden nodded. 'Would've loved to be there, but I'm afraid I leave this evening for Hampshire. Need to catch up first thing with the team on what they've been up to whilst I've been in Bath.'

Morgan shrugged. 'That's a shame. Well, we'll see you in Chawton, then!'

'You're on the tour?'

'Wouldn't miss it – would we, Rose?'

'Er – no. We wouldn't.'

'Good. Well – excuse me.' He nodded at them both and turned away.

Morgan leaned forward with the pretence of picking up her sweater so she could catch Rose's eye. 'Mad at me?'

'No,' Rose said tersely, and then she smiled. 'Of course not. I'd already embarrassed myself enough, so what does one more thing matter?'

'You did start it you know,' Morgan said, her eyes sparkling with suppressed laughter.

'Not intentionally! I had no idea I'd said it out loud!'

'Don't worry – I doubt anyone except the Doc noticed – it's not like you gave into the urge to applaud again! He was probably so tuned in to you, he was aware of everything you were doing.'

'Stop it, Morgan!' Rose wished it were true, but she wasn't stupid.

They got to their feet, and Rose looked over towards the stage. Several people had taken Aiden up on his offer, and he was presently crouched at the front of the stage talking to them.

Turning to follow Morgan, her reluctance to leave was tempered by knowing she might see him one last time on the following day. As they reached the doors, Rose hesitated and glanced back over her shoulder. Aiden seemed to be rummaging around in his jacket for something, leaving the remaining members of the audience to study the photographs, and with a resigned sigh, Rose turned and followed Morgan out into the foyer and then out into the street where they turned left to walk towards Queen Square.

They had barely gone two paces when her phone began to ring. 'Why don't you text James to meet us in *The Raven*?' Rose flipped open her phone case and stared disbelievingly at the name on the screen: *Doctor Trevellyan.*

Morgan looked up from her texting. 'Aren't you going to answer it?!'

'Oh! Yes!' Rose connected the call, putting the phone cautiously to her ear as they continued to walk along Barton Street. 'Hello?'

'Hi. It's… Aiden.' He sounded so close, Rose threw a frantic look over her shoulder, thinking for a minute he'd followed them.

'Er, hi! Did you – did you need help with something? Your laptop…'

'No, not at all. I – it's – I didn't get a chance to say thank you; you know, for… everything.'

'All I did was tell you where the photos were!' Morgan closed her phone with a snap and smiled widely, tapping a fist rapidly against her chest, but Rose shook her head, trying to hear what he was saying.

'*And* retyped my speech and rescued my *entire* presentation the other day!'

Despite her desperately fluttering heart, Rose laughed. 'Okay. But anyone could have done the same.'

'I don't agree.'

There was silence for a moment, and Rose glanced at Morgan who was staring unapologetically at her. They had reached the corner of Queen Square, and she pointed to the right to steer her friend towards *The Raven*.

Aiden cleared his throat. 'Sooo – anyway; as I said, I wanted to thank you.'

'You just did.'

'No – I mean, can I treat you to a drink or something? A meal, even?'

Rose's heart dropped in her chest, then bounded back up into place and started hammering. Would he be able to hear it?

'Are you still there?'

'Oh, yes! Sorry. That would be nice.' *Bit of an understatement.* Then Rose frowned. 'I thought you had to leave?'

'I'm afraid I do right now, but you did say you would be in Chawton tomorrow. I – well, if it works for you... I thought perhaps then?'

A jolt of anticipation shot through Rose, and she bit her lip to try and contain her smile. 'Yes, of course. That would be perfect. Do you... did you have a time in mind?'

'No. I mean, yes.' The uncertainty in his voice, after seeing his confidence on the stage, was endearing. 'How about one o'clock?'

They had reached the corner of Queen and Quiet Streets now, and she and Morgan came to a halt as she tried to take in what he was saying.

Then she remembered her friend. 'Oh! But Morgan would be – I'm sorry, can you hold on a moment?' Morgan was shaking her head fiercely and making a cutting motion with her hand, and Rose lowered the phone to her side. '*What?!*'

'What's he saying? Whatever it is you can finish that sentence '*Morgan would be happy to make herself scarce*'.'

Rose sent Morgan a beseeching look, 'He wants to take me for a drink, or lunch, as – you know, as a thankyou.'

'Of course he does!' Morgan's smile widened. 'So what's the problem?'

'Tomorrow at one, but *we're* supposed to have lunch before the tour–'

'Good! Great! Say yes!'

'But you'd be having lunch on your own! Oh.' Morgan sent her an amused look. 'I forgot; it's you. You'll be fine.'

'Yes! I'll be fine.' Morgan glanced to Rose's right. 'Hi, James. Rose is ditching me for your dishy friend tomorrow; hold on!'

Rose made a shushing motion but Morgan whispered, 'Lock him down, we'll meet you inside,' and hooked her arm through James's as they turned to walk down to the pub entrance.

Putting the phone back to her ear, Rose drew in a shallow breath. 'Yes. That would be lovely. Thank you.' Then she remembered what she'd been saying before Morgan interrupted her. 'Morgan's meeting… some people she knows then.'

'Great. See you tomorrow?'

Rose glanced up at the sky and tried to feel as nonchalant as Aiden sounded. It didn't work, so she closed her eyes and imagined his face instead. 'Yes. See you then.'

CHAPTER THIRTY-NINE

For the rest of the evening, Rose had barely been able to think of anything other than 'the phone call'. Even reminding herself that although Aiden was, intrinsically, one and the same person – a person who had seemed genuinely interested in her in the strange, other-world reality – the situation between them couldn't be more different.

Rose's preoccupation continued as she and Morgan walked into town the following morning, and it was only after they'd reached their destination she noticed something was not quite right with her friend.

'Are you okay?'

They stood with over thirty other people in the Avon Street car park, waiting to board the coach to Hampshire. There was palpable anticipation all around; everyone was chatting and smiling and clearly in the mood for a fantastic day out, which is why the uncharacteristic silence of her friend struck Rose so forcibly.

'Yeah, I'm good.' Morgan smiled at her, but Rose wasn't convinced. Her friend wasn't making any overtures to those around them yet which was so unlike her, Rose began to have doubts about leaving her alone to go and meet Aiden.

Biting her lip, Rose studied Morgan thoughtfully. Whilst some of the crowd were elegantly attired in costume, most had opted for everyday clothing, but all of them looked comfortable this mild September morning in short sleeves. Morgan wore at least three layers and was hugging her arms to her chest. Rose could appreciate this was the way it was for someone used to West Coast temperatures, but there was definitely something wrong with her whole demeanour. Had something happened after Rose had gone back to her own flat last night?

'Everyone ready for a nice ride to an old house I know nothing about?' Rose turned quickly around to stare at James in surprise. There he was, all six foot three of him, holding a cardboard tray of cups and his gaze on Morgan, whose eyes had brightened instantly as a smile spread across her face. James clearly wasn't the problem, then!

'You got us coffee? You did! You're a saint. What is it? No, I don't even care. As long as it's hot – give it to me.' Morgan helped him disentangle a cup from the tray and then peered at the other cups, smiling proudly up at him. 'And you remembered Rose's special tea.'

James shrugged. 'Her order was much easier than yours. I couldn't remember what you chose on Sunday, so I asked for the frothiest drink they offered! I may have to use another coffee shop in future to save my reputation, but my immediate concern was I'd miss you and then end up having to drink it myself!'

Morgan smiled smugly. 'Maybe if you drank coffee yourself it'd help you with the problems you said you have getting up in the morning.'

'Well, maybe if my sleep didn't keep getting interrupted by my phone going off at all hours of the night–'

'I went to bed at a perfectly reasonable time last night!'

'I had a text from you at 3am; and another, five minutes later!'

'Well, I got up again!'

Rose ostensibly inspected her tea. Did they have any idea how well they got on?

James took a sip of his own drink, glancing at his watch, and Rose met his eye. 'The crowd is looking happy enough – are you? I know you said you were looking forward to this trip.'

Rose blinked, her mouth slightly agape. James was a great boss, but his work ethic was incredibly strong. Normally elbow-deep in papers by now, here he was, passing the time of day as though he had nowhere in particular to be and hadn't seen Rose – or Morgan – in ages. Did he not remember spending yesterday evening with them?

'Yes! What about you? Everything alright at the office?'

He grinned. 'Nothing to bore you with.' James narrowed his gaze, and he eyed first Morgan, then Rose. 'Though I'm sure you'd love to hear about a love triangle which may or may not have resulted in some minor damage to one of our properties.'

'*No!*' Morgan and Rose exclaimed in unison, exchanging a glance. Surely he didn't expect to leave it at that? Time was against them, however, as someone called, 'Everyone on-board, please,' and the crowd formed itself into a neat and orderly queue trailing back from the coach door.

James checked his watch again and drained his cup, but Morgan thrust hers at Rose. 'Hold that for me, I'm going to visit the 'loo' before we spend two hours on the bus!'

Rose took immediate advantage of her friend's absence. 'James! It is our busiest week of the year, and I'm on holiday. Please tell me the office isn't in Roger's hands this morning so that you could bring my friend a coffee?'

'No, of course not.' James looked a little more serious. 'I wasn't going to mention it, to be honest, but I've sacked him.'

'*What?*! I mean, I understand why, but this week, when you're a man down already?'

'It's been an intense few days.'

'Understatement of the year!' Rose muttered under her breath, not that James would have noticed, as his attention wasn't with her. 'James, what has come over you?'

'I should think it's embarrassingly obvious.'

Trying not to laugh, Rose nodded. 'True.'

'Look, I know it looks like I've lost the plot, but I haven't.' His gaze drifted over her shoulder again, and she didn't need to turn around to know Morgan was coming back. 'She's fun to be around; lovely… *warm*; I'm having… a good time.' He gave a rueful smile. 'It's only a few more days, after all.' The smile faded suddenly, and he sighed as he met Rose's eye. 'And then I promise to turn back into the curmudgeon of a boss you know and love!'

'Good, because I miss him, and his alter ego is not good for business!' This time, Rose did laugh. It was no surprise he'd fallen under the spell of Morgan's warm and friendly manner after Mandy's iciness. He had no idea how deep he was already, and remembering he didn't know of Morgan's work visa, she eyed him speculatively. 'What if it's not just for a few more days?'

'Sorry?'

'I'm back!' Morgan smiled widely at them both, and Rose turned to look at the rapidly diminishing queue.

'We'd best go.'

James nodded. 'Yup. It's a quarter to nine; I need to get to the office. Have a great day, and say hi to Aiden for me!' He turned to leave, and Rose and Morgan walked to join the stragglers who were climbing onto the coach.

'Wait!' Looking back over her shoulder, Rose nudged Morgan's arm. James had turned around. 'Text me when you get back later, and we'll go to that Mexican place I mentioned. You can test the enchiladas.' He was looking to Morgan and then to Rose, but as he'd never mentioned going to *Las Iguanas* and it sounded like another date was in the offing, all she needed to do this time was find an excuse to leave them to it!

'I know you'll love them,' Rose said smugly to Morgan, enjoying the fact she knew for certain.

'Jenny Ashton?' Rose's eyes flew to the front of the coach where the tour guide was currently running through her list of names.

'No? No one has seen Jenny Ashton? Does anyone have her number? Would be good to check with her that she's not on her way?' The guide looked expectantly up and down the faces peering over the seat backs, but no one responded.

Reluctantly, Rose raised a hand. 'I don't think she can make it, I'm afraid.'

'Am I allowed to ask about what happened when you ran after her to accuse her of piracy and all manner of disrepute?' Morgan whispered to Rose after the guide had thanked her.

'Nope. And you never will be.' The amusement in Morgan's voice was apparent; if only she knew, thought Rose, as the engine started up and they pulled out of the car park into the morning traffic.

Rose felt a pang of sadness as the coach crawled past 4 Sydney Place and out onto the Warminster Road, though it lessened considerably as they left Bathampton behind. She missed Jane, but with a shudder she recalled those difficult days living back in her mother's house, trying to find her feet in the library, scared of losing Morgan from her life after all she'd already lost. Then she recalled her evening with Aiden, and warm memories encased her. Smiling to herself, she allowed the feeling to fill her up and, for some miles, she thought of little else.

'Look, everyone! It's Stonehenge!'

With a start, Rose glanced around. Most people were staring avidly out of the left-hand windows as the coach continued along the road. Rose felt a wave of guilt at letting her mind drift so much. She had offered Morgan the window seat, thinking she would enjoy seeing the English countryside rushing past as they made their way east through Wiltshire to Hampshire, but looking at her now, she seemed to have drifted back into the low spirits of earlier, staring blankly at nothing in particular.

'Hey.' Rose touched her friend on the arm, and Morgan started. That settled it; she was so deep in thought she had no idea where she was right now.

'You can't fool me, matey. What's up? Did – er – did something happen last night; you know, after I left you?' Surely she and James hadn't had a disagreement over the phone or something? They'd both seemed in good spirits this morning…

'No! At least, nothing… oh, I dunno.' Morgan sighed. 'I had a late-night convo with Daddy – well, late night for me!' Rose nodded. 'We were talking through the details! The visa application stuff is all going pretty smooth.'

Her subdued announcement of progress surprised Rose. 'Are you having second thoughts? About moving away from home?'

Surprisingly, this brought a smile as Morgan shook her head. 'I'm totally fine leaving home, especially if this Mexican food place works out tonight! God, I miss tacos.' She winked, and Rose laughed.

'So why does it make you so… sad?'

For a moment, Morgan said nothing. Then she drew in a long breath. 'Can't you guess? Your boss.'

'James?' Rose frowned.

Morgan nodded slowly, then her troubled gaze met Rose's. 'He's... the best man I've ever known.'

Trying not to laugh, Rose turned in her seat the better to meet Morgan's eye. If she was channelling Elizabeth Bennet, this was getting serious!

'And this makes you unhappy? Is this an American thing? We're quite partial to nice men over here, you know!'

With a rueful smile, Morgan shook her head. 'No, it's me.'

Rose was confused. 'But it looked to me like you were getting on so well!'

'We are!'

'So?' When Morgan shrugged, Rose said quietly, 'He likes you; a lot. You know that – right?'

'Not really. I mean, sure, he likes me to hang out with, or at best, for a little flirtation with someone who won't be around long – he doesn't know I'm trying to get a place here. I might not be so attractive once he knows I'm not jetting back to the US of A next week.'

Honestly, Rose thought to herself. *These had to be the most clueless pair!* 'It's not like that – not for James. Morgan, he came to see you off on a tour... on a *work*day?' Obviously unconvinced, Morgan didn't say anything, and Rose said sternly, 'Morgan; I *know* him. You said you think him the best of men – well, he is. He's a good, decent bloke and he's not into toying with people's feelings! He's single, you're single – tell him your plans; let him surprise you.'

Morgan leaned her head against Rose's shoulder, though whether it was for warmth or support, Rose wasn't sure. 'I'm scared of believing it. I didn't come here expecting to fall for anyone, let alone your boss! I can't... *read* him, y'know? He hasn't made a move – after that first kiss.

Usually, by now, if it were a go, I'd have to put on the brakes to keep things from moving too fast.'

'Well, by English standards, he's made himself extremely clear in my opinion.' Rose said, thinking of all the attentive looks and round-the-clock texting.

'I want to believe you.' Morgan's eyes lit up. 'Maybe your men here work different than the guys at home.'

Patting Morgan's arm, Rose thought about her words as the coach sailed past the sign proclaiming they were entering the county of Hampshire. Having never been to the USA, Rose couldn't comment on the cultural differences between them, but she did have one man in mind right now. The Aiden of the other reality had seemed so different to the unattainable man of her real world. With today being her last chance to see him until next year – if he even came back to the Festival again – life felt suddenly rather bittersweet.

CHAPTER FORTY

Stepping down from the coach in the car park across the road from the cottage which housed the *Jane Austen House Museum*, Rose walked slowly over to the hedge bordering the car park and stared over at the red-brick façade. She had seen it many a time, yet right now it gave her goose bumps along her arms and a churning to her insides. Why did it feel so... *personal?*

'That's it, huh?' Morgan had come to stand beside her. 'Wow. I mean, I've seen photos, but it's a lot smaller than I imagined!'

Rose smiled. 'I'm sure it might be to you. For me, I always thought it ought to be called something grander than a cottage, because by cottage standards, it isn't small at all.'

Eager to go in now, they hurried along to cross the road, went through the gate and into the small shop where tickets were sold to enter the house and grounds, pleased to have escaped many from the coach party, most of whom were booked on the morning guided tour of Chawton House Library, a ten-minute walk away. Dragging Morgan away from the extensive array of souvenirs in the gift shop, Rose led her round to the pretty, well-maintained garden, sighing with a heady mixture of pleasure and nervous anticipation.

'Awesome!' Morgan tugged her camera out of her bag and started to take photos, and Rose walked over to the other side of the garden to contemplate the house.

She had visited Chawton and the surrounding area many times, but there was no denying this felt more a pilgrimage than any other. How strange did it feel to be here, looking at a home Jane – the Jane she had met in Bath – had yet to know? How many times had she, with the utmost reverence, walked through the hallowed rooms, stared at Jane's small writing table, admired those topaz crosses, read with tears in her eyes Cassandra's account of Jane's final days and hours?

Swallowing on a sudden lump in her throat, Rose blinked, then smiled tremulously as Morgan pointed her camera at her. She drew in a shallow breath as her friend walked over to take a photo of the Pride & Prejudice rose in the border by the gate. How would it have felt had Jane – as Jenny – come on the coach tour? What would she have made of her future home, of Chawton village as it was today? Then, her eye drawn across the road, she laughed and began to walk across the grass to join Morgan. She liked to think Jane would have delighted in the absurdity of seeing that the local café was called *Cassandra's Cup* – would have loved writing to her sister about it.

'Shall we go in whilst it's quieter?'

Morgan grinned at her. 'Lead the way!'

'You can still take photos, but no flash.' Rose led the way into the first room, saying hello to the friendly lady there and leaving Morgan to chat to her; she tried to breathe steadily as she walked slowly across to the door into the passage. This was where Jane's small collection of jewellery was usually displayed, and Rose pulled out the middle drawer cautiously.

There they were! Cassandra Austen's cross and chain and, next to it, the one purported to be Jane's but, in reality, Mrs Austen's! And only Rose knew that of anyone alive today! Her skin prickling again, she walked slowly into the next room.

Everything felt different, as though she was seeing it for the first time, in a new, more intimate light. After her modest experience with the fluidity of time, Rose didn't feel far away from when Jane had inhabited this space. This was no longer simply the house of an icon, but that of a friend, and she hadn't only lived here... This was where she had become sick as well.

Not wanting to think about it, Rose tried to suppress the pressure welling up in her throat. Had she done the right thing in encouraging Jane to go back, away from modern medicine and procedures? She knew the legacy of Jane's writing was beyond calculable worth, but even so, it broke her heart to imagine Cassandra pacing to and fro over these wooden floors as the health of her beloved sister declined, and then continuing here without her for all those years...

'This is awesome!' Morgan whispered to her as she joined her. 'How did they manage to live in such small rooms?' There were a couple of other people looking at various items on display, and Rose led Morgan over to Jane's writing table.

'It's hard to imagine, isn't it? That she wrote such beloved stories in this actual room and probably at *this* window?' Her gaze drifted towards it, then back to the small table, and she smiled. 'I can see her now... when I stand here, I can picture her, dipping her pen into the ink, a smile on her lips as she gave some witty line to a character, then stopping to look out of the window at the Winchester coach flying by, wondering about the passengers, where they were headed, what their stories were...'

Morgan punched her gently on the arm. 'Hey, you're waxing lyrical today! I've never seen you like this!'

Rose gave her a watery smile. 'I'm not sure I've ever felt quite like this when I've come here, to be honest.' She couldn't explain to

Morgan why it felt so special, so intimate, this time, but she was so pleased to have her friend by her side. To make this visit alone would have been too emotional to bear.

They headed for the upper floor, but all Rose could think about as her hand trailed along the wooden banister rail was of Jane flying up the stairs to find Cassandra, to tell her of her excitement at her book having arrived from the printers, one of her 'darling children', but as she paused on the threshold into the room Jane had shared with her sister, it became almost too much to bear. Had the same hand clung tightly to that handrail as illness began to claim her and she wearily made her way upstairs to rest?

Trying to settle her emotions and push away her guilt, Rose walked into the bedroom. Morgan was studying the contents of the closets either side of the fireplace, but Rose's eye was drawn to the framed fraction of a letter by the hearth, Caroline Austen's memories of her final visit to her ailing aunt.

'This is the cutest room!' Morgan turned to face her. 'It's all so… quaint! And look at that tiny bed!'

Rose smiled, thankful for the distraction. 'I think it's a replica. It's probably so small because they had another in here for Cassandra.'

'You coming?' Morgan walked to the door, but Rose shook her head with a smile.

'Give me five minutes; I'll catch you up!'

Walking over to the window now she was alone, Rose tried not to think how captive Jane must have felt in this room as her health failed, how lonely it must have become for Cassandra Austen to return to after leaving Jane at rest in Winchester, but then she paused and looked around. It was a lovely room, small, yes, but charming and full of light. There was no air of melancholy about it, other than what she

– Rose – was bringing to it. *'And even when sick, Jane did not succumb to self-pity and despair.'* She whispered to herself. *'And she'd be unlikely to appreciate it in others!'*

A sudden soft breath of air caressed Rose's skin, and she felt the fine hairs on her arm rise; it was as though Jane, for a fleeting moment, was not far away in the mists of time, but rather standing right there – not a memory, but there beside her, only two hundred years removed.

Rose spun around. There was no one in the room but her, and a quick glance at the firmly sealed window was enough for her to hurry from the room in search of Morgan.

Closing the gate to the museum behind them, Rose and Morgan viewed the crowd of people outside the only two places in Chawton serving lunches: the village pub and the nearby café.

'Looks like the first tour is over.' Morgan pointed to the people milling around across the road. 'I'm starving! I'll grab a sandwich and see you outside the big house at two?'

Rose glanced at her watch and almost yelped. It was five minutes to the time she'd agreed to meet Aiden. She tried to shed her unsettled mood, but the thought of how close she was to saying goodbye to him did nothing to help banish the melancholy feelings gripping her since being in the cottage.

'Right. Okay. See you later.' They crossed the road together, and she set off in the direction of the church, but then Morgan fell into step beside her. 'Are you okay?'

'We seem to be asking each other that a lot the last couple of days!' Rose sent her an apologetic smile. 'Hey, I thought you were off to lunch!'

Morgan took Rose's arm. 'Here for each other, that's what it's all about!'

Feeling Morgan's friendship keenly, Rose smiled. 'I don't know what's wrong with me. Visiting Chawton has never affected me like this. Even in there.' She gestured back down the road towards the cottage. 'I've never felt so – so *overcome*, so full of sadness. I mean, there are parts that always make me sad, like the–'

'Letter her sister wrote; the one on the wall in that closet? Yeah, that got me, too!'

'Yes, precisely. That always moves me, but that's just it. It's the only thing that usually brings me down in there. I've always felt such a warm, all-embracing contentment in there, as though I can feel Jane's happiness at being back in her beloved Hampshire, in a small village, pouring out her creativity.' She couldn't tell Morgan all that had happened, of course, which must account for the bulk of her feelings, but all the same, she hadn't expected the experience to be so... *visceral*.

'Well, at least you've got a bit of time with Doctor Lovely now! I'm sure that'll cheer you up no end! What?' Morgan assumed an innocent expression.

Rose chose to ignore this, though, as usual, Morgan had managed to cheer her up, even though she was filled with trepidation over seeing him. They had come to the start of the driveway now which led down to Chawton House, and they stopped to look at it, Morgan rummaging around for her camera again.

Rose leaned on the wooden fence whilst her friend took a few shots. There seemed to be quite a few people milling around in the nearby churchyard. Perhaps she'd get away with only having a few words with Aiden? After all, the café and pub both looked to be heaving, and they'd never find a seat to have a proper conversation.

'Do you want to wait? I don't think I'll be long.' Rose and Morgan had set off down the driveway together. 'Look.' Rose pointed ahead. 'There are loads of people here – probably half the people who were at his talk yesterday! We can grab something to eat together?'

'I'm not waiting for you! I'm only here to make sure you go in there!'

They had reached the gate into the churchyard now and stopped outside.

'Don't be so – so – *cautious*, Rose! And take down your hair, for God's sake. You're not in the office now!' Morgan held out her hand for the hair clip, and Rose reached up to remove it before handing it over. 'There.' Morgan pocketed it, leaning forward to ruffle Rose's curls as they tumbled over her shoulders. 'Now you're more *you*!'

'I doubt he has a clue who the real me is!'

Morgan shook her head. 'Seems to me he already likes you; now you have to learn the same lesson as Jane Bennet, and give him a little encouragement.'

Rose almost laughed, but Aiden came around the side of the church then, several people in his wake, and her insides started doing somersaults. 'I think you need to take a dose of your own medicine!'

'What do you mean?'

'Perhaps James needs a little encouragement; just because he's not prone to being demonstrative doesn't mean he doesn't *feel*.'

'Touché! It seems we are all fools in love after all!'

Was she more of a fool than ever, though? Rose bit her lip, staring at the people flocking around Aiden. He'd always seemed so unattainable; until Jane that is. Until she'd had the chance to get to know the real man; let him see the real Rose.

'Thinking of going over there anytime soon?'

Rose fidgeted with the strap on her bag before pulling it onto her shoulder. 'He's obviously busy. Besides, what on earth am I supposed to say? *'Hey, remember me? You wanted to buy me lunch?'* The queue at the café is that long, we'd still be in it at dusk!'

Morgan laughed. 'Can't think of a more romantic time of day; imagine all that flattering light!' She winked. 'Now, come on. You'll soon think of something to say. I mean, you know so much about his work, after all! And you *are* going over there if I have to drag you kicking and screaming.'

'Morgan!'

'Go over there, Rose. Build on the morning you spent with him!'

'But that was ages ago!' In an attempt to calm herself, Rose drew in a long, slow breath.

'It was four days ago! Text me when you're done with him. And don't forget a word, I want to hear it *all.*' Morgan turned to walk away, then called back over her shoulder, 'And remember – there's no room for caution here! Throw it to the winds!'

Rose shook her head, watching Morgan making her way back down the drive. *Caution?* Okay, maybe a long time ago she'd always been cautious; but not now. You couldn't be cautious and change the world, right? And that she had done, so how hard could this be?

Swinging around, she walked under the lychgate into the churchyard. Most of the people seemed to be leaving, and Aiden was left with two women who were clearly asking him to sign something. Unsure what to do, Rose hesitated, but then he looked up and caught her eye, and taking a steadying breath, she walked towards him.

CHAPTER FORTY-ONE

'Sorry!' Finally free of any company, Aiden walked over to where Rose was hovering. 'Look, there's been a slight hitch to my day. How long have you got?'

Rose glanced at her watch, unsure if she was relieved or sorry. 'Until two? I'm on the afternoon tour up at the house.' She gestured up towards Chawton House Library. 'Meeting Morgan up there.'

'Fine; fine.' He seemed preoccupied, glancing over to where some of the dig team were sitting on the grass eating sandwiches, and she felt uncomfortable. Should she say something, make up a reason for leaving so he could be free of this commitment that wasn't going to do either of them any favours?

'The café was heaving. There are a couple of coachloads in the village today. I doubt we'll get anything quickly there, even if it's just a cuppa.'

'That's all sorted,' he dismissed her comment with a wave of his hand, then seemed to realise how grubby it was. 'Heck. Can you hold on a minute?'

Rose had no time to respond, but as he walked away from her and she turned around, looking for somewhere to wait, she caught sight of the graves of the Austen ladies, tucked away at the back of the churchyard. The memorial stone Aiden had shown her the photo of in the other reality was gone.

With a sigh, Rose turned back and immediately spotted a wooden bench facing out over the fields and went to sit on it, feeling far less of a spare part sitting down than standing aimlessly in the churchyard with Aiden's colleagues eyeing her with curiosity. How was she to recapture the rapport that had seemed to fall so naturally between them back then?

She glanced back over her shoulder as Aiden re-emerged from inside the church, wiping his hands on a towel. Unable to turn away, Rose watched him as he walked over to his discarded bag and dug around inside, clearly exchanging some banter with the team and chucking the towel unceremoniously at them as he walked back towards her.

Turning back to stare across the fields, Rose swallowed, conscious of the usual warmth filling her cheeks. She must try not to stare at him too much, but he wasn't making it easy. She was used to seeing him in his signature outfit when he came to Bath: jeans and a plain shirt – usually white – and a jacket of some description, often cord or linen. The only time she'd seen him as he was today, in well-worn Cargo trousers and a battered, mud-stained polo shirt, was on the occasions when he was out on a dig, usually for the *Time Travellers*. He looked more... approachable?

She sighed, remembering the first time she'd become aware of him. It had been about five years ago; she'd had a severe bout of flu which had kept her off work for 10 days and, bored with her own company, she'd put the telly on as background noise whilst curled up on the sofa reading, heedless of whatever programme was on.

That was until his voice filtered into the imaginary world she was wrapped in. Looking up, she'd glanced over at the telly and the rest was history. The book was discarded, the remote snatched up from the coffee table and for the rest of her time off work, Rose had watched back-to-back repeats of *Time Travellers* as it played every weekday afternoon, hoping and hoping for another glimpse of him. Of course, her first *real* glimpse of him she preferred to pretend hadn't happened! As for when she'd found out he was coming to stay in one of the flats they managed for the first time…

'Er, Rose?'

Rose looked up with a start.

'Sorry. Miles away.'

'May I?'

He pointed to the bench.

'Oh! Of course.' She grabbed her bag so he could sit down, and then turned a little so she was facing him, not that he noticed because he was busy laying a piece of white sheeting on the bench between them.

'I knew there'd be little enough time today, but I'm glad I was prepared now it's even less!' Before her eyes, he pulled a veritable feast from the carrier bag at his feet: a small selection of sandwiches, bags of crisps, cocktail sausages and some cherry tomatoes, along with a couple of bottles of water.

'There!' He sounded incredibly proud of his endeavours, and despite her awkwardness, she laughed.

'A picnic! This is thanks indeed, and well beyond the promised drink.'

'Damn!' Aiden glanced over to the other team members. 'I meant to make a flask of coffee this morning! Let me see if…' He made as if to get to his feet, but instinctively, Rose stayed him with her hand on his arm.

'It's okay; I don't drink the stuff.'

He sat back slowly, and Rose, realising she was still holding his arm, withdrew her hand quickly, the blush in her cheeks deepening.

'Ah, okay; it's good I forgot, then.' Rose frowned. 'The coffee. I don't drink it either!'

Rose laughed at his sheepish expression as he waved a hand at the spread between them.

'Here – take something to eat. What d'you prefer? We have good old BLT, ham and egg mayo and…' He glanced up at her. 'Because I had no idea whether you were vegetarian or not, cheese and pickle!'

Rose wasn't sure she could eat a thing, but she took a triangle of bread from the spread before her and a couple of tomatoes.

They munched in contented silence for a few minutes, but as it stretched, Rose became aware of it and sought desperately for something, *anything*, interesting to say. She took a swig of cold water, her mind empty of suggestion until suddenly she recalled the ease of their conversation about his work and what had inspired him when they'd had drinks at *Graze* that night. Would that work? He'd never know he'd already told her, would he, and perhaps it would fool her into thinking it was the same Aiden – the one who'd seemed interested in her, who'd told her he liked her?

She took another gulp of water. 'I know one of the ladies asked you this yesterday, but I didn't hear…' Rose faltered. She hadn't taken in the response because she'd been too busy trying to look anywhere but at Aiden. She cleared her throat; he was looking expectantly at her now. 'Would you – I mean, can you tell me a bit more about what drew you into archaeology? I think you said you started off studying history?'

He nodded and wiped his hands on the edge of the white cloth. 'My fascination with the past wasn't so much with the history in front of you, it was in what you *couldn't* see; the hidden secrets. You could walk over a field in any part of Britain and never know the enigmas buried in its depths, come across a ruin and never see the beauty of how it once looked or hear the stories that might be concealed in its stones.' As always when talking of his work, Aiden's face was animated, his hands moving expressively, but then he stopped, looking self-conscious. 'Sometimes you don't realise what's missing, what's not there – do you know what I mean?'

Rose didn't care what he meant; he could talk forever as far as she was concerned. Hell, he could read the phone directory aloud and she'd be happy listening to his voice. *Shallow. You're so shallow.*

'And so – what is the hitch today? Have you found something that was missing?' She gestured over towards his team. They seemed to be clearing up their equipment rather than returning to work.

Aiden shrugged. 'No – no, nothing!' He glanced at his watch and sighed. 'Look, I'm afraid I've got to head over to Winchester; got the call this morning; something I've been waiting on.'

'Is it – are the two projects linked then? I've seen that on TV sometimes.'

'Not at all. This…' He gestured back towards a small test pit visible near the front of the church. 'Is a commission from the local parish council to see if we can find the original footprint of the church – you knew it burnt down?' Rose nodded, trying to look as though he hadn't already told her this. 'This has gone fine – fairly routine work. But the Winchester one is more complex…' He looked away for a moment, across the open fields. Then he sighed and turned back to face her. 'Don't mind me; I'm just wishing I didn't have to go right now.'

'We were supposed to go to Winchester after the library tour; to the cathedral, you know, and College Street?'

'Yes – of course. You must be disappointed it had to be dropped.'

'I'm not too bothered. I've been before, and I'll go another time, but I do feel sorry for those who've come a long way and won't get the chance again. It's such a shame they had to close it to the public during *Festival* week!'

'Yes, I'm sure they weren't too pleased about it either, but sadly, when damage occurs in a building as old as that it has to be dealt with as expeditiously as possible to avoid the situation growing worse.' He smiled ruefully and turned to stare out across the fields. 'That's where I'm off to, actually – the cathedral itself. The consultant archaeologist was my mentor but he's away, and he asked me if I'd oversee it as I was in the area.'

'What happened?'

He turned to look at her. 'A leak in one of the windows caused some flood damage to one of the walls and the flooring below. Means repairing the window, of course, but also moving some old stones with a great deal of care.' For a moment, he said nothing, and Rose tried not to think about how every moment passing brought her closer to another long year without him. She sighed gently, trying not to stare at him and failing miserably. *Is it wrong I want to reach out and touch his face?*

'That's not unusual, of course,' Aiden said, and Rose almost gulped, then realised he was not mind reading, but merely continuing with his thoughts. 'But the timing's not great.' He paused. 'Listen, I–'

'Hey, boss!' They both turned around to find one of Aiden's team waving at them. 'We're off! See you in the morning!'

He waved a hand and turned back to Rose. 'I have to go, too. It wasn't much of a 'thankyou', was it, for all your hard work?'

'It was – it's been… lovely. Everything.'

He smiled faintly, then glanced at his watch. 'Damn. Sorry, I *do* have to go. But–'

Rose had picked up the discarded carrier bag, intending to put the remains of their picnic in it, but something fell to the ground, and she bent to pick it up.

'Ah, yes! I forgot I'd brought dessert!' Aiden took the open packet of *Love Hearts* from Rose and shook some out onto his hand before selecting one and handing it her. Instinctively, she glanced at it before popping it into her mouth, then wished she could take it out again to be certain it said what she thought it did: *Be Mine?* Hastily, before she could blush again, she swallowed it and thanked him and turned away to continue tidying up the leftover food before they both walked over to the gate.

'I appreciate you taking the time out of your tour.'

Rose shook her head. 'It was no hardship. Honestly.'

'Good. Rose,' He reached out suddenly and tucked a stray curl of hair behind her ear. 'Take care. I'll see you again, I'm sure.'

And then he was gone, walking under the lychgate and loping across the grass with his long stride towards his car. Rose watched it pull away, her heart clearly torn on whether or not to do somersaults or to sink into despair. Her time with Aiden was over, another year gone and another year to wait. But what a time it had been. It was hard to be depressed when her skin was still tingling where his fingers had brushed her face. She turned her steps towards the gravel drive to Chawton House Library, joining several others making their way up there for the next tour.

It would be all she thought about on the coach journey back to Bath; but for now, she needed to get up to the house and meet Morgan who would no doubt be keen to hear about all that had happened.

CHAPTER FORTY-TWO

The popularity of the guided tours at Chawton House Library had led to each group being split into two or three smaller ones to make the tour a better experience for all involved, and Morgan – who had turned up just as the tour was due to start and had reluctantly agreed to hear all about Rose's lunch when they had more time later – had waved cheerily to her friend as she was swept off in a different group.

Having done the tour before, Rose made a sudden decision and hung back, allowing those who hadn't to be at the front, and as soon as an opportunity arose, she slipped away from them and walked back outside.

Rose looked around, then turned and walked round to the back of the house and up into the gardens, intent on reaching the rose garden. She didn't know if she was happy or sad. As lovely as their last moments together had been, Aiden had given no hint about coming to Bath next year – what if she never saw him again… *ever*?

For almost an hour, Rose wandered among the flowers, her heart simultaneously full and lost. It was only as the faint sound of voices came drifting to her along the path from the house that she roused herself and, glancing at her watch, realised the tour must have ended.

Leaving the ghosts of the bleak futures of both Jane and her own love life behind, Rose wandered back down the path and round to the courtyard outside the kitchens where she could tell from the noise that the afternoon tea was being enjoyed by everyone.

'Yo! Rose!'

Looking up, she saw Morgan getting to her feet, smiling widely.

'How was afternoon tea?'

'Awesome!' Morgan slipped her arm through Rose's as they turned to follow some of the others from their coach party round to the front of the house and down the gravel driveway. 'How about you? You wouldn't have made me wait the entire tour if he'd proposed, would you?'

Rose sighed. 'No. And he's not likely to, is he? I probably won't see him again until next year, and there's no guarantee he'll come back then.'

'Don't give up now, Rose!' Morgan said reassuringly. 'Come on, let's have the play by play. You owe it to me for deserting me just now!'

'Yes, and I'm sure you felt lost, lonely and alone – *not!*

Morgan laughed. 'I had a blast! This cream tea thing is awesome! Did you know there's a whole debate about the pronunciation of 'scone'? Some of the ladies became quite heated! But that was nothing to the one about whether the jam or cream should go on first!'

With a laugh, Rose nodded. 'Tell me about it! I went last year and it was just the same! I still don't remember who came out the winner!'

By the time everyone had returned to the coach, the headcount had been done and the engine started, Rose had pretty much related all there was to say about lunch. After all, not a lot happened, and they'd been together less than an hour, but it seemed enough to keep Morgan happy, who was still chattering on about everything pointing to Aiden having taken a fancy to her. Rose, with a year-long abyss stretching before her, was not nearly as confident, but before she could beg her friend to let it go, Morgan's phone pinged and she began exchanging a flurry of texts.

'James says do we want to go for a drink when we get back? Says he'll meet us off the coach?'

'Why don't you see him, and I'll head home and leave you the opportunity to tell him some pertinent information about your future postcode?'

Morgan gave her a warning glance. 'No way, it's all of us or none of us. Besides, I want to wait till we're back at Laura's Place. He still doesn't always understand my *accent* and I don't want anything lost in translation. And *furthermore*, he knows how much you've been looking forward to us having this week, and he respects it.'

'Well, that's only because he doesn't know we'll soon have all the time together we could ask for.'

Morgan sighed dramatically. 'I will tell him, I swear! Tonight.' Then she grinned. 'But drinks first – we'll go, yes? All of us?'

For a fleeting moment, Rose wished with all her heart Aiden was still in Bath and included in that 'all of us', but Morgan took her silence for acceptance and turned back to start texting again.

Rose stared out of the window as the Hampshire countryside rushed by, trying not to notice the signs to Winchester as they passed and wishing she could go there now.

Then she recalled the *Love Heart* and its message. If only she'd pocketed it, she'd at least have something to hold onto, something tangible from her lunch with Aiden. If only she could believe he'd chosen that particular one from the ones in his hand…

Resting her head against the seat, Rose stared out of the window, seeing nothing of the scenery, only a whirlwind of make-believe images of what she wished were true. *If only…*

Rose woke slowly the following morning, barely moving a muscle other than to open one eye and squint around the room. Convinced of the earliness of the hour by the low level of light filtering through the curtains, she let her lid drop again, curling onto her side as she pressed her cheek into the pillow, trying to make sense of the feelings consuming her.

Had she been in the midst of a dream? She stretched languorously, hoping some strand of it would come back to her, a hint of what had triggered this sensation of inner contentment. The fog of sleep cleared and familiar sounds took precedence – the slow rumble of traffic from the street above, the birds outside her window heralding the new day – but she was still confused. Shouldn't she be depressed? Her lunch with Aiden at Chawton had been a bonus – a bounty she'd never expected before he disappeared from her city for another year – but it was over and done now.

The resurgence of memories of the previous day swept away any remaining tendrils of sleep, and opening her eyes properly, Rose blinked, then rolled onto her back. She felt... *different* somehow, as though the trip to Chawton had changed something tangible within her.

For whatever reason, she had been feeling unsettled as the bus had careered along the country roads to Hampshire, as though she didn't know what to expect, even though she'd visited Chawton many times before. It wasn't until she stepped over the threshold into Jane's former home that she had realised it must stem from her recent venture into an alternate reality, and she had been filled with a deeply satisfying sense of pride in having been such a crucial part in turning that around.

The depth of her emotion in being there in Chawton, the awkward mixture of discomfort and pleasure during her impromptu lunch with Aiden were bundled up inside her as they had travelled back to Bath.

Kicking back the covers, Rose sat up slowly. Yes, it had been quite a day; a full circle sort of day, with Rose coming to terms with emotions she hadn't even begun to suspect were warring within her before the trip.

She swung her legs out of bed and stood up, thrusting her feet into her slippers and reached for her mobile. Perhaps this was what good therapy felt like – it certainly seemed to fit with what Morgan was always trying to tell her.

Quickly checking for any messages, Rose grinned widely as she read three in a row from Morgan, sent not long after midnight. She'd gone for dinner with them at Morgan's insistence, but had excused herself as soon as she'd eaten, leaving her friend to look over yet another dessert menu as James ordered coffee, claiming she needed an early night. She knew from Morgan's knowing look as she hugged her what she meant was she needed to go home and nurse her feelings about Aiden!

Aiden… Rose walked slowly over to stand in front of the dressing table and eyed her reflection warily. In the half-light of early morning, she could almost believe he might… find her attractive? Her skin looked pale and luminous, but her hair was everywhere, of course, and she pushed it impatiently off her shoulders. His eyes had been so kind… fond, even? But what might he see in her? Morgan had said she was beautiful, but was that just her friend being – well, *Morgan?* Other than Jon, she'd never drawn the attention of anyone much. Wasn't that why she'd put up with him for so long, convinced she had to stay with him because no one else was likely to want her, that she wasn't anyone unless she was part of a couple? Believing all the negativity he threw her way, echoes of her mother's words over the years, Rose's low self-esteem had willingly succumbed.

With a grunt, Rose turned her back on the mirror. Thankfully, she had seen the light; things were changing, and she felt like she could question everything!

She jumped at the sudden ping of her mobile, and as she pulled back the curtains to reveal a beautiful autumn day, she glanced at the screen, unsurprised to see another text from Morgan: *What time are we meeting? I'm hungry!*

Rose smiled. Morgan was always hungry, and she had promised to take her friend to a café she had found serving American-style pancakes before they headed off to this morning's Festival event.

I can be with you in half an hour? Rose paused, then her curiosity getting the better of her, added quickly: *Try biding your time telling me if you enjoyed the rest of your evening!?!*

Morgan's response was rapid: another series of hilarious emoticons, culminating again in two little figures kissing. With a satisfied nod, Rose dropped the phone onto her bedside table and headed for the kitchen. Predictably, her friends were off to rather a quick start and she could not have been happier for them.

With the kettle boiling, Rose glanced out of the window where the steps led up to street level. So much had happened since she'd confronted Jane there just days ago, so much had changed.

Her mug of tea in her hand, Rose walked back into the sitting room and curled up on the sofa. Surely she must apply some caution, some restraint to these feelings of happiness? She had a whole year to get through without anything but the memories of the last few days to last her.

Hearing the chimes of the old clock on the fireplace, Rose leapt to her feet and hurried towards the bathroom. Rushing ahead in her hopes for James and Morgan's future? That was totally acceptable; but if there could be hope for something with Aiden… Rose's insides flipped over, and despite the voice of caution once more, she could feel the possibility welling inside her. If it took five more years a week at a time, Rose didn't care. It would be worth it to have his warm, dark eyes regard her the way she dreamed they could.

Rose hastily turned the shower on, turning the dial to 'cold'. She needed something to drown out her thinking – her *overthinking*. A year was a long time, as she already knew, but the first night was over; only just over three hundred and sixty nights to go, and the memories of this year might just well keep her warm for most of them.

CHAPTER FORTY-THREE

Despite her alleged hunger, it didn't go amiss with Rose that Morgan ate nothing, though she pushed the food around on her plate a few times after liberally dousing it in maple syrup. It probably had something to do with the fact she didn't seem able to stop smiling or talking – though there was nothing unusual in that, either!

'I get it!' Rose laughed, as they paid up and made their way out into the street. 'You like him. I think you *lurrrve* him!' Then she ducked, as Morgan made a playful swipe at her.

Their spirits remained high as they walked past the abbey and joined the main thoroughfare, making their way down to the lower part of the town.

'Okay, apart from my boss, what's been your favourite thing since you got here?'

'Apart from *you* and James,' Morgan sighed as they paused at a crossing. 'It's just being surrounded by the accent. Even though sometimes I get a little confused trying to decipher our common language. It's still irresistible.'

Rose merely raised a brow at her as they crossed over the road.

'Not that I'm trying hard to resist!' Morgan laughed. 'What sorts of things do you worry about in housing here if you don't have to worry about earthquake safety, anyway?'

'Well, I suppose – oh, I'm sorry – oh, *hi!* Rose smiled widely, but the woman she had accidentally bumped into on the corner threw her a startled look before hurrying on, and Morgan grinned.

'Is it normal to be so friendly to someone you've bumped into like that?'

With a rueful laugh, Rose shook her head as they continued on their way, glancing back as Mary from the library disappeared out of sight. 'No – I thought I knew her; turns out I don't!'

They turned the corner into Corn Street, and Rose caught sight of a familiar notice pinned to a lamp-post, and her present happiness faltered slightly.

Oh Prancer! she thought sadly. *How you must be missed!*

'What is it?' Morgan looked concerned. 'Rose, don't worry – I am not making wedding plans or anything; it's just that my heart hasn't stopped thumping since he... no, wait.' She sighed, placing a hand to her throat. 'Since those precious, eternal moments before he leaned down and kissed me.' She gave Rose a dreamy smile, and Rose rolled her eyes. 'He's a good kisser, you know?'

Rose struggled not to laugh. 'No – I don't know! Nor do I intend to try and find out!'

Morgan stared at her, then burst out laughing. 'Oh! Right! Yes, of course!' Then she grinned. 'Well, just take my word for it.'

I did, muttered Rose under her breath. *The first time you mentioned it; and, I think, the second. This must be the third, but – oh well.* She tucked her arm through Morgan's and urged her along the pavement towards the Mission Theatre.

'Come on, let's see if we can get you to an event suitably fascinating to take your mind off Lover Boy for an hour!'

'Don't worry, though; I know things don't always last forever.'

Rose, who had been living with those first few moments of

infatuation for a few years now, merely smiled.

'I'm not worried at all – I was a bit distracted.' Rose gestured back up the road. 'I saw a poster for a lost dog; I'm pretty sure I saw what happened to it, over by my flat the other day.'

'Aw, that's too bad. You haven't seen anything about Mr Darcy, have you?'

Rose shook her head. 'Hey, I thought James had vetoed that name for the kitten!'

'Well… who made him President? When my visa comes through, I could keep the kitten just as much as he could, and then what could he say about the name? Huh?' Morgan winked at Rose as they arrived at the theatre doors. 'And anyway, we all know I'm going to win him over, don't we?'

'Morgan…' Rose stopped, then laughed. 'Yes. We do all know.'

They joined some of their friends inside then and enjoyed a fun and entertaining hour as they were told all about the intricacies of bonnet making and pretended not to covet one of the many fabulous concoctions on display near the front of the stage.

'This is fabulous – why haven't we made our *own*?' Morgan was eyeing the display up close now the presentation had come to an end and everyone was milling around near the stage.

'Because when I suggested it as something fun we could do, you laughed at me, said I was living in the wrong century!'

This reminder of the past brought Prancer to mind – a Prancer who was now happily settled in 1803, and Rose fished in her bag for her mobile and switched it back on. Morgan, in the meantime, was trying on one of the bonnets and taking a selfie. 'Well, you shouldn't have listened to me. I want one. Can we make one for the ball?'

Taking the hat Morgan had discarded, Rose put it back on its stand. 'Weren't you listening to anything? Ladies didn't wear bonnets to balls!' Then, at her friend's pretence at pulling a disappointed face, she shook her head. 'You're incorrigible! Well, I suppose we could try! I'm sure you'll get a chance to wear it before the Festival is over.' She eyed the elegant displays in front of them. 'I've never done it before, so we can't be too ambitious.'

'How about I go straight to the source?' Morgan pointed at the lady who had done the presentation. 'She'll give us a rough idea of what we need, right?'

Rose eyed the queue of ladies in front of the presenter. 'Okay. I need to make a phone call.' She waved her phone at Morgan. 'Shall we meet outside when you're done?'

'Work stuff?'

Rose gave Morgan a look. 'If you want to talk to James, *you* text him.'

'*Fine.*' Morgan sighed, and touched her hand to her heart exaggeratedly, then laughed and turned to join the melee of people crowding around the presenter.

Rose walked out into the street, then turned and walked quickly to the end of the road and the lamp-post displaying the notice about Prancer. Keeping an eye on the doors of the theatre, she copied the number down and flicked open her phone.

Though Rose did not have a pet at the moment, her mother had once let her have a puppy, whom she'd named Bingley, but she'd not let her keep him long, insisting he was just too much work. Sadly, as Rose had been in rented accommodation since leaving home, she'd never had another chance to own a pet, but she was certain all the same she understood the heartache the elderly lady must be feeling over the loss of her companion.

Rose keyed in the number, recalling the research she'd done since her world had returned to normal. Cassandra Austen, some twenty or so years after Prancer had appeared in her life, had owned a dog named, of all things, 'Link'. Now, either Prancer had, through some magical influence of his time-travelling, become immortal, or he'd produced offspring! I mean, who named their dog *Link*?

The call connected quickly. 'Er, hello?'

Five minutes later, Rose was back outside the theatre, just as people began to spill out onto the street, the last of whom was – typically – Morgan.

'So? How did it go? Did you learn in fifty seconds how we're going to do this?'

Morgan raised both hands and waved them gleefully. '*Yes*! But we have to go to the hat store on Broad Street so we can get something to use as a base. And get some ribbons and things to decorate it with.'

'Okay; there's a great stall in the market; it'll be the best place for ribbons and so on. Let's go shopping!'

'Can we get a sandwich, too? I'm starving!'

They walked back the way they had come, but as they passed the poster of the missing dog again, Morgan gestured towards it. 'Why don't you call if you think you know what happened? Was it an accident?'

'I just did – and no, the dog… well, as I said to the owner just now, he was… taken. I – er – I saw it happen.'

'Wow! Dog-napping in Bath! And you and James told me it was so safe here!'

They crossed over and headed for the centre of town, Rose shaking her head.

'I know. Bizarre. Anyway, she seemed okay about it all. She's quite elderly, said he was always running off, escaping from his lead and even from the house. I got the impression she was a little relieved! I don't think she was up to chasing after him anymore.' Rose pointed to the right. 'We need to go this way. To be honest, she seemed more thankful she was going to save money on socks!'

'What?' Morgan laughed. 'Are you serious?'

'Oh yes; she said Prancer – that was the dog's name – used to eat them – well, typically, he'd gnaw his way through one of a pair, leaving her with nothing but odd matches. She seemed quite chuffed about that side of it!'

'Well, you did the right thing. At least she has closure, right?'

'Yes, of course. I did feel bad calling her, though. I offered to drive her to the rescue centre if she wanted to get herself another dog, but she said her daughter had it planned. Seemed as though she was keen to find herself one that would be a bit less – active!'

As they made their way towards Broad Street, Rose smiled to herself at such an outcome. Prancer had, hopefully, found a more active and willing companion in Cassandra, and the lady would get her wish and manage to adopt a non-sock-eating, stay-at-home dog who would be a faithful companion to her!

CHAPTER FORTY-FOUR

After a busy afternoon of shopping and an early evening Festival event – this time a workshop on playing the harp – Rose and Morgan had said goodnight to their friends and headed to *The Boater*, the pub just across the way from Morgan's flat, for dinner.

Not entirely sure how it happened, though she suspected Morgan's ability to text without seeming to do so might have something to do with it, James just happened to drop into the pub as they were finishing their meal, and joined them for a drink.

Rose smirked as he sat down; his foot had come to rest against Morgan's and, judging from her happy face, her friend hadn't missed it either.

'Look at what we bought!' Morgan delved into one of the carrier bags under the table, unearthing a plain straw bonnet, which she perched on her head, and a huge pile of ribbons. 'We're going to make bonnets!'

'Very fetching.' James took a draught of his pint and picked up one of the ribbons. 'How on earth are you going to use all of these? You look like you've raided the stall!'

Rose laughed. 'It was a bit like that!'

'I thought you could take some, too!' Morgan held out a few strands to him, but James looked taken aback.

'Me?'

'Not for *you*, silly! For Mr Darcy! He can play with them!'

'I've told you umpteen times; that's not his name!' James shook his head. 'And *he* is most definitely a *she*!'

'Mr Darcy and I do not agree! And I shall tell the Judge so when we are called to the Bar!'

James looked resignedly at Rose. 'Morgan's threatening to start custody proceedings if she doesn't get to spend more time with the cat.'

'I miss him!'

Rose took a sip of her wine as Morgan removed her bonnet and began extolling Mr Darcy's virtues, but the sudden ringing of her phone drew her attention, and she quickly flipped it open.

It was Aiden! Rose felt suddenly light-headed – it hadn't been a year yet... Vaguely aware of James gathering up their empty glasses and heading to the bar, she drew in a shallow breath and connected the call.

'Hello? Yes?'

'Rose?'

'Yes. Hi, Aiden.' There was a protracted silence down the line. 'Hello? Are you still there?'

'Oh, er, hi. Sorry. Bad line, I think.'

'Is the service bad where you are? Do you want to call me back?'

'No!' There was another pause, then he spoke quickly. 'Listen, I want to talk to you–.' He stopped and Rose heard him mutter an expletive under his breath. 'Sorry. Look, I'm saying this all wrong. Can you meet me?'

Rose frowned. 'In Hampshire?' It was a long way to go for a short meeting; she would look ridiculously overeager, wouldn't she? Still...

'No – no, I'm back in town.'

For a second, Rose threw a frantic look towards the door to the pub, then almost laughed out loud at her own stupidity. 'You're – you're here in Bath? I – I didn't know.' *Of course you didn't, idiot – why would you?* Feeling ridiculously gauche, Rose tried to think straight. 'But you only took the flat for a few days…'

'I managed to get in at the *Francis* at short notice.'

Rose's head was in turmoil. Seeing him again so soon had never crossed her mind, and she glanced up, only to find Morgan watching her keenly.

'Oh! It's just, I'm with friends; but I could be somewhere for around nine if that's not too late.' Rose drew on all her courage to continue. 'Where – I mean, if that works, where shall we meet?'

Morgan's eyes widened, as did her smile and she gave Rose the thumbs-up.

'Are you far from the *Francis*; shall I come to you?'

'I'm in *The Boater*, near Laura Place.'

'I know it; I'll be there at nine.' He ended the call.

Rose stared at the phone, then dropped back in her seat. What could he possibly have to say that was this urgent! At a loss, Rose observed, as casually as she could, 'Did James go for more drinks?'

Morgan narrowed her gaze. 'Who cares?! Just tell me! What was that all about?'

'I haven't the faintest idea.'

'Hmm… I'm guessing it started with 'Hi, this is Aiden', and I know it ended with you arranging to meet him here tonight…' Morgan threw Rose a shrewd look. 'What was in the middle?'

'I have no idea why he wants to meet. I mean it!'

'Rose Wallace, you are blushing!'

'That's hardly uncommon for me.'

'You've got to realise by now he might like you!'

'I don't have to realise any such thing.' *But you want to*, her heart whispered. 'It's just something to do with–.' But for the life of her, Rose could not imagine what it could have to do with if not something personal between them.

Morgan shook her head. 'I'm *so* going to enjoy telling you I told you so!'

Rose sighed as James returned with fresh drinks. 'James, you've got yourself quite a handful, you know!'

He nodded as he placed the glasses on the table and sat down. 'Indeed. And you've got a lot to answer for, because it's all your fault!'

Rose grinned, the fluttering of her insides provoked by Aiden's call settling slightly. 'Hey, I didn't force you into anything.'

'Yeah, right. You just invite your direction-impaired friend 5,000 miles from home, come up with a plan which prevents you meeting her and then conveniently forget to charge your mobile. I call it a conspiracy!'

Morgan rolled her eyes. 'Har har. You guys are *so* funny.'

Rose smiled at James. 'We are, aren't we?'

'Yep.' Picking up one of the ribbons, James started to roll it up. 'Mr Darcy thinks so, too.'

Morgan met Rose's eye from under her lashes; she knew it was one battle won and, if Rose wasn't mistaken, she was pretty confident she was going to win the one relating to her friend as well.

Morgan insisted on their staying with Rose until nine, saying she didn't want to leave her alone, so Rose found herself walking out onto Argyle Street with them just as Aiden came down the road.

He looked... she didn't quite know how to describe it; uncertain? A little distracted? Greeting them all quickly, he fell into step with her as they followed James and Morgan across the road; then, to her surprise, he said in an urgent voice, 'Look, I'm sorry to commandeer you so unexpectedly; but the truth is, at Chawton I didn't get a chance to explain...'

'Woman, I'm going to start carrying around a set of your keys everywhere I go.' James was laughing as he and Morgan tried to dig through Morgan's bag but Rose was trying to drown them both out. What did Aiden want to tell her that was so important? Why was he even here in Bath again?

'Fine with me. I'm liberated and all, but keys escape me.' Morgan turned around in a circle, her arms outstretched. 'Oh Lord; I love Bath, have I said? I can't wait to start flat hunting.'

'You're coming to live in Bath?' Aiden asked in surprise and then, after Morgan's situation had been explained, added: 'I'm jealous. I've always loved it here.' Then he turned to James. 'Your place is nice.'

'Do you want it? I've decided to sell.'

'What!? Why?' Three pairs of surprised eyes turned to James, and he shrugged.

'It wasn't my choice – living up that end of town or on the second floor! I want somewhere with outdoor space; if not a garden flat, at least a balcony of some sort.'

'Awww. You're so cute. You're thinking about Mr Darcy!'

There was silence for a moment, then Morgan was attacked by a fit of the giggles.

James shook his head. 'Probably a thought you should keep to yourself when out in public, if I'm to salvage anything like a reputation!' He sighed. 'I'm not sure what is the most unsettling: the idea of moving home to suit a stray kitten or to accommodate a fictional character!'

'But you've never been happy there, have you?' Rose met James's gaze, and he smiled ruefully.

'I suppose it was okay for a while, but I'm ready to move on now; find something that suits me better. Think I'll talk to someone in the morning about getting a valuation.'

'We have a busy day tomorrow, too!' Morgan smiled widely. 'I can't wait!'

Aiden looked sceptical. 'Not more dressing up in costume?'

Morgan shook her head. 'Sadly, no – not tomorrow, but the next day – *yes*.'

'Be careful, Ade; you'll get roped in this time!'

Aiden merely smiled faintly, but Rose was feeling decidedly uncomfortable, recalling the blank expression on the doctor's face when he'd seen her dressed up during the promenade.

'Well, there's another dance class Friday afternoon but not everyone gets dressed up for that.'

'And there's the ball that evening which should be amazing! Come with us to the ball, James!!!' Morgan turned a pleading face up to him. 'We need men! We need dancing partners! Shame to let all our finery go to waste by having to resort to dancing with each other!'

James laughed and shook his head. 'It's not exactly my scene.'

'You were laughing the entire time I was telling you about the dance class on Sunday!'

'Yeah, well; there's laughing because it's great, and laughing because it's a bit ridiculous.'

Two offended faces stared at him, and he held up his hands. 'Sorry! No offence meant! I know you love it; I know everyone who attends thinks it's fantastic and they have a great time, and I don't mean to knock that, I promise. It's just not... me!'

'But it could be!'

Aiden was grinning and James sent him a sour look. 'It's okay for you. You're not being coerced.'

'*Please*, James?'

'I don't have a costume; you said on Sunday it was compulsory!'

Morgan had sensed weakness. 'It is; but we know someone with spares, don't we, Rose?'

Rose nodded. 'Rita of *Pemberley Dreams* is here this year, and she's still got some costumes for sale.' She threw James an impish look. 'She specialises in gents' clothing, and I'm sure she'll have something fetching in your colour!'

'Give her a call, see what she has!' Morgan turned excitedly to Rose and, more to wind up James than to make the call, she reached for her mobile and flicked it open.

'As your boss, Rose, I am *ordering* you not to make that call!' James tried to sound firm, but Rose couldn't take him seriously.

'How terribly authoritarian!' She went to search her contacts, but then the screen went blank. 'Oh!' With a sigh, she looked up. 'Well, I *would* have made the call...'

To Rose's chagrin, James and Morgan exchanged a look before saying in unison, 'But you forgot to charge your mobile!'

'Can I borrow your phone, James?'

'Certainly not! Not to phone people with spare costumes so that other people can be forced against their will into wearing them... in *public*!'

Rose smiled at him, then shrugged. 'Okay; you win!'

'It's *freezing* out here!' Morgan shivered as they arrived outside her building.

'It's pretty mild for September, and you are well wrapped up for someone who's only had to walk about five yards!'

Morgan peered out at them from between her scarf and hat, her gaze drifting from James to Rose. Then she gasped. 'Tomorrow will be the one week anniversary of when we met in person!' She grabbed Rose and hugged her around the middle. 'Happy Weekiversary!!'

'Oh goodness.' Rose patted her awkwardly on the back. 'Well, at least you're not cranky when you're a bit tipsy!'

Morgan pulled away, tears in her eyes. 'How could I be cranky? I love you! You're my best friend in the whole world.' She turned around and grabbed James's arm, pulling him into a three-way hug with Rose. '*Wait!*' Morgan pulled them both closer to Aiden and swept him into the hug as well. 'I remember now! *You* were there, too! I met all of you for the first time a week ago tomorrow!'

Despite Morgan's small frame, she was surprisingly strong, resulting in them all being rather crushed together. To Rose's relief, James didn't seem to mind and Aiden appeared to be taking it all in his stride. 'Quite a milestone. Another round?'

As quickly as Morgan had started the group hug, she pulled away from it. 'No! No more drinks!'

James laughed as they all extricated themselves. 'No. Definitely no more for you! On the bright side tomorrow *is* your Weekiversary and you can celebrate it all over again.'

Morgan started to clap her hands, then looked at Rose and stopped. 'Ha, you're right; I do clap my hands – maybe it's an American thing. But I still don't see the big deal if you did it once on impulse. Really, how bad could it have–'

Rose nearly pushed Morgan at James, simultaneously throwing a slightly panicked look in Aiden's direction; he was staring right at her, and smiling faintly she turned hastily to the others.

'Thanks for the drink, James.' Her voice sounded somewhat strangled. 'Morgan, send me a text when you're ready in the morning?'

'Goodnight, guys!' Morgan launched herself at Rose, and then Aiden in turn.

"Night! James – you'll make sure she's – uh –' Rose hesitated, suddenly unsure of the situation, but James met her eye and nodded.

'Don't worry; I'll see she's settled here before I rush back to cuddle up with Mr Darcy.'

Morgan opened her mouth to respond then stopped and looked at him suspiciously, 'You're doing it on purpose now!'

James winked at her, and Rose laughed as James turned to shake Aiden's hand.

'You'll see Rose to her door, Ade?'

'Of course.'

CHAPTER FORTY-FIVE

The door soon closed behind them, and Rose welcomed the cool evening breeze brushing her cheeks.

'Back to the pub or walk?' Aiden gestured along the street.

'Oh, walk, please.'

Why was it so hard to feel at ease? As they set off, Rose tried to recapture a moment from the other reality, when she had felt freer to express herself, and Aiden had seemed to believe in not wasting opportunities. *Ask him*, urged the voice in her head. *Ask him how come he's back in town, what it is he didn't say?* If she'd been walking with the other Aiden, with the false confidence of a couple of glasses of wine inside her, she was certain it wouldn't have felt this... *awkward*. Here she was, getting yet another unexpected gift of time, and she was letting it get the best of her. She groaned inwardly.

'Are you okay?'

Aiden had come to a halt and was looking at her in some concern.

'Sorry?'

'You made a funny sound.'

Feeling warmth steal into her cheeks, Rose shook her head. 'I did not!'

Aiden narrowed his gaze. 'Yes. You did. I may be a historian and rather mired in the past, but there's nothing wrong with my hearing in the present, and I can tell you – with complete conviction – you did in fact groan.'

'Yes, well, if we're talking facts, I happen to know *for a fact* that history is...' She paused, thinking. 'Not quite as solid as you might think!' Rose nodded to affirm her statement, but Aiden just shook his head.

'Come on; let's cut through the park.' He gestured along Henrietta Street and Rose fell into step beside him.

They walked in silence for a while, and Rose could sense her heart thumping wildly in her chest. After all these years of gazing at him from a distance, she was struggling to come to terms with the change this year, not only of their having conversations – *proper* conversations – but of their progression from almost strangers to first-name terms. But what now? She knew every last step of this walk was bringing her to the end for another year, and she sighed.

'What's the matter?'

'Nothing. I mean, why should there be anything wrong?'

'You sighed.'

'I did not!'

'Are you always in this much denial?'

'No!'

Aiden grunted, then stood aside so that Rose could precede him through the gateway into Henrietta Park, but suddenly, he placed a hand on her arm, and she stopped, a nearby lamp-post bathing them in light.

'Your necklace.' He reached out to touch the cross nestled against Rose's throat and she held her breath, certain he would feel her pulse pounding where his hand rested. He raised his eyes to meet hers. 'This reminds me – we had an interesting find yesterday!'

'In Winchester?' Thankfully, his hand dropped to his side and they turned to continue their walk, allowing Rose to draw her breath. 'Was it not just repair work then?'

'In principle, yes, but that doesn't mean you won't unearth

something you hadn't planned on finding. It's one of the many reasons I love my job! Always expect the unexpected!'

Rose frowned, a hand raised to the necklace. 'But how does this remind you?'

'Do you remember me telling you about what was going on in the cathedral?' Rose nodded. 'The rainwater which came in leaked through a window – one you're probably familiar with – the one paying tribute to Jane Austen? The water found its way down the stonework and pooled there – behind and below a wall-mounted memorial.'

'The plaque erected by her nephew?'

'Precisely.' Aiden shrugged. 'It happens; yesterday, they were ready to remove it from the wall so they could treat the area needing attention – it's why I had to dash over to be on-site. And there it was – something lodged in a cavity behind the plaque.'

Rose's mouth had gone completely dry. 'Something?'

'Yes, a small box containing, of all things, a necklace. Pretty similar to this.' He gestured at Rose's. 'Though, of course, it's clearly much older.'

Her mind in turmoil, Rose stared at him. Could it be…?

'The cathedral's archivist did some research this morning.' He glanced at her and their steps slowed to a halt in the middle of the park. 'I expect you know some of it already, being such a fan. Charles Austen bought topaz crosses for his sisters. This third one is also topaz, clearly made by the same hand and in the same fashion, and of similar age, for all he can tell at this stage. What he can't tell, and I can't begin to suppose, is why someone chose to conceal it behind a memorial stone to the author.'

Rose couldn't suppose either, even though she was pretty certain she knew exactly what this cross looked like and whose it was. 'Is there… I mean, was it definitely placed there some time ago? It couldn't have been put there more recently?' She had no idea what she was suggesting, but having seen this necklace not so long ago, it was hard to imagine it existing anywhere but here and now.

'Everything points to it having been placed in the cavity before the memorial was placed on the wall. That was in the 1870s, so one has to assume it's been there, undisturbed, since then, if not longer.'

'And... so what now? What will happen to this... find?'

'It will be kept in the cathedral's archives. There's no proof of its origin beyond the circumstantial similarities in the design I mentioned and it being where it was. Everything suggests it once belonged to someone in the Austen family, but if so, they chose to place it in the cathedral, as if they meant for it to be kept there. So that's what will happen.' He smiled faintly. 'All ancient buildings and monuments have histories to tell, and myth and legend concealed within them over the centuries. It's probably the most exciting thing that's happened in the north aisle since 1850!'

'1850?' Rose frowned. 'Was there another find?'

'No – no, nothing like that. As you can imagine it's all a bit vague being so long ago, but apparently, persons unknown – they never caught the culprits – entered the cathedral in the middle of the night and were seen sometime later in the north aisle. What they were up to was never discovered, and they scarpered as soon as they realised they'd been rumbled. Rumour has it, they were planning something to do with the chantry tomb of William of Wykeham? It's a beautiful piece, much admired. There was an abandoned lamp at the scene and some tools, but no noticeable damage.'

The date meant nothing to Rose, but trying to make sense of what he'd just told her – if anything sensible could be reasoned – was beyond her when she stood in such close proximity to Aiden. Inhaling his aftershave and watching his eyes glow with enthusiasm over his subject was enough of a distraction. She would need to think carefully about all he'd said, but she wasn't going to waste the last few moments of this precious evening on trying to unravel the impossible. There would, sadly, be time enough for that tomorrow.

Aiden waved a hand. 'Shall we walk on?'

'Yes, of course.'

They strolled in silence for a moment, and Rose sought desperately for something to talk about. If they'd exhausted his work, this might be it until they said goodbye! She tried to look at Aiden discreetly, but his face was all in shadow; why wasn't he telling her what he wanted to meet about?

'Hi, Rose.'

Oh no! Now she'd been caught staring at him!

'I – er – hi!' Great. What a conversationalist!

'You remember the dig I did in Bath.' It was a statement, not a question, and he'd looked away again, so Rose felt justified in not saying anything, though her insides lurched uncomfortably, and she felt the familiar warmth filling her cheeks as they reached the gate back out into the street.

Aiden had stopped and turned to stare across the park, talking almost as though to himself. 'I wouldn't have said anything in front of the others. Up until then, I had no idea you remembered, but from your reaction to your friend's clapping...'

Rose drew in a quick breath. 'They had to redo the take; I was mortified. One of the more embarrassing moments of my life come back to haunt me in epic style.' She glared defiantly at Aiden when he turned to look at her. 'In my defence, I was a lot younger then.'

He eyed her seriously for a moment. 'Just a little over three years ago?' Nothing wrong with his memory, then.

'Okay. So not *much*; but you'd be surprised what a difference time can make!'

'Hey, I'm an archaeologist! Surprises and time go together for me!'

Consumed with her embarrassment, Rose just wanted to escape and she turned out of the gate to walk along Sutton Street. There were people sat outside *The Pulteney Arms*, enjoying their drinks and oblivious to Rose and Aiden as they passed. 'Look, I can take it from here.' She waved an arm ahead.

'I made a promise to James to see you to your door.'

Rose stopped in her tracks and spun around to face him. 'How – how did you know where I live? How did you know to walk in this direction?'

Looking a little sheepish, Aiden looked around for a moment, then met her gaze with a contrite look. 'I asked James.'

Shaking her head in disbelief, Rose took a step backwards. 'But you didn't know you'd be walking me home!'

'No; no, I didn't.' He glanced over his shoulder at the people outside the pub, then took her firmly by the arm and stepped around the corner into the mews running between Daniel Street and Sydney Place. 'He told me ages ago. But you *had* agreed to meet me after you'd eaten, so that's what we're doing.' He stepped closer to her. 'We're meeting.' Dark brown eyes met and held light grey. 'Hi, Rose.'

Rose found his closeness was intoxicating. 'You – you already said that.'

'It bears repetition. I've waited long enough to say it.'

'What… what do you mean?' Her voice came out as a whisper.

'I mean it's been a long three years.'

Rose's lips parted in surprise, but no sound came out. She closed her eyes. I'm going to wake up in a minute. *This is a dream; I know it is. The fact it all seems so tangible, so real, is an illusion.*

'Rose.'

'Yes.'

'Look at me.'

She opened her eyes, but Aiden didn't speak, just ran a distracted hand through his hair. 'I wanted to say… at least, I – damn.' He broke off. 'I can talk until the cows come home about my work, but – well, I'm not good at this; I don't quite know where to begin.'

Rose wasn't sure what 'this' was, but she did have a suggestion. 'I have a good friend – and I know of the sister of another friend – who both believe in beginning at the end. Perhaps you could try that – if it helps?'

He met her gaze seriously, then shrugged. 'Suppose it's worth a try.'

Before Rose had time to speculate on what was coming, he closed the remaining gap between them and claimed her lips with his own and without hesitation, she returned the kiss. It was one of those moments when time slows down, but Rose's heartbeat started to race, although she could hear nothing but a funny echo of what it once sounded like. In contrast, her senses were fully alert as a heady mix of incredulousness and excitement coalesced inside.

When he pulled away, they both stared at each other for a second. Then the corners of his mouth twitched. 'Yep. It helps.'

Feeling a little self-conscious and hoping she hadn't just revealed in its entirety the depth of her feelings, Rose returned the smile tentatively. 'What was that… another thankyou… for something?'

He shook his head. 'More of an apology really, for three years of bad timing.'

Aiden took her arm, and they started to walk again, soon turning the corner into Sydney Place. 'Would you believe that's how long I've been waiting to do that?'

'I don't – you can't...' Struggling for words, Rose stared at him in astonishment. 'But you were always so... indifferent.'

'Really?' Aiden's gaze drifted across the street to Sydney Gardens. 'Fair enough; I suppose that was how I wanted to seem.' He turned back to her, then ran a hand through his hair. 'Well, damn it, what else could I have done – you were wearing a ring.'

Rose blinked; did he have any idea how fast she would have kicked Jonathan out of the door if she'd had even an inkling of all this? She made a strangled noise. 'But–'

'Then this year the ring had gone; don't think I didn't notice. I almost lost it the morning you were helping me – so surprised by my turn of luck. Only, I couldn't find the words. Every time I saw you, I was filled with doubts about how much I should let on, and every time you were no longer there, I cursed myself for being so tongue-tied. It feels like I might never get it right...' Then he looked at her tenderly. 'But I've just realised whose words might help.'

'I don't understand.'

He took her hand in his. 'Rose, *it was for you alone I came to Bath. For you alone I think and plan.*' She stared at him in astonishment as he continued with words she knew well; words from perhaps the most romantic letter ever written. '*Have you not seen this? Can you fail to have understood my wishes?*' He smiled faintly. 'Didn't you work it out from the message I gave you?'

Rose frowned, then stifled a laugh when his eyes gleamed mischievously. 'The *Love Heart*? You can't possibly have expected me to understand your feelings based on a sweet! That's crazy!'

'Rose, when it comes to you, all manner of insanity takes over.' He took her other hand, too, and Rose's skin tingled in anticipation as she held her breath. Was this happening? 'Look, I must tell you–'

But before he could finish, a taxi screeched to a halt beside them and, startled, they dropped hands as they both turned to stare at it. For a moment, no one emerged and in the dark it was impossible to tell who was inside. Then the driver got out and, rolling his eyes at them, walked round to the rear passenger door.

'Got a right one here,' he said as he grasped the handle. 'Expects royal service.' The door swung open. It took the driver a moment to realise his services were still required, and he reluctantly extended his hand and helped a lady emerge from inside, and Rose gasped.

'What is it? What's wrong?' Aiden grabbed her arm, but Rose didn't turn to look at him. The new arrival looked a little harried and possibly a little older than when Rose had last seen her, as she hurried across the pavement to them.

'Thank goodness you are here, Rose. My journey has been fraught with complication, not least being conveyed at an unfathomable speed from Basingstoke. I find I do not care for some of these more modern forms of transportation, though a purpose was served in my reaching Bath ahead of my expectations.'

'Ahem.'

As one, they all turned to look at the disgruntled taxi driver.

'Ah, indeed. Would you be so kind, sir?' The lady gestured towards the boot of the car. 'I shall end this part of my journey here.'

The warm feeling wrapping Rose in a cocoon of happiness faltered slightly. 'You're... you're back? Did you take the apartment again?' She turned to look at 4 Sydney Place, but light was pouring out of the ground-floor flat. Someone else was clearly already staying there.

With a frown, she turned back just in time to see the driver deposit a heavy trunk in front of them, receive payment from a familiar-looking pouch, and return to his car.

'I have been 'back', as you call it, a short while – yet not here.' She looked around and sniffed. 'I confess, I do not miss it.'

Thinking of how small her apartment was, Rose felt a sense of panic. She would *not* go and live at home again so there was room for two of them. 'But where do you plan on staying?' It sounded a bit rude, but it had to be said.

'Stay? Oh, staying is not my purpose! I am come to fetch you.' Jane paused and looked at Aiden. 'And the archaeologist.'

Aiden's grip on her arm tightened. 'Rose, what is going on?'

'Pray, would you introduce me to this gentleman? 'Twould hardly be appropriate to journey in company if we are not acquainted.'

Rose's brain had gone into overdrive. *Where?* She wanted to shout. Where are we going? But Aiden's squeeze of her arm comforted her, and she cleared her throat.

'Aiden – I mean Doctor Aiden Trevellyan – I'd like you to meet... to introduce you to...' Rose stopped. Hadn't she just made a beginning with him? Was she going to say this out loud? She looked beseechingly at the lady, who nodded encouragingly. 'Miss Jane Austen.'

The End...

Acknowledgements

It's hard to know where to begin! So many people have helped us during the writing of this story and, in no particular order, here they are. Huge thanks to:

- Marcus Whittington and all the team at Bath Boutique Stays. Without Marcus, who shared many tales about 4 Sydney Place with us, this story wouldn't be what it is!

- Anne Buchanan, Local Studies Librarian in Bath Central Library, without whom the scenes set in the library would hold absolutely no credibility at all and who had lots of helpful suggestions on how to blend reality with our plot.

- Jackie Herring, Director of the Jane Austen Festival, for her advice and for putting on such a wonderful celebration each year.

- Douglas Walker, Heather Morris and the team at SPP in Bath, for advice, guidance, handholding and general all-round support in preparing the book for publication.

- J.K. Rowling, for creating Harry Potter, without whom we would never have met!

- Our lovely test readers, for their helpful and insightful early feedback: Diane Zimanski, Rachel Platt, Sandy Bellock Listorti, Jennifer Gray and Jenny Mattesich.

- Our equally lovely families for their support, especially Julian and Steve.

Finally, last but never least, we'd like to thank Jane Austen for everything she has brought into our lives and for being such a fun companion during the writing of this story.

About the Authors

Ada Bright

I'd like to introduce you to my friend, Ada. She likes Cheerios and bacon burnt beyond recognition (though not on the same plate) and she has an interesting sense of direction. This doesn't just apply to getting from A to B, but also in reading – she read the third Harry Potter book first - and likes to read the end of every book before she starts.

She's a talented artist, photographer and writer, but more than that, she's one of the best friends I have ever made.

Since we met 14 years ago, she's had three gorgeous children and moved house twice – from Pasadena in California to Pasadena to… wait for it… Pasadena!

Oh, and she's so cool, her name reads the same backwards too – that can't be just a coincidence, can it?

Cass Grafton

I am very lucky to be able to count Cass as a best friend and writing partner for over a decade. She likes cold wine, cats and the written word. People are drawn to the beauty of how she strings words together to create a story, but I love the humour with which she does it.

She is a poet in her writing, an adventurer in her life and the most generous host I've ever known.

Since we met, oh so long ago, she has lived in three countries and thrown more parties than I have washed dishes. She has also celebrated the joys in my life with the same love and attention as she has her own family. Though, at this point, I have to say that family is basically what we have become.

She deserves top billing here, but, being Cass, she would not hear of it. Alphabetically is simply how these things are done, and there is really no use doing anything if you're not going to do it right.

We love to hear from readers! Please follow us or contact us via the following social media links:

Our Blog: Tabby Cow   https://tabbycow.com

Facebook: Ada – https://www.facebook.com/missyadabright
               Cass – https://www.facebook.com/cassie.grafton

Twitter: Ada - @missyadabright
               Cass - @CassGrafton